Heart's Quest

by

Blythe Ayne

Heart's Quest

by

Blythe Ayne

Heart's Quest
Blythe Ayne

Emerson & Tilman, Publishers
129 Pendleton Way #55
Washougal, WA 98671

All Rights Reserved
No part of this publication may be reproduced, distributed, or transmitted
in any form, or by any means, including photocopying, recording,
or other electronic or mechanical methods, without the prior
written permission of the author, except brief quotations
in critical reviews and other noncommercial
uses permitted by copyright law.
This is a work of fiction.
Names, characters, places, and incidents are fictional.

Book, cover design & some interior graphics by Blythe Ayne
Art Nouveau graphics in the public domain

Heart's Quest
Copyright © Blythe Ayne

www.BlytheAyne.com

Paperback ISBN: 978-1-947151-20-8

[1. FICTION / Science Fiction / Genetic Engineering
2. FICTION / Science Fiction / Steampunk
3. FICTION / Fantasy / Urban] I. Title.
BIC: FM

First Edition

DEDICATION

To All Who Follow Their Heart

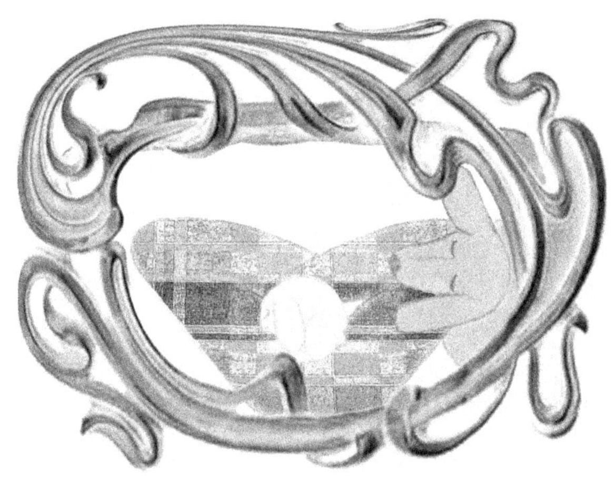

Chapter 1

Heart sat cross-legged on her cot with Violet, the little lavender rabbit, curled up in her lap, her rabbity ears twitching contentedly, while Swen stretched out on the bed, with his long-doggie snout on Heart's knee. Equuleus, the winged gear horse, stood by the window, seeming to contemplate going for a flight.

Suddenly, someone pounded on the door like he'd break it in.

All four of them jumped practically out of their skin.

"Must be Jackson," Heart observed.

"*Right*," Swen said, in an uncanny imitation of Jackson. "No one else around here …."

The banging ensued at the door again.

"… needs to pummel a door to get attention. At least he doesn't …."

The door slammed open in its frame.

"…. fling the door open before you invite him in," Swen finished, sarcastically.

Violet hopped up to stand beside Heart, putting her furry fists on her fuzzy hips, giving Jackson a disapproving look.

"Nice of you to let me invite you in," Heart added her disapproving look to Violet's. Swen didn't even bother to raise his head.

"*I knocked!*" Jackson barked.

"*We heard,*" Heart retorted.

"You needn't," Violet sputtered, indignant, "*hammer, pummel, batter, bludgeon, whack, bash and clobber the door, sir. Heart is sitting right here!*"

Heart patted the little lavender rabbit soothingly. "Violet makes a valid point, Jackson. Could you not wait for me to answer the door? Or at least, wait until I invite you in?"

"No, I could not. I *knocked*. Enough chatter. I have to get back to Earth. *Now*. I've been told to collect the dog if he's coming."

"I *beg* your …" Swen began, while Heart cried out, "*Now?! Right now?*"

"*Right now. Or sooner.*"

"No!" Heart protested. "Is there never any peace for us?"

"Apparently not," Jackson stomped up and down the room, clearly agitated to nearly his limits, the muscles in his jaw clenched. In fact, Heart noticed, the muscles in his entire body, wound up, ready to spring.

Indeed, something quite serious had developed. She stood and pulled a chair in front of her. "Sit."

"I can't."

"It's not a request, Jackson. Sit."

He took in her expression, then sat.

Heart returned to her position on her little bed, holding Jackson's gaze. "*What is going on?*"

"I am not to tell you."

"I don't care what my father says, you *must* tell me. I'll find out soon enough. *What is going on?*"

"Apparently …" Jackson hesitated, then sighed and continued. "Apparently Father Inventor's clone made clones."

"*Oh!*" Heart, Swen, and Equuleus exclaimed in unison.

"This is not good, not good at all, it will never do," Violet rattled, quivering. "Say it isn't so! How will we ever cope? What are we to do? I'm extremely dismayed, distraught, disconcerted, disturbed, discombobulated, unsettled, so on and so forth …and furthermore …."

"*Will! You! Shut! Up!*" Jackson commanded.

Violet clamped her little rabbit mouth shut, and put a paw over it for added security. "*Sorry!*" she squeaked.

3 – Blythe Ayne

"Well, I'm dismayed too," Heart added. "But … they're a further cloned generation, they'll be weak. And how many can there possibly be, two or three weak clones? Can't *The Cause of All Beings* control them without you immediately flying off?"

"There are *not* 'two or three weak clones.' There are in the neighborhood of *one thousand* clones of your father."

Equuleus whinnied, and Violet silently hopped back onto Heart's lap, curling up into a little, tight, quivering, lavender ball. Swen jumped off the bed and took over Jackson's occupation of pacing up and down the room. "*A thousand?*" he muttered. "A thousand Father Inventor clones, working for the bad guys? *We're doomed.*"

Heart said nothing in the midst of the commotion. Finally, she shook her head and said, "I don't believe it. I don't believe it, Jackson, that's a press release made up by the Purists to frighten *The Cause of All Beings*. Plain and simple. I refuse to accept it. Nor should you."

"You're wrong, Heart. It has been as shocking to your father and me as it is to you. But it comes to us via an impeccable source. In fact, there's nothing about Father Inventor's clone or clones anywhere in the news. Nothing at all."

"But, Jackson, *a thousand clones?* Really? How could it be? Wouldn't the number one clone, which we have here on Pink, which my father and

HelperFriend are reconditioning—wouldn't he have told us? With all his babble about how awesome he is, he'd not miss the opportunity to brag about this wondrous feat. Even if it was the next generation turning out clones, he'd tell us.

"Unless your 'reliable source' is an eye witness, I wouldn't believe them. And if they *are* an eye witness, *I wouldn't trust them*. Whoever they are."

"Our source," Jackson insisted, "has been eye witness to enough of the clones to know this estimate is correct. Furthermore, our source is impeccably trustworthy."

"Strange," Violet said in her muffled voice.

"Quite strange," Heart agreed. "Where are these clones supposedly hanging out?"

"It seems they're in the underground crystal matrix. Which, you'll be surprised to learn, is extremely far-reaching."

"Oh!" Heart exclaimed simply. "Horrible."

"Yes. Horrible," Jackson agreed.

Heart was suddenly awash with a deep fear for Jackson. "What can you do, Jackson, alone?"

"I can only do my best."

"But ..." Heart tried to contrive an argument, "you simply cannot fight them all, all alone!"

"And I won't. There's everyone in *The Cause of All Beings*, there's everyone in The Periphery ...."

"That's redundant. Everyone in The Periphery is in *The Cause of All Beings*," Heart pointed out.

"True."

"And how are the people behind The Wall in The Periphery supposed to help you? They're not free to move about."

"True again, Heart." Jackson nodded. "Are you seriously trying to tell me to stay here and ignore all that's happening on Earth?"

"Ahm … sort of sounds like it." Heart said quietly. "But I know you won't."

"Right." Jackson jumped up and looked at Swen. "Coming?" Without waiting for an answer, he bolted from Heart's room.

Swen and Heart exchanged a look. "You must go back to Key Man," Heart acknowledged. "Your leg is completely healed, including the bio component my father implanted."

Swen nodded. "Yes. I hardly even have a scar. Which, I must say, is rather a disappointment."

Heart chuckled. "Key Man misses you."

"And I miss him, Heart. But it's hard to leave like this. Without any warning, without a proper good-bye."

"Such seems to be the nature of our relationship, dear friend." Heart kneeled down and hugged the big hound close. "We will meet again."

"Yes," Swen agreed, neither of them sure of their words.

If what Jackson had told them was even partially true, Heart thought, the future of The Darling Undesirables, and those living in

The Periphery, as well as many other innocent beings, was in grave danger. How far were the Purists willing to go for their twisted, intolerant beliefs?

"I'd better ...." Swen moved toward the door.

"Yes. Let's go." Heart nodded.

Equuleus went out on the landing.

"I'm not going!" Violet turned her back on them.

"Why, Violet?" Heart asked. "That's not very nice."

"I'm very nice! If I don't go down, Swen won't leave. He won't leave without saying good-bye to me!"

"Oh, Violet!" Heart tried to laugh, but her voice came out almost a sob. "Your ego knows no bounds! You must realize that Swen will most certainly leave. And you'll feel terrible if you don't wave good-bye."

Violet's floppy ears trailed across the floor as she hopped down from the bed and dragged her feet to Heart and Swen. "I have nothing further to say beyond my protesting your departure."

Swen snuggled Violet. "Protest duly noted, my fuzzy friend." He turned and ran down the castle's winding stairway, while Heart picked Violet up and jumped onto Equuleus. They flew down and around, meeting Swen on the castle's marble rotunda floor below.

"Ah! I'm going to miss that sight!" Swen exclaimed.

Heart nodded but said nothing. They filed down the hall to Father Inventor's room in silent sadness.

Chapter 2

Heart saw a beehive of activity as she peered into her father's room, the back wall open to the interior of the dome, with her father, fully bio and not able to withstand Pink's environment, in his protective bell jar suiting.

She turned to Swen. "We have to get you in a protective suit before you can go in."

"Great!" Swen exclaimed with sarcastic enthusiasm, "My favorite thing!"

Heart stepped through the double baffle door into the busy space, wended her way to a cupboard, grabbed a suit, and scurried back into the hall where her friends waited.

She tried, but failed, to stifle a giggle as she pulled the person suit onto the hound body. At least he wasn't exposed to the environment that his bios could not tolerate.

"*I hate this!*" Swen's muffled voice came through the headgear.

"Still—better than not breathing," Heart pointed out.

"Up to a certain point."

Heart picked Swen up and went into her father's room, followed by Violet on Equuleus—both of whom, along with Heart, were able to withstand Pink's environment.

Clockwork, mechanical, and hybrid beings bustled about as Heart and her friends came into the space. She waved to her father, then looked about for Jackson. There he sat, obviously disgruntled, on her father's narrow cot in his ill-fitting protective suit.

Heart made her way to him through the busy throng. "What's wrong?" she asked.

"Who knows? Some something-something," he said, irritated.

"Some something-something with what?"

"The life-support system on my spacecraft. What could have gone wrong? It was fine when I got here."

"Maybe it wasn't. The Clone banged around in it *a lot* on the way here. You're lucky it wasn't dangerously compromised while you were still in it."

"Whatever. Couldn't they have figured this out before now?"

"Apparently not." Heart looked around for HelperFriend, realizing he was probably with her father's clone, as that's where he seemed to be almost all the time of late. She hoped he'd come to see Jackson off.

"I'll check with my father …."

At that moment one of the mechanicals called, "All clear."

There was a round of "all clear" from a variety of workers. Nodding at Jackson from across the room, her father was the last to agree. "All clear." He made his way to them, gliding in his bell jar, the workers stepping aside as he came.

"Ready, Jackson?"

"I've been ready, sir."

"I know, my boy. But we must not risk harming you in any way. So much hangs upon your abilities now …." he paused.

"A thousand clones, Father?" Heart exclaimed. *"One thousand clones!?!* Really, is it possible?"

"Possible and, unfortunately, probable," her father replied, frowning.

"How will *The Cause of all Beings* prevail?"

"I don't know, Heart. We can only be in this moment, and let the next moment unfold. I have profound faith in Peter and Jackson."

"So do I, Father. But I'm also pragmatic. And the odds look—impossible."

"Nice pep talk, Heart," Jackson interjected, standing. "With that, I can go anywhere, face anything."

"I'm sorry, Jackson. But I'm concerned. *Concerned!"*

They watched as Jackson's spacecraft came out of the interior of Pink's dome and into the open.

"Right. We'll chat later," Jackson muttered, and, without another word, abruptly headed for his spacecraft.

Heart exchanged a look with her father, shaking her head. They'd spoken plenty about Jackson's "socially inappropriate" behavior.

"Let's get you secure on that angry man's craft, Swen," she said. "Not that I'm entirely certain I even want you riding with him."

"Can't argue with you on that point, Heart," Swen agreed. "But he's the best pilot anywhere, begging your forgiveness, dear Heart."

"Oh, no offense, Swen. I agree with you. If Jackson weren't the best pilot anywhere, I'd not only not let you on his craft, I'd be in deeper despair over these developments. But if there's anyone who can outmaneuver one-thousand somebodies, it's Jackson."

They arrived at his spacecraft, Jackson already aboard and at the controls. Heart secured Swen in the safety harness in the back seat. "Thanks for helping, Jackson," she said, not disguising her pique.

"What?" Jackson looked back. "Sorry. Just a bit preoccupied."

"I know," Heart softened. "But please don't forget you have a passenger. A very valuable passenger."

"Yeah. Valuable," Swen added.

"I won't forget the dog. I'm going to The Museum of Scientific Improbabilities and Unpredictable Oddities first, to meet with Peter. And we all know Key Man will be at the door before the engines are cut to get his precious canine back."

"Thanks for the 'precious,'" Swen chortled.

"Being facetious."

"No you're not," Swen dared to counter.

Heart couldn't see Swen's mischievous grin in his awkward suit, but she saw it in her mind's eye. "Have fun sparring," she gave a last tug to secure the straps. "You feel safe, my friend?"

"I'm good, Heart."

She leaned down and gave him a hug, awash with sadness and loneliness. Then she stood and reached to give Jackson a pat on the shoulder, but stopped mid-gesture. Swen's barely visible eyes caught her eye—give him a hug, his look said. She shook her head, turned and stepped away from the spacecraft.

Jackson sealed up his craft, then took off the headgear and top half of the protective suit.

Heart, Equuleus, with Violet on his back and Father Inventor stood in a line, along with many other residents of Pink, waving to Jackson, their young hero, as he engaged the engines.

Without ceremony and with the smallest wave, he took off into the wide-open space above Pink, headed directly for Earth, ever-hanging overhead.

*   *

Once she was back inside with her father, Equuleus, and Violet, Heart flipped the switch that brought down the wall between her father's sparse little room and the vast dome beyond. She watched as the residents went deep inside, hanging their heads, moving slowly, depressed over the sobering news and Jackson's departure.

For some strange reason, Heart thought, despite his grouchy demeanor, everyone always seemed to like being around Jackson. Including herself, she had to admit. She didn't quite understand it, but she had to acknowledge it.

"All right, Father, what gives? Who is your, as Jackson put it, 'infallible source' for this seemingly bizarre improbability? One thousand clones? I want to know more."

"Yeah!" Violet piped up. "This improbable scenario is likely to endanger, risk, threaten, jeopardize and possibly even harm our Jackson. Which is not acceptable!"

Heart couldn't quite stifle a small giggle. "Well, she's right. It could 'even possibly harm our Jackson.' How could there be one thousand clones? How?"

Her father, climbing out of his bell jar, pulled out a chair for her to sit, then he sat on his little cot. "This is the part that's not clear. If each generation of clone has made a clone, they will reduce in efficacy rapidly. But if it's the generation after the primary one making many clones," he gestured to the interior of the castle where HelperFriend had been working with the Clone, "they'll be more of a threat."

"Maybe," Heart said thoughtfully, "it's just that your informant—whoever it may be, that I guess you're not going to tell me …."

"Not right at this time, no, dear daughter."

Heart shrugged, frustrated. "Anyway, maybe it's a case of that person being in the crystal matrix and not realizing it's mirror-like. Maybe he or she doesn't know that one looks like many."

"Wouldn't that be nice? But no, this person is extremely knowledgable about the crystal matrix. Extremely. And far beyond its reflecting capabilities."

"I see," Heart responded, in a deep reflection of her own. Most curious, this "informant"— knowledgable about the crystal matrix, and the number of Father Inventor Clones, and yet, not a Purist.

"*Ah!* So, if your informant is so trustworthy, why weren't you told before?"

"We believed there were others, but we weren't sure until just now. Apparently, they were in stasis, to be awakened by the primary clone, the one we have, if he didn't take some action at regular intervals, like push a button every so often that kept them in stasis.

"He had no need to have them all milling around. But if he was somehow removed from action, we believe he had a fail-safe means to put them into action. And now they are."

"But surely they need direction," Heart said. "The first clone is here, and I doubt his ability to do much …."

"Agreed," her father answered.

"So … Loruza and Keeper A must be the brains behind any comprehensive organized activity among the clones."

"*Hmmm* …." Her father mused.

"*Hmmmm*? That's not what I expected to hear."

"I … ahm, well, I imagine you may be right, to a certain extent."

Heart frowned, realizing she'd encountered yet another "something" that her father was not willing to reveal. "How can I help," she whispered, "if you won't tell me what you're not telling me?"

He reached out and took her hand. "Everything you do, Heart, is led by your impeccable intuition. Knowing certain details that are constantly in motion will only interfere with your internal guidance. Trust me."

"Well … I must, given I have no choice."

He smiled and patted her hand. She was neither comforted nor calmed. "Perhaps most of the succeeding generations of clones are incomplete or incompetent."

"That would be helpful," her father agreed.

"So … what if the primary clone, the one we have, gave them a directive to side with us, with *The Cause of All Beings*?"

"Very good, my brilliant daughter. That is one of our plans. Hence the non-stop attention of HelperFriend to the Clone, in his efforts to reprogram him."

"I see!" Heart said, enlightened. "Why not simply replace certain components in his brain?"

"Another good thought. But that's too tricky. Intelligence becomes so—interwoven. And with a brain such as the Clone's, where he built fail-safe measures *in himself* by both organic and mechanical means, he could as easily be destroyed as improved. This sounds weirdly immodest, but he's brilliantly made."

Heart laughed. "Oh, that *is* funny. He constructed himself, so he's not you, but he's a download of your brain, so he *is* you. Anyway, bottom line—he must be re-socialized. And the interesting paradigm is having a clockworks man re-socialize a clockworks-mechanical-bio man, to be more like a compassionate human being."

Her father chuckled. "That's about the size of it. I don't have the time to do it. And—you've socialized HelperFriend fabulously. He's more human and humane than many humans."

"I don't know how much I had to do with that …" Heart protested.

"You made him who he is," Equuleus intoned quietly.

"He was *nothing, zilch, nada, zip, nil, zero, nobody* when he met you," Violet insisted. "And now look at him! Somebody's home! He's brilliant, kind, compassionate, understanding, thoughtful, empathic. And one darn great chef."

"I had nothing to do with that last part," Heart said.

"True. Too true." Violet stuck out her tongue and squeezed her eyes down shut, recalling the time Heart tried to cook up some greens for her. "But all the rest stands."

Her father nodded. "I must concur. The other relevant factor is that HelperFriend is a clockworks man, like the clone. I see him openly trusting HelperFriend. But when I enter the room, he becomes stressed and starts to shut down."

"Hmmm, I was about to offer to take over HelperFriend's work with the Clone. But if you feel HelperFriend is doing a better job than I'm likely to, I'd better leave well enough alone."

"I think that's a good idea," her father agreed. "But, on another hand, if you were to check out how things are going with him, it might be helpful. As I say, my presence appears to cause more harm than good with HelperFriend's efforts."

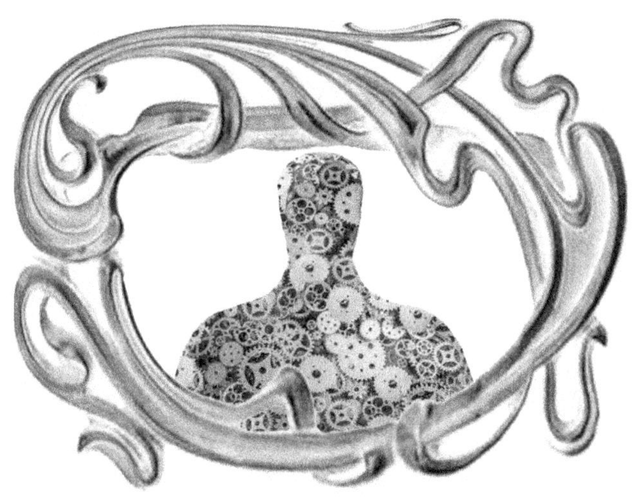

Chapter 3

Heart meandered down the hall with Equuleus and Violet alongside, silent with her thoughts—at the moment centered on Jackson. What was he flying into? Would he have enough support? Who would be his back-up?

So far, most of what Heart knew about *The Cause of All Beings* was the few people she'd met in The Periphery, prisoners behind The Wall. How would or could they possibly be of any assistance? Either there was a considerable amount going on behind the scenes that she didn't know about, or *The Cause of All Beings,* and thus, Jackson, was doomed.

She brought herself back to the present moment when they came to the little door leading to the spacious kitchen.

"All right now, off with you two," she said to Equuleus and Violet.

"Are you sure?" Equuleus asked, concerned.

"Quite. There must be as little distraction as possible while I interact with this … broken fragment of my father. I'll be fine. HelperFriend won't let anything happen to me."

"I know." Equuleus nodded. "In physical terms. But psychologically …."

"I'm sure HelperFriend will take care of me—the best he can—in that way, too."

Violet hopped down from Equuleus. "Well, I don't care what you say, I'm going with you!"

"No, Violet, you're not. The last thing I need at this moment is you babbling away!"

"*Oh!*" Violet cried, hurt.

Heart placed Violet back on Equuleus. "I'm sorry, dear. But you know perfectly well that you do rattle on, and this is a serious moment with serious business at hand. I cannot have my attention divided by anything. And you can be most distracting."

"I see!" Violet muttered.

"Take her away, Equuleus."

Heart watched as Equuleus trotted on down the hall, and then took flight when he came to the open rotunda. She turned resolutely toward the kitchen.

She had no idea where, exactly, HelperFriend and the Clone were, but she hoped they were not in the kitchen, as that seemed distasteful. She also hoped they were not in HelperFriend's rooms as that seemed invasive of the clockwork man's privacy.

As she walked through the *ginormous*, expansively white kitchen, passing closet door after closet door, a sound she knew only too well, grew. She followed the sound through a small hall she'd never seen before. She had to duck to go through the tiny doorway, wondering how either HelperFriend or the Clone could have passed this way, even with the Clone in two halves.

The familiar musical-yet-not-musical sound grew. The dark little passageway suddenly opened into a wide cavern and a gigantic doorway.

Before knocking, or even trying the door, Heart listened to the keening of HelperFriend's crying for a few moments. What could possibly be distressing him this much? What if the Clone had managed to hurt him?

She placed her hand on the opening seal. The door unlocked, then slid silently open.

In the midst of a spacious, dark, wood-braced dome with a brilliant spot light shining down upon the scene, stood HelperFriend, his back to the door. Added to the weirdness she took in the disconcerting sight of her father's clone, who looked like her father in every regard except shorn in half, the top half sitting in a chair, looking up at HelperFriend with intrigue and curiosity.

Heart came up behind HelperFriend, while the Clone moved his riveted attention from HelperFriend to her. But HelperFriend continued deep in grief, his little metallic tears of brass and copper and nickel spraying every which way, including bouncing off the Clone, who appeared to ignore them.

Heart gently placed her hand on HelperFriend's forearm, his gear hand held up to his face. "What's the matter, dear HelperFriend?"

He looked at her through his fingers. "*Oh, Heart! Oh, Heart! Heart!*"

"Yes, I'm here. Tell me what's wrong."

"Oh, making a mess of everything. My tears everywhere. *Oh, my. I'm, oh, Heart, sorry. Sorry!*"

"Are you hurt?"

"No. Yes. No. I don't know, Heart. Please tell me. Am I hurt?"

"Let's sit!" She looked around for a couple of chairs, then spied an elegant sofa against the wall in the covering darkness at the edge of the gigantic room. "Come along."

They crossed the large, open space to the sofa. Heart made HelperFriend sit, then sat, cross-legged, facing him. His crying had receded considerably, and only a few small copper teardrops fell into his lap, a relief to Heart as she didn't particularly relish being bombarded with tiny bits of metal. Not that it would be the first time.

"Tell me …."

"*Oh, Heart!*" HelperFriend wailed.

She feared he would start the deluge of tears again. She patted his hand. "Don't cry, dear. There's a solution for everything."

HelperFriend stopped mid-wail. "There is? Are you sure?"

"Pretty sure. Did the Clone hurt you, somehow?"

"No. No. The Clone … no, he hasn't hurt me. He's quite passive of late. Mostly curious. But, Heart, I don't want to tell you. You have enough to worry about without worrying about things that worry me!"

"But if you don't tell me, since I've seen you like this, I *will* worry."

"Yes. I see ... well, it's about Jackson."

"Oh." Heart suddenly felt terrible. HelperFriend hadn't been there to say good-bye to Jackson. "He just left for Earth, HelperFriend. I'm so sorry I didn't summon you so you could say good-bye."

"I know he left. I know that. It's all right that I didn't say good-bye. I watched from here. I saw his face. I know what was going on in him. He had to get on with it. He didn't need me there. I understand that. But...."

"But what?"

"What is he going into, Heart? What?" HelperFriend's face gears spun mightily, and Heart felt certain little bits of metal were about to spring onto her.

"Well, we don't know exactly, do we?"

"*One thousand Father Inventor Clones, Heart,*" HelperFriend whispered.

"You know!"

"Oh, yes, I know. I knew from him," HelperFriend nodded toward the Clone, who sat looking at them with curiosity. "Records were in his database. I cringed when I saw that information. He made two clones, and they each made two. And they each made two. And they each made two. And so on. I didn't know what to do with that knowledge.

"I was on my way to talk with Father Inventor about it when my database noted that the same information had just come through an informant. One thousand Father Inventor Clones, bent on destroying everything he ever made or developed or stood for."

"It's bad, there's no denying it, HelperFriend," Heart said, flooded with her own sadness.

"But you just said there's a solution for everything."

"Yes. Well, this one has yet to be figured out." They fell silent. Heart pondered aloud, "One thousand is awful. But, if they were each replicating in turn, why or how did it stop at a thousand? Or are there actually more—and rapidly growing—we don't know about?"

"They became weak," the Clone called from his chair. "They took great amounts of resources but were not intellectually viable, not much different from bots, really. Beautiful, but nearly mindless bots. So I turned off their replicating ability.

"There are six Father Inventor Clones, the first two generations, that are clever and intellectually viable. The problem for you is, *which six?* They all look the same. Exactly identical. *Tee-hee!* What fun, dear, beautiful Heart. Our game is not over!"

"I see," Heart whispered.

"Let us walk," HelperFriend said, standing and offering his hand to Heart.

"Yes, let's. If you're sure it's all right to leave him."

"He's harmless in his present condition." HelperFriend led the way further into the dome.

They passed through a small door and out into an open space, bathed in a cheerful yellow light, beaming down on rows of beautiful green plants.

"Oh! HelperFriend! What is this place?"

"It's where we grow some of the genetically engineered vegetables for Father Inventor, and now, for you, as well."

"It's wonderful! Full of light and beautiful green plants."

"I would have brought you here before, Heart, if I'd thought it'd be of interest to you. I thought you were only interested in flowers."

Heart laughed, stooping over to inhale the lovely aroma of the verdant plants. "You *are* a funny one, HelperFriend."

"I am? I don't understand how that can be. I never tell any jokes…."

"Funny in a dear way, not in a comedic way."

"Oh …." he answered pensively.

"All right, now, we must develop a plan."

"To make me more funny?"

"To save Jackson."

"Oh, yes. Save Jackson. That's it. That's all. There is nothing that compares to that."

"No, there's not. Now, let's look at the important information the Clone just spilled, without my even trying to get anything out of him. He said there are only six clones to have to seriously deal with."

"There's nothing 'only' about six formidable Father Inventor Clones," HelperFriend observed.

"Very true," Heart agreed. "But, *it's not one thousand*. And providing that information to Jackson will give him strength."

HelperFriend nodded. "You're right!"

"But ... it's strange ...." Heart mused.

"What's strange? What's strange, Heart?" HelperFriend asked, concern rotating in his facial cogs.

"It's strange how readily the Clone gave me that information. It's his own highly classified information. And he spouted it out to me. *Hmmmm*...." Heart tapped her chin with her forefinger.

"*Hmmmm*..." HelperFriend said in Heart's voice, tapping his chin.

Heart chuckled. "Don't distract me."

"Am I? Sorry! I'm trying to help."

"What if ... what if he lied to throw us off?"

"Oh, no, Heart, he can't lie. I disabled his prevaricating chip."

"He has a prevaricating chip?"

"Yes. Self-installed when he built his cranium for his brain."

"How clever of you, HelperFriend. You did this on your own initiative, removed his ability to lie?"

"Yes."

"Excellent. Keep your eye on that chip Helper-Friend—he'll probably try to regenerate it."

"I will, Heart. But you're right, it's *not* like him to give up information. He's never told me anything like what he blurted out to you. You appear to have power over him."

"Do you think so?"

"No surprise, Heart. You have a kind of power over most clockworks, mechanicals, and hybrids, with me in the front of the line, as you know."

"Dear HelperFriend! If I have some sort of power over the Clone, we need to develop a plan to get the most out of him, without him shutting down and refusing to say anything. This is a great start to helping Jackson."

"True!" HelperFriend agreed.

Heart and HelperFriend walked among the verdant plants under the warm synthetic light. As the lights gradually darkened to dusk they came up with a plan, finally returning through the little doorway to the Clone.

As they came through the door, they heard him making an awful sound.

"What is the meaning of this noise?" Heart asked as they approached the Clone.

"I'm trying to learn everything the clockworks man attempts to teach me."

"You mean HelperFriend?"

"Yes, that one." He nodded his chin toward HelperFriend. "But I can't quite get this last bit. Not only do I not understand the value of spewing bits of metal from my eyes, but I cannot understand how the sound he made causes it to happen. I cannot make bits of metal come out of my eyes."

"No, Clone, you'll not be able to do that. HelperFriend is quite unique. There are ways in which you'll never attain HelperFriend's greatness, no matter how hard you try," Heart knew that if the Clone considered HelperFriend superior to him, he'd wish to emulate him even more.

"I *shall* produce bits of metal from my eyes!"

"First, Clone, you must feel sadness," Heart said.

"Sadness? Sadness … *hmmm*. I'm not sure what that is. I know what disappointment is, and I've been angry. I've been frustrated. But I'm not sure what 'sadness' is."

"How do you feel about being cut in two?"

"Oh! That's easy. Angry. Quite angry. It doesn't help that this clockworks man has my legs locked away so that I can't even call them to me."

"You might possibly get your legs back. But you have much to learn. You're fortunate to have HelperFriend for a teacher, there's no one better. You needn't cry brass and copper. But you *do* have to feel sadness. Real, true, sadness."

"I think it'd be easier to cry copper tears, than for me to have a feeling filtered out of the download of Father Inventor's brain."

"*Oh!*" Heart exclaimed, shocked. She turned to HelperFriend. "Is this true? When the Purists downloaded my father's brain, did they filter out compassionate emotions?"

"That might have happened," HelperFriend nodded. "The Clone does not register compassion, empathy, or sadness on any diagnostics … while I have more than my share."

"Well, Clone, you must discover how to grow these emotions if you're to have your legs again," Heart advised. "You'll do well to continue imitating

HelperFriend, but not with that awful noise. You must *feel* the emotion from inside."

"From inside," The Clone repeated, mystified.

"You have your work cut out for you, Clone." Changing the subject, Heart turned to Helper-Friend. "Will you join us for dinner tonight? You've prepared wonderful dinners for all of us lately and then come back out here to work with the Clone. I think this evening, it would be well for you to sit and chat with my father and me while we develop further plans, following these new discoveries."

"I'd be delighted, Heart," HelperFriend said graciously.

She stood and headed for the little door in the dark outer circle of the dome.

"*Wait!*" the Clone called after her.

Heart turned. "Yes?"

"I thought we were going to chat!"

"I have things to do. And so do you—emotional insight is your assignment." As she passed through the doorway she heard the Clone say to Helper-Friend, "she's quite a delight to chat with, all fire and ice."

She smiled, amused, concentrating on how to get information out of him so she could truly help Jackson. For the moment, she would believe that she and Jackson could prevail against the Purists. They could save The Darling Undesirables, and the people in The Periphery, and all the wondrous clockwork, mechanical, and hybrid beings on Earth, whose lives, at present, were in danger.

HelperFriend was right. Although six powerful clones were considerably less than one thousand, it was quite a bit more than one compassionate genius, Father Inventor, striving to out-wit numerous iterations of himself.

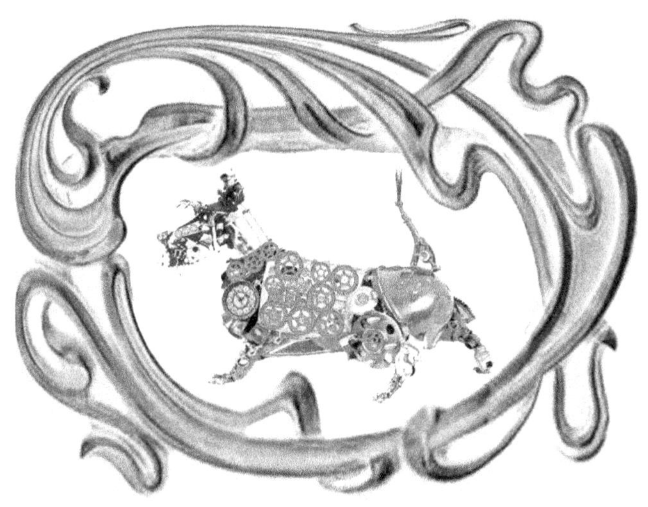

Chapter 4

"We have important plans to discuss, Father," Heart said as she entered his room. "You, me, and HelperFriend. I made a point of asking him to come to dinner since he's been spending so much time with the Clone."

"Oh dear, I invited Lady Gervi to dinner, as I assumed Helper Friend would be with the Clone. With Jackson gone, I thought it might cheer you to have her join us. But if you have confidential matters to discuss …"

"So thoughtful of you, Father. Well, hmmm, this might work out quite well," Heart said, musing. "I have a subject I've been wanting to discuss with Lady Gervi, away from the general Pink population."

"Really?"

Heart smiled but kept her mystery to herself.

*   *

Shortly before dinner, the great chimes at the front door rang throughout the castle as Heart passed by on her way to the dining hall. She'd never heard the chimes beyond the one time she'd rung them herself when she first arrived. They reverberated with an ominous sound, befitting a castle, she thought.

She slid the locks to let Lady Gervi in. Tall and statuesque, the clockworks woman came through the environmental door baffles, her little clockworks dog, Yippee in one arm, and a bouquet of beautiful metallic flowers in the other.

"I hope you don't mind my coming to the front door," she said as the locks shunted and shushed shut behind her.

"Of course not!" Heart exclaimed. "I love it, very nice to have a bit of formality now and then."

"That's what Yippee and I thought. But I apologize for bothering you, Heart. I assumed Helper-Friend would answer the door."

"I was right here, dear lady, it gives me pleasure to invite you in …."

"*Oh, my, oh my!*" HelperFriend, exclaimed, hurrying toward them. "I apologize Heart and Lady Gervi. Truly, I apologize. I ought to have answered the door! I'm completely remiss."

"Not in the least," Heart reassured him. "I happened to be passing the door when the chimes rang. It's lovely to welcome our guests."

Lady Gervi extended the bouquet of flowers to Heart. "I hope you'll accept my humble gift."

"Oh, Lady Gervi, thank you! Where did you find these gorgeous flowers, made from bits of metal and little gears—how perfectly exquisite!"

"I made them," she answered in a soft, shy voice.

"*No!*" Heart exclaimed.

"Oh dear, she doesn't mean '*no!*'" HelperFriend said hurriedly. "She means, ahm … let me see, ahm …."

"I believe she means, 'that's impressive,' or something like that," Lady Gervi said. "I've come to learn that human exclamations are often not to be taken literally."

"Precisely so," Heart nodded. "And Helper-Friend is quite literal."

"I am, it's true," he agreed proudly, "quite literal."

"But getting back to the flowers, Lady Gervi, such talent!"

"Thank you, Heart. You are too kind. They are my humble attempt to duplicate a few of the real flowers in your greenhouses. I do hope my efforts are worthy of them."

"They're amazing reproductions. And these little leaves here, and these tiny petals? Are they not HelperFriend's tears?"

"They are," Lady Gervi said. "He said if I could use these bits of metal, he would be honored."

HelperFriend looked away, embarrassed.

"Not as honored as I am to have them part of this stunning creation. Thank you, HelperFriend."

"I didn't want you to know, I only wanted to … to …."

"I understand, dear."

Yippee suddenly had something to say about it all, and launched into a speech. HelperFriend and Lady Gervi listened attentively.

'So true, so true!" HelperFriend agreed, reaching up to pat Yippee between his little mechanical ears.

"What's holding things up?" Violet squealed, hopping from the dining hall toward them. "Hungry rabbit here. Dinner's waiting. Well, you know that HelperFriend, as you laid it out, ever so long ago! Goodness, gracious, dawdling in the doorway as if there's no tomorrow …."

"We're coming, Violet," Heart laughed. "Look at these incredible flowers Lady Gervi made!"

Yippee again launched into a soliloquy, while Violet listened with rapt attention, one foot raised in mid-motion.

"Oh, my! *Really?* Fascinating. Well, all right then. My, oh my! The flowers look like the real ones. Very good, Lady Gervi. Quite excellent, I must say. Impressive, magnificent, breathtaking, awe-inspiring and furthermore," Violet turned and hopped back toward the dining hall, not waiting to see if she was being followed, "quite skilled, expert, accomplished, and masterly in workman-ship," she concluded—or so they assumed, as she disappeared into the dining hall.

"Shall we join her?" Heart asked, giggling.

"We shall!" HelperFriend offered Lady Gervi his forearm, and Heart followed, fascinated by the halting-yet-graceful gear-driven movements of Lady Gervi's exceptionally tall clockworks frame.

The wall sconces bathed the dining hall in warm, flickering, golden light, and the long dining table was covered in tantalizing fare from one end to the other.

"Lady Gervi, thank you for accepting my invitation to join us for dinner." Father inventor took her hand.

"The pleasure is mine," she replied graciously.

He led her to the chair to his left. She put Yippee down, and he scooted across the room to Violet, where they had their own little place, set with a variety of overflowing shining brass and silver bowls.

Equuleus had settled in his place by the mantle, a generous serving of his preferred greens before him.

"Look at the flowers Lady Gervi gave me, Father. She *made* them!"

Surprised, he turned to Lady Gervi. "Oh my— they're *beautiful!* That's quite a talent. How did you learn this, dear lady?"

"I looked at Heart's flowers through the wall of the greenhouses, and duplicated what I saw with bits of metal."

"Oh!" Heart exclaimed, "did you not go inside?"

"I wouldn't think of it! Those are *your* flower houses, Heart. I wouldn't think of going in."

"Nonsense. Please—go into the greenhouses any time. In fact, after dinner, we'll take a little walk among the flowers. Would you enjoy that?"

"I would love to, if you're sure you wouldn't mind."

"Quite the contrary, I'd enjoy it, very much. So that's settled—after dinner, the ladies will take a walk among the flowers. All right now, everyone serve yourselves, so HelperFriend can join us."

"Give me one moment!" HelperFriend said, dashing from the dining hall and returning in a blink with a beautiful clear glass vase. He put the exquisite flowers in it and placed them in the center of the table.

"There now!" he said, stepping back to admire them.

"Outstanding!" Heart exclaimed.

During dinner Lady Gervi shared stories of the clockworks, mechanical, and hybrid beings, their perils and successes in restoring the dome and their forays out on Pink as well, repairing the wide-spread damage after the Bot Invasion.

"We're so grateful, Father Inventor, that you and Heart and our darling Xavier put the shield in place to protect Pink and Yellow. We feel safe now."

"No need to thank me, dear Lady. I'm protected too!"

Heart, trying not to be distracted by thoughts of Xavier, uttered a small chuckle. "There is that—self-preservation."

"Is that funny, Heart?" HelperFriend asked, gears spinning into a confused expression.

"Kind of funny, HelperFriend."

"But a shield that protects Pink and Yellow from another Bot Invasion, that protects you and Father Inventor as well, isn't funny, Heart, It's just … fact."

"Also true. It is fact!"

"I think I will never quite understand some kinds of humor."

"That's the charm of humor, HelperFriend. One person's laugh is the next one's mystery."

"Interesting," HelperFriend mused.

"I believe it's another one of those expressly human perceptions, HelperFriend," Lady Gervi, said. "I, too, am frequently perplexed by what they find to laugh about."

"Quite right, Lady Gervi. So many things are funny to Heart and even her father. Although not so much Jackson …."

"No, not so much Jackson," Lady Gervi agreed.

"But still! As sober as he is, he almost laughs at a lot of things Heart says, things that leave me utterly puzzled. I have no idea what he's finding amusing."

"*He does?* He 'almost laughs' at a lot of things I say?" Heart asked, stunned.

"Have you not noticed?" HelperFriend asked. Heart shook her head. "I have not. Interesting. The next time you notice it, you must point it out. Subtly of course, but bring my attention to Mr. Serious's almost smile."

"*Ha! Ha! Ha! Ha!*" HelperFriend burst out. "I get that! I see! That's funny. 'Mr. Serious.' Yes. *Ha!*

*Ha!...*but wait." HelperFriend stopped and studied Heart's features. "You're not laughing."

"Ah, um, I … I'm laughing on the inside."

"Oh! Now, there's news! Can you laugh on the inside? How does that feel? Oh goodness, goodness, if I add 'laughing on the inside'—which I have no way of knowing when it happens!—to 'laughing on the outside,' which I can see, but often don't understand, that would imply that … you're laughing virtually all the time."

"Oh-oh! What a corner I've painted myself into," Heart sighed.

"So it would seem," her father replied, grinning.

"However, I shall ungracefully segue away from the topic and move to one of the two that are considerably more serious, but that must be addressed." Heart turned to Lady Gervi. "I've been wanting to ask you—but didn't want to when you were among your peers, although you always are, you're so beloved…."

"She who loves, is loved," Lady Gervi quoted.

"So true, so true," Heart agreed. "But, Lady Gervi, I've been wanting to ask you if you might possibly provide me with a list of the injuries of the clockworks, mechanicals, and hybrids on Pink, subsequent to the Bot Invasion. Would that be too difficult for you?"

"Oh! Oh, Heart! Oh!" Lady Gervi exclaimed, so moved, she could say no more. Yippee, who had been head-to-head with Violet in deep communication, disengaged and hurried over to his

mistress, looking up at her, whining piteously at what he took to be her distress. "No, no, Yippee. I'm all right. Heart just, Heart is going to…*Oh, my, Heart!*"

"This is why I knew we had to have this conversation away from the others," Heart said. "I'm not promising anything. Please understand, Lady Gervi, *I'm not promising anything.* More than that, I can't even suggest that anything might transpire. Further, if it's too huge of a project …."

"HelperFriend," Lady Gervi said, "if you please."

"I very much please," HelperFriend replied. Extending his left arm and pulling back his hand, a great long, narrow sheet of vellum-like paper began to pour out through his wrist. On it, Heart could see names, followed by lists of parts, with precise measurements, dimensions, and alloys.

When finished printing—*somehow!*—Heart had no clue, she glanced at her father, whose look shared her own mystification—HelperFriend tore off the list, rolled it up, tied it with a blue ribbon that he also appeared to manifest from thin air, then handed the scroll to Heart. "In addition, I've transferred this list to Equuleus's database."

"Confirmed," Equuleus noted from his place by the fire. "Somewhat invasive, but—for a good cause."

"An excellent cause," Heart agreed. "But …."

"But it's asking a lot of Key Man," her father added quietly.

"Asking a lot, and easily too much. Now, Lady Gervi, you must promise—*you must swear!*—that you will not breathe a word of this to anyone out-side of this room. You, and your little dog too."

Lady Gervi nodded. "I promise, I *swear*, Heart. You hear that Yippee? Not a grunt, nor growl, nor peep!"

To which Yippee launched upon an oration, no doubt most eloquent, Heart thought, if only she could understand it.

"Hear, hear!" Violet chimed in. "And further-more, to your adroit and succinct observations, dear Yippee, I would simply add, briefly, with great aplomb, confidence, conviction, belief, persuasion, faith and simplicity, that the promise of this poten-tial stands to improve the well-being, joy, peace, and happiness of all beings, everywhere. But most of all, on Pink."

Yippee eagerly nodded his little clockworks head, gears spinning like two-dimensional tops.

"My-oh-my!" Heart whispered. *"What have I unleashed?"*

"Good things, always, my darling daughter," her father reassured her. "Key Man will do what he can."

"And probably more than he can," Heart added.

"And probably more than he can," he agreed. "Now then, with further lack of grace or gentle segue, we had better get on to our next subject."

"Yes. We must."

"But first, tea," HelperFriend said, jumping up, and, seeming to be everywhere at once, cleared away the dinner dishes, brought in a teapot of steeping, steaming tea, and teacups, along with a tray of beau- .

tifully wrought little sweets in the shape of Yippee and Violet.

"*Ohhh! Ah! How adorable!*" everyone exclaimed. Everyone except Violet.

"*Well!*" she uttered indignantly. "*I … I mean, really! I mean! Well, words fail me!*"

Everyone broke out laughing.

"Now *THAT'S* funny!" HelperFriend crowed.

"*Definitely!*" Heart giggled.

"I beg… *I BEG*," Violet raised her voice to a squeal, "your pardon! *WHAT'S* so *FUNNY?*"

"*You*—without words, my furry friend. A most unusual event," Heart said, chortling. "Now, tell us—I'm sure you'll find words—why are words failing you?"

"Look at these … these … these *things*." She pointed at the delicacies on the silver tray. "Are these meant to represent me?"

"Of course. And darn cute they are, too!" Heart bit the head off of one of the little lavender rabbits.

"*See!* That's what I'm saying. Who wants someone to bite the head off something that represents oneself, I'd like to know!"

Yippee launched into a clear argument. Heart leaned over to Lady Gervi, and whispered, "Which side is he on?"

Lady Gervi gave her a look of pure surprise. "You don't understand him?"

"Never have," Heart confessed.

"But—how did you find me that fateful day you saved my life?"

"I followed him. I didn't need to understand his verbalized language, his body language was very clear."

"Oh my, how fortunate I am," Lady Gervi whispered.

"I assure you dear lady, whether I understood his language or not, I understood his distress. In any case, he was *not* about to let me get away!" Heart looked down at Yippee, smiling.

He shook his head and made gestures dramatizing how he'd grabbed onto her plaid pant leg and *tugged*, and would most certainly not let her go, even if she'd tried. He growled and muttered, adding to his drama.

"I see," Lady Gervi said. "I am forever grateful to you both. And, well, everyone who has shown me so much love and care."

"That's what our lives are about," Heart said, smiling at the glowing circle of loved ones around her. "Love and care. Life's greatest gifts. And because of the work that's upon us, I must ask you to again swear to secrecy, and not share a word of what's about to be discussed."

Lady Gervi looked at Heart in open trust and curiosity. "Though I don't know what you're asking me to not share with anyone, and though I've never been asked to promise to remain mute about anything before I knew what it was, I trust you, Heart implicitly.

"*You saved my life!* I owe you mine. I promise you my confidentiality without hesitation."

"Thank you," Heart replied simply. She turned to her father. "We need to talk about the Clone."

"I want you to keep your distance from him," her father began. "It's virtually impossible to know what tactic he'll try to take."

"He can be conniving, but I don't believe he's all that clever. However, I'm about to share an intriguing bit of information, with HelperFriend as witness."

HelperFriend nodded energetically.

"You don't need anyone to confirm what you say, Heart. I'll believe you."

"I know. But in case you feel I've misinterpreted what transpired, we can ask HelperFriend's opinion."

"All right." Her father looked from HelperFriend and back to Heart with curiosity. "Continue."

"I appear to have a strange power over the Clone. I don't understand it, but I must take advantage of it to help *The Cause of All Beings*, to provide support for Jackson, and to glean as much information as possible, as fast as possible, in case he changes his mind—if he can."

Father Inventor leaned forward slightly. "What happened?"

"As you know, I went to observe the Clone and when the subject came up of one thousand iterations of him, he simply volunteered that the first six Clones are the only ones with intellectual cunning.

"He further volunteered that the subsequent iterations of the clones are so intellectually reduced that they are essentially only attractive bots.

"To be able to tell Jackson—almost as soon as he gets to Earth!—that there are only six clones of major concern would surely boost his morale."

"If it's true. But, why would you believe the Clone is telling the truth?" her father asked.

"I was some distance away from him, sharing my concern about the cloned clones quietly with HelperFriend. The Clone called across to us and volunteered this information. I wasn't trying to get anything out of him. And, further, HelperFriend told me he disabled the Clone's prevarication chip …."

"He has a prevarication chip?" her father asked HelperFriend.

"He does."

"And you disabled it?"

HelperFriend nodded. "I did. It seemed wise."

"Very wise, indeed! Well done, HelperFriend."

HelperFriend fairly beamed from the praise, grinning hugely.

"So!" Heart continued, "although I don't know why he became so transparent with me, *something about me* is like truth serum to him. I must pursue it."

"I see. I see," her father said, deep in thought. "Hmmm … most interesting. Curious."

"Agreed," Heart said, also falling into a thought pool.

"*Hmmm* … agreed," HelperFriend said, the gears in his cranium spinning in studied reflection.

"It's not the least bit mystifying," Lady Gervi said. "If I may speak."

Everyone turned to her, even Yippee and Violet turned to face her, while Equuleus whinnied softly.

"His mind is a Clone of Father Inventor's. Therefore, Heart is his daughter …."

"*Oh!*" Heart exclaimed, distressed, recalling when the Clone held her prisoner in his subterranean crystal matrix, and had referred to her as his daughter.

"I know, Heart. It's unpleasant to consider, but please hear me out."

Heart nodded.

"Father Inventor has always deeply and unshakably loved you—it's a part of the fiber of his being, and it would flow through to any clone able to think and feel."

"Of course!" Father Inventor whispered.

"But …" Heart protested, "Father's brain was cloned long before I came on the scene. Long before he did—whatever he did, putting bits of bio, mechanical dark matter and dark energy together that became the 'me' sitting here, right now."

"Regardless, Heart," Lady Gervi continued, "however you came into being, he had the love of you in his heart. Something that profound and intense would be a part of *any* clone of him. I dare say none of the clones can hurt you."

"*Oh! My!*" Heart exchanged a look with her father.

HelperFriend suddenly jumped up. "*Urgent!*" he cried, unmistakably in Swen's voice.

"What! ...." Violet cried.

"Hush!" Heart demanded. The room fell dead silent.

"Urgent! The entire population of The Darling Undesirables Facility at the Gulf has been kidnapped," Swen's voice continued. *"Transmission over."*

Overwhelmed, Heart put her face in her palms.

Chapter 5

Violet and Yippee began to cry, Equuleus stood, agitated, extending his wings, then retracting them, stomping back and forth in front of the fireplace.

HelperFriend regained his voice and cried, "Heart, what are we to do?"

Heart looked up at her father, whose face still registered shock. "What *are* we to do, Father?"

He shook his head. "I … I don't know, Heart. We have intelligence of pending abductions, but not this soon. We're not prepared."

"Clearly," Lady Gervi said calmly, "Heart will have to go to Earth. That communication to Pink would not have been risked for any other reason."

"She's right," Heart said. "I must go to Earth. Directly." She expected protest from her father.

Instead, he nodded agreement. "Lady Gervi has put into words your immediate future."

"*WAAAAAA!*" Violet cried. "*WAAAAAA! WAAAAAA! WAAAAAA! NOT AGAIN! YOU'RE GOING TO LEAVE ME AGAIN! WAAAAAA!*"

"So it would seem," Heart said in an extremely quiet voice, her mind racing, contemplating all that must be done in very short order.

*   *

Lady Gervi and Yippee soon departed, Heart had Equuleus take the whining Violet up to her rooms, and HelperFriend returned to work with the Clone.

Heart and her father retired to his room and sat in companionable silence for a few moments, each considering the fast-approaching future, knowing without speaking that they shared similar thoughts.

"Jackson will be glad to have you there," her father finally said.

Heart looked up at him, but his eyes were fixed on his hands in his lap. His shoulders slumped.

Heart made a tiny chuckling sound. "I doubt it! I'll seem like a lot of trouble."

"No, Heart, he'll understand the advantage of your presence, *and* he'll be glad to have you near. But, Heart, please … please be careful. Be conservative in your moves. Think things through. Yes, you mean the world to me, but also, the world needs you. Be reasoned, thoughtful, cautious."

"I believe that I do reason carefully, and I am thoughtful. But cautious—that's absent when those I love are being abused. I take action. I will do my best to do as you ask, Father. But an entire Darling Undesirable facility has been abducted. *I must take action.* Though I may throw caution to the winds, please support me with your trust."

"Of course, dearest Heart. But my faith and my trust run right up against my fear. When it comes to you, I am not objective."

"I must see what I can glean from the Clone."

"Be careful, Heart!"

"I was his prisoner in the underground crystal matrix when he was intact and had power, and he got nowhere with me. *And* I succeeded in escaping. He'll not have any influence over me now. I need to have influence *over him!* If you would have the mechanicals get the *Heart!* ready for flight, I'll spend some time with him in the hopes of gathering some information before departing for Earth."

"If there's anyone who can do it, it's you," her father said simply.

*   *

The dusky shades of Pink's evening stole through the castle's halls like pastel thieves, as Heart stole along with them, heading to interrogate the Clone. If only she could understand the Purists' motivation. Why did they even care about how others chose to live?

She *did* agree with them that the "Longevity Experiments" that brought the Darling Undesirables into being *must quit*.

No more experimental, defective children spawned in labs, in test tubes. It was horrible. Unforgivable. But the solution was not to destroy those who already existed. Could not the two opposing factions come together, realizing they both pursued the same goals? Kindness. Peace. Joy. Love.

She arrived at the tiny door, passed her hand over the lock and heard it slide back. She opened the door, entering the dark, cavernous space. The darkness did not help improve her frame of mind. She felt strangely lonely and tired.

HelperFriend, sitting by the Clone, saw her enter and nodded.

Heart pulled up a chair and sat before the Clone. "We have a lot to discuss."

"Excellent! I'm delighted to discuss anything with you, Heart," the Clone said, with a charm that was not quite disarming.

*   *

Heart tried to get over the disconcerting sight of what appeared to be her father, cut in half. To be this close to the Clone, with the unsettling visual, and the memories of the last time she sat this close to him, added to her discomfort.

"I'm waiting," the Clone said, with a look of anticipation and curiosity.

Heart inhaled, cleared her mind of the distracting thoughts, and began to think, instead, of what she needed to learn and how she could extract the information she needed.

"All right, Clone, I have something very important to discuss with you. But, first let me ask you, what's more important *to you* right now than anything else?" Heart assumed she knew the answer, but she wanted him to understand there was room for negotiation.

"*Ah! Brilliant!* Brilliant foray, my beautiful daugh … Heart. Giving me the illusion of power!"

"Not the illusion. The possibility."

"Interesting!" The Clone closed his eyes.

Heart waited for several seconds. But it appeared as if he'd gone to sleep. "Clone? Are you awake?" She tried to keep the urgency out of her voice, but the clock was ticking. She had Darling Undesirables to rescue.

"Yes," he answered. But still kept his eyes closed.

"What are you doing?" Heart asked.

"I'm imagining that my answer to your question is my reality."

"Will you answer my question?"

"Yes."

"Please continue," Heart urged.

His eyes flew open and he looked directly at Helper-Friend. "All right. But the clockworks man must leave."

"Why?"

"Because I have a trace of pride left, in this disgusting, humiliating condition." He gestured to where his legs would be if they were attached. "And, as I'm at least smart enough to know that what I wish for more than anything will not be granted to me, if I'm to tell you anyway, I'd like no one but the two of us present."

Heart exchanged a look with HelperFriend.

"I don't like it, Heart. He can't do anything to you physically. But why does he want me absent?"

"Perhaps it's as he says. You disabled his ability to lie. Let's honor his request. A little show of faith on our part demonstrates the behavior we'd like him to emulate. Go, take a relaxing walk in the vegetable garden. I'll call you if I need you."

HelperFriend stood. "I'll take a walk, but it won't be relaxing."

Heart returned her attention to the Clone and tried to puzzle out his enigmatic expression. "What does this strange look mean?"

"It's the answer to your question. You asked me, 'what is more important to me right now than anything else?' And the answer is, more than anything else, now, and in the past, and in the future, it's all the same … what I want more than anything, is that you love me like you love Father Inventor."

"*Oh!*" Heart jumped up in shock. She paced back and forth in front of the Clone. "Oh, you *are* clever! You certainly have managed to say something I would never—*could* never—have anticipated. Brilliant move yourself, Clone."

"It's not a brilliant move. It's the simple truth. I've invented so many things in the hopes of somehow ending up with you caring for me like you do him. He always beats me at everything."

"Well, of course. You're just his clone." Heart was immediately sorry she'd said that with such force. "I mean …."

"You mean precisely what you said. And it's true. I know it can never be. But you asked me what is most dear to me, and that's the answer. I'm frustratingly only able to tell you candid truths, Heart. There's something about you that makes me tell the truth. No matter how much I wish I'd simply *shut up*."

Heart sighed. Was it true? Was it true that he could only tell her the truth? "All right then, what is the second most pressing desire you have?"

"You know what that is, Heart. I'd like to have my legs reattached. Poor legs, under lock and key, unable to move about. It's quite cruel, you know."

"Don't try to work me, Clone."

"I'm not. My legs, of which I'm fully aware, I feel them as if they were attached, and yet I also feel them over there, in that cupboard, wrapped in chains, with a lock and key on the chain, and a lock and key on the cupboard door. I've called and called to them, but no matter, they are unable to free themselves.

"They are, you know Heart, in part bio, and it is not good for them to not move about. They need to exercise, even if I command them to move about in this 'bisected' manner. Yes, I would love to be intact. But, barring that, it would be good to let my legs exercise."

"*Hmmmm …*" Heart contemplated what the Clone said, and what he said made sense. "Have you mentioned this to HelperFriend?"

"Repeatedly. But he doesn't believe me. He is clockworks. Clockworks can be put away for decades, centuries, and brought out, given a squirt of oil, and off they go. But not so for bios like you and me. True, I'm considerably less bio than you, beautiful Heart. But I built bio components into myself, and those components need the care and attention that all bio components need." He paused but kept his studied gaze on Heart.

"I will discuss this with HelperFriend and my father. I'm inclined, at this moment, anyway, to let your legs move about on a regular basis so they get the exercise they need to not atrophy. I agree that that's … inhumane. My motivation is always to do no harm to any sentient being if harm can be avoided. But …."

"You want to know if there's a way to distinguish the six greater clones from the hundreds of lesser ones."

"Yes. That's one question."

"For me, there's a sort of magnetic force between any clone and myself. The higher level the clone, the stronger the pull. This will not work with you, nor anyone else."

"Obviously," Heart said, disappointed.

"I really cannot stand to see you sad. I don't know what it is. It's a sheer immense discomfort that makes me want to change how you feel. I'm at cross purposes between the directives, socialization, and programming I've been given by the Purists, conflicting with a drive to see you happy. Just that simple.

"You'll be able to know lesser Clones by their eyes. The lesser Clones are not capable of engaging in complicated conversation. Not like you and I are, Heart."

"So," Heart recapped, "I'll know immediately if I've encountered a lesser clone. What if I come face to face with many clones?" The thought of a phalanx of Father Inventor clones advancing upon Jackson was unbearable.

"They, like me, will not be able to hurt you. But they will probably capture you."

"And hand me over to Loruza and Keeper A."

"It's possible, Heart. I would hate to see that. Loruza is quite frankly crazy. And *jealous!*"

Heart restrained herself from commenting on the Clone's own expertise on the subject of insanity.

At that moment, HelperFriend stepped back into the space, cocking his head toward the front of the dome—she knew that meant the *Heart!* was ready for take-off. No more time for interrogation. The Clone would have to come with her.

"All right, now I must ask my burning, *burning* question. If I were to take you to Earth, will you attempt to do me harm?"

"Take me to Earth? Take me to Earth? *You are taking me to Earth?*"

"It seems I must."

"No, Heart. I don't want you to go to Earth with all the trouble that's brewing there now, it's not safe for you."

"But that's why I must go. If I do, will you do me harm?"

"I cannot."

"Will you do Jackson harm?"

"Given the opportunity, I would. After all, *he cut me in half!* But as I'm cut in half, I couldn't do him much harm, could I?"

"You could rally your minions."

"I can rally my minions from here, Heart."

"No, you can't. The shield …."

"The shield keeps physical harm from Pink and Yellow, as well as certain types and levels of other energy waves. But I can work my way around it, and have already been somewhat successful. *Oh, blast!* There I go telling you another one of my secrets. You make things quite difficult for me, you know that, don't you?"

"That's what I want to hear." She stood. "I must go now and get things organized." She went to HelperFriend.

"Excellent. And are you?"

"Me?"

"You're going with me to Earth. I need you to oversee the Clone."

"Oh, boy, I'm going to Earth!"

"It won't be all fun and games, HelperFriend."

"So … it'll be some fun and games?"

"*Augh!*" Heart cried, no time to explain the figurative meaning of her comment. "Just get yourself and the Clone ready. We'll have to find a way to secure him in the *Heart!*"

"I'll do it, Heart, don't worry about that," HelperFriend assured.

She passed through the gigantic door, locked it, then ducked through the little door, and headed for her father's room.

Chapter 6

Her father appeared to be in the same position she'd left him, although she knew he must have done a hundred things while she was gone.

"Was your conversation with the Clone a success?" he asked.

"It was. He told me how to distinguish the most challenging Clones from the weak ones. He told me that, whether I like it or not, he considers me his daughter, and he cannot harm me. Nor can he lie to me. Then I asked him what he wanted more than anything in life."

"Did he tell you?"

"He did. But what he wants, he will never have."

"And what is it?"

"He wants me to love him like I love you."

"Oh, now, there you have it, darling daughter. Your most challenging challenge."

"What do you mean?"

"If you can come to love him in a caring and unconditional way, you will have done some significant growth."

"*Oh, Father!*" Heart exclaimed, frustrated with confusion. "I could never feel about him the way I feel about you. I mean … it's just not in me."

"You don't have to feel the same about him as you do me. But if you arrive at a place where you're able to know, to *deeply know*, that you can love him, unconditionally, even while disapproving his behavior or beliefs, then you'll have made my work worthwhile.

"All my inventions and creations and dabbling with sentient clockwork beings, and sentient mechanical beings, and all my work with dark matter and dark energy—has one ultimate goal …."

Heart looked into her father's amazing, wise and brilliant eyes. "That love, and only love, must be at the core of one's motivation. That in all of life, there's but one ultimate realization—to love and to be loved," she said.

He grinned, his face alight. "That's it perfectly, Heart. You've been called to a supreme test, to be in close proximity with the one being you are more likely to hate than any other. He has done many things to tear the calm and beautiful lives of innocent beings asunder. He is responsible for Xavier's death…."

Heart gasped. The thought had not concretely crossed her mind. But, yes, this was true.

"And even, *even* at that, if you can find the place inside yourself where you experience unconditional love for the Clone, then you'll be able to heal wounded places *in yourself*."

Heart listened attentively to every word her father uttered, realizing that a moment of reflection, no matter how dire the situation, would serve her. She must remember patience and contemplation.

"I hear you, Father. And I'll be attentive to counsel I receive from those I respect."

He moved to sit by her on the little cot and took her hand. "I can ask no more. You're wise and loving. Those qualities are a strong foundation for anyone. With them, you're prepared—as much as anyone can be—for the future that comes flying toward us."

He released her hand and stood. "And, as the future comes flying toward us, we must move toward it. I've had a couple of the mechanicals checking the *Heart!* over, and it's ready to go. I asked the Plant Folks to take care of your flowers. They're thrilled, of course, with the assignment."

"Thank you, Father. But my biggest concern is …."

"I know. Violet."

"She's going to screech when she learns that not only Equuleus and I are going to Earth, but Helper-Friend as well."

"HelperFriend too?" He sat back down beside her.

"Yes. HelperFriend and the Clone."

"Oh, no! Why the Clone?"

"Because I don't have the time, nor the focus right now, to ask him everything I need to ask. Just easier to take him with me. He can't hurt me, he can't lie. And with his legs here on Pink, he's can't go very far."

"I see …" her father said. "Yes. I see …."

She suddenly realized he was puzzling together passages from *Ourbook*—like everyone always seemed to have to do when she made any sort of announcement or took a particular action. *So irritating!* She hated the feeling that all her efforts, thinking, and planning were, somehow, predetermined, and not only predetermined, but written in a book! For everyone to read and to seem to know her next move before she did!

"Not *Ourbook*, please!" she finally protested.

"I'm sorry, Heart. I know it irritates you when anyone has an insight around all that's happening, but *Ourbook* allows for many choices, which lead to different paths. You *are* making your own decisions, leading to one path unfolding and the others closing. As you make your choices and decisions, passages in *Ourbook* stand out with lightning clarity."

"So, I'm not a robot with only one behavior," she couldn't resist the edge of sarcasm, "I'm a robot with several possible behaviors. Just call me Helper-Friend!"

"Heart," her father said, disappointment in his voice, "you insult the powers of intention, yourself, *and HelperFriend.*"

Shamed but still irritated, Heart looked down.

Her father stood and pulled her to her feet. "Give me a hug and go gather your things. About Miss

Violet, I suppose we'll impose upon Lady Gervi and Yippee to 'adopt' her for the time being."

Heart cheered up. "I hadn't thought of that. Yes, if they're up for it, that will solve the lavender rabbit problem. Now I must organize and solve all the other problems that face me." She hugged her father and hurried up to her rooms, chatting with Helper-Friend via her communication device, on the way.

"I'm headed up to my rooms to gather a few things, including a winged horse and a lavender rabbit. The horse comes with us, the rabbit will stay with Lady Gervi and Yippee, if they'll have her."

"Oh dear," HelperFriend said.

"I know. But once she settles in, it'll be fine. She and Yippee are great friends," she said as she entered her rooms.

"*WHO* is a great friend of Yippee's?" Violet squealed, hopping up and down on Heart's bed.

"*You* are, you funny rabbit."

"Oh, well, yes, that's true," Violet agreed, greatly mollified, settling down. "I am his very best friend."

Heart nodded. "That's why we're having you stay with him and Lady Gervi for a while. That is, if it's all right with them."

"Of course it'll be all right with them! Why wouldn't it be all right with them? They ought to feel privileged!" Violet jumped down from the bed and hopped about, full of indignation.

"But, wait a minute! *Wait-a-min-ute!* What do you mean, you're having me stay with Yippee and Lady Gervi? What-da-ya mean?"

"I'm going to Earth *right now*."

"Don't go, Heart! I have a *baaaaad* feeling." She leapt onto the bed and hopped up and down and up and down. "*DON'T GO!*"

"You know I must, Violet."

Violet stopped hopping and jumped back down to the floor. She quietly walked across the room to Heart. Looking up at her and cocking her little rabbit head, her long lavender ears flopped coyly around her face. "All right then, all right. That's fine. But take me with you. That's an obvious choice. Obvious. You don't want to be without your own little Violet, do you?"

Heart picked Violet up and went to her closet. "No, Violet, I don't want to be parted from you." She put Violet down and brought out her small travel bag. She put her two plaid outfits in it, went into her bathroom and gathered a few essentials, then moved about her rooms, deciding what she might need to take with her, which was almost nothing.

"I'm not going on a vacation. I must stay incredibly focused. I'll have no time for you. You'd be bored within one Earth day …" Heart stopped mid-sentence, reveling in those words—a real Earth day! Dawn and dusk! Day and night!

"No I won't, Heart," Violet protested. I won't. I'll be quiet and patient and so happy to be there."

"I don't even know what all I'm going to have to do, or where I'll be …."

"Doesn't matter. I'll be fine."

"Yes, for sure, you *will* be fine, because you'll be here, either in my father's room, or out in the great dome with The Folks, staying with Yippee. It'll be fun for you. You'll forget me in a few Pink days."

Violet, who had followed her around the rooms, turned her back on Heart. "Oh, now you insult me. My goodness, as if I could ever forget *you!* The person who left me here and went to Earth, the person who said terrible, dreadful, awful, deplorable, egregious, heinous, and unforgivable things to me right before she left."

Heart put down everything she was holding, picked up Violet and sat with her in her lap on the bed. "We will never forget one another, dear Violet. Father advised me to take extra care, and because I want to be in your life and in his, I will do so. I know it's sad and not easy for me to go into—well, I don't know what, for sure.

"But we must do as we're called to do, and you must think positive thoughts, that Jackson and Peter and I and everyone who believes in *The Cause of All Beings* will come out triumphant. You must picture that good prevails. All we desire is that everyone be allowed to live the life they imagine for themselves, without impinging on the life of anyone else.

"That's the dream, Violet, and that's your assignment. To keep the dream steady in your thoughts, to hold it pure."

Violet calmed in Heart's embrace. "All right, Heart, I will do it. I will. I understand. I can be calm and brave, even here, from the distance, I can send you safety and strength. And love. I will do it. I don't want bad words between us before you leave, if you must leave."

Heart hugged Violet for a long, long moment. Then she stood, setting Violet on the bed, and returned to gathering what little she would take with her.

Finally, she turned to Equuleus, who stood silently by. "Ready?"

He nodded and passed through the door. Heart shouldered her bag, picked up Violet, then climbed onto Equuleus. He flew around and down, around and down, in the beautiful, pale pink light of the castle's rotunda, the three of them silently wondering if they would ever do this again.

Chapter 7

Heart saw the *Heart!* in front of the dome through her father's windows as they entered his little room. The spacecraft always gave her a start when she saw it. Would the time ever come that she would not first think of Xavier, processing a stab of pain?

She returned her attention to the commotion in her father's room. He had apparently chatted with Lady Gervi about taking care of Violet, as she and Yippee were there. Yippee leapt about, chattering in his strange language. It seemed to Heart that she could almost understand him. Was he not saying, "we'll have so much fun, my Violet friend," in among his other sounds?

Heart slid off Equuleus and put Violet down by Yippee. "Yes, the two of you will have a lot of fun!"

Everyone fell silent, looking at Heart in surprise.

"You understood him?" Lady Gervi asked.

"I believe I heard him say, 'we'll have so much fun.' Among some other … ahm, words."

"That's exactly right, Heart!" Violet looked up at her as proud as if she'd taught Heart "Yippee-ish" herself.

"Well, then, maybe it's not so difficult."

Yippee danced around Heart, voicing a soliloquy of apparent intense and fervent meaning, though Heart could not translate a single word. She nodded politely, but it became evident that she had no idea what to reply.

"So true, Yippee," Lady Gervi said, filling in the awkward silence. "You've said it neatly! All right now, I believe we must leave Father Inventor and Heart to organize her journey." She moved with her fascinating statuesque, gear-driven grace, both fluid and lurching, to the back door baffles, Yippee at her feet. "Come along, Violet."

But Violet remained standing in the middle of the room, quivering. *"I can't!"*

"You must," Heart stooped over and picked her up, placing her in Lady Gervi's arms, then whispered in Violet's ear, "I will wave a special wave with the *Heart!* just for you."

She turned and moved to her father, her back to the door, filled with sadness. Her whole life with Violet passed through her mind in an instant, flooded with the emotion of how dear her little friend had become.

As Lady Gervi, Yippee, and Violet exited through the back baffle, HelperFriend came in through the hall. He looked at Heart and Father Inventor's somber expressions. "What? What's wrong?"

"Nothing to worry about," Father Inventor said. "Just a sad parting between Violet and Heart."

"Oh!" HelperFriend exclaimed. "A difficult parting. But Lady Gervi and Yippee will take excellent care of her."

"I know," Heart nodded. "I know they'll take good care of *her*. But what will she do to *them?*"

Everyone chuckled softly.

"How are things at your end, HelperFriend?"

"The Clone's reaction is unbelievable. If his legs were attached, he'd be jumping up and down like Violet. He's quite excited and has asked me thirty-two times since you were there when we're leaving."

"Are you exaggerating?" Heart asked.

"Exaggerating what?" HelperFriend asked, his cogs whirring into a frown.

"Thirty-two times?"

"Oh … *oh!* Yes, precisely thirty-two times. You know me Heart, quite literal. Yes. Thirty-two times. I *wish* I was exaggerating. Do you know how *boring* it is to have a being as intelligent as the Clone ask the same question again and again as if something is wrong with his programming?"

"Perhaps there *is* something wrong with his programming," Heart said.

"I checked, hoping it was so. At least then there'd be an excuse. But, no. He checks out fine. He's simply crazy-excited to be going to Earth."

"Even without his legs?"

"Even without his legs. He said new legs can be had. But getting to Earth is the great challenge."

"Perhaps we ought to reconsider taking him," her father said. "He may be more dangerous than you think."

Heart recalled the way the clone, in two impenetrable—or supposedly impenetrable—metal boxes, himself cut in half, still managed to almost murder Jackson on the flight to Pink. "What do you think, HelperFriend?"

"A lot of emotional nuance gets by me, Heart, as you know, but, it seems to me that he's just happy to be going to Earth. You can't blame him. He's been stuck with me in that dark dome since arriving here. After you talked to him he brightened up. I'm sure that the promise of more conversations with you took him out of his depression."

"I see. Still, I wish there were a way to sedate him."

"I could try to hypnotize him," her father suggested.

"That might work. That's what you did when he was trying to kill Jackson on the way here. If you could suggest that he go to sleep until further directives, and he slept all the way to Earth, that would be a relief."

"Let's try it," her father said, heading for the hall.

Heart, her father, HelperFriend, and Equuleus paraded through the kitchen, then down the dark hall, and finally arrived at the tiny door. Heart and her father passed through it, but HelperFriend led Equuleus around a corner that Heart had not before noticed in the dark, and down a different hall. Heart and her father came through the larger door at the same time as HelperFriend and Equuleus came through a door partway around the giant domed room.

In his place, as always, sat the Clone, attentively watching the sudden activity.

"*Ah! Company!* Come in! Come in," he called to them. "Lovely to see you all. Excuse me for not standing. I know it seems most rude, but you see, I have no legs!" He broke out in uproarious, crazed, laughter. "*No legs!* Funny, yes, my amazing mirror image, Father inventor?

"Please, everyone, have a seat," the Clone continued. "Come down to my level. But, wait, are we going to Earth now? If so, then never mind, no sitting, we must get on the move. No, no, wait. Something's up. There's no need for all of you to be here. *Hmmm ...*" The clone's eyes closed down as he gave the situation some deep thought. "*What's ... going ... on?*" he asked, his voice racked with suspicion.

"Nothing to worry about," Heart tried to sound reassuring.

"Are you going to take me to Earth, or not?"

"I am, Clone. But I don't want any trouble from you. So, to be perfectly transparent, my father is going to talk with you for a while, to assure a calm journey for everyone."

"Hypnotize me. He's going to try to hypnotize me. Not necessary. I'll be quiet and perfectly well behaved."

"Yes. That's just what we want," Heart agreed. She pulled a chair in front of the Clone. "Here you go, Father. HelperFriend, Equuleus, and I will move over to the sofa and leave the two of you to chat. When my father is satisfied, we'll leave." She moved to the wall with HelperFriend and Equuleus.

While her father talked in soothing yet authoritative tones to the Clone, Heart reflected upon her own immediate concerns. She'd have to check the magnetics that would hold Equuleus to his place against the wall. She and HelperFriend would have to secure the Clone, somehow.

Then she thought about HelperFriend. Would he sit next to Equuleus? She didn't like the idea of Equuleus having to tolerate additional magnetics.

As if reading her mind, HelperFriend said, "I hope I get to ride copilot, Heart. You will let me, won't you?"

"*Yes. I will!* That solves the problem of Equuleus having to tolerate more magnetics to keep you in place."

"Thank you kindly," Equuleus said quietly.

"All right now, my biggest concern is getting the Clone firmly secured."

"No problem, Heart. If he's hypnotized, he'll be calm. I'll tie him to the wall, and he'll stay put."

"And if he's *not* hypnotized, you'll tie him to the wall, and he'll stay put," Heart said, distracted by the serious interaction between her father and his mirror reflection.

Her father said something with earnest intensity to the Clone that she saw was more than merely hypnotizing him. He was giving the Clone fair warning of some sort as she watched the Clone's eyes grow wide in surprise, and then his shoulders slumped, as if utterly defeated. How small and pathetic he suddenly appeared.

What could her father have said to him?

Soon, thereafter, as her father continued to talk, the Clone's look became far-away and absent.

"Look, Heart," HelperFriend whispered. "The Clone is hypnotized."

"Yes. He's not faking that, it's obvious even from here."

Chapter 8

They headed back to Father Inventor's room, HelperFriend easily carrying the hypnotized Clone, who, for once, was perfectly silent. Heart's father climbed into his bio-safety bell jar, and they stepped outside.

As they moved to the *Heart!*, The Folks stopped their activity and joined those who were already out-side, expressions of hope and joy, fear and triumph, on their many clockworks, mechanical, bio faces. An overwhelming emotion of happy-sadness hung in the air, everyone hushed and nearly motionless.

As Heart walked by them—these hundreds of beings of every sort, every one of them with their own unique sentience, intelligence, and emotions— a sudden unsteadiness reached into Heart. Their love and concern and trust was greater than ever before, and rocked her to her core.

They depended on her. And—*she was not that powerful!* She was not that "grand!" She was not that … whatever it was they believed her to be. She didn't feel like an impostor, because she'd never, ever said she was some kind of warrior, some kind of savior. But now she discovered herself in that role—driven by two desires of her own: to take care of Eye and to be with Equuleus.

The events that fell one upon the next as a result of her determination to fulfill those two commitments, cascaded through her mind in a flurry.

She put her hand on Equuleus's back to steady herself, and, although touching him did have that effect, the surge of his emotion—the same as hers—nearly brought her to her knees. The gathering gasped as Heart faltered.

She felt their compassion, support, and love for her, and for Equuleus, and took strength from it.

She was not alone. She had a mission, *but she was not alone!*

She came to the open hatch of the *Heart!* HelperFriend went in first with the Clone and, Heart knew, would determine a safe-for-everyone means of securing him. She finally gathered her courage to turn and look at her father.

Inside his bell jar, his look of worry and love was unguarded. He reached out his protectively covered arms, and she moved into his embrace, the bell jar between them.

"I love you, Heart, my own heart. You must take care of yourself."

"I will. I will. I love you, too, Father. We will be together again."

With a dark feeling that she may not be saying the truth, Heart turned, braced herself, stood tall and strong, put her hand on Equuleus, not to steady herself, but to show everyone, including herself, that she was ready to take on whatever the near future held. That she would save the missing Darling Undesirables. That she would do whatever she could to quell the minions of the Purists and the Clone. That she would serve *The Cause of all Beings*.

"Heart, Heart, Heart …" the crowd murmured.

Heart raised a hand in acknowledgment.

"Heart, Heart, Heart …" the murmuring swelled.

Heart gathered her courage to look for Violet in the crowd, but she could not see her.

"Heart, Heart, Heart …" the crowd affirmed.

Heart finally saw the tall and graceful frame of Lady Gervi moving through the crowd. With understanding, everyone moved aside, letting her through. Heart could even hear Yippee, at Lady Gervi's feet, crying a shrill, but understandable, *"Heart, Heart, Heart …"*

But, she still could not see Violet.

Then Lady Gervi came to the front, and, there in her arms was the sweet Violet, having shed so many lavender tears upon Lady Gervi's black gears, that her arms sparkled with a violet luminescence.

Reaching her little, furry, rabbity arms toward the distant Heart, Violet shrieked in her high-pitched voice, *"WHO DO WE LOVE?"*

"Heart! …" the crowd roared.

Heart smiled what she hoped was a happy, but she knew it was sad, smile at Violet, and, with Equuleus, turned and entered the *Heart!*

"WHO DO WE LOVE?" Violet repeated.

"Heart! Heart! Heart! …" the crowd thundered.

She and Equuleus entered the *Heart!* Equuleus settled into his place, and Heart adjusted the magnetics that would hold him there. She checked on the Clone, still with his far-away look, strapped safely in the corner.

The chant outside fell into a steady rhythm as, wordlessly, Heart gave HelperFriend a thumbs up, and he secured himself in the co-pilot's seat. Seeing Violet shed her copious tears, HelperFriend whispered, *"Oh! Violet!"* Bits of metal began to spring from his eyes onto the instrument panel. "Sorry, Heart, sorry."

"That's all right," Heart whispered in return, wishing that she, herself, might shed some tears. But she'd rarely cried in her life – the last time had been for Xavier.

HelperFriend reached down for the little box at their feet. He gathered up most of his tears and opened the box. *"Stars! Stars! Stars!"* the child voice of Heart exclaimed from the 3-D image in the box. HelperFriend poured his tears in the box to accompany the ones that had been put there before.

"Ready?" he asked, replacing the box and sitting up straight in his co-pilot's place.

Heart studied the plaid of her outfit for a few moments. *All the threads glowed.* They reflected the many roads she'd traveled converging upon this moment. "Ready," she replied, firing up the engines.

They slowly taxied past the crowd, Heart waving, smiling as best she could, but refusing to make eye-contact with anyone. Even her father. *Especially* her father. *"Love you,"* she whispered. *"Love you all …."*

Then, with a mighty surge, she brought the *Heart!* off Pink's surface and it leapt into the sky. Hoping there was still some lavender skywriting smoke left that she'd asked the mechanicals to install previously to tease Jackson with her frivolous ways, she now made a giant heart, releasing the decorative trail, as promised to Violet.

She made another pass close above the residents of Pink, and, even at the distance, couldn't miss Violet leaping up and down upon Lady Gervi, waving.

"Oh! Poor Lady Gervi!" Heart chuckled.

HelperFriend joined her. "Thank goodness, she's calm and patient."

Heart nodded, "Maybe it'll rub off on Violet." They both broke out laughing at the absurdity.

Heart then saw Geometria at the very, very end of the line of Pink's residents, holding aloft his mystical box—now a pyramid of molten gold and platinum, the intense metallic colors roiling in the form, shining a beacon in Pink's twilight dusk.

She nodded to him. Yet more evidence that she was not now—*and would not be!*—alone.

She felt energies greater than any she understood gathering in the wings of time, rustling at the edges of the stage of Life.

She looked up at Earth, hovering overhead, and as she did so, Equuleus said quietly, "home."

"Yes," Heart agreed with a rush of joy and longing. "Home."

*   *

A strange sense of urgency and peace settled over Heart on the journey homeward. She hardly thought about the fact that she was now, well and truly, captain of her own ship—even named after her, if not by her own doing, nor even her preference.

Flying solo, with a clockworks man, a passenger, not a pilot, in the co-pilot's seat. With her beloved clockworks, winged horse. With a weird and disconcerting iteration of her father, hardly half the man he used to be, she thought, with a small wry chuckle, tied down in the back, seemingly quite content with whatever swirled around him.

"You laughed," HelperFriend said.

"I did?"

"You did! You laughed. At nothing. Nothing is happening at all. No, no, that's not correct. Much is happening. We're flying to Earth, which is a lot, a lot, a lot. But not funny."

Heart glanced over at him and noted his cranium gears spinning, but not dangerously so.

"I can't find in my mind …" he paused, and she heard a clicking sound.

"Are you all right?"

"Yes. I'm trying to find something now to laugh at. But I really can't."

"It is a bit obscure, HelperFriend."

"Yes?"

"Thinking about him …" She nodded her head to the back.

"The Clone?"

"*Ummm-humm.*" She put her finger to her lips.

"Something funny …."

"There's a saying, 'he's not half the man he used to be,' meaning, well, in psychological terms. Sorry, HelperFriend, it was a ridiculous passing thought."

"*Oh! Oh, I get it!* I really do get it. Because, he's not, because … he's not. Physically."

"Right."

HelperFriend puffed his chest up. "I got it! I got something obscure that you found funny. I'm quite pleased with myself. I'm ready for human society."

"Ah, well, there might be a few more things you will learn, my friend. But I'm impressed that you understand that little bit of my strange humor."

"I remain quite pleased with myself," HelperFriend insisted.

Heart chuckled again.

They continued in quiet companionship for the rest of the journey, while Heart plotted a variety of logistics and maneuvers in her mind.

After all, she'd not had time to plan anything beyond the brief discussion with her father about where to land—they'd agreed that she'd land at The Museum of Scientific Improbabilities and Unpredictable Oddities. But they also agreed that it didn't feel quite right nor quite safe.

The Clone posed problems.

However much she always felt at home with Martha and Key Man, she would go anywhere else in the world to protect them, if such were the concern. With these many preoccupying thoughts, at last, they drew near Earth, and she could feel the pull of its gravity.

It made Heart happy. Earth would *always* pull her near.

"*Uhhhhhh….*" HelperFriend groaned.

"What? What's the matter?"

"*Odddd feeeeling. Heaaaavy… heeeaaaavvvvyyy … Is it wrong?*"

"It's Earth's gravity." Heart studied Helper-Friend's gears from head to chest to arms and down into his hands. They appeared to be functioning perfectly. "It looks like you're all right. We've talked about Earth's gravity. It's so lovely." She breathed deeply, filled with joy. "So lovely."

"Yes. But I didn't know it would *feel* like this, Heart. If you say it's all right, I'll make adjustments. I was more worried about you."

"Oh darling HelperFriend, I'm *so* fine. I love the gravity. And I love to watch the sun setting." She gestured out the viewport at the glorious sunset, not quite looking like sunset from where they were at present, high above Earth, but the wondrous lace of golden-orange clouds around the sun spoke more than any words Heart could contrive.

"Oh, Heart, Oh Heart, is that all right? All those colors and all that stuff around the sun? Did it break? It looks like it's spilling out!"

Heart laughed. "Such poetry my own HelperFriend. It's fine. It's beautiful. Surely you've seen pictures of sunsets …."

HelperFriend's gears whirled audibly. Heart knew he was thumbing through his vast data banks of images. "Oh, yes, of course. I've seen it many times. But, somehow, this is different."

"Sure, it's different. It's real!"

"Very good. Now that I know it's considered beautiful, I can see the beauty. Beautiful, beautiful…"

As HelperFriend chatted to himself about the gravity and the beauty, Heart became aware that the Clone seemed to be stirring. "What's he doing?" she interrupted HelperFriend's monologue, needing to keep her attention upon navigation.

HelperFriend looked back. "Ahm, he's stirring about. He appears agitated. Perhaps the gravity is making him come out of his hypnosis."

"Excellent deduction, HelperFriend," Heart said. "I can't let him distract me at the moment. I must navigate."

"He can't get loose, but I'll watch him." HelperFriend turned the seat around. "Too bad to miss the sunset," he mumbled. "Just when I was beginning to appreciate it."

"There'll be other …."

Heart was interrupted by a bleep followed by Jackson's voice reverberating through the *Heart!* "Can't do anything without having to worry about you!"

"As always," Heart replied, droll as she could muster, "glad to see you too!"

"Follow me," he ordered.

"Right," she said, in a flat-voiced imitation of him.

"Not landing where previously planned?"

"Right," he rebutted. "What the … what is all that racket?"

"The ahm …" Heart became aware that their conversation may be eavesdropped upon. "The half-man wants to play."

"The half … oh no. It's not even remotely possible that aboard the *Heart!* is …."

"Possible. Probable. True." Heart looked over at HelperFriend and crossed her eyes in exasperation.

"Oh, Heart!" HelperFriend cried, "That's— I've never seen you do that!" He looked at her and forced the gears in his eyes to pull to center. "How do I look? Do I look like that?"

"I'm afraid it's a completely different sort of look on you …."

"Will you stop jabbering?" Jackson ordered. "Honestly, Heart, all you need is any sort of creature around you to babble on."

Heart inhaled sharply to retort, but then, remembering the bad place their arguments tended to go, she clamped her mouth shut, exhaled slowly, then said in a voice considerably more calm than she felt, "I have you in sight. Following, sir."

"Right. Turn on your Dark Energy Highway running lights."

"Yes, sir." Heart flipped on the lights.

Silence reigned, except for the almost rhythmic thrashing of the Clone, Heart glanced over at Helper-Friend, who kept his eyes on the Clone.

Heart followed Jackson's vehicle, and they eased down onto the Dark Energy Highway. The sun had set. They passed over The Museum of Scientific Improbabilities and Unpredictable Oddities. Heart sighed heavily, sorry to leave behind her hope of finally spending a night in Martha's darling cottage.

"The Museum of Scientific Improbabilities and Unpredictable Oddities," HelperFriend whispered in awe.

Heart nodded. "Do you know it?" she asked quietly.

"Oh, I know it, Heart! I know! I was inert in that closet in the castle's kitchen, awaiting your arrival for—for a long, long time.

"But I had my receptors watch you and Equuleus come in the aurora borealis, the mechanical aurora between Pink and the rotunda of The Museum of Scientific Improbabilities and Unpredictable Oddities. Oh! That's the first time I ever knew fear, fearing you would not make it. Fearing the terrible, terrible bomb the Purists sent up in the aurora would destroy you.

"But you prevailed, Heart! You did then, and you will now."

"Be quiet, clockworks," Jackson commanded. "Follow close, Heart. We land near The Wall. Not too close, but near enough that you must follow me precisely. The landing is not unlike your landing in The Periphery. In the woods, but with no one on the ground to guide us, and it's night. I don't want you plowing into me as we land, so be attentive."

"Oh!" Heart exclaimed. Beyond that, words failed her.

"After landing, we'll taxi for some distance. Follow me. And I mean, follow me, no matter what."

What could that mean? Heart wondered but kept her question to herself. "Will do."

Jackson dropped from the Dark Energy Highway and turned off all but faint running lights. Heart followed his moves as closely as she could. Then Jackson flew down into dark woods.

Heart, filled with trepidation, followed. Jackson's vehicle, considerably smaller than the *Heart!*, it navigated the narrow passage with relative ease, but it was a significant challenge for Heart.

Suddenly, Jackson was on the ground, and, just as he'd said, he taxied along at a good clip. Heart brought her craft gently down behind him.

"Wow, Heart!" HelperFriend sighed, *"amazing!"*

Concentrating with every fiber of her abilities, and more that she pulled from she-didn't-know-where, she nodded wordlessly, hoping that she continued to earn HelperFriend's admiration, without tearing the *Heart!* and trees apart in the dark.

A solid rock wall appeared before them. Heart began to brake, but, much to her shock, Jackson's vehicle drove right through the wall, and, with a faith that exceeded just about any she'd ever experienced, she did as he'd commanded, and followed.

Chapter 9

As Heart passed through the illusion of a wall of stone, she saw Jackson continue to taxi into a vast cave. There was an ambient light that she couldn't quite figure out, but she refrained from asking questions. She simply did as she'd been told, and that was to follow Jackson.

"To my right," he commanded, "and cut engines."

Heart pulled alongside his vehicle, and shut off the engines, looking over at HelperFriend—his expression of mystification reflected hers. She turned off the magnetics holding Equuleus in place.

"May we disembark?" she asked Jackson.

"Of course."

She flipped the switch opening the hatch. Equuleus stood and stepped out, while she and HelperFriend unlatched themselves and joined Equuleus. She put her arm around Equuleus's neck, bracing herself for the reprimand from Jackson.

He came around his vehicle toward them. "Amazing piloting, Heart. I can say nothing less than that."

Heart was dumbfounded with astonishment. "Well, I ah … I don't know what to say. Thanks? I was braced for an angry tirade."

"No. I'm through with angry tirades. They are emotionally expensive and have no discernible pay-off."

"Oh, oh, someone pinch me. I must be asleep!"

"You want me to pinch you, Heart?" HelperFriend asked, hesitating. "Are you sure? I believe I can affirm that you are, quite truly, awake. I would much prefer not to pinch you, nor to have anyone else do it. In any case, Equuleus cannot, and, no, I don't think I can allow Jackson to pinch you. I believe if he tried I have a program that would stop him by force. And I'd really, really rather not be compelled to do that. I mean, I …."

"*Will. You. Shut. Up!*" Jackson articulated.

"I don't mean it, HelperFriend," Heart clarified. "I mean, Jackson gave me a huge compliment, and then he missed a perfect opportunity to tirade. It seems unreal. So I jest that I must be dreaming, and suggest that someone wake me up by pinching me."

"Oh! Yes, all right then. My response is another instance of my taking your comment literally."

"It is."

"*Beeeeee quiet!* Or I *will* pinch someone!" Jackson walked back and forth before the three of them, appearing to Heart to be gathering his calm.

"Quiet, sir. Yes, sir. But—*where the hecky-heck-heck are we, sir?!*" Heart dared to ask.

Jackson stopped, turned and looked at her with an utterly bemused, wrinkled brow. *"Hecky-heck-heck? …"* He shook his head in exasperation.

Heart couldn't contain a sly grin but kept her mouth shut.

"It might interest you to know, Heart, that we are in your father's secret laboratory."

"Oh!" Heart raised her arms toward Jackson, simply stunned by the information. "Oh! Jackson, truly?"

"Truly."

"Something familiar," HelperFriend muttered.

"My father's laboratory … wonder of wonders …." She fell silent, in awe.

"Something familiar," HelperFriend repeated. "Something familiar here."

Jackson turned his attention from Heart to HelperFriend. "Yes. It's likely, clockworks man. It's likely your core brain was first conceived, developed and synthesized here."

"So, I too, am home!" HelperFriend cried.

"Oh, HelperFriend!" Heart turned to him. "Oh, HelperFriend, don't start crying! But, this is such a priceless moment."

"I'm going to cry, Heart. There's no stopping it." Bits of metal began to sprinkle over Heart.

"That's all right, I understand. My goodness, what unanticipated information!"

Equuleus wrapped his neck around Heart and HelperFriend, saying nothing, but whinnying softly.

"Equuleus! This must be where you were created, as well!"

"It does feel familiar, Heart."

Jackson tapped his foot. "Right. There'll be time for tears and celebration, etcetera, later. But right now, we have work to do, Heart. Or, at least I do. I have to get back on my mission. However, Father Inventor insisted I be the one to bring you here, although any mechanical could have done as well."

"No, Jackson. No mechanical would have sufficed, and you know it. I could never have followed someone I don't know, blindly, like I did you. My father knew that, and you know it, too."

Jackson nodded curtly. "No doubt. I won't belabor the point. We're here now, and I must give you some information. The sooner, the better. I'm on a mission. Every moment counts."

"Of course. We are at your command."

"Right. Follow me." Jackson turned on his heel and headed into the complete darkness of the cave. The threesome followed obediently. "Follow my voice. Illumination is constrained for a short distance."

Heart followed Jackson's voice in the total darkness, still stunned, thinking, I'm in my father's original laboratory, where he imagined his first inventions. Where he animated and conceived sentient clockworks beings. Equuleus and surely* at least some parts of HelperFriend.

Though unnerving to walk in pitch-black darkness, one hand holding HelperFriend's hand, and the other on Equuleus's back, it was even more shocking to step into a blinding light that suddenly blipped on.

"Shield your eyes, if they're sensitive."

"Thanks for the late warning." Heart covered her eyes with her forearm for fully half a minute while the blindness abated. As she lowered her arm, she noticed she appeared to be the only one discomfited by the light. "I see the clockworks beings are not bothered by this unnaturally intense light, but why are you not bothered, Jackson? And you can see in the dark!"

"I've had ocular implants."

Heart thought of when she first met Jackson in The Periphery, when Zack turned her and Swen over to him, to save them from The First Turning Point Battle, and how Jackson plowed through the near-jungle-like undergrowth of terrible, grabbing vines that had Swen and Heart repeatedly all but hobbled, yet Jackson strode ahead as if he were on a sidewalk.

"The First Turning Point Battle, when Swen and I tried to keep up with you. I couldn't imagine how you were able to move without faltering. It was because of ocular implants."

"Right. Now, let's get to business." He waved his hand, and a table slid out of the wall, along with two backless stools on either side of the table.

"Perfect," Heart said. "But where are you going to sit?"

"Oh, Heart, don't make him mad," HelperFriend said. "You know perfectly well he means for the two of you to sit."

"Of course I know it. But you must be in on this conversation as well, and sit with us."

Jackson waved his hand over another panel, and another little backless stool appeared from the wall, ten feet away. "Sit, clockworks man," Jackson commanded.

HelperFriend brought the stool to the table and sat beside Heart, his cranium gears churning with an erratic sound.

"Jackson," Heart said, making a small nod in HelperFriend's direction.

Jackson took in HelperFriend's obvious distress and sighed deeply. "What must be done?"

"Just … calm your energy. You can be very scary. Right now your energy…."

"DON'T SCARE HEART!" HelperFriend said in a terrible voice of many voices. He jerked to standing, the small stool flung several feet distant. "I am programmed to protect Heart. If you are scaring her, I cannot control my programming, Jackson, sir. I assure you, I am equipped to do you great harm, which, emotionally, I do not want to do. But I have no power to contain it past a particular threshold, which has been triggered by Heart uttering her fright."

Jackson stood and backed away, and Heart stood too, not knowing which terrifying body to address first. She read in Jackson's look a clear—and quite unusual—expression of indecision.

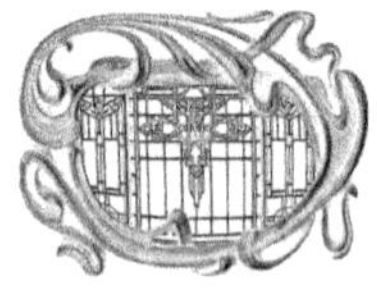

Chapter 10

She turned to HelperFriend, and cautiously put her hand on his frighteningly tense forearm. She felt the intensity and power of his gears beneath the surface with a forcefulness that she'd never known he had.

No timid butler now!

She recalled the traumatizing and unbelievable experience of watching the little donkey, Lolly, transform into a gigantic and terrifying creature at The First Turning Point Battle, completely engulfing her bio mother, Molly, to protect her.

"It's all right, HelperFriend. I was not being literal. I am not afraid of Jackson."

HelperFriend remained tense, ready to spring. Heart had no idea of his capacity, and she didn't want to see it now, wreaked upon Jackson. "Jackson is protecting me too."

HelperFriend immediately relaxed, as if every one of his gears took a breath.

"Jackson is not threatening you?"

"No. He's tense because he's on a mission, which we've interrupted. He needs to get back to it. I observed that his energy is frightening, but I didn't mean *to me*."

"*Oh!* Literal. Again!"

Heart laughed nervously. "Yes, dear, that's you being literal again."

"Very good." HelperFriend retrieved his stool and placed it by Heart. The three of them sat again, uneasily.

Heart glanced over at Equuleus. He ruffled the gears of his wings. *"That was close! He has power even I did not realize."*

"Good to know!" Heart thought back. She exchanged a look with Jackson that said essentially the same thing.

"I apologize, HelperFriend," Jackson began, "for conveying a message that called your resources into action. I would never initiate combat with you, and, as Heart affirms, I am duty-bound to protect her, just as you are. But I must say, I feel greatly relieved to know you have potent abilities to protect her, and that the threshold of calling these powers into action is fairly low.

"As I understand it, all Heart has to do is say, 'I'm afraid' or 'I'm scared,' and you are programmed—

against any argument other than her own—to protect her to the limits of your ability."

"You've said it precisely, Jackson," HelperFriend nodded, his gears clicking calmly in their usual butler mode.

"Excellent."

"Very excellent," Heart agreed. "But I wonder why neither you nor Father informed me of this fact?"

"Need to know, Heart," HelperFriend said. "You've never been threatened when I was in your proximity. Had I been out on Pink's terrain with you during the Bot Invasion, you would have seen my full abilities. As it was, I was in anguish, holed up in the Castle, distressed along with Father Inventor at your distance. I begged him to let me go to you, but he knew I could not get to you before being destroyed myself, out in the open with the crazed bots."

"*Oh my, oh my, oh my!*" Heart took several deep breaths. "Too much to process. If you had been there, you would have prevented me from bringing Xavier back. But I didn't save him anyway."

"But you saved us all, Heart," HelperFriend observed quietly.

"Yes," Jackson agreed. "We have had this discussion before, Heart. You completely saved Pink and its residents when you activated the shield."

"Well …" Heart fell silent. *Too many memories!*

"Right. Can we get back to the present moment and present concerns?"

"Please, let's do," Heart agreed, relieved to put the memories back in their box, and tucked away in the cupboard marked "Xavier." "What's the mission you're on at present, Jackson?"

"You know I can't tell you. Suffice it to say, it's something you would much prefer I was doing, rather than sitting around here having tea and crumpets with your merry tribe."

"I see no tea and crumpets," HelperFriend observed. "If, Jackson, you would be so kind as to inform me of the whereabouts of the kitchen—although I do seem to have an idea where it is—*hmmmm* … I'd be ever so happy to bring tea and, if there are any supplies, quickly make some crumpets."

"Dear HelperFriend," Heart said. "Again, Jackson is not being literal. He's being sarcastic."

"Right," Jackson agreed. "Although, I have to say, eating something seems like a good idea. I haven't in some while."

"Well, then!" HelperFriend exclaimed, "are there any supplies here?"

"Probably. Father Inventor left suddenly. He'd have supplies in a Stasis Lock, which he invented around that time, so its contents would be viable."

"All right," Heart said. "HelperFriend, if you have a mind map or can otherwise find the food preparation area, please be so kind as to bring something for Jackson."

"Very good." HelperFriend moved down a hall as if he knew exactly where he was headed in the vast cavern.

Heart returned her attention to Jackson. "Now then! Lovely repast on its way. You were telling me about your current mission …."

"No, I was *not* telling you about my mission."

"Then I want to address the missing Darling Undesirables of the Gulf Facility."

"How do you know about that?"

"I know all!" Heart intoned, mystically.

"So it would often seem. But, really, Heart, how do you know about that? It's supposed to be absolutely under wraps. To protect all the Darling Undesirables."

"Swen sent us a message."

"*Dangerous.*"

"I know."

"Which is why you're here now," Jackson reasoned.

"Yes. I came to Earth to talk with you—neatly done since you're the first person I meet, thanks to my father. And secondly, to find the missing Darling Undesirables."

"I see," Jackson said. "The first reason is fine, but you're not to get involved with the second. I cannot compromise your safety. As long as you're here in your father's lab, which is impenetrable to search devices, I know you're safe. Your father had me bring you here, and this is where he intends for you to stay!"

Heart nodded, then shook her head. "Sweet. But unlikely. I have my own resources, more so now, with the revelation of HelperFriend's power."

Right then, HelperFriend returned carrying an elegant silver tray, laden with steaming teapot, tea-cups, saucers, little plates, delicate silverware, and warm, freshly baked, little savory cakes.

"So fast, HelperFriend!" Heart exclaimed.

"Yes, yes!" HelperFriend put the tray on the table between them, giddy with delight. "I can't tell you how inspiring it is to touch Father Inventor's early inventions—many are most certainly original prototypes." As he chatted he placed everything on the table with simple formality.

"Thanks, HelperFriend," Jackson said, devouring a small cake in a single bite.

"Most welcome," HelperFriend answered, happily trilling like a meadowlark, he poured them piping hot cups of tea.

"I trust the flavor is acceptable? As you said, the kitchen is well-stocked with foodstuffs, all in three gorgeous Stasis Locks. My receptors qualified them as 'acceptable human consumables.'"

"Your receptors are correct," Jackson acknowledged, wolfing down two more delicate cakes with even less ceremony.

"We must accept that Jackson's approximation of manners is an indicator of his appreciation, Helper-Friend," Heart noted wryly, watching Jackson with uncertain fascination.

"Oh, I do, Heart, I do accept his appetite as an indicator of his appreciation. Very edifying, indeed. Also, I'm quite relieved that I did not have to restrain him when I misunderstood your meaning, Heart."

"*Hah!* Yes. I'm sure Jackson and I are both relieved that it did not come to that. Yes."

Jackson nodded. "Agreed. Right. Do you think I might take some of these—whatever they are, along with me? I often forget to eat, or what's available is so awful I'd *rather* forget to eat."

"But of course! Let me make more." Helper-Friend hurried off, practically delirious with joy.

"You sure know how to warm a clockworks butler's gear-driven heart," Heart observed.

"My pleasure." Jackson slowed his cake devouring for a moment to quaff a cup of tea. "You're not eating."

"Too … entertaining watching you." Heart sipped her tea. "So, as you've learned that I know what your mission is, will you not give me some details?"

"No. I will not."

"It would be helpful."

Jackson actually stopped eating. "In what way?"

"'Need to know,' Jackson. If you won't help me, I can't divulge my knowledge. I guess we're on the same side, but at a stalemate in being productively helpful to one another. Seems odd. But … I'll live with it."

"Heart, don't do anything foolish."

"And if I say the same to you?"

"That's different."

"How, Jackson? *How?*"

"I'm a trained peace-keeping member of *The Cause of all Beings*. And you're … you're *Heart*."

"I *do* know who I am. But, apparently, you do not."

"Oh, Heart! Don't tax my thinking like this. I can't stay focused if I'm worrying about you. I mean, I *can* stay focused, but it's stressful. Will you please not add to my stress?"

Heart looked down into her cup of tea, but no answers arose to the surface. "I suggest you put me out of your mind and continue with your duties, clear-headed. But … as long as things are as they are, as long as the world is so out of balance, as long as we each have our calling to which we must respond, it seems I will add to your stress."

She paused, then sighed. "But please know, Jackson, I don't mean to. I mean to make your life easier. My wish is that your life be one *not* centered on keeping peace for all beings. That all beings, or most of them—of us—keep *ourselves* in balance, keep peace on our own. And that your life is about whatever gives you pleasure, whatever gives you joy."

HelperFriend came back with a beautifully wrapped package radiating a delicious aroma and handed it to Jackson.

Jackson peeled off his nearly invisible backpack, tenderly placing the bundle within. "Thanks, Helper-Friend. That's something to look forward to," he said, keeping his eyes down.

"Don't eat it all at once," Heart teased, touched by Jackson's pure human simplicity.

"Well, I probably will," he teased in return. "I thought I had a long list of things to tell you, but your information changes everything."

"I agree. But I have a few things to tell you, which I will do succinctly, as I, too, sense, your urgency. It happens that the Clone, being an iteration of my father, cannot, despite the brainwashing of the Purists, set aside the deep-seated devotion to me, *his daughter*.

"Further, HelperFriend cleverly disabled the Clone's prevaricating chip—so he cannot lie. To anyone. He can keep silent, but he cannot lie. But, with me, he's apparently compelled to tell the truth. The challenge for me is to ask the relevant questions.

"Anyway, that's how I learned, which I feel may be of extreme importance to you, that, although there are one thousand clones of Father Inventor, there are only six that can pose particular difficulties. The rest are dressed up iterations of bots."

"Only six," Jackson said flatly.

"I know. Six is bad enough. But it's not one-thousand. Anyway, I thought it important enough to pass on to you."

"You could have sent me that information from Pink."

"Not acceptable, Jackson, and you know it. The added probability of interception …."

"Right." Jackson nodded.

"*I'm always right!*" Heart crowed.

"Yeah. No. Not quite."

"Yes! Name one exception!"

"Coming to Earth without Equuleus, and almost dying."

Equuleus whinnied agreement.

Heart turned to him. "Whose side are you on?"

"The side that takes care of you, which is not always you!" Equuleus retorted.

"You're ganging up on me," Heart laughed.

"Going out on Pink's terrain right before the Bot Invasion," Jackson continued with his list.

"Yes," Heart countered. "And as you've just noted yourself, contributing to saving Pink and its population."

"Not *'contributing to.' Doing.* You saved Pink and Yellow and their populations from the horrors of more Bot Invasions," Jackson acknowledged.

"Well, whatever I did, I did through love—with a bit of insurrection."

Equuleus whinnied, and Jackson made a sound not much different, while HelperFriend clarified. "I feel I must agree with the majority, Heart and point out that you are motivated by a character trait consisting of more than a *little* insurrection."

Heart shrugged. "Perhaps. But further discussion must be postponed. Jackson, are you going to give us a tour of where we are?"

"I've never been here, Heart."

"You've never been here?"

"No. First of all, although I knew of it, I didn't know where it was. It's been under your father's lock and key for these many years, hidden by the rock wall hologram. He gave me the hologram's precise location, which I held faith would work as I flew toward the rock wall."

"You've never been here," Heart repeated, aghast. "I followed you blindly, through the woods, when you, yourself, were flying blindly. And through what looked like a rock wall—blindly."

"That sums it up." Jackson stood. "I'm to remind you that we are not far from The Wall—so if you explore …."

"Which of course, I will …." Heart interjected.

"Which, of course, you will, be mindful of the sensation of dark energy. At least you have your two guards to assure your safety." He headed back down the black hall. "I want to check on the Clone before departing."

Heart, Equuleus, and HelperFriend followed. "It would be nice to have some light in this hall," Heart observed.

"Not necessary Heart," HelperFriend said. "I can see perfectly. Not to worry."

"All right," she said, grabbing his hand as the lights behind them blipped off. "*Sooo* dark, though."

Heart hurried after Jackson even though she could see nothing, afraid that he'd jump into his vehicle and disappear without a good-bye, wondering why she even cared.

As she hurried, she heard the Clone suddenly begin to scream. Was he was being murdered—*again!*—by Jackson? Though why Jackson would harm their possibly greatest informant was inexplicable.

"Running, now, in the dark."

"I got you, Heart," HelperFriend said, holding tight onto her hand as they ran through the darkness. They soon came to the clearing, where the Clone outside the *Heart!*, stood on the ground, looking up at Jackson, screaming, *"Get away from me! Get away! Monster! Terrorist! Abuser! LEAVE ME ALONE!"*

Jackson stood three feet away from him, arms folded, not moving.

"What ..." Heart rushed up to them, *"What is going on?* What did you do, Jackson? Why did you take him out of the *Heart!*?"

"I haven't touched him. He was as you see him, having figured out a way to move about, trussed up in straps and chains."

"Get him away, get him away! Vile murderer!" screeched the Clone.

"He is not a vile murderer, Clone. Be quiet!"

The Clone softened his tone at Heart's command, but he continued to protest. "He *is* a vile murderer. He killed some of my lovely bots."

"Ugh!" Heart said. "Those sad, mindless, white things ...."

"My children. My own, my very own, creations. Having nothing to do with Father Inventor."

"I should hope not, Clone. They are certainly not lovely."

"Beauty is in the eye of the beholder, Heart. You are beautiful, I won't argue that, a blind person knows it. But my creations, they are my own, they are devoted to me, and they are *beautiful to me.* Anyway, look what that monster did to me! He cut me in half!"

Heart nodded. "Yes, what it took for him to get you under control was dramatic. But, he's not a monster. You're fortunate you were not dismantled bit by piece to help repair the wounded and maimed Folks on Pink after the Bot Invasion. So be quiet and count your blessings. Or I'll dismantle you myself!"

A look of petrified fear came into the Clone's eyes, much like the look Heart saw when her Father talked with him before hypnotizing him. That must have been what he said—that he'd have the Clone dismembered, component by component, if he caused Heart any trouble.

"You wouldn't!" the Clone whimpered.

"Don't push me. And *be quiet!*"

"You wouldn't take me apart. We've become friends. And, even if you don't acknowledge it, you are my daughter. You wouldn't hurt me."

"I'm *not* your daughter. I'm Father Inventor's daughter. You are his clone. End of story. But quite problematic is you moving about. I can't have that. We'll have to discover a way to keep you constrained."

"I wasn't going anywhere," the Clone argued. "Where would I go? I wanted to be where you were. You were having tea, and I wanted some. And, of *course,* I wanted to see if I *could* move about. Even without my beautiful legs. So sad, my poor legs."

"Do you want me to do something with him?" Jackson asked. "I gotta get going, but I can't leave you alone with him if he's figured out a way to move about."

"He's still chained and tethered. Although I'd sure like to know how you got yourself loose from the wall, and how you move about without legs or use of your arms."

"Oh, well, I'm sorry to say I simply pulled the latches from the wall. Left maybe a couple of small little holes. Then I sort of hop like this." And the Clone—*somehow!*—hopped, chains and tethers, and all.

"He's very strong," Heart acknowledged. "We'll have to find a secure room to lock him up in. And, might it be possible for you to program some kind of alarm that would let you know if he moves about, HelperFriend?"

"Of course. And if Equuleus wouldn't mind, I could program it to inform Equuleus immediately, as well."

"Good idea," Equuleus agreed.

"Now, then, Clone. Do *not* cause us grief," Heart said.

HelperFriend programmed an alarm on himself, connected to the Clone, then shared it with Equuleus. "I ought to have done that before," Helper-Friend said. "But as he never moved about before, I didn't know he could."

"There wasn't anywhere to go before," The Clone protested. "I just wanted some tea."

"Do you want me to put him somewhere before I leave?" Jackson asked, becoming ever-more fidgety to get on the move.

"Not necessary, Jackson. HelperFriend will take care of him, and you must be on your way."

Jackson climbed into his vehicle, fired up the engines and pulled around, facing the hologram stone wall.

Heart waved, feeling a rush of sadness. Ah! Jackson! The thorn in her side! Her friend!

She stood looking after his vehicle until she could not hear the faintest rumble of his engines. Everyone, even the Clone, waited in silence while she stood poised, her hand still raised at the empty space, which she didn't realize until she came back to herself, looking down at the Clone. Here, beside her, stood the mind that had created much of the danger her thorny friend was now about to face.

As her father had observed, it took a great lot of fortitude to feel compassion for him. "Bring him, HelperFriend," Heart said in a rush of chilled anger. She headed toward the black hallway, then with a second thought, climbed onto Equuleus. "Be my eyes, dear Equuleus."

"Gladly."

She heard HelperFriend heft up the Clone and follow her. The Clone chattered in a quiet voice, but his babble seemed not to be relevant to Helper-Friend, as he made no response.

"Probably trying to defend himself," Heart said quietly.

"It has that tone," Equuleus agreed.

In the few moments of flight in the dark hall, Heart thought of how lovely it would be to fly over Earth on Equuleus in the night, taking in all the sweet, soft, dark energy lights from homes and highways below.

Just to have a calm, contented life, doing good deeds, loving and being loved—please let that not be too much to ask, Heart silently prayed.

Chapter 11

They came back to where they had been having tea, the tea cold, but a few beautiful little cakes still sat on a platter.

"Heart, you didn't have any of my little cakes!" HelperFriend said, with, perhaps the slightest edge of hurt in his voice.

"I know, HelperFriend. But I'm going to have them now! I was focused on Jackson." She slid off Equuleus, sat on the little stool and bit into one of the cakes. "Oh, my, HelperFriend, this is truly delicious! No wonder Jackson inhaled them as if he'd never eaten in his life." She sipped her cold tea. "Even the cold tea is delightful."

"Let me heat it up. But what shall I do with this?" He held the Clone out in front of him, while

the Clone eyed the tea and cakes with obvious longing.

"Oh, set him down on the stool across from me.
Not that I'm in the mood to have anything to do with
him right now."

HelperFriend placed him on the stool. "Now,
don't wiggle around, or you'll go crashing to the
floor, and Heart may have me leave you there."

"Umm," Heart agreed, doing her imitation of Jackson by inhaling another little cake. "You can count on
it. I'll leave you right there. No tea, no cakes."

HelperFriend took the teapot. "I'll be right back."

"I just wanted to be with you," The Clone chattered. "I even said to myself, don't move, it will not
go well for you. But I couldn't help it. You all were
having fun. And I was there, all alone."

"We were not having fun. We were trying to
figure out how to stop all the trouble you and the
Purists have caused. Really, what's the matter with
you? Besides being an insane megalomaniac, that
is."

"*I am not!* Just because I realize my brilliance and
power doesn't mean I'm crazy!"

"No. *Being crazy* means you're crazy, with or
without brilliance and power. Now, be quiet. I have
things to think about. And lovely cakes to devour.
Let me have some peace." Heart scooted the little
stool up to the wall, leaning back against it and
moving so the Clone was out of her view.

"You don't like me," he said quietly.

"That's an understatement! But we'll let it suffice
for the moment. Now *HUSH!* Or I'll have Helper-

Friend stick you in a cupboard. I'm sure there are plenty of them in the kitchen if I know my father."

The Clone shut up.

Heart tried to sort out why she felt so sad. Strangely, deeply, sad. And lonely. Disturbingly lonely. Why? She had the fantastic blessing of both HelperFriend and Equuleus with her. But she had to face the fact that—however strange it may seem!—she felt a great, lonely void, with Jackson gone.

If he hadn't come in the first place, she reasoned, she'd be fine. But coming and chatting and sharing their human-ness, even if sparring, then leaving left this—*gap!*

Or—*oh dear!*—maybe she felt lonely *because of the sparring*. She'd really have to consider herself a sad case if what she liked about Jackson was arguing.

Hmmmmmm….

She took her mind to other matters, by force. She tried to work out where they must be, re-running the journey to the interior of this rock or mountain, or whatever it was, again. She'd been on a heading to land at The Museum of Scientific Improbabilities and Unpredictable Oddities when Jackson appeared. He'd taken her in the general direction of The Darling Undesirables Facility at Long Prairie, but they'd headed slightly north, and soon landed. So….

Heart had the flash of realization that she was undoubtedly as close to The Mystic's cottage in The Periphery, on the other side of The Wall as she could be, and still be on *this* side of The Wall.

That meant she was as close to Eye as she could possibly be, while still on the free side of The Wall. Surely this contributed to her intense sense of loneliness, knowing intuitively she was but a short distance from Eye.

The thought made her sad and happy all at once. She'd tried hard to keep thoughts of Eye out of her mind, her precious childhood companion who had helped her through so many trials. She knew he was happy, and she'd accomplished her first most important goal—assuring his safety by having him, and Butterfly, taken to The Mystic's charming forest cottage.

He was so near! If not for the fact that the dark energy in The Wall would paralyze her, she suspected she'd be out of this cave and off into the woods, making her way to The Mystic's cottage.

But there *was* the dark energy in The Wall, preventing her from crossing, in addition to the fact that she had Darling Undesirables to save. But was there significance in the proximity of her father's laboratory to The Mystic's cottage? She'd ask him one day when life was more settled.

HelperFriend had been standing by her with the tray of tea and cakes for, she now realized, several moments. So entangled in thoughts, she wasn't even aware of his presence.

"I'm sorry, HelperFriend. Have you been there for long?"

"Fifty-two seconds. Fifty-three. Fifty …"

"That's fine, not necessary to count. Why didn't you say something?"

"You were doing important thinking." He placed the tray on the little table. "May I pour you a cup of tea?"

"Yes, please."

As HelperFriend poured the tea he asked, "Shall I pour the Clone some tea?"

"Yes," Heart said, begrudgingly. "And I guess you'll have to release one of his hands. But stay close in case he gets ideas about hopping around and doing damage."

HelperFriend released the Clone's right forearm. He remained passive, and wisely so, Heart thought. Equuleus came to sit by her and she fed him one of the lovely little cakes.

"Very nice, HelperFriend," Equuleus said.

HelperFriend's facial gears clicked happily. "Not often one gets a compliment from the great winged horse himself," he chirped.

Heart grinned but said nothing. She watched the Clone sip his tea quietly, and seeming, for the moment, so like her father. "You are fashioned after the most amazing human being alive. Won't you come out of darkness and serve those who live in love and light?"

The Clone helped himself to one of the small cakes, clearly enjoying it, in silence. But he finally answered Heart. "I believe I do not, and perhaps cannot, understand your feelings regarding love. I would like to think that the feelings I have for you are love. But as you vehemently dislike me, I have logic parameters that dictate that another must return my feelings in kind, or they are invalid. And light? Well, what is light? You mean some figurative notion, not literal daylight or room light, so, again, I don't know how to quantify it. It doesn't make sense to me.

"I'm motivated by an understanding of what serves me, and a feeling that what serves me would serve others. I'm not someone else. I'm me. Therefore, it seems to me that what I think, what I feel, what I desire … all would be best for others as well.

"The tea and the little delicacies are exquisitely wrought, HelperFriend. You may or may not recall, Heart, that I fancy myself an outstanding chef, and so, as rare as a compliment may be from the gear horse, one from me is actually more meaningful. Or, at least, that's how I would determine it.

"One thing I must acknowledge, none of you share my values, and yet—I'm not free to leave. It may serve me to shut down."

Heart thought about the ramifications of an inert Clone when the very reason she went to the trouble of bringing him along was to pick his brain. She couldn't lie and pretend to like him. But could she do as her father advised and make an effort to feel compassion for him?

"You don't understand the immensity of the pain you've caused me," Heart said. "I know I can't make you understand. But I'm no better than what I criticize if I treat you with disdain. I will attempt to be more humane with you, and set aside my negative thoughts and feelings as much as I can."

"There's no particular cause for celebration in your words, Heart," the Clone replied. "But you imply it'll be a bit better than the way you've been treating me."

"I'll try. But for your part, please do not move about without our knowing. If you would kindly agree to that, I'll work to shift my behavior."

"All right, Heart."

With but two little cakes left, the Clone took one, and Heart fed the other to Equuleus.

"Let's go exploring," Heart suggested, while HelperFriend cleared the table.

"Excellent," HelperFriend said. "I've been hoping you'd say that!"

Equuleus whinnied his agreement.

"Well, now, I'd find that most interesting," the Clone agreed.

"Ahm, I'm sorry, Clone, you cannot go with us. I don't know what we'll find or how difficult it might be to navigate some passages. I'll need HelperFriend's full capacity, and not preoccupied with moving you."

"I could ride on Equuleus."

"Perhaps. But not this time. You'll have to stay behind, but remember, you agreed not to move about without my knowledge."

"Well, actually, I didn't. I said 'all right' to your comment that I not move about, not that I would *refrain* from moving about."

Shocked, Heart studied the Clone for a few moments. "Now, Clone, that's a sideways lie, and you're not supposed to be able to do that. So you'd better think again about your agreements, and the result of them." She stood. "But, for the time being, I'll find a place to lock you away. Shut yourself down if you must. I'm not negotiating with a liar."

Angrily she started to head in the direction HelperFriend had come with the tea tray. "Come along HelperFriend, let us find a stronghold for this truth-twister."

"Wait, Heart!" the Clone called.

Heart ignored him, stomping down the hall, muttering to herself. "The nerve. I try so hard, and just … some beings are beyond redemption."

"Yes, yes, just so, Heart. He does not deserve your kindness. Ahm, actually …" HelperFriend followed along behind Heart. "Actually Heart, Heart, you've passed the kitchen. It's, ahm, back here."

Heart turned and came back to HelperFriend. "See how counterproductive anger can be, HelperFriend? It's not good!"

"I see. But I understand your anger. I think maybe I'm having an emotion something like anger too. I disengaged his prevaricating chip, and yet, yes, he told you that 'sideways lie.' A lie of omission, isn't it? Well, now I have the alarm, so if he moves more than a couple of feet on his own, it will go off. But what if we're far away, exploring or doing something important?"

"I'm beginning to wonder if I ought not to have brought him. If he shuts himself down, the very reason he's here will be over."

"Not so, Heart." HelperFriend gestured over a nearly invisible pad on the wall, and an equally nearly invisible door slid open.

They stepped into a glowing white kitchen, so familiar to Heart, a near duplicate of Pink's kitchen. "Oh! HelperFriend! Does it not feel like home?"

"It does, Heart. It makes me quite happy."

"Ah, my friend!" Heart felt joy rush through her and closed her eyes delighting in the moment. "Who cares about that ridiculous Clone? We will be happy, in spite of everything!"

"And because of everything," HelperFriend added.

"*HelperFriend!*" Heart exclaimed, filled with wonder at his ever-growing wisdom.

"Yes?"

"You're amazing!"

"*Oh!*" His facial gears clicked and swirled, and Heart could have sworn his cheeks actually took on a rosy hue. "If the Clone shuts himself down out of spite, that will be fine, because he won't be able to awaken himself. But *I will.*"

"*Really?*"

"*Really.*"

"That's a relief!" Heart gave him a big hug.

HelperFriend gently returned her hug. "Shall we explore now?"

"Yes, after we figure out where to put the Clone."

"No problem. I'll put him where he went when he first came to Pink." Heart followed HelperFriend to a sleek white door with a compression locking system. HelperFriend gestured over a pad along the door panel's edge, the door's seals swished a release, and the door slid open. The sound reminded Heart of all the seals on all the castle's exterior doors on Pink.

"That sound, HelperFriend."

"I know."

"My father had been working on his escape to Pink for a long, long, time," Heart said softly, trying to picture what his life must have been like.

"Yes, Heart. All these inventions—although great for adding luxury to life on Earth, they're essential for his life on Pink."

They stepped inside the small room. "The Clone will be in stasis in here," HelperFriend said. "We can take the chains and tethers off, and he'll be fine."

"You are such a genius!"

"No, Heart. Your father is such a genius. But I know how to take advantage of his genius."

"Which is a form of genius."

"Well …" HelperFriend appeared at a loss for words. "Let's go exploring," he added, changing the subject.

"Yes, let's!" Heart agreed.

A few minutes later the Clone had been put to bed, and Heart, with her two intrepid companions, moved deeper into the interior of the mountain.

Chapter 12

A subtle, light, flickering like candles although there were none present, came on as the three of them moved into a massive hall, where no one had been for many and many a year. There was no ornament or diversion of any sort.

"*Uhhhhh ….*" Heart suddenly felt herself go completely limp as her knees gave out from under her. She looked down at the plaid of her sleeve and saw its slight glow had flattened out to a dull monochrome.

"*Dark energy!*" Equuleus exclaimed.

HelperFriend quickly picked her up and hurried back the way they came.

Regaining consciousness, Heart saw the metallic colors of her plaid begin to pulse. "I'm all right, HelperFriend. You can put me down now."

He gently put her down, but she still felt dazed, and she sat on the floor. "Well, that's disappointing! I was so looking forward to seeing my father's laboratory."

"Equuleus and I can continue, Heart, and report back to you. I'll show you 3-Ds along the way," HelperFriend suggested.

Heart nodded. She couldn't help thinking about how very close she must be to The Mystic's little cottage.

Equuleus picked up on her thought. "Yes, Heart. Only a few minutes walk for you, on foot."

"What?" HelperFriend asked.

"Eye," Equuleus answered.

"Oh! I see!" HelperFriend projected a 3-D map of the underground path before them and then projected it to the ground above. There came into view the dusky night of the forest, and in the near distance, The Mystic's adorable little cottage.

As Heart peered at the image, The Mystic, shadowy, with the pale light from the cottage outlining her, came into the doorway. She looked around. Heart could tell she knew they were near.

Then The Mystic reached down, patted the ground, and looked toward Heart, smiling.

"Oh, HelperFriend, look—*The Mystic!*" The image faded back to the map of the underground cave. "Thank you, HelperFriend. Even if I can't go to The Mystic's cottage right now, you've shown me this incredible ability to map places where there are people I care about. Do you think you can do that with the missing Darling Undesirables?"

"I don't know, Heart. I knew I could project maps, but showing the real world … I didn't know I could do that."

"Maybe it was The Mystic."

"Maybe. But I had your mind picture of her little cottage, and we're close to it. *And* she's someone you know personally. Finding missing Darling Undesirables you don't know, in a place that none of us knows—that's completely different."

"*Hmmmm* …" Heart contemplated for a few moments. "I wonder if I could get the Clone to think of a map where the missing Darling Undesirables might be, and perhaps you could project it, Helper-Friend. Let me try to pick his bio-mechanical brain to see what we might discover." She jumped on Equuleus. "Let's return," she urged.

"Fly?" Equuleus asked.

"If you would like."

"I would *love!*" He leapt from the ground, and much to their surprise, the entire cave lit up brightly with a flowing rainbow of colors, swirling and whirling around them, as if the interior of the mountain itself filled with glee.

"*Ha-ha!*" HelperFriend shouted, running along below. "*Ha-ha!* Beautiful!"

Equuleus began to fly in circles, and the lights started to hum the songs of the stars, in the belly of the Earth. Pinpoints of brilliant light appeared around them, and suddenly Heart recognized constellations. There Ursa Major, there Virgo, there Aquarius, there *Leo!*

"Oh-oh-oh! Equuleus! The stars!" All the zodiac appeared as they circled, with great swaths of aurora borealis, weaving among the celestial display.

Heart and Equuleus flew around in the mountain's mystical, celestial ether, with HelperFriend giggling and dancing and jumping higher and higher, up to meet them.

Time stood still.

But slowly, slowly, the aurora dimmed, the stars faded, the song softened, and the giant cave returned to its subtle, yet friendly, soft lights.

Equulcus then flew back to the little table, landing softly. Heart slid off Equuleus as HelperFriend rushed up to them. *"Oh, Heart, Heart! The lights, the music, the stars!"*

Heart nodded, but, for the moment, could not speak. She wrapped her arm around Equuleus' neck and leaned into him, but finally found her voice. "Yes, HelperFriend quite—*magical!* I suppose we just witnessed the basis for the Mechanical Aurora Borealis between The Museum of Scientific Improbabilities and Unpredictable Oddities and Pink."

"Oh! Of course!" HelperFriend agreed. "It wasn't only beautiful, it made me happy!"

"It made me happy too, dear friend. And it reminds us all that Father Inventor loves us, and, to honor and support his love, I must be about my mission to find the missing Darling Undesirables. So anticlimactic to have a chat with the Clone now, but we must try to access any map he may have in his mind to help me find the missing Darlings. If I can get him to think of a map, I hope, HelperFriend, you might project it behind him, so I can see it, but without him knowing what you're doing."

"I can try, Heart. I'll do my best."

*　*

HelperFriend brought the Clone to Heart at the little table.

"How many years have passed?" he growled.

Heart was tempted to say "four hundred," but knowing, though that might give her a small bit of satisfaction, it would serve no great purpose. She told him the truth. "You were in stasis a very short while, as I have some questions. First of all, are you aware that all the Darling Undesirables are missing from one particular facility?"

"I've seen a news blip to that effect."

"What is your personal knowledge of this event?"

"What do you mean? If I've seen the news blip, I have personal knowledge."

"Do not be coy, Clone. It won't serve you."

"You want me to give you confidential information. But without specific questions, I cannot answer specifically. Even though I cannot speak a direct untruth, my programming is in a double bind, because I'm also programmed not to give confidential information."

"Hmmm …" Heart considered her next question.

"Do you know all the Darling Undesirables facilities?"

"Yes," the Clone answered. The air around HelperFriend lit up like a small town, with a map of all the Darling Undesirable facilities. Heart felt her entire body clinch in fear at the clarity of the Clone's database.

"Do you know which of the Darling Undesirables facilities has had every child kidnapped?"

"Yes."

The Darling Undesirables Facility at The Gulf lit up, and the other Darling Undesirable facilities faded away.

"Do you know who is behind this kidnapping?"

"Yes."

Heart did not expect any visual to accompany his answer, but a clear image of Loruza hovered over the map of The Darling Undesirables Facility at The Gulf.

"Oh!" Heart gasped, try as she might to stay neutral.

"Are there any of the six primary clones, as you mentioned, involved in this kidnapping?"

"Yes," the Clone said, becoming ever-more agitated, but unable to keep from answering.

"How many?"

"Two."

Heart inhaled deeply, about to ask the question that was the point of all the other questions, as she led him, she hoped, to where he would give her the information she needed.

"Do you know where the children who were kidnapped from The Darling Undesirable Facility at The Gulf are at this moment?"

"Yes."

"Where?"

The Clone remained mute, struggling between keeping his mouth shut and blurting out the answer. But it didn't matter, because the map glowed golden behind him. Heart gasped again at the information that became revealed.

"Thanks!" She said to the Clone, jumping up. She turned to Equuleus. "Ready for a serious flight in the night?"

"*Absolutely!*"

"Will you accept a download of this map, Equuleus?"

"With pleasure."

Heart watched in awe as the map poured through the air, scrolling from HelperFriend's forehead into Equuleus' forehead.

The Clone turned his head as far as he could, to see what was going on, just in time to see the last bit of the map disappear into Equuleus's gear-whirling cranium.

"*Augh!*" he cried. "Once again, I've betrayed my creations and my supporters."

"And have, hopefully, done a good deed for many innocent children."

"*Deformed* children," the Clone retorted.

"Have you looked in the mirror lately?" Heart asked, unable to resist the dig.

"Oh, you are mean, Heart. I was beautiful before Jackson hacked me in half."

"And every, single Darling Undesirable is beautiful, as well."

"Yeah. Even that pathetic, eyeless deformation of your sad little friend, right?"

"Watch it Clone. *You could be next.*" She leapt on Equuleus. "Put him back in storage, HelperFriend. And remind him how lucky he is to be in only two pieces."

"I will most certainly do that, Heart." He picked the Clone up and headed directly for the kitchen, but paused when Heart looked back at him, waving, as she and Equuleus passed into the black tunnel. He almost dropped the Clone in his longing to wave back.

"Take care of yourself," HelperFriend called to her in his thrilling many voices, which sounded all around her in the few moments of blackness. *"IIIIIIII LLLLLOOOOVVVVVE YYYYOOOOUUUUUU!"*

"I love you, *tooooooooo*," she called back.

*   *

In a few moments, they flew by the *Heart!* and Heart thought fleetingly that she ought to take the *Heart!* leaving Equuleus behind with HelperFriend.

But wise or unwise, she wanted to pursue her mission on Equuleus. It felt right. Like everything that led up to this moment—this moment when she and her heart, housed in the great and loyal chest of her beloved gear horse, the two of them as a unit, flew to rescue Darling Undesirables.

They burst through the hologram of the rock face out into the night air among the forest trees, among the fragrant night-blooming flowers. They flew along the narrow path that she and Jackson had flown on the way in.

Seeing now how remarkably narrow the path was, she could only wonder how she possibly succeeded in flying along this path without damaging the trees and the *Heart!,* when the thought came to her that perhaps some of the trees were holograms as well, as the path barely accommodated Equuleus's wingspan.

"*Agreed,*" Equuleus thought, picking up on her contemplation. "Too narrow for the *Heart!* Some of the trees must be holograms."

They came to the edge of the woods. Equuleus shot up high into the sky, with an intention of not being seen.

Heart looked down at her plaid, every color glowed with an intensity she'd never seen. If she had any doubts about her present maneuvers, they were dismissed. Her plaid let her know there was no choice other than the one she now made.

"I can't believe that they are hiding at The Darling Undesirables Facility at Long Prairie. How is it no one sees them or knows they're there?"

"It looks like they're underground."

"In the crystal matrix. Of course." She sent a message to HelperFriend, letting him know where they were headed, realizing that he'd already sorted that out.

"I know," his reply zinged back. "At least you know the territory!"

Grateful for his observation, Heart released her first reaction of disappointment, her longing to never find herself at that depressing place again.

But, the truth was, she *did* know it, like the back of her hand. She even knew the essential layout of the underground. She could save these children.

"Aren't you going to tell Jackson?" Equuleus interrupted her thoughts.

"Eventually."

"You can't do this alone, Heart."

"No. But …."

"Yes?"

"I want to see where the children are, and see what I can accomplish on my own."

"Going it alone, you risk endangering the children."

"Going at it with Jackson and company blazing away with weapons also endangers the children. I'd like to see who's where, first. Do you think I'm wrong?"

"No, Heart. It's a difficult decision. I'll let you sort it out. It'll take a while to get there, which gives you time to plan."

Incongruous, the balmy and gorgeous night against the thoughts of what she might encounter when they arrived at The Darling Undesirables Facility at Long Prairie.

Oh, would she never have a life free of that sad, sad place, even if there was a huge advantage in being familiar with it? At least the knowledge that the original occupants, all the precious Darling Undesirables she grew up with, were safely in the care of Peter—*or someone, somewhere!*—after being swept up into the Gargantua and taken to parts unknown, gave her peace and joy.

But she must concentrate now on what she *might do*, and what she *must do*, making numerous decisions as they flew.

What was the plan of the Purists regarding the Darling Undesirables from the Facility at the Gulf? They'd been so adamant that they wanted to destroy all Darling Undesirables, which would allow them to uphold their other insane statement, that they would never *touch* a Darling Undesirable, from a weird superstition that their anomalies were contagious.

But now, obviously, if they had kidnapped the entire population of the Darling Undesirables Facility at the Gulf, they were "touching" Darling Undesirables. Unless they used the clones for the kidnapping—another obvious possibility!

However accomplished, Heart reasoned, they must have an ever-more devious plan up their evil sleeves to make off with the children, hiding them in the crystal matrix under The Darling Undesirables Facility at Long Prairie.

And, furthermore, by whatever means they succeeded in this evil deed, the next burning question was, how did they arrive at The Darling Undesirables Facility at Long Prairie *without being seen?*

How?

The two Darling Undesirables Facilities were over an hour apart on the Dark Energy Highway. Even if the children and keepers were piled into the facility's air buses, it would take two or three trips to transport them all.

Had no one seen all this activity? With the peacekeeping forces closely watching the Darling Undesirable facilities everywhere, how did the Purists carry this off?

"*Underground?*" Equuleus entered her thoughts.

"*Underground? UNDERGROUND, Equuleus? Are you suggesting that the crystal matrix runs that far?*"

"*Why not? That far and maybe farther.*"

"And maybe even farther!" Heart exclaimed. "You're a genius!" She pictured the part of the crystal matrix she'd experienced and imagined how it might continue from there.

"But, if they're on foot in a tunnel, it would take *days* to get to The Darling Undesirables Facility at Long Prairie."

"Perhaps they're walking some distance, then surfacing in small numbers and getting into vehicles to be taken the rest of the way."

"Possible," Heart mused. She tried to picture this scenario, wondering where they might surface, unnoticed. But she suddenly saw with strange clarity, the subterranean crystal matrix. *She saw a road!*

Equuleus whinnied and bucked in the air as he picked up on her visual. "Where did that picture come from?"

"I'm not sure, Equuleus. I think it might be The Mystic. A very clear image."

"Or maybe it's your own abilities."

"Maybe." It seemed possible, given her concern for the Darling Undesirables and her experience with the crystal matrix.

If it were true that all the Darling Undesirables of the Facility at the Gulf and their keepers were in the crystal matrix under The Darling Undesirables Facility at Long Prairie, and if it were true that there was a highway underground, then coming from both sides would be a powerful strategy. But would Jackson listen to her if she tried to tell him? She feared he'd be so angry with her for leaving her father's laboratory that he would not.

She decided to continue as she'd first intended— go in solo, reconnoiter, *then* tell Jackson what she found.

"Just ahead," Equuleus broke into her thoughts.

The dark outline of the only place Heart had known as home throughout her childhood came into view, small and far away.

"We'll set down in the woods outside the fence."

Equuleus flew gracefully down among the trees and landed in a small pouf of dirt and ferns. Heart slid off, then Equuleus curled up into a ball among the ferns, all but invisible.

She noted where he hid, then turned and stole toward the fence that enclosed her luxurious childhood prison—trying not to think about the fact that she was possibly running headlong into a dire situation with no backup. No one other than two clockworks beings had any idea where she was.

"Call me if you need me!" Equuleus demanded in her thoughts.

"All right," she replied, knowing she would not risk him if everything suddenly turned into a disaster.

Chapter 13

ow I wish I had Swen, my ever-faithful fence-crossing companion, with me now! she thought as she came up to the fence. He'd dig a tunnel under the fence in moments.

It was strange to see the place in total darkness. Even the ever-lighted night lights were extinguished. She came to the fence and noticed that it was much shorter than it used to be! She readily pulled herself over it, into the grounds, chuckling with the realization that the fence wasn't shorter. She was taller!

If the eternal night lights were turned off, she surmised, the motion detectors were probably not working as well. However, not willing to gamble on that probability, she set her mind to shapeshifting across the grounds to the small garden building.

When she arrived at the back of it, she moved around the building to see what had become of the damage she'd done to the otherwise gorgeous and pristine garden of Keeper A.

Much to her surprise, there was no hole. Someone had filled it in. Who would have done that?

Loruza and Keeper A, of course!

She walked onto the ground where the hole had been, and fell through, landing upon something soft. In total darkness, Heart realized that the appearance of ground was holographic. She simply must get used to the fact that the Purists had access to many of her father's inventions, none the least being holographic images.

She'd fallen upon the bed in the room the Clone had constructed for her. He'd finally done something that was a benefit to her, she thought wryly. Not only would evil never ultimately prevail over good, it sometimes served it!

Heart now had to determine the layout of the crystal matrix beyond her previous experience, and discover where the children were hidden. Then she must figure out how to get them out.

The other advantage of the hole in the ground was that when she was ready to communicate with Jackson to help her, she could return here to move away from the blocking of the crystal matrix and reach him through her star necklace in the open air of the hologram.

She moved stealthily across the room toward where she knew the door was, although she could see nothing. When she came to the wall, she felt for the door frame. *There!* As she'd hoped, the door readily slid open. The only reason it had previously been locked was to keep her inside.

She crept along the hall, anticipating the subtle lighting along the edges of the floor to come on. But they did not. A good thing, but a strange thing. Why didn't the lights come on? Had they been intentionally turned off? Or was there no power?

If there was no power, the children were suffering. If the lighting was intentionally turned off, it implied that the Purists anticipated invasion, *and were prepared.*

In any case, she must watch her step, and count steps, too, in order to return to the hole in the ground—her means of communication and escape.

She continued to slip along the wall, her hand occasionally lightly touching it to her left. When she anticipated she would come to the great room where the Clone had first appeared, the wall did, in fact, fall away underhand and she felt the openness of the cavernous room.

She didn't want to think about that moment when she first saw the Clone, but it came unbidden. The vision of him coming and coming and coming toward her down the eternally long hall replayed in her mind. At first, she'd believed it was her father, that, as threatened, he'd been kidnapped by the Purists.

Heart had finally realized it was the mirror-like reflection of the crystal matrix that gave the illusion of him moving toward her without getting closer, and that, in fact, he'd been coming down many halls to her.

As she'd sorted that strange fact out, the knowledge struck her that *this was not her father*, but the Clone, the horrible bots came out of the walls and restrained her.

She now stood still in the open space listening intently, hoping that the bots or the clones or the Purists, whichever of them might be here, didn't have a means of seeing her in the dark. She was utterly vulnerable, unable to shapeshift into something she couldn't see.

What was that? A small sound, a bit like a whimper, or … what? She moved toward the sound, reaching for the wall to help guide her. She finally found the wall, but in the same moment, the sound stopped. She continued to move in the direction of the sound.

An insight began to wash over her. This crystal matrix cave, and the cave of her father's laboratory where she'd just come from, were strikingly similar. True, the crystal matrix was mirrored, but, thinking about the wall from which the little table and backless stool had come, it *felt like this wall!*

Did that mean that her father had made this subterranean environment too?

If The Darling Undesirables Facility at the Gulf was connected to The Darling Undesirables Facility at Long Prairie, which appeared to be true, then was it not likely that The Darling Undesirables Facility at Long Prairie was connected to her father's laboratory?

And if so, *why?*

She'd always believed her father had nothing to do with the creation of the Darling Undesirables. That his turncoat scientist employees had taken his work and distorted it for their own gain. That they'd let the world blame Father Inventor for all the sad and broken Darling Undesirables when he was completely innocent.

But what did this underground crystal matrix mean? The more she thought about it, the more she knew it was of her father's making. And … what about Pink? The interior of the little moon was the same, a maze of below-surface tunnels.

So … if there was a subterranean matrix of tunnels uniting the Darling Undesirables facilities to Father Inventor's laboratory ….

The whimpering began again, slightly louder. She must put away the terrible thoughts for now, and attend to the children.

She must do what she could, even if she had *no one at all on her side*. Even if her father, even if Helper-Friend, and even if … *even if!* Equuleus turned on her, she would defend to the end the Darling Undesirables. Though she wasn't sure of the outcome if Equuleus, caretaker of her physical heart, turned on her.

As she neared the sad whimpering, Heart heard another sound. Disconcertingly, the sound of adult, male voices.

Was it clones? Could it be the Darling Undesirables' keepers?

She pulled herself up against the wall, and none too soon, as, down the tunnel from the opening under the garden shed, and into the great room came Jackson with three peers, dressed in combat gear. Their large movements caused floodlights to turn on, glaring, the light bouncing crazily against the mirrored crystal matrix walls.

Instantly, Heart shapeshifted into the wall, a particular challenge as it reflected herself. She trusted that she'd succeeded in becoming mirror-like. In any case, preoccupied with their mission, they'd not be expecting to see her.

"*Damn!*" Jackson growled when the lights came on. "Be still. Perhaps they'll turn off."

The four of them stood like statues, and, after a few moments, the lights blipped off.

"All right now, men, our mission, of course, is to save the children. But priority one is to watch for Heart. If I know her, she'll soon be here."

Even in the midst of her profound shock at what he said, *in every way!* that he thought she'd be coming here, that she was his priority one— she was overjoyed to hear him say, candidly and as a matter of fact, that the mission was to *save the children*. Not to capture them, or … or anything worse. At the moment, with the insight of the crystal matrix and her father's lab being quite similar, and maybe, even connected, she didn't trust anyone.

Jackson's clear cut directive kept her faith in him, and she'd reveal herself to him eventually. But not just yet. She still wanted to know where the children were first.

She would follow Jackson, she'd be an invisible soldier, on a mission to save children for *The Cause of All Beings*.

A strange, faint glow issued from each of the four men, no doubt another invention of her father's, Heart surmised. It was a kind of light that would hardly be detected by a surveillance system, but that allowed them to move about in a dark or near dark environment.

With Jackson in the lead, they crept right by her. She could feel Jackson's body heat, his tension, and edginess, as he passed but inches from her. He paused for a moment near her and cocked his head as if listening. She felt certain he was mystified by sensing her immediate presence.

There was something incredibly thrilling in the moment, Heart thought, as both of them were charged with energy, focusing on the intensity of their mission.

They were more alike, she realized, than she'd been willing to acknowledge.

A small whimper issued again from the bowels of the crystal matrix. Jackson moved on, his men following. Heart trailed after. The faint light issuing from the four soldiers was perfect—all she need do was follow until they took her to the children, or she felt they'd passed them, and she would go off on her own.

The whimpering, though, was a perfect homing device. Soon they all arrived at a closed door, beyond which the sad sound ensued.

Jackson gestured to his men to fan out.

Of course, Heart saw, his first thought—*and wisely so!*—was that this was a trap. The three men moved, even in the darkness, like a well-oiled machine, equidistant from one another, surrounding, protecting, Jackson.

Jackson cautiously reached to slide open the door. Heart stepped right behind him, ready to move into the space immediately at his side—whatever the room may hold.

"*Ah!*" one of the men sighed.

Heart knew he'd picked up on some aspect of her shapeshifting.

"*Hush!*" Jackson hissed.

"*SIR!*"

Jackson ignored him. Grateful, this time at least, for his single-minded focus, she stepped through the door with him, shapeshifting into him as much as she could manage.

They walked, lock-step, down a short hall.

At the end of the hall were two doors, the sad whimpering coming from the right. Jackson paused, listening. Heart listened too. She knew now that what she heard was a real, living, frightened child. Even so, Jackson put his right hand on a weapon on his chest and cautiously attempted to slide the door open, but it would not budge.

Heart thought of the door at the kitchen in her father's laboratory. She reached out to make, she hoped invisibly, the same gestures HelperFriend had made over the pad alongside the door. Much to her relief, the door slid open.

Jackson looked in shock at the door frame, but the raised volume of the piteous crying took his attention. He must have decided the crying was a child and not a trap, as Heart saw him move his hand from the weapon to a torchlight. He clicked it on and held it aloft.

In the bright spotlight that he slowly revolved around the room, dozens of frightened eyes looked up at him.

"*Men!*" Jackson called, groping on the wall for a room light. The three men hurried into the room as the light came on. "We found our treasure!"

Heart hoped she remained invisible while noticing that several of the Darling Undesirables saw her. Even if they were missing body parts, they were particularly capable of seeing the unseen and hearing the unheard.

The three men stood back, waiting for orders. Jackson, surprising Heart yet again almost as she'd never been surprised in her life, knelt down on the floor with the frightened, broken children and gathered up as many of them as he could hold, patting them, cuddling them, talking to them softly, gently, lovingly reassuring them.

More of the children came to him, and, somehow, he kept finding room to embrace them all, as they calmed, the fear leaving their eyes. She gaped in amazement when she saw tears spring to Jackson's eyes. She looked around to see how his men took their leader in this open and vulnerable state.

Every one of them shamelessly let tears of sadness and joy fall.

Heart felt her heart, at distance, in Equuleus, in the woods, turn for the second time in her life….

As she fell, hopelessly, completely, and totally, in love.

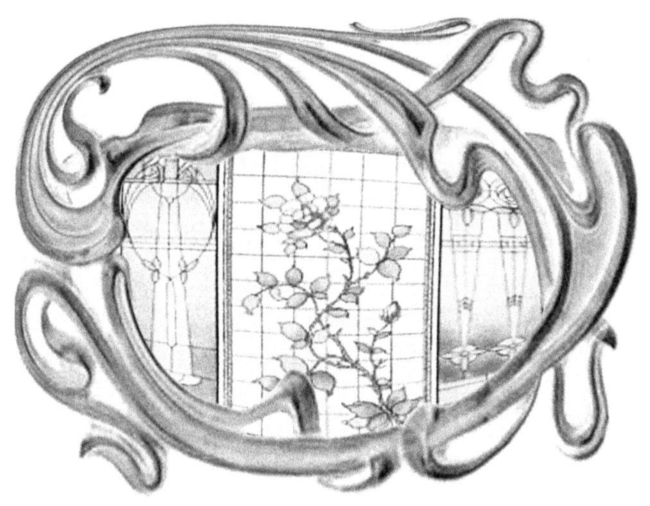

Chapter 14

Still holding an armful of children, Jackson turned to his men and spoke softly. "We have to move swiftly. I don't know how long we've got to hustle these kids out of here."

"Are there any keepers, sir? Any adult caregivers?"

"Right," Jackson said, very Jackson-like. He looked down the little girl closest to him, with an angelic face, but an unnaturally long, and many-jointed neck giving her a snake-like appearance. "Are there any keepers here, Precious One? Your keepers, did they come with you?"

The little girl nodded, and with a sinuous, unnerving motion, twisted her head around, looking fully over her shoulders, as she pointed to the door across the hall.

Jackson nodded to one of the men. "Check it out."

He stepped across the hall and pulled, tugged, and shoved on the door, to little avail.

Heart realized that she now must reveal herself as she couldn't possibly go unnoticed to cross the hall and open the door. She pulled herself from the wall, right before Jackson's eyes, causing him to jump up with a small yelp, still holding the little girl.

The little girl giggled, and many of the children joined her with gleeful giggles.

"*You!*"

"Well, yes, *me!*"

"I tried to tell you, sir," the soldier who had seen the ripple of her shapeshifting spoke up.

Jackson shook his head. "I always have an empath on my team—however, I don't know why, if I'm not going to bother to listen to him."

Heart stepped across the hall, made a series of gestures over the pad by the door, which slid open. Out came six anxious women and two equally anxious men.

"Thank you, thank you," they muttered as they hurried across the hall to the children. Much scurrying and cries of joy and cuddling ensued—Heart reveled in the beauty of the love.

It had almost never been this way, above ground, when she was resident at the Darling Undesirables Facility at Long Prairie. The keepers would act like they loved the children, but it was a rare individual who truly cared.

The Darling Undesirables were a challenge, she understood, with disconcerting physical deformities, and many of them with severe mental disabilities. But right at this moment, when everyone's lives were at risk, the room bubbled with joy and love, as each and every little flower was hugged, and held, and patted and reassured.

"Excellent," Jackson decreed. "Now, let's get outta here. How far is the Gargantua?"

The empath closed his eyes. "Two minutes, sir."

"That's a long time. Let's get on it."

"Yes. We must. Bots in the hall. We're going to have a challenge."

"The Gargantua!" Heart exclaimed. "Will it drop down those gondolas?"

"Yes," Jackson answered.

"Only two at a time?"

"No. There's twenty, and they can each hold two, or three children and a keeper."

"But we only have eight keepers, and we can't send children up without an adult. So that's three rounds."

"You'll be going with them," Jackson said. "That'll help."

"Sure, I'll go a couple rounds, then with your men and yourself, that'll work out pretty fast."

"We won't likely be able to do that. Well, maybe one of my men. But I'm thinking we'll be pretty busy." He shouldered a couple children, and Heart picked up a couple of little children as well.

"Move out!" Jackson commanded.

The group of keepers, carrying as many children as they could, and herding the rest, did as he ordered, following Jackson, with his men taking up the rear. Side by side Heart and Jackson went down the dark hall, his and his men's torchlights providing minimal light.

But as they moved, there was the unmistakable slippery, slimy sound of bots ahead, coming toward them. Heart braced herself, handing off one of the children to the keeper behind her, and grabbing one of the children Jackson held, trying to figure out how to get the other one, in order to free him up.

One of the oldest children, who understood what was happening, rushed up and took the small child Jackson held. Jackson rushed forward, unsheathing a weapon.

Heart dreaded the children witnessing the combat, but it appeared it could not be avoided, when, suddenly, a door opened in the wall, and Heart was pulled through, with the children she carried.

The door slammed shut. Heart turned to see herself staring face to face with the face of her father.

*   *

Heart's first concern being the two children she held, she turned and tried to block the door before it slid shut, but to no avail. Then she looked deep into the eyes of the clone facing her. As she feared, he was no doubt one of the higher level clones. Intelligence and wicked glee shone in his eyes.

"Let me set the children out," she begged.

"I don't care about those … them. They were only used to bring about this very event—*to capture you!*"

"All right then, you've succeeded. You don't want the children, let me set them out."

"You must think I'm one of the stupid clones. I am not! I'm not going to let you go."

"I won't leave. Just let me let them out. I'll stay."

"No. Stop arguing." His gleeful smile turned dark.

Heart, hoping that Jackson was still inside the crystal matrix as she could reach him through her star necklace if he was, while at the same time, hoping he had escaped, set the children on the floor, and, under the ruse of attending to them, turned her back and activated the necklace.

"You won't get away with kidnapping me by opening a door in the hall and grabbing me and these children and then slamming it shut. *Please* let me put the children in the hall, and then you can tell me why you feel you need to capture me."

She released the button and listened carefully to the sounds on the other side of the door, grateful to hear the last of the children, keepers, and soldiers hurrying down the hall. They all, except these two sad little children, had gotten at least that far.

She stood and turned to the lesser clone, shielding the children behind her. "What do you want with me?"

"I can't believe I'm the one to capture you. I can't believe it," he said, giddy and a bit ridiculous sounding. He clapped his hands as if he'd made the winning move in a game of chess.

"Well, now that you have me, what are you going to do with me?" She studied his expression again and had second thoughts about him. "You're not one of the two original clones, made by the Clone, are you?"

"My originator is great. Very great. He is but the second generation. I am but the third generation. And I have been honored by fate, by glorious fate, to capture Heart. Oh, auspicious day. Auspicious day." His sing-song voice sounded like he was quoting.

"Are you repeating a wisdom statement, Venerable Third Generation Clone?"

"Yes. Yesyesyes. Oh, they said you would know. So amazing. I can't believe, I can't believe …."

Heart thought back to her father's attention to "the Clone" on Pink, when he so successfully hypnotized him. She made eye contact and held this clone's gaze.

"Yes. So amazing, this blessing upon you, Venerable Third Generation Clone. Blessings upon you. I trust that you understand and recall every step you must perform after capturing Heart, Father Inventor's daughter. Do you remember all the steps?"

The clone looked a bit confused.

She began to "recite," making everything up as she went, having no idea what she was saying. She only knew she had to keep a monotone. She had to confuse the clone.

"Step one, you must thank Heart for her presence. Step two: you must offer her a beverage. Step three, you must give her a sumptuous repast to her liking.

"Step four, you must provide her with a room, appointed with items to her particular liking, and the room, also, must be to her particular liking. Step five, you must provide entertainment, you must sing and dance with proficiency.

"Please recall that if you fail on any of these, points, if Heart is not satisfied, you will be dismembered by your superior clone.

"It is not acceptable to be unsatisfactory with Father Inventor's daughter. Are you prepared to fulfill your duties?" Heart concluded.

"Ah, ah," the Clone groaned, "ah, what, what, what is 'sumptuous?' And the, repeat, repeat, repeat …."

"First, you must take Heart to her rooms to see if they are acceptable to her."

"Yes. Let's go to your rooms." The Clone opened the door, and as much to Heart's surprise as the clone's, Jackson stood on the other side.

"Most tiresome having to do this," he said, wielding his saber and cleaving the clone in half, grabbing up the two children, and yelling at Heart, "Great hypnosis. You almost had me in a trance."

She looked down at the halves of the Clone as he continued babbling. "The meaning of sumptuous. I will see you have a sumptuous meal, as soon as I know what it is. I'll have the bots gather sumptuous for dinner. It will be delicious…."

She ran down the hall after Jackson. "Everyone out?"

"No. Impasse with the bots. They're still ridiculous and ineffective, thank goodness. But they're succeeding in keeping us from getting out."

"Have everyone go the other way."

"What other way?"

"One-hundred eighty degrees. Down the hall the other way. What was my room still has a big hole in the ground, covered over with a hologram of grass and roses, like the stone hologram covering Father's laboratory."

They came to the thrashing muddle, keepers trying to shield and carry the children, children crying, the bots waving about with their sickly white, shapeless bodies, Jackson's three men doing an amazing job of fending off dozens and dozens of bots.

"About face!" Jackson commanded. His men, at the forefront of the melee, turned one-eighty and directed everyone, as much as they could, the opposite direction. The bots, yet more confused when there suddenly was no one to slap at, started beating up on one another.

"They really like to do that," Jackson observed.

Funny! Heart thought, with the added fleeting thought that she would laugh some another moment.

As they scurried down the hall, Jackson apprised his men of the situation, and, Heart saw, also barked the directions into his wrist, reaching it around the wee child he held, knowing that Peter could not hear him until he cleared the crystal matrix.

They poured into the subterranean room, that, Heart knew, was open overhead.

"Say it again, Jackson. It's open."

"Heart!" she heard Peter's voice through Jackson's communication device. *"Heart!"* he cried again.

"Yes, Peter. If you have the coordinates of my voice, drop the gondolas, project them to eight feet below ground level. Visual is holo."

"Got it!"

"We'd better .…"

'Stand back everyone," Jackson commanded, while everyone backed out of the room. *Slam! Bang!* The beautiful, life-saving gondolas appeared before their eyes.

Jackson, his men, and Heart rapidly loaded the gondolas up with keepers and children, telling the keepers to return to gather more children.

Heart wished she was outside, looking up at the black, gigantic Gargantua as the gondolas zipped the children up, safely into its belly. But she was awash with relief at every gondola that appeared to rip through the ceiling.

Then down came another ten gondolas, quickly loaded, and up they went.

Meanwhile, the bots had sorted out where their prisoners were and came shoving their way down the hall, slapping and waving and grunting and groaning.

"The bots are going to push into the room, and we'll get hit by the gondolas." Heart said.

"Adjust to three feet below ground," Jackson commanded, "then gradually loose tension."

The next set of gondolas zipped through the hologram and hovered above their heads. The keepers, Jackson, his men, and Heart pulled the gondolas down and they were filled, as the bots began to crowd themselves into the room.

"Got to close the door, but I'll be on the other side," Heart said.

"No!" Jackson protested.

"I'm the only one who knows how to do it."

Jackson turned his fury on the bots, slashing them in half, left and right. "We're … almost … there. Get in the next gondola, Heart. There are only six children left. You take two," *slash, slash, slash,* "Dirk, take two, and there's one keeper. That's it. Dirk, return. Heart, you stay on the Gargantua."

"WHAT? NO! Are you crazy? No. I'll take the children up," The gondolas appeared. "And I'll return with Dirk."

"Do as I say, Heart!"

"I can't," she grabbed two of the children and jumped into the gondola. "Equuleus is in the woods. I *must* return."

"Equuleus? What do you mean?"

"You know. My winged horse." Her gondola and the two others zipped up through the hologram and into the night air. Faster than thought, it sped upwards to the unimaginably gigantic Gargantua. She looked overboard to see Jackson and his two men appear to come right through the earth among the rose bushes.

Grinning broadly, she was sucked into the belly of the high-in-the-sky whale.

Chapter 15

Heart could hardly process what she saw when the gondola sucked up into the Gargantua. Incredible activity stirred and swirled all around. There were lovely, warm, bright lights as far as she could see. All sorts of beings were doing all sorts of things. But, right at this moment, the ones near the gondolas were picking up and cuddling the children, hugging the keepers, scurrying around the gondolas, which were being rapidly put away in their neat cubby holes.

Two clockworks women, their facial gears spinning in delighted, friendly smiles, took the children from Heart's gondola. A mechanical man came up and offered Heart his hand.

"No," Heart said, looking around for Dirk. As she did so, she thought she caught a glimpse of someone familiar off in the distance, turning sideways, watching the gondolas intently, most conspicuous because she wasn't moving in the midst of all the movement.

The mechanical man continued to hold out his hand, bemused.

"No," Peter said, coming through the beehive throng. "Thank you, Wilker, thanks," he said, smiling at Heart. "Dear Heart! What a surprise to see you! And yet not, I guess."

Jackson's voice came urgently over Peter's communication device. "Keep Heart there, Peter."

"I can't, Jackson. It's …" he grinned and shrugged at Heart as if to say, sorry you have to hear this. "It's not time yet."

There was a long pause from Jackson, then, "Right," he said, so utterly Jackson-like that both Peter and Heart chuckled, even though Heart was purely mystified by the comment.

Dirk appeared at Peter's side and got into the gondola with Heart.

"So good to see you, Heart," Peter said. "Take care of yourself, and I really mean, *take care*. I love you, little girl." And then he winked at her, just like, *oh so long ago!* he had the first day her whole adventure began. He winked at her and looked just like the sweet, shy doorman at The Museum of Scientific Improbabilities and Unpredictable Oddities, the day she and her peer Darling Undesirables first visited. The day she first saw Equuleus.

"I love you too, Peter." And, to give him a chuckle, she blinked both her eyes like she had the first time they ever talked, when she tried to imitate his wink, having never had anyone wink at her before, though, of course, she'd mastered the art long since.

She did indeed hear his delighted guffaw as the gondola fell out of the Gargantua like a baby guppy, into the sea of the night sky, and she and Dirk flew straight toward the ground. Heart saw that the gondola hovered over solid ground, and she and Dirk jumped out. She followed him to the back fence, where Jackson waited with his two other men.

"Get out of there," Peter's voice sounded suddenly urgent and concerned. "Purists are roaring down the crystal matrix road."

Jackson, his men, and Heart jumped over the fence. Heart ran toward the woods and Equuleus. "Where's your vehicle?" she asked Jackson as they ran.

"Pretty much where I parked it the last time you and I were here."

"Equuleus is there, in the woods. I'll follow you."

"Equuleus can't keep up with me."

"Then project a map of your destination to him, and we'll catch up."

"Heart, I put you in your father's laboratory, and that's where I mean for you to stay."

"Oh, Jackson … *blah, blah, blah!* I have a father, don't try to be one too. Give us your destination."

"No."

"Then we'll wander around the sky until we find you, I guess."

"Sir," Dirk said, "I believe it's best to give the winged horse the coordinates. It's only half the distance of the lab, and, well, the storm is gathering."

Jackson stopped in his tracks. The night, fortunately, was quite dark, but the little moons, Pink and Yellow, and *their* moons, glowed sweetly in the sky. Heart looked up to them, sending love to her father, and … and everyone there.

Jackson followed her gaze. "Right," he grumbled. "Right, right, right. Sending coordinates. But briefly, so as not to get intercepted." He continued on his flat out run to his vehicle, his men close upon his heels.

Heart ran into the woods, thinking to Equuleus, *"Ready for take-off, and receive coordinates from Jackson."* She scurried up to him, as he leaped to his feet. Jumping on him, Equuleus tore through the woods, and the moment he came into the clearing, he ascended into the night sky.

Heart saw Jackson's vehicle hovering above the tree line, and worried about him risking detection, but, she knew, he was making sure he had a visual of her on Equuleus.

"Coordinates received," Equuleus said.

Heart held onto her star necklace, and repeated, "coordinates received," to Jackson.

He appeared to fly slow, and Heart hoped it was not to keep an eye on her, although she was sure that was precisely why. *"Go, Jackson!"* she whispered, to herself.

As if he heard her, his vehicle shot away, into the dark, dark night.

"Are you good, Equuleus, are the coordinates clear?"

"Perfectly clear. The destination is a glowing point on the map, and getting a little brighter as we go."

"Excellent!" Heart relaxed and took in the night, the chilly but invigorating night, so grateful for everything, at the moment. Grateful to be part dark energy and dark matter, as, otherwise, she'd not be able to fly, high in the sky. Grateful for her mystical plaid, that, as she looked down at it, pulsed brightly, as if breathing.

Energies were building. She could feel them all around her. As much as she wanted to believe she determined her own actions, there was a strange, compelling sense that she was also being led. She didn't like it, and, yet, oddly, she did.

Most peculiar!

But that all paled at the most important thought. "We saved the children, Equuleus. We saved each and every one of the Darling Undesirables of the Gulf, and their sweet, amazing, keepers, too!"

"Truly wonderful, Heart. What about that clone?"

"Ah! You picked up on that did you?"

"Of course."

"Well then, you probably know that Jackson dispatched him in short order, in the only way he seems to know. The poor thing there on the ground, in two, still trying to fulfill his obligations. But, most importantly, the Darling Undesirables are all safe in that flying city."

Equuleus shuddered under her. "Kind of scared the wits out of me when it came overhead. And, you know, I don't scare easily."

"I did tell you the Gargantua is—*gargantuan*."

"You did, and thank goodness. I quickly realized that it was what made the sky black, not that the stars had all instantaneously died."

Heart chuckled. "It's breathtaking inside, Equuleus! A city. Every kind of being, hustling about, loving the children, smiling and happy and friendly."

"Like on Pink," Equuleus observed.

"Yes. Exactly like on Pink." Heart couldn't bring herself to mention the one human she thought she saw at a distance. But it couldn't be possible, could it? She needed to set the thought aside.

"And what about that *other event* that occurred?" Equuleus asked.

"What other event?" Heart asked evasively, this being the *second* subject she didn't want to discuss.

"You know."

"I do. But for now, let's keep it quiet. Too much is going on. It's too surprising. Too distracting."

"It's love, Heart. Only love. The core of what you, yourself teach, the core of all of life and all of being."

"Nothing 'only' about love, Equuleus."

"True."

They flew on in companionable silence, Heart enjoying beyond measure the sight of the golden, dark energy lights in the homes below, cozy, safe, charming.

She hoped it would stay that way.

But Dirk's words, "a storm is gathering," stuck in her mind, and in her feeling body. She knew it to be true as she summoned her courage.

Chapter 16

Jackson's voice came to her in the midst of her reverie through her star necklace. "Hurry, Heart. Have Equuleus speed it up!"

"Why?" she asked, sorry to have her sweet reflections disrupted.

"Because—because I say so. And because, I mean to try and save your life, you intractable girl."

Equuleus responded to Jackson's comment without any order from Heart, putting on a burst of speed that startled Heart. "*Ahhh!* I didn't know you had this speed in you!"

"When it's life or destruction, I do."

"Yes." Heart recalled Equuleus's incredible ability to accelerate, when they were in the mechanical aurora, escaping the dark matter bomb of the

Purists, and, also, when she had him fly to get to the plummeting *Heart!*, to attempt to save Xavier.

If this were a moment anything like those, then it was good that Equuleus responded immediately to Jackson's command.

"Do you know something I don't?" Heart asked Equuleus.

"Yes. Hush. Let me concentrate."

Heart knew Jackson was watching their progress closely. "What does Equuleus know that I don't?" she asked him.

"He sees blips on his dark energy map, Heart. The Purists are on the move, and they're on their way here."

Heart heard a strange humming and even began to feel it in her body.

"*Augh!*" Equuleus cried.

"What?"

"That sound, that vibration, it's tapping my energy."

"Come, Equuleus," Jackson called. "You're almost here."

Heart looked to the ground in the near distance, and as she did so, blue lights winked off.

"Sorry, Equuleus. Automatic shut down. You're all right. Continue on your heading."

Equuleus put on yet another unbelievable burst of speed. Although now, everything was black around her, Heart could feel Equuleus descending. The warmth and scent of the loamy earth rose up around her, and she could see the dark forms of buildings some distance ahead.

Suddenly the humming turned into a screech, while high-intensity lights blasted on from behind. She knew Equuleus was suffering from this sound, as it began to hurt her, as well, in her bones. But on he flew toward the dark buildings.

There, she saw a small blue light. She knew this was Jackson, risking his life and the life of how many others, she didn't even know, to guide Equuleus.

She dared to look over her shoulder and gasped in shock and terror. At some distance, but approaching at a phenomenal speed, were phalanx of impossibly bright lights, lighting up the sky behind them like a terrifying dawn from another dimension.

"Good, good, Equuleus, the little blue light. It's Jackson."

"*Yes,*" Equuleus said in her mind, with a single purpose, driven to the light.

The impossible sound, the screeching, augmented, and Heart wondered at how the Purists, themselves, could tolerate being in the center of that pain-inducing sound.

The blue light winked off, Equuleus touched ground, and ran, pell-mell, to where it had shone.

"Holo wall," Jackson said. "Come through. Quickly. It is closing. I cannot override it."

Heart trusted Equuleus to leap through the holo image of a wall that she could now barely make out. But, with curiosity and fear, she watched as the wall appeared to slowly thicken, hoping Equuleus, too saw the closing thin circle in the wall.

Should they even try? What would happen to them if they slammed into a stone wall at this speed?

What would happen to them if they stayed out here, with the fast-approaching ranks of the Purists' warcraft?

She didn't have time to process the thoughts any further than that as Equuleus leapt gracefully and with confidence through the closing holo, pulling in his wings as tight as possible, protecting Heart's legs. Even at that, Heart heard a sickening dragging crunch, as Equuleus's gear wings were closed upon by stone. He landed on what sounded like a stone floor, but everything was in total blackness.

And total silence.

"Are you all right?" Heart asked as the screeching horror of hellish sound was closed out with the closing stone wall. "The stone hit your wings. Are you all right?"

"We're here, that's what's important," Equuleus answered, but his voice didn't sound quite right.

"Are you all right?"

"Yes. I'm fine."

Darkness and silence surrounded them. Equuleus didn't move, and Heart became concerned about his total stillness.

"Equuleus?"

He remained silent, but Heart knew something was not right.

"*Ahh!*" Heart heard Jackson's voice come from nearby. "Not good. Sorry, Equuleus. I had no control over the holo gate."

She saw the intense blue light hurrying toward her. But she didn't move. She had a feeling that she had better not move as there was something wrong with Equuleus.

Jackson finally arrived at her side. "Oh, *not good!*"

Heart, then, could not bear to look down. The tone in Jackson's voice frightened her.

"Right. Ahm, Heart, get down carefully."

She let the pins retract from her thighs, and slid off Equuleus. Then, with fear, turned to look at Equuleus. Both of his wings were hanging down, nearly touching the ground. She could see in the faint blue light, several gears, bent and smashed, realizing the same must be true of his other wing as well.

"Oh! Equuleus!" Heart breathed, terrified for him. *"Equuleus!"* She turned to Jackson. "What are we to do?"

"I don't know. What must we do, Equuleus? What is the extent of the damage, can you tell?"

"I do not know. I've never been damaged like this."

"We need to move into the interior to be safer," Jackson said. "Can you move?"

"I believe so. But you'll each need to hold up a wing. I think it's very bad if they drag."

"Of course, dearest, of course!" Heart gingerly lifted the near wing, while Jackson went to his other side and held up the other wing.

"Follow the blue light, Equuleus. It'll take us to the interior. We have clockworks medics." Jackson tapped on his communication device. "Incoming injured— clockworks horse. Standby clockworks medics."

"Equuleus?" Heart heard someone exclaim in response. *"Equuleus! Oh!"* the excited voice continued. "Medics, prepare, Equuleus, incoming injured."

Heart had forgotten what it was like to be a "celebrity," though that had been her life when she lived at The Darling Undesirables Facility at Long Prairie. But, of course, Equuleus would be a "celebrity" among clockworks.

If his fame made them take special care of him, that's all she cared about.

"I wish WonderMan One and WonderMan Two were here."

"Yes," Jackson agreed. "But we do have excellent medics."

"My beautiful Equuleus," Heart cried as a wide door slid open to a light-filled room, with every sort of being rushing about, everyone seeming to have something important to do.

But her mind was on Equuleus.

An extremely impressive, eight-foot-tall, graceful clockworks man rushed up to them. Heart was reminded of Lady Gervi.

"Look at you," he cried. "Gorgeous Equuleus. Dear, dear, the stone holo, I think must have almost closed on you." He stepped in front of Heart, taking the wounded wing from her.

"Yes," Equuleus said, voice much subdued. Was he in pain? Heart couldn't imagine it. She couldn't bear it.

"Well, you performed a miracle to get through the closing stone wall. Your entry was quite symmetrical too, as …" he walked around Equuleus to his other side with gear-driven grace, "the other wing is almost identically damaged."

"*Oh!*" Heart exclaimed in despair.

"But that's a good thing," the clockworks doctor said, stroking Equuleus's neck. "Had the injury not been perfectly symmetrical, it would have been very bad, with severe damage on one side. This way it's superficial on both sides." He looked down at Heart on the other side of Equuleus. "And most likely would not only have rendered his wing completely useless but might have injured you as well, miss."

He stopped, took a second look at Heart, cocked his head in a strangely HelperFriend-like movement, looking at her from the corner of his gear eyes. "Heart? Is it Heart?"

Heart smiled, curious that he would suddenly realize that it was herself on Equuleus. "Yes."

"Heart and Equuleus! Oh, my pleasure." He reached his amazingly long arm across Equuleus's back to shake her hand. She took it, smiling. "Who else would be on Equuleus?"

"Well, now, that's a perfectly reasonable question. I didn't process it. I'm very literal. A thing has to be in front of me before I can think it through. But then, when it is, I'm good at attending to it." He seemed to have a second thought. "That is to say, I will take superior care of Equuleus."

"I trust you will," Heart nodded. "I have a clockworks friend who is quite literal, so I'm fairly used to it. Although sometimes it's confusing to have to explain certain things that seem obvious."

"I dare say that's true!" He turned his attention back to Equuleus. "But for now, let us take care of our Equuleus, and see what might be done to get him back into perfect shape." He reached around

Equuleus, and, keeping both wings from touching the floor, started to lead him away, while Heart followed. "I'm sorry, Heart. You must not come along. Not only is the space quite confined, but, well, you need to stay with Jackson."

Heart looked across at Jackson, standing a few feet from her, now that Equuleus had been taken away.

"Jackson," she cried, "Equuleus!"

He stepped over to her and, much to her surprise, put an arm around her, even among all the bustle and witnesses. "I know, Heart. I'm so, so sorry. But he'll be all right. Out of commission for a while, but all right. I don't know much about clockworks medical attention. I know they're very good at repair and healing here. Beings from everywhere, all over Earth, come here."

He walked Heart back out of the busy, light-filled infirmary, and the wide door slid shut behind them.

"We have a lot to talk about, a lot to plan, with almost no time to do it."

They stood in the darkness, Heart, miserable with a guilt that now began to engulf her. If only she hadn't ridden Equuleus in the first place! She could have taken the *Heart!* She would have been able to move faster, and Equuleus would now be in her father's laboratory, safely with HelperFriend.

"I'm *so* terrible," she said quietly.

"Have you not been listening to me?"

"You said we have a lot to talk about."

"All, right, Heart. You must put aside your feelings of guilt. I know how your mind works. I know you're thinking about how you ought to have taken the *Heart!*, if you had, Equuleus would not be injured now. But, you must stop those thoughts and come into the moment. You *did* ride Equuleus, he *is* injured, he *is* being taken care of.

"Now, at this moment, we must put our minds to the fast-upon-us battle to assure that all of us see a tomorrow."

These hard, and unarguable words snapped Heart into the moment. "All right, Jackson. I'm … I'm with you. By the way, we're standing in the dark."

"Yes. That's as it must be." He reached out and took her hand. "There's a bench here, against the wall, we'll sit and I'll catch you up a little, but, as you can guess, I must, almost immediately, be else-where."

"Well, I'm guessing you need—*right now!*—to be elsewhere."

"Being elsewhere right now is my second prior-ity. My first priority, and even more, my first direc-tive, is to watch over you."

"*Oh!*" Heart gasped.

"Don't act as though that surprises you."

"It doesn't surprise me. It shocks me."

"Well, don't let it. Anyway, to get to business. The Purists are now overhead and surrounding us. We are impenetrable, as you may understand, by virtue of how the closing holo immediately clamped shut upon the sound weapon. But, even as we speak, they are bombing us. We have intentionally drawn this activity, in order to deplete their stores of weaponry.

"But you never know when the opposing forces have developed new weaponry. At present, we appear to be safe …."

"Where are we?"

"We're at a The Darling Undesirables Facility at Mountain's Edge, a facility that was closed down many years ago."

"There are Darling Undesirable facilities that have been closed down?" Heart said, amazed.

"Yes."

"But I thought the population of Darling Undesirables was increasing?"

"Not so. The needless experimentation has slowed considerably, ever since you came on the scene. Because, quietly, subtly, Father Inventor continues to develop solutions to longevity that do not require physical experiments. He can extrapolate results with the physical experiments on computer simulation."

"Oh! So … I don't even know how to say this with caution, given the hurried circumstances, but when I realized that there's a crystal matrix uniting the two Darling Undesirable Facilities at the Gulf and Long Prairie, and, then maybe Father Inventor's laboratory, I can't help wondering …."

"No Heart, you're wrong. He built the crystal matrix under Darling Undesirable facilities to try and *stop* the experimentation. Or at least to keep a close eye on it, and to, as I say, be sure to get all the data so that, eventually, the experiments would have no reason to continue. Which has been the case for years now. Darling Undesirable facilities have been closing, quietly closing, right and left."

"But the news—forever saying that another Darling Undesirable facility has opened."

"Lies. All lies. Do they ever say where those facilities are?" Jackson asked.

"Well, no. But I accepted what they said, that they had to be secret, to protect the innocent children from the Purists."

"Nothing, Heart, is as it seems."

Suddenly the building all around them, rocked.

"Well, that's not good," Jackson whispered. "They've figured out a way to make a synthetic earthquake, to shake us to the groun if they can't bomb us. I don't think that will succeed, either. But, I have to say, I'll be curious to learn if my engineers have managed to make our buildings completely earthquake impervious."

The building seemed to jump, and Heart felt herself rise from the floor and the bench, and land back down, hard.

"Sublimation," Jackson noted. "Pretty sophisticated. I guess I'll have to go out and disperse them. They're becoming an irritation."

Heart giggled nervously. She wasn't afraid for herself, but she couldn't help but worry about Equuleus being delicately worked on with the floor moving side to side and up and down. "Equuleus," she whispered.

"It's probably not helpful to the doctor, I'll grant you. Right. Off we go." He turned on his little blue light, leapt up and ran down a hall.

Heart stayed where she was.

Jackson looked back at her. *"Come along!"*

"I … I don't want to …."

"You don't want to leave Equuleus. I should have known. But, you must come with me, Heart. I know you won't be able to resist going back in there, and you mustn't. And I must keep you in close proximity, or I can't concentrate, wondering where you are and what you're doing."

"Well," she stood and took a few steps toward Jackson, realizing that, if she paid close attention, she could return to this spot. Though difficult in the dark, not impossible. Also, it was true that she was keeping Jackson from his duties. "But," she tried to argue, running to catch up to him, "if I were here, you'd know where I was because I'm not going to leave Equuleus."

Jackson grabbed her hand again and dragged her along at a good clip. "True. But I want to be able to tell Peter and Father Inventor that I have you in sight. You're distracting both of them, especially your father, as you can imagine."

"Oh dear, I'm such a problem."

"Yes, Heart, you can be a problem sometimes. And," Jackson paused, "you are the solution."

Chapter 17

As they ran, they also flew up into the air a couple more times, causing Heart great anxiety about Equuleus.

"How have these old buildings been made impervious, Jackson?" Heart asked as they ran.

"The scientific details are a bit of a mystery to me, Heart. Just as you are."

"What does that mean?"

"That means that Father Inventor has applied dark matter and dark energy to these buildings, in ways that make them nearly indestructible. Just like you."

"I see! Very …" they flew up into the air even farther, and came down harder, with the floor still raising toward them as they landed, *"ouff,"* Heart let out, "brilliant of him!"

"As always. *From Pink,* he's been doing these experiments on the various closed Darling Undesirable facilities, especially remote ones, like this one, which is the most remote and the most experimented on by him. And now it's the most populated."

"Other than the Healing Station, it appears virtually abandoned," Heart said. They ran down some steps and across a causeway that seemed to Heart like it might be an underground connection to another building.

Jackson said nothing as they ran through a doorway, up another flight of stairs, and stopped before a huge door.

"The current population of The Darling Undesirables Facility at Mountain's Edge," he said, opening the door.

What Heart saw reminded her of the first time she went into her father's room on Pink when the outside wall had been raised, and she saw hundreds and hundreds of clockworks, mechanical, and bio beings listening to her father's instructions.

And here, now, she processed the shock of seeing hundreds, no, *thousands*—all sorts of beings—at 3-D computers along the walls, or attending to vehicles of every type and description, like the population itself. There was an indescribable mingling of humans, mechanicals, and, Heart guessed, hybrids, along with a few, but not many, clockworks, all working in subdued lighting.

"*Oh, my!*" Heart whispered. "*My!*"

"*Sir! Sir! Sir!*" various beings called at the sight of Jackson, rushing up to him. "What ought we to be doing?"

"What damage from the earthquakes?" Jackson asked.

"Nothing so far, sir. Everything is intact. The buildings are handling it, but the components—it's stressful."

"Right. We'll have to put a lid on it then. Orange, blue, orange," he commanded.

"*Yes, sir!*" The humans and mechanicals went running off to accomplish whatever his color-coded command meant.

Jackson turned to Heart. "I must get out there and halt the bad guys. I really, really hate this part of the mission. I don't want to harm human and mechanical pilots in the Purists' war crafts."

"No clockworks?"

"Almost never. There are not many clockworks left on Earth, they're mostly on Pink. And on Yellow, too, I assume. Most clockworks on Earth are in permanent stasis, in museums. The liberation of sentient clockworks is part of our plan. But, for the moment, they're better off where they are until we get the world sorted out."

Heart chuckled. "Yes. Always a good idea to get the world sorted out! Why is that—about clockworks being kept in stasis? You've seen HelperFriend be powerful and ferocious, much to even my surprise."

"That's part of the problem—they tend to be unpredictably emotional. And, well, you've got to be able to function, single-minded and cold. Cold focus, we call it."

"You've got that down, for sure, Jackson," Heart said. "Just on the off chance no one ever told you."

"Right," Jackson said, with, Heart noted, cold focus. "I must go out there now and work on getting the Purists to change their minds." He ran toward his vehicle, which Heart noticed in the midst of the motley stand of vehicles.

Heart ran alongside him. "I'm going with you."

Jackson made a small explosive sound. "Yeah. No."

"*Yes*, Jackson. If I can't be with Equuleus, I need to be doing something."

"You need to be safe, Heart. I haven't had a moment to tell Peter and Father Inventor that you're here, intact."

"But Equuleus is not."

"He'll be fine. Quite honestly, if he keeps you on the ground, that's fine by me."

"Don't even say such a thing!"

"Well, you know what I mean." He jumped into his vehicle, looking down at Heart, rushing around to climb in, he locked the doors, while Dirk hurried up to grab onto the passenger door, giving Heart a look of bemusement.

"Locked, sir."

"Keeping out the stowaway. She's good at that!"

He unlocked the door, Dirk jumped in, and Jackson waved her away. She stepped back, watching sadly as he taxied to the far end of the gigantic building, followed by a few dozen mismatched vehicles, lining up.

Whether Jackson liked it or not, Heart knew that she had to join them. *Why else was she here?*

She ran to another vehicle and jumped in, just as the mechanical copilot jumped in the other side.

Heart was glad he was a mechanical. He would not give her any argument like a human might when he saw who was at the controls.

She fired the engines, as the pilot ran up. She waved him to the vehicle behind, and began to taxi in line with the others.

The mechanical copilot did a double-take when he realized that his pilot was on the ground, and someone else, *who?* Was at the controls.

"*HEART!*" he fairly yelled when he recognized her.

"Yes. I'm right here. You needn't yell."

"*HEART!*" he yelled again.

"*WHAT?*" Heart yelled back.

"*It's you!*"

"I know. But, I think we'd better pay attention to what we're doing here, now, don't you?"

"Oh!" The mechanical snapped to attention. "Yes."

"Please give me a fast thumbnail sketch of what we're headed into, and how we're to handle it." Great, Heart thought. I have to encounter the only super-emotional mechanical, anywhere.

"Oh. Oh dear. I'm only a copilot, and I've only done a couple of simulations. I'm not the best …."

"You're the *only*," Heart pointed out.

"Oh, not so good …."

"Is the simulation onboard?"

"Yes!" The mechanical punched some buttons, and a 3-D came up in front of Heart.

"Fast forward through it," she commanded.

She watched intently as the simulation showed the same bright-light vehicles she'd seen outside. A subdued, but horrible sound began to accompany the simulation. "What's with the noise?"

"That's a tolerable simulation of the sound weapon that the Purists use."

"How is it dealt with?"

"Mechanicals can turn the sound off, by pressing on our temple. Bios have a device. I hope there's one here. My pilot, you may have noticed, is also a mechanical, so we don't need them."

He turned around and began thrashing through things behind his seat. "Not this …" *thrash, thrash.* "No, not this either, …" *thrash, thrash.* "Ah, here's one."

He brought out a deep blue helmet. "You push this button and it will completely block the sound. Then you push this button on the instrument panel, which brings up a shield around the vehicle that blocks the vibration."

He pointed to a switch on the instrument panel. "This is *our* recently devised and newly installed sound weapon."

Heart watched her copilot and the 3-D simulation at the same time. The toggle on the instrument panel directed and deployed the sound weapon. A little primitive in design Heart thought, but she knew if her father developed the science behind it, it was infallible. "How does it work? What does it do?"

"No one knows, Heart. It's never been used! If we must use it, it'll be the first time."

"Very interesting. It might work perfectly. Or we'll be causing uncontrolled death and destruction, or maybe we won't phase them in the least, and they bring us down."

"Well, that wouldn't be very nice," the mechanical said.

Heart laughed. "No. It wouldn't. What's your name, you most unusual of mechanicals?"

"You can call me Mick. You'd better put your helmet on." He handed it to her. "We're next, and you'll want it engaged." He pointed down the runway, Heart saw at some distance apparently another holo, as, one by one, the sad band of mismatched terrestrial and spacecraft appeared to fly through the wall.

"How do you know when to go through the holo?"

"Our vehicle will automatically accelerate and be shot out into the sky."

"Oh boy, Mick, that sounds like a lot of fun."

"Does it?" Mick sounded confused.

"Sarcasm, Mick."

"I see," he said thoughtfully. "I've heard of sarcasm, but I'm not sure I understand it."

"Not necessary." Heart pulled on the helmet, then fumbled to find the button on its side. Mick put her finger on it, as she taxied slowly behind the vehicle before her, which suddenly shot forward and appeared to be sent right through the wall.

"Here we go!" Heart crowed.

"*Fun!*" Mick said.

Heart glanced over at him, and his hard metallic face softened into a beautiful smile. He didn't understand sarcasm, Heart thought, and that couldn't be all bad.

The simulation she'd been studying switched off, and the 3-D showed a view of the spot where they were. She saw the mechanical push a button on his head, and then she heard his voice inside her head.

"The 3-D will now show the actions we ought to take, given the position we're in. It's more or less automated. Of course, you can override it, if you want."

Heart was about to ask how, when she was thrust deep into her seat by the force of the vehicle being propelled out into the night sky. She hardly noticed the holo wall, it happened so fast.

And there she was! Flying in the night sky, lining up in formation with the four previous vehicles. She noted the next vehicle coming into formation beside her.

Looking ahead, she saw two other sets of six vehicles moving toward the bright white lights of the Purists' phalanx. Their paltry ranks seemed ridiculous against the innumerable opposing forces. But she was in it now. Her rumination suggested that this might not be the wisest move, and perhaps she ought to have listened to Jackson while the listening was good.

But she would make the best of her abilities, along with complete faith in her father's inventions. He'd not so thoroughly safeguard the buildings below, without equal attention to this sad fleet of protectors.

It was good to be in the middle of her group so she could imitate those around her as much as possible, and the 3-D seemed fairly active. She hoped Mick would also be helpful.

"Why aren't The Purists taking action against our first craft?"

"They can't see them. They're cloaked. We can see each other, but they can't see us. If one of their empaths senses us, then …."

"One of their empaths? What do you mean? They're Purists. They don't believe in empaths."

"They don't believe in a lot of things that they do or have or … *believe in!* They don't believe in genetic manipulation, and they are at the center of it. What about their bots?"

"Yes, Mick. What about their bots? You're absolutely correct. They're … hypocrites." Heart watched the 3-D overlay as a red moving line appeared. "What does this red line mean?"

"Sorry. I need to be telling you what to do. The red line is showing you where to go to get into formation. The system has figured out you've not done this before. I forgot about the red line. I've only seen it once when I *attempted* to pilot during the simulation—I saw the red line a lot. I'm not a natural pilot. But I'm an acceptable copilot."

"More than acceptable, Mick. And thank you." Heart zipped along the red moving line and came into formation. The red line disappeared.

"What's happening?"

"We'll come into a pentagon shape with our sound weapons strategically pointed at the invaders. Then, at Jackson's command, we'll activate our weapons. In theory, the sound will cause many of the opposing forces to fall from the sky. Our ground forces are ready to gather the fallen. They'll be taken in and medically attended to, whatever their form. Bot. Mechanical. Human."

"We'll be contending with the enemy spacecraft remaining up here in front line battle. Of course, we hope they'll be so disabled by the first sound weapon blast that there's not much battle to ensue. But, as this is the first time we're using the new sound weapon, we'll soon discover how it works."

"Goodness …." Heart whispered, worried for Jackson, concerned for all her peers in *The Cause of all Beings*, surrounding her, and sad and concerned for all those in the hovering spacecrafts below, continuing to drop sound bombs, in the hopes of stimulating an earthquake large enough to destroy the buildings. "How many craft will we be in total, once the pentagon is formed?"

"Twenty pods, six craft per pod—one-hundred and twenty."

"And how many of those light and sound Purist's vehicles are we now flying above, would you guess there is?"

"I'm sorry, Heart, I cannot guess. Because I know. There are one-thousand twenty-four."

"Well, *hmmm*, interesting," was all she could bring herself to say.

She watched silently as the formation continued to become defined. Finally, she could see the pentagon shape of her peers, the small, ragtag, seemingly hopeless—but intrepid and persevering!—believers in *The Cause of All Beings*.

Suddenly, Jackson's voice came through her helmet, sounding as if he was in her head. *Disconcerting!* She pictured him in his craft and tried to imagine what was going through his mind this moment. Well, she knew what was going through his mind at this very moment.

THE MOMENT.

She knew he was utterly and completely in the moment. On his mission. Doing everything in his superlative power to quell the advance of the Purists against the life of freedom and self-realization for each and every being. Not even, probably, thinking about all those details. Simply single-mindedly attending to the perfection of the formation, the aiming of the sound weapons, the actuation of their power.

A power understood and channeled by her father.

Heart waited with a quiet intensity, still taking in the training of the 3-D before her, showing her where the sound weapon was located on her craft. Where the activation switch was located on her instrument panel. How to deploy the weapon. There followed a simulation of the result of deployment. Little lights simply winked out.

The tutorial included a running percentage of "effectiveness" beneath the simulation. It quickly reached one-hundred percent. Heart was sorry to reflect that the result would likely be considerably short of that.

The simulation blacked out, and she thought it was through. But another simulation started to play, with a consideration of the mission being only fifty percent successful. It showed various battle strategies and evasive maneuvers. It included a scenario in which her craft tucked its virtual tail between its wheels and scurried back into the big, safe, building.

An unlikely choice for her, she knew.

"Is there a ten percent tutorial?" Heart asked Mick.

"Ten percent for them or us?"

"Us."

"Ahm …we're not likely to be in the last ten percent, if the battle rages that badly." Mick fussed with the 3-D. "Here. It looks like the best odds the program gives us is to be still in flight at twenty-three percent, at which point we will be downed, or have retreated."

"The system does not know me, Mick."

"*Oh!*" Mick said with delight. And awe.

"Can you put in a variable?" Heart asked.

"I can put in some variables."

"Put in 'Heart is pilot.'"

"*He-he-he!*" Mick chortled. "*He-he-he!*" he chortled again, a mechanical sound, and yet so charmingly gleeful. "Here goes."

Heart watched with interest as the simulation blacked, then seemed to struggle with coming back up. It blinked the pentagon formation several times. Highlighted their craft in the formation. Then blacked again. Words scrolled in the air between Mick and herself: "Not a possible option. Heart is on Pink."

"Can you enter, 'proceed with simulation?'"

"I'll try."

Soon the words scrolled between them: "Cannot conceive viable simulation with Heart, Father Inventor's 1-1-2080 at helm."

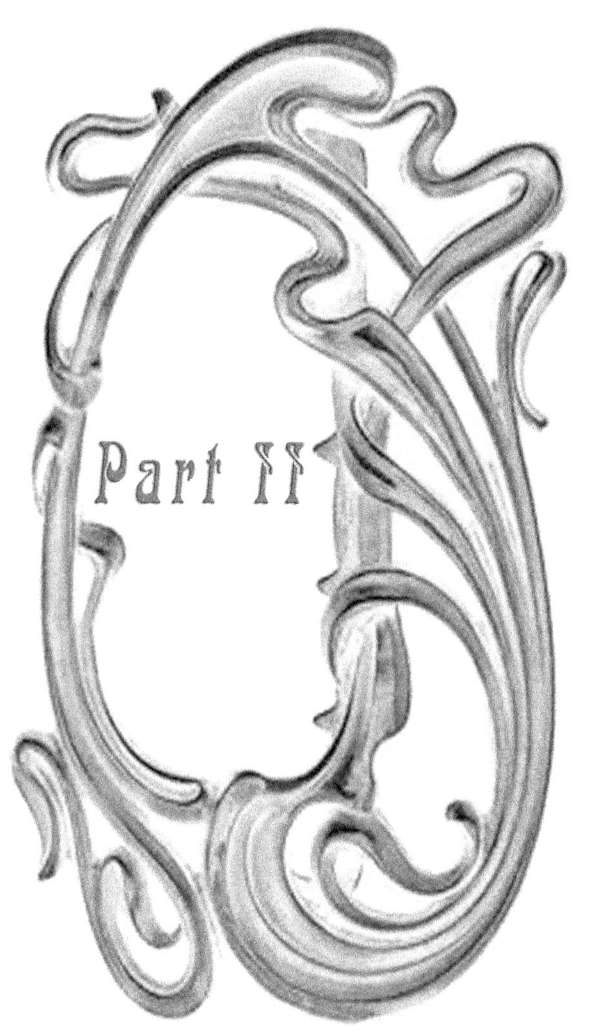
Part II

Chapter 18

Heart, anticipating a simulation that would at least be interesting to see, was shocked by this information. "*What? ....*"

Jackson's voice came loud and clear in her head, via the helmet. "Ready. Position sound weapons."

There followed an interminable pause ....

"X-4-5, adjust."

Heart looked to the pod to her left and saw that, sure enough, one smaller vehicle had its sound weapon perhaps three degrees out of line with the others in its pod. It made a small adjustment.

"Excellent," Jackson said.

"Sorry, sir. Calibration is erroneous. Manual, visual adjustment. Thought it looked wrong."

"Concentrate," Jackson said calmly.

At that moment, the light vehicles below released a joint volley of encapsulated sound bombs. They hit the ground in force, and, at a count of two, Heart watched in fascination and dismay as the entire building below raised visibly from the ground, even at this distance and in the strange light.

She could only think of Equuleus.

Wonderfully, she heard in her mind, *"I'm all right, Heart. A bit unnerving, but we all handled the building's temporary flight."*

Heart relaxed.

Jackson commanded, "Activate sound weapons."

Heart flipped the sound weapon's switch on, at the same moment as her peers, and watched in horror and fascination at what transpired—considerably different from the picture the simulation had shown.

Hundreds of the Purists' craft fell, in slow motion, but the vehicles clearly had no control over the falling motion. Trails of brilliant light dripped to the ground—with the stunning effect of a rain made of light, as the little vehicles sank to the ground.

She felt a pressure she'd not even been aware of release from her skeleton and surmised that this was, despite the protections, the effect of their sound weapons that could not be entirely subdued.

The 3-D stats noted that the Purists had been reduced by thirty percent with this first foray!

"Seems successful," she said to Mick, her attention taken by the activity on the ground below—dozens of medics and others came pouring out of the building, rushing up to the felled vehicles, quickly removing the pilots.

"*Monumentally successful!*" Mick cried. "Thirty percent, completely disabled. And, look, that slow descent. Probably one-hundred percent capture of the felled!"

At that moment, the 3-D corroborated Mick's observation "*ONE-HUNDRED PERCENT CAPTURE!*" scrolled across their vision.

Heart saw human forms, along with the multi-limbed, thrashing forms of bots being led, and in some cases, carried, into the building.

"*But—wait!*" Heart exclaimed, looking more intently at the activity below. "Those aren't … humans."

"No," Mick, said, "they're bots. Bots and … oh! They're … they're …."

"They're my father's clones! *Now* we know where they are."

"Your father's clones? The Purists cloned his brain, but …."

"Yes, and that 'brain' built a body, a bio and mechanical body, through directives to mechanicals the original clone brain hypnotized. And *that* clone cloned himself twice, and those two each cloned two, and those two cloned … anyway, there ended up being somewhere around a thousand clones, of diminishing powers. But apparently able to operate these little warcraft."

"Well, we have quite a few of them now."

"What will become of them?" Heart asked.

"They'll be 'psychologically reconditioned,' we call it. There's not much to bots, they don't really have a central brain, and they're easy to re-train. They're predominately bio, with a bit of dark matter, but no mechanicals. No clockworks. Not a bio like you—well, never mind that, there's no bio like you, Heart. But, not bio like fully human bios, and yet—still bio."

Heart had never thought about the bots in those terms. They were more like her father, and Jackson, and The Mystic, and Zack, and all humans, than they were like mechanicals or clockworks.

"What about the clones?" Heart asked. "What will be done with them?"

"That'll be interesting," Mick said. "Various generations of clones. *Very interesting!* They'll be psychologically reconditioned. Sooner or later, they'll be reconditioned, and then they'll be so helpful to our cause."

"Well …" Heart said, unable to say more. In the midst of battle, she became flooded with joy. "*Hundreds of helpful Father Inventor clones!*" she whispered.

"Yes," Mick whispered back, imitating her. "*Hundreds of helpful Father Inventor clones!*"

Heart's attention was drawn to the Purists' vehicles in the air beneath them. She watched as they began to regroup into another formation. But her attention was captivated by a peculiar dark area in the midst of two circular formations.

"What do you make of those dark areas, Mick?"

"Yes. I noted those two areas myself. There are cloaked craft there."

"Oh! In the center. The two primary clones," Heart recalled her conversation with the Clone. "Protected! Cloaked and protected, Mick. They are the two primary clones. They're the brains behind the maneuvers. We need to neutralize them."

"How?"

"Pods one, five, nine, thirteen, seventeen—eighth formation," Jackson commanded.

Jackson's pod one and the four others rose up through the midst of the Purists secondary formation. Heart watched in horror as several of the craft in these pods were hit with direct explosives, and went spiraling to the ground.

Where was Jackson? *Where was Jackson?*

She heard his voice, still amazingly calm amidst the ensuing confusion. "Formation eight. Keep focus."

Heart held her position, trying to decide what best to do. She saw Jackson had lost two craft from his pod.

In a blast of sound that broke through her protective helmet, the sky burst into blinding light. Her craft flung from its position and tumbled end over end. She worked frantically to regain control, observing Mick doing the same, adroitly manipulating the controls at his command. Gradually the little ship slowed its frenetic head-over-heels headlong spill, slowing, then, finally, stopping in black, dark space.

"Are we all right?" Heart asked.

"Seems like it."

"The ship?"

"Acceptable parameters of function."

"*WHAT WAS THAT?*"

"Don't know. A new weapon, it would seem," Mick answered.

Heart looked around. They were completely alone in the sky, not another craft to be seen.

"Where *are* we?"

"Our instruments are still reeling," Mick noted. "Hold. Hold. There, stabilizing. Ahm … hmm … we've been thrown an impressive distance!"

"*We must get back!*"

"Right." The instrument panel's magnetics were severely skewed in the tumble, which Mick efficiently adjusted, while Heart watched the 3-D replay of the event.

A flash of light, and then the craft tumbled. "Yeah," Heart said sarcastically. "I know that, I was here. Still feel a bit dizzy. But *what happened?*"

The 3-D went blank. "All right, all right! Be that way. Are we able to get back on our heading, Mick?"

"Yes. The craft's compass and magnetics are still a bit off, but mine are all right, I'll compensate for the amount the craft is out of sync. We ought to see the conflict in, four, three, two …."

"*One!*" Heart saw the skirmish in full force, straight ahead. "Good work, Mick. Ready?"

"Ready."

She hoped to hear Jackson as they approached, but there was no sound beyond the clash of weaponry against craft. "Do you see Jackson's craft, Mick? Can you see it?"

"Looking … looking … *there!*"

Coordinates came up on the 3-D. Above her, and above the second tier of the Purists' crafts, she saw Jackson's craft. Well, she couldn't see that it was his from here, but took Mick's word for it that that was Jackson, his pod now down to three ships.

She paused flight at a distance to comprehend the conflict's full panorama. She saw few of their own craft in the action.

"Looks bad, Mick."

"It does."

"How many of our peers went reeling out of the territory like we did?"

"One moment. *Forty!*"

"That's a lot! Are any of them functional?"

"Checking. I receive signal from … twenty … twenty-six. Fourteen remain at large."

"Are the twenty-six returning?"

"Ahm, several are confused which direction to head. Their instrument panels worse off than ours."

"Can you send a homing signal?"

"I will. Sending signal to come to home in on our ship."

"Excellent, Mick. All right. What tactic ought we to take? We no longer have a pentagram."

"If there's only one craft on a side, it is—in theory—adequate to deploy the sound weapon."

"All right." Heart studied their formation. "I see three sides. We can be a fourth, but little point without a fifth."

"Pod three, ship three, align," Jackson commanded. "Pod one, return to first formation, for sound weapon deployment of first level."

"That's us, pod three, ship three. He's joining us," Mick noted.

Heart flew the craft to position, the only craft on that whole side of the imagined pentagram.

In a flash, Jackson flew across from her. "Ready," he commanded, "align weapon."

Heart joined the rag-tag formation in aligning her craft's sound weapon.

"Deploy!" Jackson's command came, calm and clear.

Much to Heart's surprise, they succeeded in making a significant blast, even with their severely reduced numbers, and, once again, hundreds of the Purists craft rained gently in streaks of trailing light, to the ground below.

"Oh, that was satisfying." Heart felt triumphant. "Even with our paltry numbers, we …."

She was cut short. In shock and dismay, she saw Jackson's craft take a direct hit, and plummet from the sky.

With neither word nor thought, she tore after him, down and down, to the ground below.

Total mayhem reigned on the ground. Medics and clones and bots and downed craft littered the ground. Flashing, disorienting lights created bas relief distortions of everything, whether moving or still.

"Where is he?" Heart asked Mick, feeling nearly frantic. "Where did Jackson's craft crash?"

"One moment," Mick said, with mechanical calmness. "Here it is." Mick brought the coordinates up on the 3-D.

"Input coordinates, Mick. Override all else."

"Affirmative." Mick input the coordinates.

Heart knew the craft would do a better job of going direct, where she would continually try to avoid hitting the moving and the still. On automatic, everyone would simply have to get out of her way.

Through the darkness, the blinding flashing lights, the haze, Heart finally spotted Jackson's craft.

"There he is!" she cried, fear crawling up her spine. *Please do not let him be … like Xavier. Please!* She prayed to any god or energy that might be attending to their battle.

She pulled her craft to a stop by Jackson's vehicle, nearly destroyed, although the cockpit appeared intact. But Heart saw no motion inside his cockpit. She jumped out and ran to open the door, with Mick, at her side, running to the other door to rescue Jackson's copilot.

Heart carefully unharnessed Jackson, pulling him from the wreckage. In the darkness, she could see he was bleeding from nose and mouth. But he was breathing! Mick had carried Jackson's copilot to Heart's side.

"Let's get them inside, now!"

"Right!"

"Ahhh …" Jackson moaned, unconscious, but in pain.

"The sound weapon, It's killing him!" Mick cried, distressed.

"Where's his helmet? It must have flown off in the wreck." Heart ripped hers off.

"*No! …*" she could barely hear Mick shout.

She shouted to him, but couldn't even hear herself, "*I can take it better than he can! My dark matter ….*"

"*OH!*" She saw Mick mouth. He reached across and pressed a spot on her temple. All became quiet. Then she heard Mick's voice, "You're more mechanical than maybe you realized. Can you hear me?"

"*Perfectly!* Great insight, Mick. You're a genius. Let's get them inside." They carefully put the two men in the back of their craft and, just as they were about to jump inside, they looked at each other, stunned.

Something profound had happened—sudden total blackness, total stillness. The hundreds of lights from the Purists' craft winked off, *en masse.* The sound weapons stopped.

Heart and Mick looked up.

The stars above had disappeared. All the spacecraft, on both sides of the conflict, hung in mid-air.

Overhead, over it all, over everything, hummed the Gargantua.

Gorgeous, Heart thought, the Gargantua! There will be no more battle this night!

Thank you, Peter! she silently prayed in gratitude. Then his voice came in her head. *"Pod one, ship one, Jackson! Jackson!"*

"*Peter!* Heart here. Can you hear me?"

"Heart! Where are you?"

"On the ground. Jackson shot down. Not good. Unconscious. We're retrieving him and copilot, taking them to medics immediately."

"*You are our Angel!*"

Heart jumped into the pilot's seat and strapped herself in, while Mick did the same on the opposite side. "What does that make you, Peter? You've saved us."

A roar interrupted their conversation. Though Heart could not be sure, it seemed that the remaining airborne ships of *The Purist* cadre left.

"It would not have been so easy if the numbers hadn't already been reduced by half. Excellent work, Mountain's Edge forces. Stand down." He paused. "I see some of your craft at distance, heading this way."

"Yes, Peter. They deployed a weapon that threw us head over heels for many miles. Hard on instruments."

"And pilots," Peter observed.

"We maintained. Will you put down?"

"No, Heart, as much as I'd love to, we have only two more Darling Undesirables facilities to gather aboard, and need to get it accomplished before the Purists regroup. The report of this terrible interaction took me off my route. But, dear Heart, our meeting is not too far in the future."

"I'm glad to hear it." Heart brought the engines roaring to life and lifted off, heading to the aircraft holo-portal. "Now to attend to Jackson. See you soon, dear doorman!"

Peter's chuckle faded as the Gargantua disappeared from the night sky as silent and mysterious as it had arrived.

Chapter 19

"Inform medics of Jackson and his copilot's urgent condition," Heart ordered Mick.

"Will do, Heart." As Mick made contact with the medics, Heart looked over her shoulder at Jackson and his copilot. Both unconscious. But—*both breathing*.

In moments Heart passed through the holo, and, once inside, the engines barely stopped, Heart leapt out. Two clockworks medics hurried up.

`They removed Jackson and his copilot gently from the vehicle, and placed them on the floor, before doing anything else. With equipment from backpacks they carefully went over their bodies to determine the extent of injuries.

"Not small, but both will survive."

Heart sighed a sigh so deep, and so full of relief, that she surprised herself.

"We'll take them to the infirmary now," one of the medics said.

"Of course. I'll come along," Heart said.

"You needn't. They'll be fine. You probably saved their lives."

"Very good to hear," Heart said. "But, I'm coming along, just the same."

"Don't you know who this is?" one medic said to the other.

"Should I?"

"*It's Heart!*"

"No."

"Yes."

The disbelieving medic looked hard at Heart. *"Heart! Heart! You're Heart!* You're here. How did you get here?"

"On Equuleus. Who is also in the infirmary, and I need to see him, as well."

"Oh, my g-g-g-oodness," the stunned clock-works man stuttered. *"H-h-h-heart!"*

"Yes, dear clockworks man. Now, to fix Jackson."

"Heart and Jackson," the clockworks man said softly, in awe, while he picked up Jackson.

"Just two people, dear clockworks man. Just two people."

"No!" he said firmly. Not 'just two people'. What we witnessed this night in battle proves that!"

*   *

Heart scurried through halls filled with a soft blue light now that peace reigned, with the medics.

Jackson's injuries were not life-threatening, and she would now get to be with Equuleus. Yes. Almost happy in this particular moment.

Soon they were rushing down the hall where she knew the infirmary to be, and, even if she didn't, the rushing about of every sort of medic, and every sort of injured made the fact clear.

Everyone seemed to know Jackson was on his way, and the path cleared as they came.

"Please wait here," A doctor said to Heart when they came through the infirmary doors.

"Where's Equuleus? How is Equuleus?"

A sweet, clockworks nurse came up to Heart. "You may see him. Follow me."

Jackson had been whisked away from her. She stood looking after him until he was carried through a doorway that opened and shut quick as a blink.

She followed the nurse.

"I've so enjoyed attending to Equuleus," the nurse said. "He's so refined."

"Oh, yes, Equuleus comes from another time when good manners were as important as intelligence or wealth among caring beings. I can see why you appreciate him, it's like that here. And it's like that on Pink."

"Oh! Pink! How I love Pink! I'd love to go there one day. Assuming it's ever a possibility."

"Hmmm," Heart replied thoughtfully, tucking the information away. "What's your name?"

"I hope you don't mind that I took a name for myself."

"I don't mind in the least. In fact, I think it's a good idea."

"Well, I'm known as Nurse GoodHeart."

"I shall remember you, good Nurse GoodHeart."

Nurse GoodHeart opened a door to a small room, where Equuleus lay reclining, appearing deep asleep, which was quite unusual for him.

Heart put her finger to her lips so as not to awaken him. She warmly took Nurse GoodHeart's clockworks hand, and was delighted to feel the warm clicking of her gears under her fingers.

The nurse stole out, and Heart sat beside Equuleus, studying his poor wing that faced her. Although it appeared to be properly in place, there was no denying that too many of the gears were destroyed for him to fly.

Much to her surprise, given all she worried about, all she had to think about, all she had to accomplish, she felt herself sink down to lie on the floor by Equuleus, and slip into a deep sleep of her own.

"Sleeping on the job," Equuleus said sometime later—she had no idea how long.

She jumped up and threw her arms around his neck. "Both of us! Sleeping on the job. How are you my beautiful, beautiful Equuleus?"

"Not nearly as beautiful as before." He looked down at his wing.

"Not to worry! Key Man will make you good as new."

"Yes. I know. But for now, my pride …."

"Your pride? Be very proud, you saved my life, and yours, as well."

"Only to have you go out there and try to lose it again!"

"Sort of true, dear Equuleus. But it was my mission. If I hadn't, Jackson probably would not …."

"What happened with Jackson?"

"Shot down. He crashed badly. My copilot and I brought him and his copilot in. The medic said we saved their lives. So it all works out, it all makes sense, in the end." Heart sighed, the thought that truly nagged at her refusing to abate. "But, what *does* bother me immeasurably, and I feel terrible, and guilty and just about can't stand how awful I feel, is bringing you in the first place.

"I could have taken the *Heart!* And I don't quite know why I didn't. It would have been faster, and safer. But, no, I had to endanger you! What was I thinking? I wanted to have that ride in Earth's night sky!"

Equuleus whinnied rather loudly for an infirmary, and shook his mighty head. "*I wanted to go, Heart*. I would have been unhappy if you'd taken the *Heart! Very unhappy!* You're not one bit to blame."

"Oh," Heart sighed, "I guess we both did it. The important thing is, you're all right, and Key Man will fix you. Now I need to see how Jackson is doing."

"I'm coming with you." Equuleus stood.

Heart cocked her head and grinned. "Not quite as subtle, but, all right, let's see if we can pull off sneaking in to see him. Wherever he may be."

She peeked out the door. The infirmary had settled down considerably and the hall was virtually clear. They tiptoed—Equuleus quite gracefully tiptoeing—down the hall and toward the last place she saw Jackson. She encountered a large and somewhat grouchy medic.

"Where are you headed with that clockworks horse?"

"We're looking for Jackson."

He did a double-take, looking at Heart. "Oh! You're Heart!"

"That's true," Heart agreed.

"Come with me."

Heart and Equuleus followed obediently.

"I probably ought not do this, but it feels right to me." He led her down three different halls and finally opened a door. "So nice to meet you!" he whispered, then turned and disappeared down yet another hall.

They stepped into the room. Heart stepped up to the side of the bed, and there, sleeping like the proverbial baby, lay Jackson breathing deeply, with a sheer release of tension that Heart had never seen on his face.

"Oh! So pretty!" She continued in her whisper, but could not contain her surprise at his relaxed beauty. His frown gone. The lines around his mouth gone. His eyebrows unknit. The line of his beautiful cheekbones and jawline much more noticeable without the teeth-gritting tension she was used to seeing.

Oh! How delightful it would be to look in his eyes when he felt utterly relaxed. To see him calm and in the moment….

"*He is beautiful,*" Equuleus agreed.

She gently took Jackson's hand and simply stood there for a few minutes. Equuleus went to the corner and sank down to rest on the floor. She looked over her shoulder at him, concerned.

"Still a bit tired. But I'm all right."

After her study of Jackson for those few minutes, she gently put his hand down, and joined Equuleus, sitting by him on the floor.

So lovely—as long as Jackson would be all right—so lovely to quietly be here together. Not doing anything. Not thinking anything. Not *having* to do anything, not in this moment, at least.

And then, he woke up and spoiled the moment.

"Right!" he said, sitting bolt upright. "What? Oh. Dream. A dream. Right. Got to get at it." He didn't see Heart and Equuleus behind him in the corner of the room.

Heart watched with an almost wry smile, mingled with sadness, as the worry and stress lines came back into his face as if they were part of his mission. Worry lines on his forehead. Tension lines around his mouth, and his teeth-gritting, working his jaw muscle.

He started to stand but fell back on the bed. "Something not quite right with me. Well, that's not acceptable."

He moved slowly to sit sidewise on the bed and finally saw Heart and Equuleus. "Hmmm, where'd you come from?"

"Clearly, we just this instant teleported ourselves through this wall." Heart grinned. She would never, ever tire of teasing him when he asked questions with obvious answers.

"Would it not be polite to knock first?"

Both Heart and Equuleus giggled.

"Touché," Equuleus observed.

"Whose side are you on?" Heart laughed. Oh, she loved the teasing.

"Who brought me in? It's all a blank after a point."

"I brought you in."

"What do you mean?"

"You crashed. I had my copilot track you. I came to the ground, and my copilot and I saved you and your copilot. You're welcome."

"What are you saying?"

"In the battle. Do you recall being in battle last night with hundreds and hundreds of Purists?"

"Of course, Heart. Don't be patronizing."

"No. No, don't mean to be patronizing. You may possibly not remember anything from last night."

"I remember the battle. I remember my craft getting hit. I don't remember anything after that."

"The short version is, my copilot and I saved you."

"Why do you keep saying that?"

"Because it's true."

"But you weren't in the battle."

"But I *was* in the battle."

"No."

"Yes. There must be some 3-D or recording somewhere of the events. I was in pod three, craft three. There was a big blast of, what my copilot, my amazing copilot, Mick, said was a new weapon. It threw a lot of us—forty, to be precise—for many miles, and disrupted our magnetics and compass. But fortunately for me, Mick made adjustments according to his compass, and brought me right back in time to see you take a direct hit."

"Mick? Your copilot was Mick?"

"Yep. And he deserves a medal."

"He always messes things up."

"Well, give him a chance to shine, and he's brilliant. We wouldn't be talking now either one of us, for that matter, if not for him. You crashed. It was mayhem on the ground. Black night, brilliant flashing, blinding lights, a haze from everything. Mick got your coordinates, I followed them, I pulled you from your wreckage, Mick rescued your copilot.

"At that moment, Peter came with the Gargantua, neutralized the weaponry of what was left of The Purists' craft, then left to rescue the residents of the last two Darling Undesirable facilities. And now, here we are talking. For which I am extremely grateful."

"Well, so am I. But bemused. So you bumped someone, got on a craft and joined the battle," Jackson reasoned.

"Right," she said, imitating him like she so loved to do.

"Don't tell me I owe you my life."

"You owe me your life, Jackson. So stay in bed until the doctor tells you you can get up."

Jackson looked around the room. "Where's my …" He saw his communication device across the room, and stood to retrieve it, and almost fell. "What is *wrong* with me?"

"You crashed. From the sky. In battle. You silly boy!" As Heart ranted, she jumped up, pushed on Jackson so that he fell back into bed, then grabbed his communication device. "I know I ought not give this to you, because it will make all those hard lines in your face come back."

"Hard lines?"

"But I know if you don't have it, the hard lines are going to come into your face anyway. So, here. But stay in bed." She handed the device to him.

He clamped it to his wrist. "Hard lines?"

"Yes. Hard lines. The lines that come from saying 'right,' like that's the beginning and end of any discussion."

He looked distracted away from the conversation at something obviously disturbing on his communication device. "Righ …" He caught himself. "Yep. I say 'right.' You're right." The hard lines came into his face as he looked at his communication device again.

"What is it?" Heart finally asked.

"The Purists are rallying in The Periphery."

"*Oh. No!* But their numbers are so reduced, I can't imagine it, even if their weapons work at all after Peter neutralized them last night."

"Apparently they have recovered and, though reduced, are regrouped. I have to …" He tried to stand but fell back on the bed again.

"The only thing you have to do is recover."

"Aren't you worried? About Eye, and Butterfly?"

"Not really. In my father's laboratory, Helper-Friend projected an image of the other side of The Wall. Did you know my father's lab is close to The Mystic's cottage?"

"Yes."

"Anyway, I saw an image of her, and she sensed we were present. She leaned down and patted the Earth, because, of course, I was underground. But I think, too that she was letting me know that they were safe. She knows about the underground. So they're safe.

"You're not the only person who can protect others, Jackson. You won't be protecting anyone if you run around when you need medical attention."

He put his head back on the pillow, looking resigned. "Who can I mobilize?" he wondered quietly.

"That's it. Figure out who you can send in your place."

At that moment, a dazzling beam of light shot through a little, high up window, landing with full force on Heart. "Oh! Dawn! *Dawn, Jackson.*"

"That's right, Heart. Dawn."

"I wish you could go watch it with me."

"We'll watch some other dawn. But for now, why don't you and Equuleus go out and enjoy the rising sun? I know how you love dawn. Then come back and tell me about it."

"W-e-l-l …" She hated to leave him. But she really wanted to see the dawn. She and Equuleus could stand in the light, in the Earth dawn. Without hiding. She imagined the sun on her face. "But, wait … there'll be … wreckages. I don't imagine Equuleus or I want to see that."

"The wreckages will be cleaned up. Everyone not attending to the injured brings in the craft as fast as they can manage. Highest priority after life forms. The team here is outstanding. They repair our ships and return them to the fleet. Then they'll scour the Purist ships for any new technology, as well as any information that might be gleaned about their maneuvers, then alter their identification and add them to our fleet."

"Really? Quite the undertaking, given how many craft were brought down. But the good news is, they *floated* to the ground. What a sight!"

A shadow of a smile dared to hover over Jackson's features. "It was an amazing sight. The success of Father Inventor's new sound weapon intervention exceeds our expectations."

"I guess that's what Peter used when he brought the Gargantua in. Everything stopped on both sides, instantaneously."

"Well," Jackson visibly relaxed a body-wide tension, "that's good that Peter came." He closed his eyes in obvious fatigue.

"You're tired. Equuleus and I will go enjoy the sunrise for a little while. But you must stay right here, in bed. Don't move. Remember, *you owe me your life.*"

"You're unlikely to let me forget it."

"That's right!" Heart and Equuleus went to the door.

"We'll be back in a few minutes with a detailed report." Heart looked back at Jackson.

"I expect nothing less."

*　*

Ħeart and Equuleus wandered through the halls with the morning sun stingily creeping and peeking in through small, high up windows all along the halls. This must have been the most miserable Darling Undesirables facility Heart thought, with this miserly attitude about light—prison-like.

She finally found the front door and stepped out into the courtyard, the stone enclosure—*again!*—blocking the sunlight. She moved toward where she recalled the holo entrance to be, and when she arrived, she met a mechanical gateman.

"Could you open the holo gate and let us step outside for a few minutes?"

"Why?" he asked as if her question was the most peculiar concept he'd ever heard.

"To watch the sun rise."

"To watch the sun rise? Why?"

"Because it's beautiful."

"Is it?"

"To me and my clockworks horse, it is. So … could you ….?"

"I could. I have the power."

Heart realized then that this mechanical was a simple drone, without complicated reasoning. She'd confused him with what amounted to complicated reasoning.

"*Open the gate*," she commanded.

"As you bid," the mechanical replied. He pushed a series of levers and switches that caused the giant circle of stone wall to open out.

"Leave it open until we return." She and Equuleus stepped through.

"As you bid." He stood at attention at the controls.

She and Equuleus moved out onto the rocky terrain. There were scrubby trees dotting the landscape.

But, other than a few trees and lots of rocks, there was not much else to see.

Except the sun. *The glorious, gorgeous sun!* Running, as it further crested the horizon, across the rocks and trees, turning their grey sameness into hues of orange and yellow and fuchsia, the rocks and trees dancing in the beauty of the light.

"Oh … Equuleus," Heart breathed.

"Yes, Heart. Beauty."

"Beauty, and Earth and *Earth-air*." Heart closed her eyes, raising her face to the sun, letting it pass into her. Beloved sun! She inhaled and exhaled deeply for several breaths, then sighed contentedly, after which she found a big, flat, east-facing rock to sit upon.

She sat, put her elbows on her knees, her chin in her hands and quietly drank in the peaceful, morning, here in this place she'd never been—*wherever she was!* In this place where the sun arose, just like it did in every, single other place on Earth.

Equuleus sat quietly beside her.

After a while she sighed deeply and stood. "I suppose we'd better get back to Jackson before someone comes along and tells the mechanical to close the holo gate."

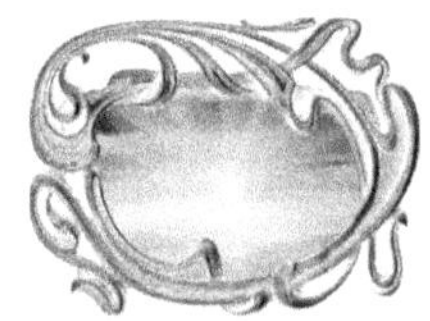

Chapter 20

They meandered back to the holo gate and found the mechanical just as they'd left him, hand on the switch, waiting to be told what to do next.

"Shut the gate, mechanical," Heart said when they came through.

"As you bid."

The circle of stone closed again. Equuleus visibly shuddered, hearing the stone clanking shut.

Heart silently stroked his neck, then they went back inside to rejoin Jackson. Much to Heart's surprise, the tiny, high up windows had scrolled down to nearly the floor, each with a deep window seat, low enough that even a small child could sit there and enjoy the day.

"The windows, Equuleus!" The small high-up windows of the night were, obviously, for protection. The warm, glowing, sunlight put Heart in a spectacularly happy frame of mind.

She looked over to Equuleus, and, even with his wounded wings, he looked phenomenal, the light glinting off his many gears, his walk proud, his step high.

They turned the corner of the second hall then down to the third hall, to the end.

"*Oh … no!*" Heart whispered as they approached the open door to Jackson's room. There she saw a rumpled, empty bed. On the bed was a tiny piece of paper with a cramped bit of writing.

Thank you, Heart, for saving my life.
I still owe it to you.
I'll have to pay the debt some other time.
Duty calls.
J.

She ran from the room and down the hall, Equuleus alongside.

"What are you going to do?"

"Try to stop him."

She dashed into the infirmary. "Where's Jackson's doctor?" she asked the first medic she encountered.

He pointed to the tall clockworks doctor who had attended to Equuleus. "Same doctor for a clockworks and a fully bio?"

"He's very good," Equuleus said.

Although the doctor was in consultation, Heart unceremoniously interrupted. "Jackson left!" she exclaimed.

"Oh, he probably went to breakfast. He's fully bio, you know, and needs to eat a lot, and regularly. Especially when healing."

"No. He left. Please try to stop him from flying out."

As if to humor Heart when he was certain he was right, the doctor contacted the aircraft bay. "Is Jackson there?"

"No, sir," came the reply.

"See?" He said to Heart. "Just as I said."

"You missed him," the voice at the other end continued. "He just left in the most high-powered craft we had, since his was destroyed last night."

"*Ohhh* …" Heart cried.

"Oh no," the doctor said. "This isn't good. I wanted him to get bed rest for a couple days and keep tabs on the potential brain damage from the sound weapon."

"*Ohhhh* …" Heart cried again. "Brain damage?"

"I don't think it's as severe as his copilot's injury. We're about to perform brain surgery on him. But I certainly wanted to keep Jackson resting. He's bio. He ought not push it."

n   And he said *she* was headstrong! She'd jump into a vehicle and follow him if she didn't have to cross The Wall. But, as it was, she couldn't. The dark energy would bring her down.

She had no choice but to let Jackson go on in his head-strong way, and trust that he was in better condition than the doctor seemed to think.

When she reflected back on how he couldn't even stand by the bed, she wondered how he made it across this building and the next, to get to the aircrafts.

Determination! That's how he did it. That's how they both did everything they took on. And she now needed to move upon her own determination—which was to get back to her father's lab. To get into the *Heart!* with HelperFriend, and get to The Museum of Scientific Improbabilities and Unpredictable Oddities.

She may wish Jackson were here. She may wish he'd stay in that comfortable infirmary bed for a week. But he never would!

She could be grateful that, at least, Jackson was on the other side of The Wall. Because, although she believed that The Mystic would take care of Eye and Butterfly, Jackson would take even better care of them all. The Purists would get nowhere near them.

As long as he didn't kill himself first, running around with a bleeding brain.

She went into the hall removed from the hubbub and pressed the communication button on her star necklace. "Jackson ..." she called, knowing he would not answer even if he heard her. "I know you won't answer. But if you hear me, please, please take care of yourself. You won't do anyone any good if you augment the brain injury you sustained.

"I didn't want to tell you this, but when I pulled you from the wreckage of your craft, you'd lost your helmet and you sustained a brain injury. *Do not push,*

Jackson. I talked with your doctor. He's quite alarmed that you've run off. Please, please take my words seriously, and assign to others everything that you can. Over. Out."

She turned to Equuleus, who stood patiently by her side. "Well, my friend, Jackson has his mission, and we have ours—it's time to make our way to The Museum of Scientific Improbabilities and Unpredictable Oddities, by way of my father's lab. Does your map show the subterranean path from here?"

"It does."

"Then let us be on our way." She paused, thinking she perhaps ought to tell someone that she was leaving. But who? Everyone was busy taking care of the captured and injured from the previous night's battle. But it did cross her mind to say good-bye to Mick, and to thank him once again for his remarkable help, to let him know that she believed he saved her life, and Jackson's as well.

"Are we going to pass near the aircraft hangar?" she asked Equuleus.

"Right *under* it."

"I'd like to say thank you and good-bye to Mick."

"Easy enough, it's just up the next set of stairs."

They soon came to the stairs. "I'll be right back." Heart ran up the flight of stairs and came into the wide-open hangar, where all the aircraft damaged the night before were being rapidly repaired. Heart looked around for Mick, but she didn't see him.

She hailed the workers on the nearest vehicle. "Hello there—can anyone tell me where Mick is?"

They paused in their work. "He left!" one of them replied.

"Left? What do you mean?"

"He went with Jackson, in our best vehicle," another answered. "They left quickly, but Jackson mentioned he was going into The Periphery and recruited Mick on the spot. He said he needed a copilot and was recruiting Mick, for outstanding valor in last night's battle."

"Can you imagine that?" another worker chimed in. "Mess-up Mick came through when it was real battle—when it *really* mattered."

"*He certainly did!*" Heart agreed. "Thanks!" She turned and ran back down the stairs to Equuleus, hugely relieved—Mick would take good care of Jackson.

"Ah my friend," she said as she ran up to Equuleus, "Jackson recruited Mick to be his copilot."

"That's good news," Equuleus replied.

"As good as it gets, under the circumstances. Now then, to get you repaired. How long will it take us to return to my father's laboratory?"

"Well, if I could fly, it would only be about an hour." He projected the 3-D map in front of them. "Here's the underground crystal matrix we're about to come to, right ahead. Fortunately, it's quite direct between here and the laboratory. But still, without flight, if I'm running, it'll take several hours."

"If *you're* running. You mean if *we're* running. I won't ride you and deplete your energy yet more. I can run fast, but not as fast as you. So that slows us some more."

"I'll be all right with you riding."

"I won't hear of it. So, it may take the better part of the day. We'd better get moving." Heart was hatching a plan to join Jackson in The Periphery once Equuleus was in Key Man's clockworks healing hands. She'd have HelperFriend fly the *Heart!* over The Wall into The Periphery, with herself wrapped up in her paisley blanket.

"That's quite the plan," Equuleus noted.

"Stop peeking into my mind!"

"Do you *have* any idea how loud your thoughts are? *Sheesh!*"

"All right, all right! Point made. I suppose my thoughts about getting to Jackson to watch over him, as he won't watch over himself, are fairly noisy."

They came to the crystal matrix. Not mirror reflecting like beneath The Darling Undesirables Facility at Long Prairie, it had an inbuilt gentle light.

"Let's go!" Heart stepped onto the road, and they began their long-distance run.

The soft, mysterious light made the journey dreamlike from the outset. Thoughts floated through Heart's' mind as she ran, but they seemed to all have the same import. Nothing caused her anxiety. Thoughts about Jackson over-exerting himself felt calm as if there was nothing to worry about.

They ran and ran. Heart recalled that first time she'd ever run in her life, with Swen, when she ran away from The Darling Undesirables Facility at Long Prairie—how amazing it had been to run and run. How surprised she'd been to be able to keep up with Swen, a bio, mechanical dog, a newshound, built to run without stopping.

Apparently, she, too, was built to run without stopping, if necessary. All the dreamy thoughts that floated through her mind seemed, also, to be resolved. Any thoughts that were problems, solutions came to mind. Any thoughts that were projects how to complete them came to mind. Everything appeared so easy, so obvious.

And, though it seemed like they'd just stepped onto the crystal matrix, before long she heard Equuleus say, "Here we are!"

"Where?" Heart asked, trying to pull herself out of her trance state.

"At Father Inventor's laboratory. The doorway is straight ahead." Equuleus snorted. "It looks like we'll come right into the kitchen. HelperFriend will be waiting for us. I told him some while ago we were on our way since you were in your altered state."

"Altered state?" Heart tried yet harder to pull herself out of the lovely, dreamy place. "But, how can we possibly be there? We've only just begun running."

"We've been running, non-stop, for almost five hours, Heart."

That snapped Heart right out of the dreamy place. "How is it possible?"

"Something in that light, Heart, took you on a magical mystery ride the moment we began running."

Heart giggled. "That's true. But, Equuleus, it was so lovely! I had solutions to all my problems, answers to all my questions!" She paused at the door, reaching out to open it, but hesitating. "And I have the strangest feeling that all the answers and solutions will disappear when I open this door."

"Like in dreams, every night."

"Oh, Equuleus! So wisely said!" She put her hand over the pad by the door to make the gestures that would cause it to slide open. "But, I guess I must do it."

"Remember, Heart, they are there, in your 'dreamplace'—all those answers, all those solutions. They are there. You've understood them once, in that calm and quiet place. They remain there, waiting for you to 'wake them up,' when needed."

Heart took her hand away from the door, turned to Equuleus, and wordlessly, hugged him tightly. What he said was from the depths of the truest truth. So much so, no words could suffice. Leaning into him, taking strength and comfort, she then turned and slid the door open.

*   *

HelperFriend was practically jumping up and down on the other side of the door. "What were you doing? You just stood on the other side of the door. I've been waiting for you for hours, and when you come, you just stand there!" HelperFriend's little metallic tears of joy sprinkled all about them, pinging off Equuleus's gears with a light, chiming sound.

"I'm sorry, HelperFriend, I had to 'decompress' for a moment. It was an amazing experience, that run, in the crystal matrix. But I'm so happy to see you. Although it's not been two days, it feels like months!"

"Exactly!" HelperFriend agreed, frantically trying to pick his tears off Heart's plaid outfit, and trying to gather them up off the counters and floor. "Sorry, sorry, Heart!"

"That's all right, my friend, I love your beautiful tears." A little bell jar sat on the counter. "Let's put them in here, they're so pretty." She pulled off the lid with a soft "*snuck!*" sound, and HelperFriend poured his tears in, where they jingled sweetly.

"But Heart! Equuleus has been injured!"

"Yes, he has."

HelperFriend walked around Equuleus, looking at his damaged wings. "Oh, sad, sad. What a pity!"

"It'll be all right, HelperFriend. We're going now to Key Man, and he'll repair Equuleus in no time."

"I see. And I'll stay here?"

"No. You're coming with us."

"I'm coming with you?" HelperFriend asked in surprise and delight.

"She has an ulterior motive, don't be too overjoyed."

"Well, I am overjoyed, if I'm to go with you. I don't care about an ulterior motive. My only business with Heart's plans is to see that they become fulfilled if I can do so."

"*There!*" Heart nodded to Equuleus. "That was in the dream-space, and it's also in my real world!"

"True," Equuleus agreed. "No argument."

"What are we going to do with the Clone?" HelperFriend asked.

"How has he been?"

"He remains in stasis. Not a sound or rustle from him."

"Let's leave him that way for the time being. We have a lot to do, and I need not to be worrying about him." Heart, coming fully out of trance and into the responsibility of the moment, left the kitchen, with HelperFriend at her elbow and Equuleus at her heels.

But she did an abrupt about-face and walked back into the kitchen. "I need to take a peek at him, and then I can move forward."

"Sure, Heart." HelperFriend went to the Stasis Lock, entered the combination, and opened the door a crack. Heart peered inside where the Clone stood, eyes open but unseeing.

Heart nodded to HelperFriend and stepped back. He locked up the Stasis Lock tighter than a drum.

"Let's go!" She scurried out to the *Heart!* and opened the hatch, turning on low magnetics to hold Equuleus in his place, checked everything over, turned on the banks of dark energy chargers to make sure the *Heart!* had a full running charge, with HelperFriend at her elbow every step of the way. She was about to tell Helper-Friend to strap himself in, when a thought crossed her mind.

"Wait! It's mid-afternoon—not a good idea to take the *Heart!* out in broad daylight."

"No, Heart, you're right. It's not," Helper-Friend agreed. "With all that's going on with the Purists right now, you need to be especially careful."

"What's going on with the Purists?"

"They seem to be mobilizing, or trying to mobilize, everywhere. But the interesting thing is, the non-purist humans are not liking it. They are not taking to it. There's conflict between them."

"Really? That's different. Humans who are not Purists have, in the past, been apathetic to their rant, simply staying clear of them. But if there are difficulties, we'll wait until the sun sets to depart. Now, it seems like a perfect idea to go out and watch the sun set. Can you believe it, Equuleus? Today we watch the sun rise and the sun set. A full day of peace."

"Oh!" HelperFriend exclaimed while Equuleus whinnied.

"We watch the sun rise and the sun set, the first full day of peace," HelperFriend and Equuleus recited together.

"Ourbook," Heart observed.

"Yes," Equuleus agreed.

Heart sighed deeply. "Well … I trust it portends good things."

"It does," HelperFriend said quietly. "Let us watch the sun set."

They climbed into the *Heart!* Heart taxied it through the holo wall and out among the trees in the woods, where they got out of the *Heart!* and took a short walk.

Heart patted the beautiful bark of the nearest evergreen. "Trees are so—*patient!*"

"Just so, Heart," HelperFriend agreed. "They watch the world go by, standing in their place. They say they are important watchers."

"Are you communicating with them Helper-Friend? "

"Aren't you?" HelperFriend asked in surprise.

"Well, no. Not directly."

"The one you're touching, just told you it loves you. Further, it said, 'be thoughtful and patient.' You really didn't hear it?"

"I did not. And I'm sorry that I cannot. But it's amazing, HelperFriend, that you can talk with them."

"It seems quite ordinary to communicate with these large, intelligent plants … very strange that you cannot."

"I shall have to put more focus in communicating with trees," Heart said, watching the deep shadows creeping among them like a stealthy robber, putting in the giant rucksack thrown over its shoulder all the light of the day.

"But for now, it's time to head for The Museum of Scientific Improbabilities and Unpredictable Oddities."

The three of them returned to the *Heart!*, but not without Heart pausing before entering, and turning to the trees. "Thank you for watching over us," Heart whispered. "We truly need it!"

Aboard the *Heart!* She secured Equuleus, made sure HelperFriend was strapped in, then sent a hasty note to Martha and Key Man. "On our way—looking forward to a night in the gingerbread house!"

She dared not say more than that with all the Purists' activity. But she knew it would be enough. For sure Peter, at least, if not also Jackson, had informed them that she, and her two compatriots, were on Earth.

Chapter 21

The journey was quick and, thankfully, uneventful. But, *oh!* How Heart loved the night sky. Her beloved Earth beneath, and her adored second home, Pink, glowing in the sky above. She thought of her father up there, inventing in a frenzy, disabling the Purists weaponry, virtually as fast as they came up with it, it seemed.

Soon she could see the dark yet familiar outline of The Museum of Scientific Improbabilities and Unpredictable Oddities. She quickly put down in the landing area behind the museum, looking in anticipation toward the back door. Sure enough, there stood Martha, Key Man, Swen, rather much leaping about in poorly controlled, dog-like delight, along with WonderMan One and WonderMan Two.

So warm and home-like to see them! She turned off the magnetics holding Equuleus in place, and unstrapped herself, at the same time, opening the hatch.

She heard HelperFriend mumbling, "So want to meet Key Man, can't wait to meet Key Man," fumbling with his safety latch in his excitement.

Heart leaned over to help him, while Equuleus stood, snorting and whinnying.

"Where is he?" she heard Key Man demand as he came up to the hatch. "Where is Equuleus? Injured? How injured?" His voice utterly agitated.

Swen by his side, reassuring, "I'm sure it's not too bad, Key Man. Jackson would have said."

"Swen's right, Key Man. Equuleus sustained only minor injuries," Heart called, finally succeeding in moving HelperFriend's hand out of the way enough to unsnap the latch.

Equuleus stepped out the hatch and whinnied again as Key Man threw his arms around his neck. Finally, HelperFriend stood and followed Heart out the hatch. Heart got down on her knees to give Swen a gigantic hug. "Missed you!"

"Missed you more," he answered.

Martha and the WonderMen hurried up to join them.

"What happened?" Key Man demanded. Equuleus extended his wings as far as they would go, given the damaged gears. "Oh, my, that's too bad, Equuleus. But, yes, an easy fix, thank goodness. I'm curious how that happened!"

"Flying through a closing stone holo entrance," Equuleus answered.

Key Man, Martha, and Swen gasped, picturing what that must have been like—and realizing how close it must have been for a much more terrible result.

"Well," Key Man said soberly, "I'll have you perfect in no time!"

"That's what I told him," Heart said, standing. "Everyone, I'd like you to meet HelperFriend, my right-hand man."

Key Man finally pulled his attention from Equuleus and looked up at HelperFriend. "Stunning! Aren't you beautiful!"

"Careful, Key Man, you'll make him cry, and his tears pinging off all your keys will make quite the music. On second thought, that would be lovely! You're his hero, for what you did for Lady Gervi."

HelperFriend extended his hand to Key Man. "So honored," he said.

Key Man took HelperFriend's hand.

"So honored," HelperFriend said again. And, sure enough, his brass and copper and nickel tears began to spring from his eyes, pinging all over Equuleus's gears and Key Man's keys. "So honored."

Heart closely watched his facial gears, but they were clicking in joy, not overload, even though he was repeating himself.

"Don't know what else to say. What you did for Lady Gervi, I can never thank you enough. So amazing. Amazing." He continued to pump Key Man's hand.

Heart reached out and patted him on the shoulder. "Very sweet, HelperFriend. I'm sure Key Man sees that you adore him. I believe you might release his hand now."

"Oh!" HelperFriend dropped Key Man's hand. "Sorry. Very sorry!"

Everyone laughed—except, of course, Wonder-Man One and WonderMan Two, who almost never chuckled at anything.

"It's fine, HelperFriend," Key Man said kindly. "I'm exceedingly pleased to meet you as well. I've heard wonderful things about you."

"You have? From where? From who?"

"Heart, of course."

"You told him about me?" HelperFriend looked at Heart in astonishment.

"Certainly."

"Oh! My! I'm … I'm very touched."

"Let's go inside, shall we?" Martha suggested, heading for the back door.

"Yes. I want to begin on Equuleus's repair immediately," Key Man agreed.

Everyone followed Martha inside, while Heart kept her hand on Swen.

"You won't mind if Equuleus and I stop off in my workroom to begin repairs?" Key Man asked.

"Decidedly not," Heart affirmed. "I love being here, but my mission is to get Equuleus in perfect working order, so he can fly, good as new."

"Perhaps better," Key Man added. "Brand new gears, well-tempered metals, and I've developed lots of ways for clockworks to run even more smoothly.

You might be able to put on a burst of speed that surprises even you."

"He did that the other night. I couldn't have been more amazed at the speed he was able to reach, instantaneously. Saved our lives. I'll let you two catch up."

Martha, Heart, HelperFriend, and the Wondermen stood in the hall, continuing to chat.

"We came because Key Man didn't know the extent of Equuleus's injuries," WonderMan One said.

"We're quite relieved that the damage is superficial and repairable by Key Man," WonderMan Two said.

"And we're so happy to see you, Heart!" they said in tandem.

"Me too you, my wonderful, life-saving Wonder-Men."

"But!" WonderMan One said, "We are most especially honored and pleased …"

"To," WonderMan Two said, "meet *you*, HelperFriend. Such a beautiful, beautiful, clockworks being!"

"We would really love," WonderMan One added.

"For you to teach us how to cry!" WonderMan Two concluded.

Nodding and smiling at their comments, HelperFriend jumped back in surprise at this last. He shook his head. "I'm terribly sorry to disappoint you. I could not teach you how to cry, as I have no idea where it comes from, or why. I would teach myself how to stop if I could. It's quite distracting and interruptive at times."

"Oh no," Heart protested. "Don't ever stop crying, HelperFriend. It makes you special and reminds everyone of the important moments in life.

"And I must agree with the WonderMen—you are amazingly beautiful!"

"*Goodness*," HelperFriend held his head down. "I feel shy from all this praise. I fear I cannot fulfill your expectations."

"You already have more than fulfilled my expectations, in so many ways, HelperFriend. But, all right, we'll take the spotlight off you for now. Goodnight, dear WonderMan One and WonderMan Two." She waved at them as they went in lock-step tandem, down the hall, and around the corner to the clockworks wing of the museum.

Martha turned to Heart. "You mentioned something about staying in the gingerbread house?"

"Yes. I confess, my greatest fantasy." Heart noticed Martha giving HelperFriend the slightest sideways glance, and read her meaning immediately. As graceful as he was, he still was used to spaces the size of castles and caves. And Martha's tiny house was—not.

"I wonder, HelperFriend, if you'd like to spend the night with Equuleus and Key Man?"

HelperFriend's eyes spun nearly out of his head. "I would, Heart, I surely would."

"I think there's a lot you can learn from him about clockworks, being one yourself. But," Heart put her finger to her lips.

HelperFriend nodded energetically. "No more babbling adoration, Heart. I got it out of my system. I'll be perfectly quiet. Silent and learn."

"That sounds excellent. Let's see if that works for them."

Heart knocked on the slightly ajar door.

"Heard every word, we'd love to have him," Key Man said.

Grinning—but silent!—HelperFriend ducked into Key Man's workrooms.

Heart turned to Martha, herself grinning. "Just us girls … and Swen!" What an incredible opportunity, Heart thought. What were the odds that she would ever end up with only Swen and Martha?

They stepped out into the sweet evening, a breeze blowing in the trees, the leaves patting together, an approving audience.

"Let me park the *Heart!* so it's a bit less conspicuous," Heart said.

"Sure." Martha and Swen stood to the side while Heart moved the *Heart!* into covered parking. She shut off the engines, picked up her little bag of personal belongings, rejoining Martha and Swen. She looked across the street to Martha's darling lavender and yellow gingerbread covered house, sighed deeply with great contentment, then the three of them crossed the street. Martha opened the front door. "Welcome to my humble home."

Heart stepped through the doorway and took in her surroundings. The walls were covered—solidly covered—in 2-D and 3-D images of Father Inventor's clockworks and mechanical creations, in old-fashioned two-dimensional, still photo images of clockworks, mechanicals and hybrid beings, as well as photos of humans.

"Oh my! Oh, my!" Heart whispered, wandering around, studying the pictures, one after another. She finally came to the mantle, and it, too, was covered in image after image of one sort of being after another. But she stopped stock still at the photo in the middle of the mantle.

She stood mesmerized by an old, old picture of a beautiful young couple. Instead of looking out at who-ever took the image, they were looking into one anoth-er's eyes. Deeply, deeply in love. Impossible to miss.

"My … my …." Heart could not bring herself to finish the sentence. She turned to Martha and Swen, and raised her hands, slowly, toward the image.

"Yes, dearest Heart. Your parents. Your mother. Your father. So young, so beautiful. So, *so* in love."

"My … my …." Heart still could not bring her-self to say the word aloud. But she let herself feel it. Her parents. Parents. Together. In love. Romantic love, that strange, unwieldy beast. That strange, and beautiful *Force*.

She didn't want to move. She wanted to stare at this image until it made up for an entire child-hood, the one she never had. The one where the three of them were a family. Where they went on picnics, where they went to visit aunts and uncles and cousins, where they went to visit their clock-works friends and their mechanical friends.

But, no. No matter how long she stood here with that dream, is was not her real dream. Her real dream had Eye, and, now, Equuleus, and her father. Swen. Martha. Key Man. She was a Darling Undesirable because she didn't have a heart. But her heart was in Equuleus.

And she had two—known!—genetic parents. Darling Undesirables did not have known, genetic parents.

"It's—very confusing," she said aloud.

"I know, Heart. I know it's confusing for you. But not for much longer. *"When a myriad lights fall from the sky like a gentle rain, the day of clarity is at hand,"* Martha quoted.

"Oh! Oh, Martha. The battle at the Facility at Mountain's Edge—that's what happened. The Purists' aircrafts fell softly. That was my very thought, it looks like a rain, a soft rain of lights. None of them were hurt. Their weapons were disempowered, rendered useless."

As always, Heart didn't want to have to imagine that *Ourbook* was viable. But this quote—not cryptic and impossible to understand, causing dissension everywhere. No. It said what really happened. Plain and true.

"Martha! How did you know? About that battle?"

"Jackson relayed the reference. We knew what it meant."

Swen nodded solemnly but kept his silence.

"Yes. What it meant. 'The day of clarity is at hand'—for me, or for everyone?"

"I believe, dear Heart, they are one and the same. *"Clarity for the one with a heart of hearts is clarity for all with hearts afire for Love and The Cause of All Beings."*

"*The Cause of All Beings*—that's from a quote? From *Ourbook?"*

"Yes. It's from a quote in *Ourbook.*

"I. Have. Much. To. Learn."

Martha's round eyes closed down into their sweet half moons of joy in her beautiful smile. "Dear Heart, we all have much to learn!"

"I haven't even begun," Swen affirmed, his tail wagging, but still, Heart could feel his concern for her.

Heart drank in the picture of her … *parents!* … once again. She looked beyond at the many, many other images on the mantle and the walls, but she didn't want to take in any more of them at the moment. She wanted to sit and absorb that one precious picture, taken at that one precious moment, so very, very, long ago.

And yet, the light of love was still alive. Still touched her as she stood there, absorbing it. Them. Herself. Her life.

"I need to just … sit," she said. She turned away from the image, and, as she did so, it appeared that Martha was doing something with an image frame.

"Come," Martha said. "Let's go into my little old-fashioned kitchen, and I'll brew an old-fashioned pot of tea."

Martha extended her hand, and Heart took it, gratefully, as if she needed to be led through the forest of images of all the beings, all of whom seemed to have their eyes fixed upon her.

She looked down at the frame that Martha had touched, but there wasn't any image in it at all. She put her other hand on Swen's head. She was glad he was here. Quiet. Attentive.

They went through to Martha's charming, old-fashioned kitchen. Martha pulled out a slightly rickety, but quite serviceable wooden chair. "Sit, while I put on water to boil."

Heart sat and Swen put his head in her lap. Heart watched in fascination as Martha bustled around her kitchen, gathering one antique thing and another, and proceeded to engage in a ritual to make a cup of tea.

She named each item as she used it, but Heart, still preoccupied with the image on the mantle, barely heard her, and certainly could not have repeated what she said, even if everything in the world depended upon it.

Finally, Martha sat down at the little table, next to Heart and poured a diminutive cup of tea.

"Very compelling," Heart said. "Your tea ritual. It's a pity HelperFriend wasn't here for that, he would dearly love it."

"I'll invite him then, one day."

They sipped their tea in silent reverie, while Swen, in continued contentment, all but purred as Heart scratched between his ears.

But Heart had something she needed to address. It would not be easy to bring up this talk with Swen, but it *would* be good to hear what he had to say.

She fumbled with her shoulder bag of personal items. "I, I want, I mean, I need to talk with you about this."

She pulled out her own little album of 3-D images. "This album was in my fake room that the Clone built under The Darling Undesirables Facility at Long Prairie. I put this album together ages ago when I was a little girl. So—when I was trapped in the Clone's crystal matrix room, I sat down and looked at the pictures, one after another. Which I don't think I've ever done. I'd put an image in, and then leave it at that.

"But, as I say, trapped there, underground, I picked it up and looked through it." Heart opened it and held it so Martha and Swen could both see the images.

"First of all, I noticed all the appearances of you, Swen. It surprised me because you never mentioned having gone to every one of my public appearances. Then there are all these pictures that you're not in. So, at first, I didn't think much of a News Hound being at many of the events that 'starred' the two most famous Darling Undesirables, Eye and myself.

"Then I realized that the images where I didn't see you were images you'd taken of me, yourself. So, with lightning clarity, I understood that you'd been watching me my whole life. A little unnerving to discover this about one of your best friends who claimed to be very truthful, but never bothered to mention this fact."

"Still, I thought there may be a 'need to know' basis in this, and I've been, more or less, all right with it, knowing one day I'd be able to sit down with you and ask you to tell me the truth."

She looked down at Swen expectantly. He sighed deeply and glanced at Martha. She gave a tiny, little shrug and a tiny little nod. "Yes, Heart, you clever girl. I was assigned, from the day you were left on the doorstep of Keeper A's home at the Darling Undesirables Facility at Long Prairie, to watch over you. Yes. It is true."

"Why didn't you tell me?"

"I didn't tell you because I was instructed not to tell you unless you specifically asked. Which you have never done until this moment."

"Who instructed you?"

"I've had different communicators. But behind them all is your father."

Heart contemplated Swen's answer for a few moments, decided it was the truth, and satisfactory for the moment, and plowed forward.

"Then I came upon my new discovery."

Right at this critical moment, Martha leapt up. "Want another cup of tea?"

"What? No, Martha, I don't right now want another cup of tea. I want to have this conversation with you. Please don't run off or change the subject."

"All right." Martha came and sat back down next to Heart, but Heart sensed a definite tension from her.

She turned the 3-D album back to the first page. "Here's what I saw, that'd I'd never noticed before." She pointed to the image of a woman cloaked in drab clothes, old-fashioned sun-glasses, and large hats in picture after picture, standing in the back, in every single image.

"*Keeper A!* Everywhere I ever went, Keeper A was there, in the back, watching me. And watching Eye, I guess. *So. Creepy.* I've been … I can't get over how it bothers me. We always had our keepers and attendants with us. There was no need for Keeper A to be there, except for some creepy, unpleasant *Purist* intention.

"Keeper A was always so mean. Cruel even, you know. Putting Eye in the deprivation tank. He almost lost his mind. But if she had something devious in mind about me, why didn't she *do it?*

"Clearly, she and Loruza are in this together."

"I see what you're saying, Heart," Martha said. "It'd be unnerving to make this observation. But, really, the woman in these pictures, I wouldn't be able to say they're all the same woman."

Swen remained mute.

Heart looked at Martha, disbelieving. "It's *clearly* the same woman. Even the same glasses and … *hmmmm.*" Heart was stymied. Hurt. Mystified. Why would Martha not agree with her?

"It seems like kind of a reach," Martha went on. "Anyway, what does it matter now?"

"It matters now, Martha, because—and ought I even tell you this, because I find this conversation strange and unsupportive—it matters now, because I'm positive I saw Keeper A on the Gargantua when I took up those two children in a gondola. I saw her, down a long hall, all sorts of activity swirling around. But she stopped in the midst of everything, and still as a statue, looked at me, hard for a moment. Then looked away. Then I was dropped like a stone in that little gondola back to the ground.

"But *I saw her*. I saw Keeper A on the Gargantua. I'm sure she and Loruza are the brains behind the Purists. So the Gargantua, the heart of *The Cause of All Beings* is infiltrated by the Purists."

Chapter 22

Martha reached out and patted Heart's hand. "All right, Heart. All right. You're no dummy. I have to take you seriously, and I am, now. I am. I'll take this up with Key Man, and we'll, we'll figure out a way to ... I don't know right now, Heart.

"Your information is disconcerting. I need to think about it. Is that all right with you? Will you let us consider what you've sorted out, and let us take it from here? And Swen, too, of course. His insights are always tempered and brilliant."

"What else *can* I do? I had a talk with Jackson about my suspicions of my father when I realized that the crystal matrix unites all the Darling Undesirable facilities with each other *and his laboratory.*

"But Jackson was vehement that my father built the crystal matrix after the turncoat scientists built the

Darling Undesirable facilities because he hoped always to bring an end to the Darling Undesirable facilities and also to keep tabs on the science they were discovering.

"So I decided to believe Jackson, with caution, and, quite frankly, hypervigilance."

"*Oh! Heart!* How can you even for a moment think such things about your father?" Martha said, truly dismayed.

"I've lived a life where lies are truth and truth is lies. That's how."

"*Oh!*" Swen exclaimed, standing up on all four feet.

Martha gasped. "*She will reveal the truths that are lies and the lies that are truths,*" she quoted.

"Well," Heart said with an edge of sarcasm, "We're on an *Ourbook* roll tonight, are we not?"

"We seem to be," Martha agreed. "I must apologize, Heart, for not taking you seriously. It's just—your information shocked me. What's your reaction, Swen?"

"Heart is very bright. Quoting *Ourbook* directly is a bit of a surprise. But, then again, no, it's not."

"All right now, Sweetie," Martha said, "I'm fully bio and have not eaten for many hours. I must have nourishment to keep my chubby little body in its best form. So, I hope you won't mind if I heat up some soup and make a couple little cheese sandwiches for us. Swen, what would you like?"

"Not hot soup and a cheese sandwich sounds wonderful!" Swen said, chuckling. "Oh, Heart, so glad you're here. All sorts of treats for me. And, to tell the truth, I'm very glad to tell the truth. I don't like cloaking stuff, especially when I have nothing to hide."

"I'm glad you're glad." Heart reached down with both arms and gave Swen a super-hug. She felt a weight fall from her. It was a huge relief to have Swen remove this untruth between them, and to tell Martha what had been bothering her.

"As you know," Heart went on, "I don't much need to eat, and HelperFriend made me a lunch so I've eaten today. But the thought of a companionable bowl of soup and a bit of sandwich here in your," Heart finally looked around at Martha's kitchen, *"absolutely adorable kitchen!* will fulfill another part of my fantasy about staying in the gingerbread house."

After a delightful supper during which Martha and Swen regaled Heart with story after story of events that happened in the museum, mostly having to do with children asking amazing or hilarious questions, and a few anecdotes about themselves and Key Man, they agreed to call it a night.

Martha took Heart and Swen up to a minuscule room for a fairy, with pale green and white flowers on the walls, and a pale green carpet. The tiny sliver of bed, piled high in white and green pillows and comforters looked like a wonderful place to relax and think.

"Sorry, Heart," Martha apologized. "It's hardly big enough for a mouse to turn around in. But—you asked for it!"

Heart gave Martha a huge hug. "I love this fairy room, Martha. It's even more perfect than what I tried to imagine."

Martha's face turned into its happy round circles. "All right my dear, sleep tight. I'll see you with the morning light." She went down a short flight of stairs to her own room.

"All right, sleep tight. I'll see you with the morning light." Heart whispered, turning out the light. She

went to the small window, and Swen padded alongside. They looked out. Heart was surprised to see that
she could look right into Key Man's workrooms. All
the lights were on, and the lights were on in the shed
out back as well. She could see HelperFriend standing as if mesmerized over Key Man, who was working with a shining gear. Equuleus sat off to the side,
watching them in pure contentment.

"Oh, Swen, what a picture! It warms me into the
deepest depths of my being. How sweet, how magical
to have this little peek into the joy of those three."

Swen nodded "And how sweet, how magical if the
three of them were to see us in our moment of joy."

"True," Heart agreed.

She moved back to the bed and turned on the bedside light. She then zipped open her bag and pulled
out the precious scroll wrapped in the blue ribbon.

"I had thought I would have HelperFriend take me
to The Periphery tomorrow and join Jackson. Equuleus is safe and very much at home here. But my own
mission has become quite clear to me in this moment.
With Lady Gervi, I started, and I need to finish, the
job of repairing and healing the residents of Pink. On
this scroll are the wounded and damaged from the Bot
Invasion, on Pink."

She slipped the ribbon off the scroll and unrolled
it for Swen to see. "Do you think Key Man can be
recruited to help?"

Swen looked at the long list. "Show him this, and
you won't be able to stop him!"

*   *

Much to Heart's extreme shock, she slept! She woke early in the morning with the delicious sun pouring across all the pile of pristine white and pale green bedclothes and pillows on the tiny bed, where her feet hung over the end and her arms fell out the sides. But still—*delicious!*

She looked over the edge of the bed, and there, curled up very dog-like on the pale green little circular rug, lay Swen, snoring lightly.

Could I not stay here forever? She wondered. *No!* Came the resounding reply. She had to convince Key Man to go with her to Pink, but first, he'd have to gather everything on the list and maybe make a few items. He'd have to sort out who would handle his responsibilities while gone. Maybe the Wonder-Men. Martha couldn't do everything.

As it was, Martha got up earlier than ever every morning to take on Peter's duties, opening the museum. They'd hired a temporary doorman, but Heart heard he was not friendly. That was not acceptable for The Museum of Scientific Improbabilities and Unpredictable Oddities!

She hated to wake Swen, so beautifully enjoying his sleep on the soft little rug. But the room was so small there was no place to put her feet to even stand up other than on his hide.

He apparently became aware of her dilemma as he snorted and looked up at her. "*Barrrk-ahh-what?*" He shook his head, his long, floppy, ears dancing around his muzzle. "Oh! Good morning, Heart. I was having a great dream. Doggie, but great."

"Well, you *ought* to have 'doggie' dreams!" Heart laughed. "But! As long as you're awake, let's get at this day. I have to show this list," she pointed to the scroll on the bedside table, "to Key Man. And see if he's finished making Equuleus beautiful. And a million other things! If Key Man agrees to go to Pink, will you be going with us?"

"What a question—try and keep me from it!"

"All right, then, up with you. You're in the only place I can put my feet!"

"*He-he-he*," he chuckled. "I have you prisoner in the sweet little fairy room!"

"Oh! That's what I called it in my mind last night when I came in here, a fairy room."

"See? I know you so well." Swen stood, lazily, stretched his paws out far in front of him, and wagged his tail high in the air.

Heart drummed her fingernails on the bedside table, feigning exasperation. "*Time is passing!*"

"Arrr … Heart, take a moment to stretch."

"I will, when I can get up."

"Stretch where you are—feet and arms hanging over the edge in every direction. You're too big for this bed!"

"I know it. But that still didn't prevent me from sleeping, *really sleeping!* Like I almost never do. Something so comforting in this little pile of bedding and pillows."

"Lovely, Heart, that you slept so deeply in this little fairy room. There's something about this tiny space that feels like you to me. It's rather strange. Do you know what I mean?"

"I do, Swen. This room feels almost unnaturally familiar. Deeply familiar. As if I've been here before. But I have not."

They both paused in the sweet but disconcerting thought.

"So …Heart …." Swen said very quietly.

"What, my dear canine friend?"

"I … I am sorry to have sort of 'betrayed' you by not letting you know I was a protector of yours from the moment you were placed on the Darling Undesirables Facility at Long Prairie's doorstep. It always bothered me, even though I knew it was for your own protection. There were times when it was quite difficult."

"I can imagine, Swen. Because, well, because it seems to me like it's dog nature to be transparent. It seems to me that a fully bio dog would not even comprehend the essence of lying."

"There you have it, Heart. That's exactly right. I still don't feel comfortable about it, and I need your reassurance that you're all right with my not telling you the plain truth before. That it hasn't damaged our friendship."

"No, Swen. It has not damaged our friendship. If some other things become revealed that you've kept secret, then that will become a different matter. But for now, I'm content knowing that you dedicated your life to protecting me, from the beginning. And that it was important to others, to my father anyway, that I not know it.

"I suppose, if I'd known, I would have always been looking for you in the crowd. It would have interfered with my performance, that's almost certain. But—you don't have any other secrets you're keeping from me, do you?" Heart laughed, sure she was only teasing him.

"Well, Heart, now, you're poking at, what you called my 'doggy-ness'—there are, in fact, things I know that I cannot tell you. I mean, literally cannot. They are locked so I cannot reveal them, but facts I know that, once again, call into action my abilities to protect you, if necessary. Please don't be mad at me."

Heart sat up, cross-legged in the tiny bed, and looked down at her friend. "No Swen. I'm not angry with you. But I am angry that you're being used in this manner. As if your feelings don't matter. It's just wrong. Who's behind this programming of you?"

"Well, that would be central to what I can't reveal, wouldn't it? But, Heart, it's not an intellectual challenge. I mean, it probably resembles the shortest distance between two points."

Heart nodded. "I see. And my father is going to get a serious talking to in the very near future."

"Oh, no, Heart. What have I done? See, I can't be held responsible for anything!"

Heart leaned over and patted Swen. "Not to worry. Everything will be fine. But now, we must get in motion." She flung her legs over the edge of the bed, and Swen leapt up and out the door.

"*Sheesh! Dangerous!* All right, I'm out of your way. I'll meet you downstairs."

"Quietly. I don't want to wake Martha."

"I'm sure she's been up for hours, and is at the museum, welcoming another day of curious museum-goers."

"And here I lie, like a big, lazy lump!"

Chapter 23

Sure enough, when Heart got down to the kitchen, there was a note on the table:

GoodMorning Heart!
I trust you slept well in the tiny attic room.
Help yourself to anything in the kitchen
for breakfast. I've set out some options."
Hugs,
Martha

Heart giggled as she looked over the various containers Martha had placed on the table. She wasn't the least bit hungry, but it was interesting to see the numerous options Martha offered. It was a little like being at The Darling Undesirables Facility at Long

Prairie. There had always been lots and lots of food, and many choices.

Heart turned to Swen. "Anything here for your breakfast?"

"Not if you're not eating. And it looks like you're not."

"Nope. Not hungry. I ate twice yesterday, which is quite unusual for me."

"Key Man has my particular dog-preferred breakfast waiting for me, I imagine."

"Then let's go!" But as Heart moved through the house, she could not resist stopping and standing before the picture of … her … *parents*. She still had a hard time thinking the word, even silently to herself.

She studied the image for a few moments and noticed something she hadn't noticed the night before. Her father was reaching out and gently touching his beautiful wife, and she had her hand over his, where he touched her. And there, where they touched, there seemed to be a glow, a bit of light.

But perhaps it was only the sunlight, pouring uninhibited, through the entire house. Heart turned from the picture, knowing that she would come here again to stare at it. Maybe even, one day, she would screw up the courage to ask Martha for a copy of it.

She and Swen stepped through the front door. Heart took a mental picture of herself, standing with Swen on the adorable front porch, surrounded by the profusion of curlicues of wooden decoration as if the house itself were bright and smiling. She looked down at her plaid, the one with bronzy-golden hues. Curiously and enchantingly, it took on the lavender of the house's gingerbread, glowing.

"Heart!" Swen exclaimed. "Heart!"

"What, Swen?" she asked, unable to take her eyes off the glowing plaid.

"You glow! You're in a bubble, an amazing, glowing, lavender bubble!"

She looked at Swen. "You too, Swen. You're glowing too."

"Glow contagion—I caught it from you!"

"The house likes us."

"Well, it ought to!"

Heart became aware of someone waving and looked up. Key Man stood on the other side of the street, waving at them. Beside him strutted Equuleus, expanding and contracting his wings, their pristine new, shiny gears glinting in the morning sun.

Heart clapped in glee, seeing her beautiful Equuleus showing off as only he could do, grandstanding and parading—a parade of one!—back and forth in front of her.

"You're lavender!" Key Man called to them.

HelperFriend was jumping up and down in delight, so happy, Heart knew, words failed him.

"We know—the house has caught us in its spell." Heart giggled. "Equuleus is *be-uuu-ti-fullll!*"

"Isn't he?" Key Man called back.

"All right now, Swen, we must leave the gingerbread house!"

They jumped off the porch and ran across the heavily oak-lined street. Heart stroked Equuleus' wing. "Better than ever, just like Key Man promised."

"Better than ever," Equuleus agreed. "And he made some adjustments that give me an ability to accelerate fifteen percent faster. It's amazing.

"I went for a 'test flight' in the night. Oh, Heart, it was magnificent. And then I spied on you in that little room. I was glad you were in that tiny room at the top of Martha's tiny little house. There you slept in the far too tiny bed with Swen curled up on the little rug. The sweetest picture."

Heart and Swen exchanged a look, recalling their conversation of the night before.

"It was sweet, Equuleus. I slept as almost never before. As if I was in my own little room. It felt so safe and familiar."

Martha stepped out the back door. "What's everyone doing out here?"

"Drinking in the sun," Heart answered. "I'm telling them about how I had the best sleep ever."

They all went through the back door.

"I'm glad to hear it. Now then," she said when they were all standing in the hall outside Key Man's workrooms, "what's the plan for the day?"

"I'm glad you asked." Heart pulled the ribbon-wrapped scroll from her bag and handed it to Key Man. "Do you have any of these parts?"

Key Man took the list, while HelperFriend, Heart feared, would explode with delight to see this list in Key Man's hands.

Key Man slipped the blue ribbon off the scroll and mumbled as he read through the list. Then he looked up at Heart, over to HelperFriend, and back to Heart. "Oh, Heart!"

"This is the list of the Folks on Pink, who were damaged and injured in the Bot Invasion, that took Xavier from us. Halt and lame, they've rebuilt Pink's dome, their home, and where the spacecraft and so many other things are housed. Selflessly, they've worked, knowing that every scrap of well-tempered metal, every viable gear, must go into the dome, not into their bodies. Knowing that they may never again be able to fully move, or be fully functional.

"When I gave Lady Gervi her leg, they went wild with delight, shouting cheers and shedding tears. No one begrudged her beautiful recovery. They each felt it in their own personal way, so happy that their beloved Lady was restored to her full statuesque beauty.

"Will you not bestow on them a life of quality, without deformity, as only you can, dear Key Man? As only you know how."

"Oh … Heart." Key Man was awash with emotion and could say no more for a few moments. "I would be honored to do this for Lady Gervi's friends. *So honored!*"

"Does that mean you'll go to Pink with me, as soon as you get these bits and pieces together, to perform this service?"

"Of course it means that, Heart. There's no other way!"

"*OH! Yay! Yay!*" HelperFriend cried, trying ever so hard to contain himself. "Oh, Heart! Heart! Everyone on Pink, whole again. Oh, Key Man, Key Man! Oh …."

Heart watched HelperFriend closely, hoping the excessive emotional input would not cause him to crash.

"It is wonderful, HelperFriend. But we don't want you to blow a fuse that Key Man will have to fix before getting to this list."

"Right, right you are, Heart. I do feel a bit over-over-over …."

Heart led him down the hall and had him sit on the floor, and she sat with him. "Just relax, dear HelperFriend. Think about counting. Let's count … one, two, three, four …."

HelperFriend continued to say "over" several more times, but finally, he started counting, picking up with Heart where she was. "Twenty-seven, twenty-eight …."

"Very good, HelperFriend. Just keep counting for a while."

Heart rejoined the group, who watched the interaction silently.

"How did you know to do that?" Key Man whispered with reverence in his voice.

Heart shrugged. "It just came to me. I really don't want him to short out like he did once, and my father had to reset him. Without him here, I'm not sure we could reset HelperFriend. And he'd be awfully awkward to carry about, as he's very *big and heavy!*"

She turned to look at him. He continued counting, his gears slowed their frenetic, jerky pace. "I'm going to let him do that for a few more minutes while we get at our work. It looks like he'll be all right. He'll be very happy to join us, and be extremely helpful as well, once his gears calm down."

"He's certainly emotional," Key Man observed.

"He is that!" Heart agreed. "I don't know why that is, but I do know I really love it about him. Even though there are these occasional moments when I must watch over him, he spends all the rest of his time watching over me. It's much more than fair."

Martha gave her a big hug. "As always, your thoughts are about love and care first, and other matters second."

"Well," Heart said, "that's as it should be. Now, Key Man, what do we need to do to get to Pink as soon as possible?"

*   *

Key Man went to work, gathering and organizing the components on the list, plus adding to it anything he thought might make the repair even more effective, given the parts needed. In addition, he asked Heart dozens and dozens of questions about each individual as he contemplated the repairs.

Heart was sorry to have to say that, in many cases, she did not know the details. It pointed out to her how modest and amazing all the residents of Pink were.

"They built themselves," Heart told Key Man. "My father took all those bits and pieces up to Pink with the thought of eventually putting them together, making new clockwork or mechanical, or partially bio beings.

"Then he heard noises on the other side of Pink. He went there, opened up the massive door to the interior of Pink where he'd dumped all these parts, and there was this population of beings, who had made one another, looking out at him.

"Can you imagine what that moment must have been like for my father?"

"It must have been amazing," Key Man said, stopped in mid-motion. "I know what I feel hearing the story. I think I feel a bit overwhelmed, like HelperFriend."

Heart laughed. "Yes. I feel like HelperFriend sometimes, too. And speaking of HelperFriend, I think I'll go see if he's ready to stop counting."

Heart went into the hall where HelperFriend patiently sat, counting.

"One-million-two-hundred-thousand-and-sixty-six,one-million-two-hundred-thousand-and-sixty-seven, one-million-two-hundred-thousand-and-sixty-eight …" he counted.

Heart sat down by him on the floor. "Hi, Helper-Friend."

"One-million-two-hundred-thousand-and-sixty-eight—no, nine … one-million-two-hundred-thou-sand-and-seventy …."

"HelperFriend, It's Heart. Stop counting."

One-million-two-hundred-thousand-and-sev-enty-one …"

"Stop, HelperFriend."

One-million-two-hundred-thousand-and-and-and …"

"Command: HelperFriend, stop counting."

HelperFriend stopped counting. His gears purred softly.

"Are you all right?"

HelperFriend looked at her. "Oh! Hi, Heart. I was just, hmmm, I was counting. But that doesn't seem very important. I wonder how I thought that was helpful? It seemed while I was counting that it was important."

"And it was. I wanted to see how far you would count in an allotted amount of time. Now, would you enjoy doing something else?"

"I would, Heart. I like to be constructively busy. You know that about me."

"Very good. Key Man is putting together all the components needed to help the injured on Pink. And we could use your help."

"But, Heart, that's exactly the assignment I want! That's exactly what I want to be doing!"

"Let's get at it, then." She stood and HelperFriend jumped straight up to standing from sitting on the floor. "You must be the most agile clockworks any-where, HelperFriend."

"Do you think so, Heart? That seems unlikely. I'm sure there are many clockworks who are much more agile than I am. But I'm glad you think that of me. I shall work to be the most agile clockworks anywhere."

"That's not necessary, HelperFriend. The amount of agile that you are is perfect."

They hurried down the hall and out the back door where Key Man and Swen were poring through all the gears and bits and parts in the little shed.

"Here we are, ready to make your work easier, Key Man and Swen," Heart said cheerily.

"Excellent," Key Man took his eyes from the list and gave HelperFriend a moment's study. "Looks like you're ready to help, all right."

"I'm always ready to help!" HelperFriend affirmed.

"I showed you how everything is laid out in here last night, HelperFriend, when we were working on Equuleus, so I imagine you recall that?"

"Yes, indeed. Even more, I made a map." HelperFriend projected the map in the space between them. "As such, I can look at everything from the sides, or the bottom, or exploded view, to see where even the tiniest metal bit is located."

"You did? Why didn't you tell me that last night?"

"I was being quiet, as Heart directed. To not be annoying or distracting. I'm very literal, and, although that *still* seems to me like a good thing, it, apparently, can cause difficulties."

"So—you're saying you can find any part?"

"Quite quickly, yes."

"Well," Key Man looked at Heart, "perhaps we might let Swen and HelperFriend work on gathering components, freeing me to check them over and organize them."

"I believe we could. Let's stand back and watch for a minute."

"I've been reading the part description, and Key Man wrote down numbers after them," Swen said. "So I'll read the number, and, hopefully, you can find it, HelperFriend."

"Yes. I'll find it."

Swen read a number, and HelperFriend produced the gear in seconds. Swen read several more numbers, and HelperFriend produced every item in seconds.

"Truly amazing," Key Man sighed. "They're going to be way ahead of us."

"Just lay each set of repair parts in its own pile, HelperFriend, and I'll bring each pile in to you Key Man, one by one, you can check them over and we'll then put them in a container for transport, in the same order as on the list."

Both Heart and Key Man watched in stunned silence as HelperFriend zipped about, picking out parts as Swen read, and putting them in a pile, then on to the next one.

"They'll be done shortly."

"There's no part 99-XX-99," HelperFriend said, looking dismayed.

"It's true, HelperFriend, that I do not have some parts. Some parts will have to be contrived. Can you memorize which parts are missing, and for which repair pile, HelperFriend?"

"Certainly. Very easy."

"Which brings up another point, Heart. Will there be a possibility of any metal to fabricate with, once we're there?"

"It's limited, Key Man. Just about all viable metal is in the building. It is stronger than it used to be though, my father said. So, that's good. But there is a pretty big heap of distempered metal."

"Some of that may be usable for our purposes. And I'll take some to fabricate with, as well."

Before long, all the parts were safely organized and stowed in a large container. HelperFriend lifted it easily and carried it to the *Heart!*, setting it by the hatch, while Heart calculated the dark energy charge.

"Well, Swen and Key Man hardly have to be accounted for, they're so light. But that container …" she continued crunching numbers, "makes it a close call to get to Pink with this load on one charge. Not a big problem. Might have to have a craft come out and give us a boost, but we'll be very near. If Pink had Earth's gravity, it'd be no problem at all."

She looked at Key Man. "Who's going to take your place? Poor Martha, left alone!"

"We talked about it, and chatted with Wonder-Man One and WonderMan Two. They're going to take on my duties around the museum, other than clockworks repair, of course. And, also, they're not good at the front door as they scare so many people, especially children."

"Ah, that's too bad!" Heart exclaimed. "They're so sweet!"

"But intimidating."

"True. True. If you don't know them, that's true."

"Anyway, Martha and I sorted that out early this morning, while you and Swen slept in, as well as *another, important subject*," Key Man added with emphasis.

"Yes?" Heart said quietly, knowing, of course, what he referred to.

"Know, Heart, that your concerns are not going unattended to nor unacknowledged. Trust me on this."

Heart nodded. "All right, I will trust you, and Martha."

Key Man sighed as if hugely relieved. "Let's get this project in motion, then!"

"I'll open the hatch. HelperFriend, if you would please figure out what will go where, and how to gently secure Key Man and Swen,"

Heart stepped outside, went to the *Heart!* and opened the hatch. Then she stepped out and went to look at Martha's little house across the road. That one night had stirred so many thoughts and feelings and even, it seemed, memories. Deep and far away memories.

But how? How could that be?

She suddenly missed Jackson. *Massively!* Missed him as if there was some particular reason to miss him. Was he all right?

What was this feeling?

She couldn't resist. She had resisted, ever since the terse few words she sent him and he had not even bothered to reply.

She thought, fine! Just fine! Don't reply. Why would you? We've never been close, really.

All that she had argued with herself before slipped away in this moment of her emotions in an upheaval. But—there was also the possibility that the Purists had intercepted her communication.

Finally, she activated her star necklace, "We're departing for a small moon. You may not be interested. Just wanted … wanted … someone to know."

She disconnected. She had wanted to say, "I wanted *you* to know," but she couldn't bring herself to say it. Lost courage at the last moment.

Ah, this thing called love. The easiest—and sometimes the hardest!—part of life.

She took one last lingering look at the safe, precious, gaudy-beautiful cottage across the street and turned.

There stood Equuleus. Silent, patient, waiting. Loving.

"He's … he … don't worry, Heart."

"It's not worry. It's, well, I don't know. It's the unknown."

"Life is full of unknowns, Heart. But Jackson? No unknown there. For Jackson, first the missions, which are all to protect Heart. Whether near or far, protect Heart. Then, next, Heart. That's all. He's not more complicated than that."

They walked toward the *Heart!* "I do believe he's more complicated than that."

"Nope!" Equuleus insisted as they joined everyone standing in a line by the *Heart!*

"You all look like you're about ready to go somewhere," Heart teased.

"We are, Heart," HelperFriend said enthusiastically. "We're ready to go to Pink. Did you forget?"

"No, HelperFriend. I couldn't forget. I'm teasing."

"Oh, yes, of course. Teasing. I see. Literal HelperFriend, once again. Let's see, because we're all lined up here, ready to go, so you 'tease' us by saying the obvious. Yes. I see."

"Very good, HelperFriend!" Heart smiled. She walked around the *Heart!* checking it out. Used to having the crew on Pink do this, she wasn't entirely sure of every detail she was to check, but she made her best effort.

"I'm learning what *you* find amusing," Helper-Friend said. "The part where *I* find it amusing too seems remote."

"You'll get it, over time. And then you'll be cynical like the rest of us. All right, everything looks good. Let's board and get tied down. I see the parts container is no longer on the ground, so I guess you got it secure?"

"Parts container secure, Heart." HelperFriend said.

"Did you sort out the seating arrangement for Key Man and Swen?"

"Yes. I was going to let Key Man have the copilot's seat, but I really do believe I ought to be there as I know more about piloting."

"Agreed," Key Man piped up.

"So, it's not too refined, but the only reasonable option is to tie them down where I had the Clone."

"Oh, Swen."

"We're fine with it, Heart. We understand the constraints of the space. Swen and I are together, and that's all we need."

Swen nodded energetically. "That's all we need! We don't want to lose time trying to devise something more complicated, we just want to get there."

"True, we do. All right, all aboard! Where's Martha, isn't she going to see us off?"

At that moment, Martha stepped out the back door, breathless. "Oh, didn't want to miss you! Didn't want to miss you! I had a customer chattering on about a trip to the seaside, and I'm standing there thinking, I'm needing to say good-bye to my friends who are taking a trip to a *mooooooon!*" Her eyes, her mouth, her little, round button nose, her whole round face, all rounded in to the *"oooooo"* of the moon.

For some inexplicable reason, everyone, all at once, Swen and Equuleus, and KeyMan and Heart all repeated, *"mooooooon!"* and then broke into giggles.

Martha gave everyone, in turn, a short-person gigantic hug. "Travel safely, heal many, be sure to return, Key Man. I can't run this show alone, and the WonderMen are nervous about their duties. Ever since that child fainted at the sight of them, they've not been their same jovial selves."

Jovial selves! Heart exclaimed to herself.

"I'll wave to you tonight," she said, stepping away from the *Heart!*

"And we'll wave back!" Heart entered the craft through the hatch, and her interesting mix of passengers followed.

She watched as HelperFriend secured Key Man and Swen, then she adjusted the magnetics for Equuleus, who positioned himself against the wall, then she and HelperFriend secured themselves in their pilot and copilot seats.

"And, we're off!"

The engines roared, and the *Heart!* leapt from the ground, rising as vertically as she dared fly, high in the sky, rapidly leaving below the dark energy highway and everything—and *everyone*—else.

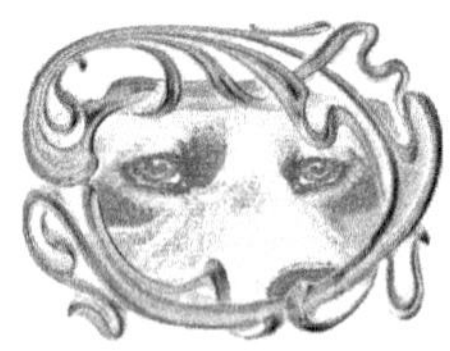

Chapter 24

Partly because she still wasn't clear on who might be able to eavesdrop on any communication she might have, and partly because she wanted to surprise the residents of Pink, she didn't tell them of the *Heart!'s* imminent arrival until just before she knew they would spot her themselves.

"The *Heart!* is inbound," she told her father. "Including a cargo of surprises."

"I'm so glad you're coming," her father said, sounding particularly pleased, but not particularly surprised.

"Someone spoiled my surprise," she said, disappointed.

"Only a short while ago, so, yes, I was surprised. I've not told anyone yet. Haven't had a chance. Of course, they're now all …."

An uproarious cheer sounded in the background.

"They're now all," her father raised his voice to be heard above the noise, "aware of your near arrival."

Heart grinned from ear to ear, hearing a shrill *"She's MY Heart!"* above the din. Ah, Violet! But of course, she was Violet's Heart, and no one had better give her any contest about it.

"All right, passengers, bios Swen and Key Man must first put on protective suiting against the environment. When we land, I will release Equuleus's magnetics. HelperFriend and I will release our safety harnesses, and I'll retrieve suits for the bios."

"Oh, great, I almost forgot this part. Dog in human suit."

Heart grinned, delighted with her secret.

Soon the *Heart!* landed among the fanfare. She taxied slowly, while all the residents of Pink, cheered.

HelperFriend began to spurt tears, joyfully moved by his people welcoming him home.

"My goodness!" Key Man said quietly. *"My goodness!"* he said more loudly as he could barely see from his position in the back of the *Heart!* the crowds smiling and cheering. Those he came to heal sat in the front row, as everyone moved aside to let them through. "Oh, Heart! My, my goodness. I have work, wonderful work, to do here."

"Indeed you do, Key Man."

She finally taxied to a stop, turning off the engines. They'd made it without having to top the dark energy, which was convenient. She grinned and waved to her father in his bell jar, Violet hopping from Lady Gervi, nearby, to Father Inventor's bell jar.

"Heaaaaart!" she squealed, somehow, above the din.

Heart shut off Equuleus's magnetics, released her safety harness, stood, stretched, went to the wall and slid open a door, retrieving two white environmental suits, so glad that she'd had a variety of them made to stow aboard.

But she was proud of one in particular. She fussed about like she wasn't sure what she was doing, though, of course, she knew exactly what she was doing.

"See if this works for you, Key Man." She handed him a suit with little airlock buttons on the arms and legs which allowed them to become longer or shorter, as needed. She helped him pull it on, and showed him how to work the buttons. Soon he stood before Heart, grinning through his visor.

"Now I'm a real spaceman!" he crowed.

"It looks like it!" Heart agreed.

Swen had watched, feigning disinterest, but, of course, ever the newshound, he paid close attention.

"All right, Swen, let's see how this fits you."

She held up the suit she'd had made for him.

He studied what she held in her hands and then leapt up and ran around in circles, even in the crowded space. "For me? A dog suit? For me?"

"For you, and only you, my special dog friend."

"Oh, help me put it on, help me!" But he kept running in circles.

"You have to stand still!"

"Well, of course. Sometimes it seems my dog-part runs away with me!"

Everyone laughed.

"What's so funny? What's so funny?" Violet screeched. "Come out of there right now!"

"We'd better do as the lavender rabbit demands." Heart flipped the switch to open the hatch. "Ready?"

"Ready!" everyone chorused.

Out they came. Equuleus to wild cheers, Swen to surprised yells of joy and cheers, HelperFriend, sending metal tears into the happy crowd, and then Heart took Key Man's hand and walked down the hatch ramp with him.

It always fairly took her breath away at their kind and generous, boundless love. Although only her father knew who the short man in an environmental suit was, the crowd cheered ever more wildly, and then began to chant, "Heart! Heart! Heart!"

She grinned and bowed, then raised her hands. "Dear friends … thank you … thank you …"

They continued to roar, but, finally subdued enough so she could be heard to say, "I want to introduce you to my friend, Key Man. He is the one responsible for making the beautiful limb for our beloved Lady Gervi."

The crowd went crazy at this information, yelling and cheering, but finally, the chant broke over them all. "Key Man, Key Man, Key Man!" They pushed Lady Gervi to the front. She stood, holding Yippee. And Heart saw that she was almost quivering.

Ah! It was too much for her—to meet her hero, Heart understood in a flash. She released Key Man's hand and went up to Lady Gervi, led her inside her father's little room, and had her sit on her father's cot.

Both Lady Gervi and Yippee looked up at her gratefully, but wordlessly.

"I understand, my friend. It's too much. In front of everyone, and without any notice. You stay right here, and we'll all have a nice chat in a little while when the excitement calms down."

"Yes, Heart. Yes," she finally managed to say. Yippee found his voice too, apparently expressing gratitude as well.

"Listen, though, to what we are about to say."

"I will, Heart. I'll listen."

Heart went back outside. The crowd had become utterly silent.

"Thank you for that wonderful welcome to my amazing friend, Key Man. Of course, he has wanted to come and visit you, to meet the wonderful Folks of Pink. But that's not all."

Heart turned to HelperFriend, who had moved to stand beside her father, and Violet was doing her dance of "look at me" all over his head and shoulders but had managed to be quieted.

"HelperFriend, if you would kindly bring out the container."

HelperFriend put Violet in Father Inventor's hands extending from his bell jar, and went inside the *Heart!* He came out with the container, and Heart held up the scroll that HelperFriend had himself printed out, at Lady Gervi's request.

She walked close to the crowd, letting the scroll unroll, letting them see what was on the list. As the clockworks, the mechanicals, the bios that were most injured were the ones in the front row, as Heart walked by, there were gasps, and cries and shouts and singing.

"Yes, my beloved friends. Let us soon begin. We have brought with us nearly all the parts and pieces needed to make you all physically whole again. After you so bravely gave of yourselves during the Bot Invasion, this is the least we can do for you, in gratitude for your devotion.

"Gather yourselves, and we shall soon begin. Let us allow Key Man to become acclimatized for a while. We'll have to make a space where he can work, that is protected from the environment, but those are just little details.

"The big news is, we are going to make all The Folks on Pink whole again!"

Heart thought for a minute that the residents had truly, collectively, lost their minds, and was almost concerned for their safety, and Key Man's.

They rushed him, and Heart as well, lifting them up they formed a giant circle, chanting, *"Heart and Key Man, Key Man and Heart, Heart and Key Man, Key Man and Heart!"*

Flattering as it was, she would prefer to move forward with the work.

Much to her surprise, HelperFriend came to the rescue. He came into the circle and lifted Key Man away from those carrying him, acting as though he was joining in, but when the circle came around to Father Inventor's door, HelperFriend neatly stepped inside and deposited Key Man in the room and stepped back outside.

Heart grinned. Totally by accident, Key Man and Lady Gervi were now alone together.

HelperFriend came and retrieved her from the shoulders of adoring residents of Pink as well. "Put me down by my father, HelperFriend."

He did as she bid, and finally! Violet was able to get herself in Heart's arms.

"Why are you ignoring, spurning, slighting, snubbing and disregarding me?" Violet cried as the circle and the chant of The Folks continued.

"I never ignore you, Violet. There's no future in it."

"A great truth you have spoken," Violet said simply.

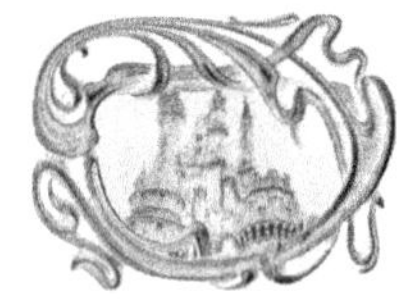

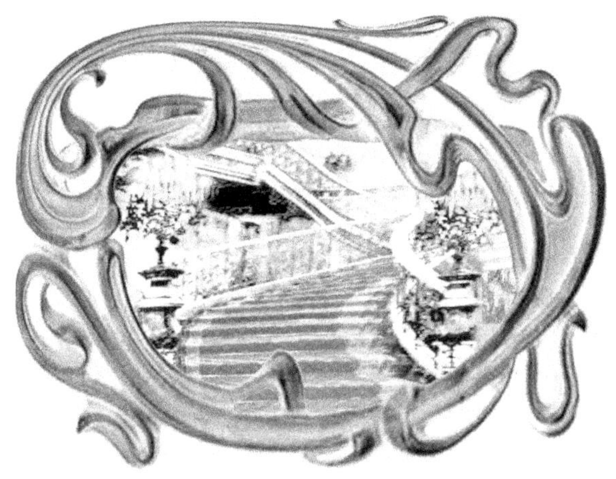

Chapter 25

Once the delightful shock of what was about to transpire had worn down a bit, all the clockworks, mechanicals, and bios of Pink pulled together—with Pink's WonderMan One and WonderMan Two heading up the project—and built an environmentally safe room for Key Man, while Father Inventor made adjustments on the few residents needing repairs or rebuilding, for whom a human environment was unsafe.

As used to their ability to do amazing things as Heart had become, their present manifesting surprised even her father.

"Look at them!" he exclaimed, standing at the window of his room, appreciating the beautiful, spacious and bright white-domed room they were putting the finishing touches on. "Much nicer than this little room I made for myself."

Heart laughed. "I guess you'll have to move out there."

"Well, curiously, I like my humble little space and my rude little cot. But I probably will have them join the two spaces, so I can take advantage of it if necessary." He looked at her intently.

"What? Is my hair standing on end?"

"Hardly, dear Heart. It's … oh, what can I say? You amaze me! You amaze me!"

"But, Father, you knew I was going to do this, when I had HelperFriend make the printout at dinner."

"Well, yes, I knew you intended it, and, one day, perhaps it would come about. But, no! There's no waiting around with you!"

"It was my mission, along with doing what I could to save the Darling Undesirables. Which Peter has completed with the life-saving Gargantua." For a moment she thought to tell her father what she'd told Martha, about the infiltration of the Purists in the Gargantua.

The worst infiltration—*Keeper A!* But strangely, and unhappily, she still had a niggling little doubt about her father. Hating it so much, but not able to dismiss it.

And so she kept it to herself. But, as soon as she could wander off without being noticed, she went into the library. She'd not been there in a long time, and one of the reasons she avoided the room was the very reason that she *was* going there now.

To look at the glowing image of her biological mother. Subdued golden lights came on as she moved stealthily to the mantle. There, this beautiful, blonde and delicately beautiful woman. Yes. It certainly was the same woman as in the image on Martha's mantle. Younger. Maybe even under twenty.

Maybe even, Heart thought, stunned, breathless, maybe even the same age as she, herself, was now.

She looked harder and harder at the picture, an old-fashioned 3-D image. When Heart moved, her mother went from smiling to looking dreamy-eyed, out of the frame, but not at the person in front. No, her vision looked off into the distance.

Heart wanted to see herself in this woman's features. But she did not. Her features were more like her father's—so much like her father's, her bone structure, the shape of her eyes, her nose, her mouth, that there was no denying paternity. But—maternity? Open for argument. She was, after all, a test tube baby. Any bit of genetics could be her mother.

But there was something very, very disconcerting about the image of this supernaturally beautiful woman. Something quite unnervingly familiar. She knew someone who looked like this. But search her memory with details, she could not come up with who it was.

Which was another reason she avoided looking at this picture. It didn't look like herself. But it *did* look like someone she had known. Or interacted with … somehow.

Troubled yet more, with no answer to her deepest, most burning questions, she returned, slowly, in contemplation, to her father's room, intending to go back outside where everyone was—Equuleus hovering overhead, making sure the smaller, quickly built dome for Key Man's work was coming together properly.

Add to that, HelperFriend's direction of the entire event with the amazing leadership abilities he was rapidly developing, and Violet, of course, bossing everyone around and mostly getting underfoot, shouting at everyone for almost stepping on her.

As she approached her father's room, she heard the low murmur of two voices—her father and Key Man, one entirely bio and the other, too bio to be out in Pink's environment, and thus, they were alone together.

"She's so amazing, Ray!" Key Man said.

"She … she is that," her father agreed, deeply emotional. "Always has been amazing."

Key Man chuckled.

Ray! Key Man called her father, casually, by his shortened first name! She didn't know anyone who did that. Then Heart grinned sheepishly, inadvertently eavesdropping on their private conversation about her.

"And brilliant. I remember when she was about five, she came to me and said, 'I just learned that your entire name is Kevin Edward Mann. And that means your initials are 'K' 'E,' and you carry all these keys. So your name ought to be 'Key Man.' Well, Martha and Peter were standing right there so ….'"

"So you became Key Man. How is it I never heard that story?" Her father asked. He laughed softly, but there was only sadness in his voice.

They … *they were not talking about her!* They were talking about some other girl. A girl who made her father very sad. When was that? Who was she?

Some other little girl that made her father sad. Did … did he have a daughter who … maybe had a heart like her mother's and died? Was Heart, herself, a surrogate daughter, not a real daughter at all?

And, clearly, her father and Key Man, or Kevin Mann, whoever he was, whatever his name, had known one another for a long, long time. Given that her father was 250 years old, give or take, this other girl could have been two hundred years ago!

She had no idea, had never thought about—how old Key Man was.

She was about to turn and leave this totally disturbing glut of unimaginable conversation when Key Man said, "Well, you have excellent, excellent reason to be proud of her now."

"I know, Kev … I mean *Key Man*, I know." She heard her father stand and go to the window. "Speaking of proud! Look at what these amazing beings have done—while we've been sitting here babbling, they've almost completed your workspace."

"Very good, I can't wait to make these beautiful beings whole."

There was a long, companionable pause, during which Heart mulled over the information that this "she"—whoever she was—had given two of the men she most loved in the world reason to be especially proud of her. Now. In the present.

"And then, there's Heart," Key Man said softly.

"*Ah, yes. Heart!*" Her father sighed, as if with an even greater sadness.

"Why—why are you sad?" Key Man asked.

"Heart is such a light—such a joy. And, such a surprise! What will she do next? I keep asking myself. Then she does something that simply astounds me."

"True, true," Key Man agreed. "And there are things you don't even know, that we don't have the time to go into right now."

"I don't doubt it. Like this, now with you here, healing all Pink's wounded! *Amazing. Amazing.* But …."

"But what, my friend?"

"*What I did to her,*" he whispered so that Heart could barely hear. "Her heart, putting it elsewhere. In a clockworks creature. Making her so abnormal. Willfully doing that to her."

"*Oh!*" Key Man registered surprise, as his keys clanked about in, Heart assumed, a shocked response, which she shared. "I … you … *Goodness!* You surprise me, Ray. You did that to protect her. No one faults you. You wanted to keep Rose's memory alive, in Heart. You did everything in your power to protect Heart.

"And it worked! Anyway … and, more importantly, I don't think she has any thought like that. I haven't heard, no one has heard her say … no, Ray.

"I think, well, I think several things. She could not have stayed at the Darling Undesirable Facility if she was whole. And then what would have happened to her, with the world so crazy about the Darlings at that time? And, given everything, as you know, not the best option, but she was *safe* and looked over. And, when she learned that she *did* have a heart, housed in the loving and intrepid Equuleus, she bonded with him more closely than any of us had even hoped for.

"She has all our hearts, Ray, yours, mine, and … well, I don't need to tell you, you know. She has all our hearts."

There was no verbal response, but Heart could picture her father nodding.

"And in this last minute of our tiny window of being able to confide things privately, I'll let you know that I believe a light has been lit between Heart and Jackson."

Her father snorted. "There's a fire there, for sure. I never saw two people, and I mean, humans, so at odds. He says yes, she says no. She says maybe, he says absolutely. It's exhausting to be around the two of them in the same place if you want to know my truth."

Key Man chuckled wryly. "Love and hate, Ray, hate and love. A cycle, a circle. But Heart and Jackson are so much alike – both looking for love, not believing in it, braced for challenge. But nobody, and I mean, nobody, can do what the two of them do when together. They don't even know their power, it's unstoppable. When they figure that out for themselves that together they are capable of doing more for this world than anyone, that will be a great day!"

"Well," her father said, walking across the room, then turning and pacing back again. Heart pulled back further into the shadows. "If he would be loving and kind, and if she loved him, and he made her happy, it would make me quite happy. He's our wild urchin, is he not? Where did he come from? We don't even know."

"He is our wild urchin all right," Key Man agreed. "Always escaping both your and society's efforts to do a gene panel on him. We told him he was Xavier's cousin—at least they were cousins in their hearts. Maybe he just … fell from the stars."

Heart had heard all, and, in fact, more than, she could handle. She turned and slipped to the front door, stepping through the baffle, she went into one of the greenhouses, grateful that it was synthetic night inside, and sat among the flowers. She didn't even talk with them like she always did.

She simply sat. Her mind, completely blank. And yet, she could feel it blazing, as all that she'd heard tried to find places to rest, and where it couldn't— which was all over the place!—she felt it blaze new trails, new connections.

Her recent little indignant chats with Martha and Swen were ridiculous in the face of the enormous truths she'd never been told.

She had no idea how long she sat like that, in a trance state of mystification, when she heard Equuleus, flying about the greenhouse, then Violet, on his back, squealed, "Heart! Heart! What are you doing in there? Come on, it's amazing. Key Man has begun. It's amazing."

Swen loped up with HelperFriend, "Oh Heart!" HelperFriend called, "I'm so *haaaaaaappy!* You've made us all so *haaaaaaappy!* Dear Heart, come out and share the happiness!"

"*Bark-bark!*" Swen said, "*Arrr*, I mean, Yes, Heart. See I'm sharing the happiness so much, I slipped into dog-talk."

Heart couldn't help but smile. She couldn't help but be happy too. She had accomplished this mission, and now Key Man would fulfill its final details.

Whatever her history, whatever she did know or did not know, she would continue on her path. Did she need to know every detail about her life?

Did anyone, ever know every detail of their lives?

Life was a mystery from one end to the other, and all she could do was make it better, where ever, when ever, she could.

"Hearrrrrt!" Violet added with a grand finale squeal.

Oh, how she loved these four amazing beings! What had she to complain about, or wonder, or waste her time thinking about?

Grinning, Heart stood and exited the greenhouse. "What's all the racket? My goodness, can't a person sit in meditation without all this noise?"

"Oh, sorry-sorry-sorry-sorry," HelperFriend, apologized, stepping backwards, facial gears spinning, troubled.

Heart rushed to him and put her arm around his shoulders. "I'm teasing, you big goofy. I love it that you've come to rescue me from my blue funk. Wasting my time reflecting on things I don't know! So silly, while, right now, wonderful things are happening. History is being made on Pink. Key Man is going to bring the entire population back to how it had been originally imagined by the population, itself."

She took HelperFriend's hand, and headed toward the far end of the castle. "I wouldn't miss a minute of this, for all the worlds in Alpha Centauri!"

"What would you do with all the worlds in Alpha Centauri, Heart? If you had them, what would you do with them?"

"Precisely! Such a wise question, HelperFriend. What would I do with all the worlds in Alpha Centauri? Much better to be present for Key Man, right here on Earth's little Pink."

Heart gasped as she came around the corner of the castle. The newly built dome was sparkling white. How the residents had managed to do that, when everything was a wash of pink or lavender, she couldn't imagine. How they got it to sparkle, she couldn't imagine, either. It was an amazing touch.

But what really took her breath away was the line of Pink's residents, each standing with their particular parts, patiently standing, with their broken bodies and broken smiles, waiting their turn, with all the patience of saints. Calm, relaxed. Happy.

Sad and wonderful, all at once. Their missing arms and legs, their giant holes in their chests, their smashed heads, missing eyes. To see them together, separated out from everyone else, their tragic wounds in one, long, line—Oh, Heart thought, why did I wait so long to get this done?

"If not for you," HelperFriend said, as if she'd asked her self-critical question out loud, "If not for you, Heart, when would these broken, tragic friends of mine ever have become whole? *When, Heart, when?*" His sparkling metal tears sprayed in every direction.

"Father Inventor is working day and night to save Earth's population from the confused beliefs of the Purists. And that's as it should be, Heart. That's what he must be doing. But for you, Heart, this," HelperFriend waved his hand along the line of the remarkable sight, "might *never* have happened!"

"Thank you, HelperFriend, for your kindness. Thank you."

"No, Heart. I'm not being kind. I'm telling the truth. I may be naïve and I may be remarkably literal. But I *DO* know the difference between someone saying a kindness, and telling a truth."

Heart nodded at his uncomplicated wisdom. He was right. It was possible that the residents of Pink, off-world, far away, and not even known to exist to most of Earth's population, much less the devastation they experienced from the Bot Invasion, would never have the attention they needed and deserved, if she hadn't done what was in her power to do.

Heart and her band of devoted friends hurried up to the dome. Leaving her friends to commune with those in line, Heart went in through the double baffle, into the pristine clean and light interior. Key Man was industriously attaching a hand, removing badly smashed, tiny gears, and accomplishing the delicate work of replacing the exquisite, delicate gears he'd brought on the *Heart!*

"What can I do to be helpful, Key Man?"

He glanced up at her. "You've done so much already, Heart. Take a break."

"No way! Think you're going to get all the glory for yourself? *Nahhh*, not going to happen! Tell me what to do."

He chuckled. "All right, all right, I'll share the glory. You can help each one exit, and ask them how they feel. We've got stations out the back baffles for everyone to recover in, or to address complications.

"Lady Gervi is out there. My, she is amazing! She's double-checking on everyone's recovery, but if you could help them through the baffles and get them settled, that'd be fantastic. That way, your father and I can stay right here and stay focused on the healing."

"Where *is* my father?"

"He's gathering materials for bio components. He says, he can do some of the necessary bios right here and now, but some will need more attention."

Key Man patted the clockworks man he was working on. "There you go my friend, good as new!" He helped him stand. Heart walked the clockworks man to the back baffles, and led him through, listening to the seal as she went, making sure it was adequate to protect Key Man and her father.

"Oh Heart," the clockworks man cried, "thank you, and bless Key Man. Look at my beautiful hand! Look! I never thought this could happen."

"It *is* beautiful!" Heart agreed. "You needn't thank me, but it is good to give Key Man a blessing. He's going to need all the blessings and energy we can imagine for him!"

"So true, Heart. I will have everyone send him strength, stamina, and energy. But we must make sure he does not push too hard! After all, he's mostly bio, and bios have their limits."

"That will be wonderful, dear, if you rallied everyone to send Key Man your special clockwork, mechanical and hybrid energies. Such a wonderful idea!"

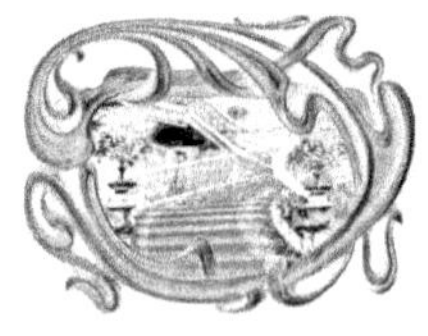

Chapter 26

They worked tirelessly, and it did seem as though Key Man was graced with an unnatural degree of energy, patience, and stamina. Each being presented a new challenge, which, Heart knew, he loved. And then each and every one of them was so sweet and loving and appreciative, there was energy in that loving exchange, as well.

Key Man and her father worked tirelessly, right through Pink's dusky night and pale day, again and again, until Heart, herself, began to worry about them, not even taking a break for a bit of refreshment.

She finally went outside the front baffle and told HelperFriend to make a meal for Key Man and her father, and he scurried off to do as he was bid.

Then she turned to the line—still reaching off to the horizon. "I hate to have to say this, but Key Man and my father must take a break. I am going to insist that they do so. They are bio and they need nourishment. I know you all understand."

The entire line made murmurs of agreement, with a couple of them piping up saying, "we were wondering when they would stop," and "we've been worrying about their ability to continue."

"Thank you, thank you," Heart nodded. "Your kindness and patience are much appreciated." She went into her father's room, only to see Key Man and him standing, wolfing down the beautiful repast HelperFriend had made for them.

"This will never do! HelperFriend, bring that little table over here by the cot, and bring that chair."

HelperFriend unceremoniously dumped everything that was on the little table onto the floor.

"*Agh!*" Father Inventor cried. "My work!"

"Sorry, sorry. I'll put it back, exactly as it was." Then HelperFriend brought the chair to the table.

"Now, sit you two! It is not a break if you don't take a break!"

They sat, not pausing in their eating for a second. "What about that one with the …" Key Man said.

"Right, with the 'birth defect' you might say. That was beautiful work. It wasn't a part of her injury from the Bot Invasion, so the parts weren't in her hand, but you contrived that piece from one of your keys! Genius! A delight to observe."

"As are you, my friend!"

Heart couldn't help grinning. They made a fantastic team. She stepped out into the dome to check if there was anything she could put in order or better organize. She saw Lady Gervi through the back baffles. Within the quiet moment, she was talking with Yippee and Violet, both of them looking up at her attentively.

Heart stepped out to join them.

"You're doing wonderfully, Lady Gervi, making sure everything with everyone appears to be in good working order."

"Oh, I'm not doing anything special. But Key Man. Oh, my, is he not the most amazing being? The most amazing being!"

"That he is, dear lady."

"Amazing, amazing," Yippee said, quite clearly.

"Oh, my!" Heart exclaimed.

Lady Gervi laughed lightly. "Yippee has quite fallen in love with Key Man."

"Well, then! Key Man is fortunate!" Heart said, thinking, perhaps Yippee had fallen in love with Key Man, but he was not the only one!

Their chat was cut short with the return of Key Man and her father to the dome. "My goodness, if I don't stand right over them, they will not do as I say!"

The healing picked up where it had left off. But, miracle of miracles, as it seemed to everyone, there finally came the moment when the last, sad, broken mechanical came through the baffles. He had no bio components, so Key Man and her father performed the repairs together, and, whole again, Heart took the little mechanical man through the back baffles.

When she returned, both Key Man and her father were looking expectantly toward the door. But no one came through the front baffles.

Heart stepped through the baffles and came back in. "There's no one there—the two of you have made whole all the damaged beings on Pink!

"Take a load off and celebrate!"

Key Man and Father Inventor looked at one another and began jumping up and down like schooboys. "We did it! We did it!"

The way they said it, and the look exchanged, gave Heart the impression that they had said this at another time—who knew how long ago?—over some triumph perhaps equally as relevant.

They stepped outside where HelperFriend stood with his hands upheld, like, what am I supposed to do?

"Everyone is healed, fixed, repaired, whole, HelperFriend. Time for some of your mystical music.

"Oh, oh, oh, oh, oh, Heart! Heart! Heart! Everyone, everyone is whole?"

Heart nodded.

Amazing, celebratory music broke over the entire terrain of Pink. Everyone gathered from everywhere to the front of the castle, in front of the Healing Dome as it had come to be known. Wild and graceful dancing ensued, from unbroken bodies, filled with an unlimited joy.

Suddenly, Heart saw Swen in his white dog suit, break through the crowd, a strange expression on what she could see of his face through his visor— probably much like when a newshound was fast upon a breaking story, she thought.

"Heart!" she saw him mouth, although she couldn't hear him.

He came up to her, and she leaned down to hear him. "Watch this, but we need quiet. *WE NEED QUIET!*"

Heart hurried up to HelperFriend, unable to tell from Swen's energy if it was good news or bad.

Whatever it was, it was huge!

"HelperFriend, stop the music, stop the music!"

He looked at her, completely mystified, and unable, without giving his very logical mind a reason why the music should stop, to shut it off.

"Swen has something important to show us. We need quiet!" she shouted above the din.

The music *SHUT. OFF.*

Dancers were practically hanging in mid-air from the shock of no sound.

Her Father and Key Man, nodding and grinning in front of the healing dome, having donned their protective suiting, gave her curious looks. She shrugged and waved at Swen, who was trotting over to Key Man, to be near him. Heart, with HelperFriend, rushed to them. Equuleus, flying above the dancers, and performing his own gorgeous ballet, with Violet stuck on his back like a burr, landed nearby.

"*What, what what!*" Violet began to chatter. "We were having a very good time, an excellent, delightful, marvelous, outstanding ...."

"Hush, Violet," Heart ordered.

Raising her little lavender rabbity eyebrows, Violet hushed.

Swen moved out in front of everyone, who crowded around him in a semicircle.

"Give him space, give him space," a few folks said, and everyone moved out a bit. But not much!

"I've been so busy with the healing, that I've not even looked to see if there was any communication from anyone. Very unlike me. Anyway, I was just now catching up, when I came to this news story."

He projected the 3-D high up so everyone could see.

The newshound on the 3-D was saying, "A great day here on Earth for all those who support *The Cause of All Beings*, which, and this newshound agrees, is anyone with heart and sanity.

"The day started with rabble-rousing and trouble-making in the streets from the Purists, all over the world …"

3-D snippets of different rowdy crowds flashed by.

"*Ohhhh …*" All the residents of Pink cried in dismay.

"It was more than any peace-keeping force could staunch …"

More images of clashes with the Purists and vastly out-numbered uniformed Peace Keepers.

"*Nooooo …*" All the residents of Pink cried louder.

"But then," the news hound's voice came over the images, "something happened," he said in hushed tones. "Something wonderful happened!

"A little girl walked out into the street, in front of one of these bands of rabble-rousers and she said— this newshound was right on the scene, eye witness to this world-changing event, which I shall never forget—she said '*Each One Reach One.*'

"She walked up to one of the Purists and started talking with him. Who knows what she said? But he changed. He changed right in front of my eyes!

"Suddenly, from all the houses, from the cars, from the streets, from the offices, all the people, the regular people, went into the streets and faced the Purists, faced them, bold and brave, even though many of them were beaten, many of them were hurt, many of them were abused.

"But the people, regular people, came from everywhere and, in the end, stopped the Purists in their tracks. By sheer numbers, chanting *'Each One Reach One'* by determination and by, I dare to suggest, the Power of Love and Kindness, *Each One Reached One*."

The 3-D flowed overhead, showing people in all parts of the world, advancing upon the Purists, taking hits, being beaten, falling before the illegal sound weapons that some of the Purist groups waved about.

"*Ahhhh! …*" All the residents of Pink cried, horrified.

"But people," the newshound continued, "the *PEOPLE*, came on, in endless phalanx of human forces, dividing and conquering, breaking up the Purists, even the bands of outlaws with illegal sound weapons, were brought down. The people were prepared. They had something they were saying that caused many of the Purists to stop where they were and join the other side, or just quietly walk away."

"*Yay! Yay! Yay! Yay! Yay! …*" The residents of Pink hollered and yelled, jumping up and down. Then they became hushed as the newshound continued.

"So remarkable! Is it not?

"This news hound had to dig deeper. What had the little girl said? That's what I had to know, to make this news story complete.

"Well, it turns out that the little girl is the much-adored baby sister of the Purist she approached. So, of course, he hesitated.

"And what she told The Purist, her brother—*wait for it!* What she told The Purist, Ladies and gentlemen and children of All Beings and All Faiths, is that *she is almost half mechanical!*

"Which was, of course, the first shocked look on his face."

The 3-D of the Purist's look of shock hovered as big as Pink's moon above the residents of Pink for a long, long moment.

"*Yay! Ohhhhhhhhhh, yay!*" The residents of Pink said softly, reverently. How they were touched!

Heart felt her own bit of internal mechanicals turn as if pulled by a magnet. She felt she might actually begin to cry. *This was too, too, too wonderful!*

"But then," the newshound continued, "that little girl revealed the greatest reveal that could ever be revealed to change this torn and troubled world.

"You see the next look unfolding on the Purist's face as he tried to protest, but the little girl tells him something more, and we see his second look of shock ...."

The Purist's second look of even greater shock hovered above them, larger and longer than the first.

"*What? What was it? What was it? What did she tell him?*" All the residents of Pink whispered.

Heart *knew*—deeply knew—what the little girl told her brother.

"The little girl," the newshound intoned, "gathered her courage and told her brother that he, too, *is not pure bio*. That he, too, is, *in part, mechanical*. You see him trying to resist it, but she tells him, right there in the street, the secret that the family had hidden the whole of this young man's life.

"She tells him that their parents had produced genetically unviable children, and they had opted to have them saved, by the integration of mechanical parts with their bio components."

The Purist's look moving from disbelief, to argument, to shock, to acceptance replayed again and again, overhead.

"The little girl refused to be interviewed on vid, but she talked with me for a few minutes privately. She said she reminded her brother of the times they'd talked about having memory blackouts, and that her parents finally told her the truth.

"This lie has been perpetuated many times over, but thousands of people, seeing how the Purists have taken society down, have revealed the non-bio components in their children and in themselves.

"This has led, today, to long, long lines at hospitals and doctors' offices and wherever they can get a 'component output,' as many people are learning what their components are.

"Well, I'm a newshound. You name it, I probably have some of it in me. So, I'm obviously not objective when I say, "Hooray for *The Cause of All Beings!* Harry Hound, over and out."

The surface of Pink exploded with joy-filled cheers and shouts and tears, even more dynamic than the interrupted dancing.

And, Heart thought, laughing and yes, even crying with everyone else, including her father and Key Man, it was celebration for a good cause. *The Cause of all Beings!*

Swen looked over at her, then trotted up to her side. "There's another, amazing news story that I'm pretty sure you'll want to see. You and your father and Key Man, and Equuleus."

"Yes?" She looked at Violet, dancing with Yippee some crazy rabbity hip-wagging dance, twirling her long, lavender ears around one another and unwinding them.

"Let's go inside." She nodded her head to Equuleus who came to her side, then got her father's eye. Key Man had already been watching the interaction between Heart and Swen with interest. They quietly slipped into her father's room.

"Swen has another news story to share with us," Heart said as she closed the second baffle.

"This would have been the big news if it hadn't been overshadowed by the even bigger news. I know you all want to see this as soon as possible."

He projected the 3-D into the semi-darkness of the room. Harry Hound appeared. "I would have thought this story would be the biggest news in some while, but other news has recently overshadowed it. Even so, this story is near and dear to my heart, as I know it is for many of you."

There appeared lots of empty buildings, empty sidewalks of various Darling Undesirables Facilities.

"Today it has been announced by several sources that the last two remaining Darling Undesirables facilities have been completely vacated. All the residents, according to reliable reports, are aboard the city-sized Gargantua."

An artist's rendition of the Gargantua, wildly ill-conceived, of a triangular, sort of brown and mountain tall, structure appeared, instead of the five-sided, sleek and black behemoth of the Gargantua. Everyone in the room chuckled. Even her father, Heart observed. So … he was familiar with the appearance of the Gargantua.

"Although," the newshound continued, "with the tempering, if not the complete undoing, of The Purists´ movement, this is not quite the issue it was with the constant threat of harm to the Darling Undesirables, and, although they have been well cared for in all the facilities, the stigma upon those children will now be removed.

"It's reported that some of them may even be adopted by genetic relatives, who are unaware of their existence.

"Anyone who wonders if there's a Darling Undesirable related to them is encouraged to contact The Darling Undesirables Home Project. Your query will be held in strictest confidence.

"Though a quieter story than the pacification of the Purists, in this news hound's personal opinion, it's a huge move in the social evolution of our planet."

"Harry Hound, over and out."

"What a guy!" Swen said under his breath.

"I can only imagine that Harry Hound was one of your closest associates when you were active in your career," Heart observed.

"He was the best, and he remains the best. How did the world find out about that little girl? Harry. Bravely shot the story that changed the world, and he's also telling the world that it's not only an option but a wonderful opportunity to make a home for our Darlings."

"We did it again," Key Man whispered, looking down, but, obviously talking to his life-long friend, Ray.

"It would appear so," her father agreed, as, unabashedly, tears streamed down his face. Heart moved to sit by him on his little cot. She took his hand and held it, utterly wordless. She felt more emotion pouring through her than she could hardly handle.

They did it.

And—so had she.

Chapter 27

A few minutes later, but long enough that they bonded over the moment, Violet crashed in upon them, forcing the interior baffle a crack open, though it was more than she could handle.

"Where is that big lump? HelperFriend, come here and *HELP!*"

"No," HelperFriend said from outside. "They are … no, it's not right."

"Oh for goodness sake, what's the matter with you?" She made a great shove and managed to fall into the room.

"What are you all doing in here? What's going on? Look at your faces. Goodness, like you've had a visitation from, I don't know. I don't actually know what I'm saying. Why aren't you outside?

Why aren't you dancing? Why are you hiding in here?

"Why, why, why? *Akkk!* You're boring! Come on, Heart, outside. Reason to smile. Not these strange, serious faces." She turned to leave indignantly, but there was no way she could open the door from the inside. "*Akkk!* Can't even leave indignantly. Heart, open the door if you please."

Heart laughed. She could always count on Violet to say the wrong thing to make her laugh. She stood and opened the door. "There you go."

Violet stood in the doorway so that it couldn't close. "Now, as you're up, come on out. Everybody's wondering where you are."

"No they're not," Heart protested.

"Well, actually," HelperFriend said from the other side of the baffles, "they are. And they're wondering where Key Man and Father Inventor and Equuleus and Swen are, as well."

Heart turned to the room and shrugged. "We are wanted."

"Nice feeling," her father said, as they all moved to join the ongoing celebration, adding to it their own, very special, triumph.

*   *

Ħeart knew the celebrations would go on and on, and why not? There was much to celebrate.

But there was much to reflect upon, as well. She slipped away from the merriment to walk behind the castle, to the little hillock she liked to sit and lean against while having a chat with Xavier. She hadn't even been out here in some time—could there be a more perfect moment for reverie?

"Ah, Xavier, so much has happened!" As she looked at the little glowing moon, she thought she could make out the pale colors of the flowers she'd had Jackson place with Xavier.

"I suppose you know it all, though. The Purists, depleted and defeated, the Darling Undesirables, all aboard the Gargantua, though I don't quite see how they will live there in an ongoing way. New, strange information from eavesdropping on my father and Key Man.

"But the one thing I must tell you, because it's the right thing to do—I mean, you're gone, and, well, it's all quite confusing, because I do still have feelings for you.

"It seems, and again, this is another thing I feel confused about, it seems I've fallen in love with Jackson. I'm not going to get into a long chat about everything I've gone through coming to this conclusion. I'm not even going to go on about how I've tried to argue myself out of it. I'm going to leave it at—it seems I've fallen in love with Jackson.

"What about Jackson? you might ask. How does he feel? I'm sure that if I can't see myself clearly, he is even more opaque. I don't expect you to solve anything here. I only thought it right to let you know."

As she fell into comfortable silence looking up at Pink's moon, she felt certain that as she stared, Xavier's face glowed, very, very faintly, but taking up the whole surface of the moon.

It was, at least, a sweet illusion.

She then heard the murmur of a couple of voices approaching. Not wanting to startle whoever it was, she sat still and quiet.

"Well, my dear Key Man," she heard Lady Gervi say, "I wanted to take this quiet walk with you because I have an immense request."

"My goodness, Lady Gervi, what could you possibly have to ask of me?"

"I could ask Heart, it's true. But, before doing that, I thought I'd run it by you, see what you think, and discover your advice."

"Oh, this is getting grander by the moment. First a request, and now advice."

"Dear me, I believe I'm making the subject bigger than it objectively is. I think I must just blurt it out."

"Yes, why not. There's only the two of us here."

And me, Heart thought ….

"I …" Lady Gervi still hesitated. "Let us sit on this little bench," she interrupted her own sentence. "It's outside the window of the room where Heart— sweet, sweet Heart—allowed me to convalesce after she and Yippee found me under the pile of stone that fell from the castle parapet during the Bot Invasion.

"My injury was terrible …."

"I know, Lady Gervi!" Key Man interjected.

"But my convalescing—changed me profoundly."

"I see," Key Man said with a tone that implied he didn't see a thing.

Heart heard them settle on the decorative and romantic little bench, and wished with all her might she could dare to turn and look at them, sitting there together. Key Man barely four feet tall almost the same dimension around, and Lady Gervi nearly seven feet tall, with lanky, long, gear limbs.

"Well, you don't see yet. But I'm about to make it more clear."

Heart couldn't wait to hear what had so profoundly changed Lady Gervi, and what her point would eventually be. If she made it!

"Heart had HelperFriend bring me books. Physical books. She asked me if I could read. I honestly didn't know if I could. I'd never had occasion to, that I could remember.

"HelperFriend brought me thirty or forty books, and I read them."

"You read them," Key Man repeated.

"I read them all. You see, I could read."

"Well, Lady Gervi, that's quite an accomplishment, reading thirty or forty books in a fairly short while."

"Yes. Short while. I had them all read long before dinner. I asked HelperFriend to bring me more books, and so, with Heart's approval, he brought me armloads of books, and I read them about as fast as he could bring me more and put the other ones back."

"Oh! Now, I say Lady Gervi, that's some reading!" Key Man said, about as impressed as Heart had ever heard him.

"Then I read hundreds of books that were not physical, on the 3-D."

"I'm speechless!"

So am I, Heart thought, although she *did* know that Lady Gervi had read voraciously while in the castle, she did not know, what her point was going to be.

"So, my point is, I would like to, ahm, love to … ahm, emigrate to Earth."

Heart heard, well, nothing from Key Man for too, too long. She almost stood thinking they had gotten up and moved. Although how, without making a sound.

"Key Man?"

"I'm, I'm trying to put together your reading with this last statement."

"Sorry. It seems so obvious to me. I was perfectly content to live here before I did all that reading. But now, I … and you know how dearly and deeply I love everyone here, but I … I feel … I mean, I've so fallen in love with Earth, for one thing. And I would love to go to a place where beings get together and study, or talk about books, or … something like that. It's not … that'll never happen here."

"Oh! Now I do see. I do see. *Hmmmmmm …*"

Heart could hear his synapses firing all the way to where she was.

"What are you thinking?" Lady Gervi asked.

"Well, my question was going to be, where would you live, what would you do? But then I thought, but wait, we need some help at The Museum of Scientific Improbabilities and Unpredictable Oddities."

"Oh! Oh my! Too amazing. Too amazing!" Lady Gervi exclaimed. "That was exactly my next question. Do you think there might be a job for me at the museum?"

"Great minds think along similar lines, my dear."

"Yes. My dear," Lady Gervi replied.

Wait! Heart thought. What's that tone?

"I think we can try to put through your request," Key Man said. Followed by a strange silence. "Is it possible," he asked softly, "is it at all possible you … have feelings for me, as well as Earth?"

"Not possible, dear Key Man. Ever since you created this beautiful leg, that so matched my other one, and I could feel your creative genius running through it, I … I fell in love with you."

"That's because," Key Man replied, his tone ever softening, "I became utterly fascinated with the beauty I imagined you must be, from the grace of that gorgeous limb. I asked Heart as many questions as I could about you, without, I hoped sounding sort of ridiculous.

"Then, when I saw you—and I did, the instant we landed—I was—that was it. I was gone, head over short little heels for you, on sight.

"But all of that is nothing compared to how I've really fallen in love with you during the healings. How kind you are. How solicitous. How intuitive."

"Oh, Key Man!" Lady Gervi cried. "And we both have dogs!"

Heart almost chuckled out loud. It was true! How different their dogs from other dogs and how different their dogs from one another didn't matter in the least.

They both had dogs!

Then it was far too quiet for far too long, and Heart knew that they were sealing the moment with some gesture of affection, though with Key Man's protective suit it would, of necessity, be most chaste.

Well! Love! It will always find where it means to go, Heart thought. They might look like the most improbable couple. But their values and feelings and character and personalities—a perfect couple!

"So sweet," Key Man murmured.

"Ummm," Lady Gervi agreed.

"We'll have to find Heart and convince her to take you and Yippee to Earth. We'll have room, as the parts container is now empty."

They got up and wandered off. Heart hoped they were not extremely intent upon finding her immediately.

And she also hoped she would act appropriately surprised and joyful when they asked her if Lady Gervi and Yippee could go to Earth on the return trip.

*   *

As it turned out, neither Key Man nor Lady Gervi was the least bit shy about announcing their romance.

"And," Key Man said quite enthusiastically, "given that the container of repair parts is now empty, there's plenty of room for Lady Gervi and Yippee to come back to Earth with us."

"I can't argue," Heart said, trying to contain her grin. "But, tell me how all this happened. We've been working around the clock, when did you and Lady Gervi even have a chance to discover love?"

"Ah, Heart, you're the one who preaches love. You know it will always find its way."

"Yes, my dearest Key Man, I tend to have great faith in love. Well, with all the changes on Earth, I'm anxious to be there. So I'm waiting on your go-ahead to get ready to leave."

Key Man nodded. "I want to assure that everyone's healing is successful before leaving, although your father is entirely capable of handling any complications if any arise."

"He is, of course." As much as Heart wanted to get back to Earth, a sadness washed over her at again separating from her father. "We'll leave for Earth as soon as you say."

And thus it was only one more Pink day before Heart was checking over the *Heart!* in preparation for departure.

Suddenly, she had quite the passenger list. Various adjustments needed to be done to the *Heart!* And she had a couple of Pink's most talented fabricators help her figure out who would ride where, and how to accommodate them.

They welded in the back two seats for Key Man and Lady Gervi and installed safety harnesses. Beside Lady Gervi they constructed two little compartments, one for Yippee, one for Violet.

Yes, Heart said to herself, despite Violet's noise and distraction, she could not leave Pink, this time, without her.

Or because of her noise and distraction. Not to mention how inseparable she and Yippee had become, it would be a cruelty to part them. But, of course, she didn't *tell* Violet she was taking her! Oh, not yet!

Then, alongside the compartments for Yippee and Violet, a compartment for Swen. Slight magnets were built in for this whole seating matrix, which could be increased if necessary.

Then Heart had the fabricators divide the cupboard spaces: a space for Lady Gervi and Yippee's things, a space for HelperFriend's things—whatever they may be! A space for Violet's things, which, Heart knew, would be a big argument about all she'd "have to take."

And then, yes, she could no longer stand her guilt over that sad bit of sentience, in stasis in her father's laboratory, she had a hidden away space, double-metal lined, with extra metallic harnessing, built for the Clone's legs. They would not be visible to anyone, which, there was no denying, was a disturbing sight.

But during the entire process, she could not relinquish her great sadness that her father was not also coming. She knew he could not simply abandon all the beings on Pink who needed him there as a parent, as a friend.

She could not extinguish, nor even subdue, the great sadness in herself that she had no idea when she might return to Pink. There would be so much work for her to do on Earth now. But oh! Pink and all its sweet, kind, loving, emotionally transparent, darling residents had taken up a place in her that would never, never go away.

Ah! Two homes! Always missing one, while at the other. She looked up at Earth, ever and ever over-head, gorgeous green and blue. Soon, soon to be there, *and to live free!* It was a compelling, magnetic, thought.

She cleared her mind of the conflicting thoughts, the confusing feelings, and focused, again, on all she must attend to.

Celebration still reigned over Pink as all the beautiful, newly healed residents strutted happily about, hugging and being hugged, adoring and being adored, one by all and all by one, no one really realizing that Heart was preparing to leave this safe harbor.

She was glad that was so, as she slipped about, taking care of details. Only the two mechanicals who assisted in all the details had an idea that something was up, sworn to silence. And the passengers—with the exception of Violet—knew what was pending, and they, too, kept quiet about their departure, join-ing in the celebration as if there was no tomorrow.

But, sure enough, tomorrow did arrive. Heart sat quietly outside the *Heart!* in its place inside the dome, trying to think nothing, having gone over the list of what needed to be done for the last and final time.

Geometria appeared, suddenly, beside her. "Ah! Heart! Leaving us … so soon."

She looked down at the mystical being, holding his geometric box. It rested quietly at present in his hands, a slightly rectangular box, lavender and pink, blue and green floating upon its surface, looking rather much like an open box.

"Yes. Of course, you know exactly what's about to transpire," she answered, looking curiously at the little box. "Tell me, am I seeing correctly? Does your geometric shape look like an open box?"

Geometria looked down at the shape in his hands, feigning surprise at its presence. "Well, hmmm … this shape … oh! These colors—see how united Pink and Earth are. Finally. Finally comes the day, I see these colors coming together, as I sit next to you, dear Heart. You have brought it all together.

"And the box? Well, what will you put in it? The future unfolds," the box flattened out to a flat, two-dimensional surface, much to Heart's surprise, as she'd never seen Geometria's geometrical shape be anything other than three-dimensional. "And the past folds up." The flat shape rolled up and seemed to disappear right out of Geometria's hands.

But he still held his hands as if it remained. "Just because it cannot be seen doesn't mean it's not still here. All that you have done, Heart, is still here. Has changed the shape of things forever."

Geometria stood. "Well, I must be off and away. The celebrations continue, and I really am having such a good time. Thank you, Heart, for that."

"Well, ah, you're welcome, Geometria. I will miss you!"

"Not necessary, my own Heart. Not necessary …." He faded into the dark recesses of the gigantic dome.

Soon, Heart stood too. She must do one or two things, then it would be time to get her passengers aboard.

She wandered through the residents of Pink, calling to her, smiling and dancing, as she wended her way through the dome, then outside to the front of the castle.

She came to the first greenhouse, stepped through the double baffle, and walked among her wonderful, aromatic, friendly, comforting flowers. Here they had grown, and here they would stay.

There had arisen a group known as "Heart's Flowers Folks" among the residents, and she knew they would always care for and cherish her beautiful flowers. But, oh! It was hard to leave them! She must be strong and say good-bye, giving them love now, and knowing she would send love in the future, as love knows no distance.

She caressed several of their cheerful faces as she passed along the little path, but she knew she dared not stop, for fear of never moving again. Oh, some part of her could sit here forever!

She passed through the back baffle and went into the neighboring greenhouse, smiling a sweet, sad smile, recalling the day she and HelperFriend and Equuleus first erected the greenhouses.

Such memories were being created, and, at the time, she didn't even know it. At the time, she was sad at the thought of never being on Earth again.

And now, the day had arrived when she was sad, not knowing if she would ever be on Pink again.

"Keep this for everyone," she said, stooping over to kiss a delphinium. Then she exited through the front door baffles and did not look back.

She entered the front door of the castle, where Equuleus waited for her. "It's not easy," he said sympathetically.

"No. Much harder than one would have thought. Shall we?"

"We shall, we must."

Heart jumped on Equuleus, and he swept up and around, and up and around, in the Castle's rotunda, in the mystical fragile pink light of Pink, Pink's silvery little glowing moon peering in at them through the curved windows above.

Equuleus alighted with a gentle swoosh on the landing and they went into Heart's rooms. She wandered through them, looking for anything she must take. But there was nothing. Everything she wanted or needed was still in her unpacked bag, in the *Heart!*—her plaids, the paisley blanket, her little photo album. She picked up a couple of odd little bits she'd seen Violet attached to and put them in a small satchel.

She turned to Equuleus. "And you, Equuleus, anything from these rooms you would like to take?"

"Only you, Heart. That's all I need."

She patted him as they stepped back out onto the landing. "One last time," she said. Equuleus leaped from the landing and took a long, long time to sweep down, and down and down, lazily as if he had all of eternity.

HelperFriend appeared below, with a satchel on his shoulder, ready to depart, sending tiny metal tears in every direction, making delicate chiming music off the marble floor and mahogany balustrade. "So beautiful, so beautiful, so beautiful!" he repeated.

"Thank you, HelperFriend. Are you all right?"

"Yes. No. Yes. No. Oh, Heart, I'm all right and I'm not all right. How can that be? How can that be? I'm very literal. This is … not possible. It's … not possible!"

"Oh yes, dear friend, it's entirely possible! Equuleus and I are having the same feelings. We're all right and we're not all right. We're looking forward to being on Earth, we're not looking forward to not being here. That's part of life. To have conflicting emotions, and to do the wisest thing possible, anyway."

"I see. I see. Well, no, I don't exactly. But, what do we do with these conflicting emotions?"

"We do the next thing, and the next thing, and the next thing. Right now, I need you to quietly put the Clone's legs aboard the *Heart!*, make sure they are secure. Have they done anything lately?"

"No, Heart. They're completely inert. Not making a single move or anything." He cheered visibly, having a specific assignment.

"Very good. If you would slip them into the *Heart!* without being seen and get them stowed away, that would be helpful."

"I can do that. I can go the back way. No one is out back now, they're all still celebrating."

"Then, if you would collect Violet, kicking and screaming, until I tell her what's about to happen, I'm sure. But, as you know, I don't want her going off on a million different tangents before we're ready for take-off. I'm giving Key Man and Swen our sign that we're ready and they'll gather Lady Gervi and Yippee.

"I'll be with my father, in his room. When you come with Violet, I'll signal the mechanical who's standing by to bring out the *Heart!* And then, we'll be off."

"Oh, Heart!" HelperFriend began to cry again.

"One thing at a time, dear HelperFriend. Right now, Clone legs in the *Heart!*"

"Yes!" He scurried off to the back of the castle. Heart slipped off Equuleus and the two of them walked down the long hall toward her father's room.

She stepped into the library on the way, went up to the mantle, kissed her fingertips and pressed them to the image of her young and innocent mother, turned and walked swiftly out of the room, to continue down the hall, past the dining hall, past the kitchen, and then, into her father's room. The two mechanicals who had been making the improvements on the *Heart!* were chatting with him.

"We're ready," she said.

One of the mechanicals nodded, and turned to taxi the *Heart!* out. They had been all business, but now, both of their metallic faces reflected the sadness pervading the moment.

"Thank you," she said to them, which felt woefully inadequate.

"Oh, Heart, no! Thank you!" the nearer one said. "You've done so much for us, and we … we …."

"We love you," the other one said, and quickly exited through the door baffles.

"Yes, we love you. We all love you!" And he followed his partner.

"I love you too," Heart said. "I love you all, too." Looking after them, almost unable to turn to look at her father.

But she finally did. "Oh, Father, how can I leave you? How?"

He came to her and put his arms around her. "Ah! My girl, my amazing girl! You're not leaving me, you're going to your future. I am always with you, you know that, don't you?"

"Yes. In this poetic, pretty way, yes. But in the 'what has HelperFriend made for dinner?' way, no."

He chuckled. "You are *sooooooo* lovable!"

"You too, are *sooooooooo* lovable." But she felt strange that he seemed not really to be processing her departure. It left her feeling a bit unhinged.

"*What. Is. Going. On?*" they heard Violet screech.

Heart looked toward the door, and there stood HelperFriend, holding Violet, who squirmed and wriggled—and protested. HelperFriend looked in, not knowing what to do.

"Come in," Heart called to him.

He came through the double doors and stood awkwardly, looking from Heart to Father Inventor, while Violet did the same.

"I repeat," Violet cried indignantly, "*what is up?*"

Heart saw the *Heart!* taxi out through the dome, all the celebrating Folks becoming somber at the sight.

Key Man and Swen, in their protective suits, came into the little room behind HelperFriend. Key Man stepped around HelperFriend, and Heart stepped back to let him give her father a parting hug. "Be well, my friend," her father said.

"And you. Until we meet again," Key Man replied.

Violet, still facing away from the outside windows and not seeing the *Heart!* outside, looked at everyone in turn. "*You guys are going to Earth!* And you have this hulk holding onto me so I can't go ballistic, bonkers, loco, cuckoo, nuts. *Well*," she squealed at a new level of previously unheard squealing, "*I. Can. Still. Go. Nutty-raving!*"

"You're going with us," Heart said quietly, rolling her eyes.

"I. Ahm. *What?*" Violet said, bemused.

"You're going with us. Though I'm a little bit, right now, wondering why. And I'm sure, if you're going to act out anything like this on the journey, my passengers will wonder why you're with us, as well."

"*No!* You, Heart, you're taking me with you to Earth?"

"I am. Unless you want to stay here."

"Stay here? Why would I do that? What's for me here? Well, Yippee, that's true. It'll be hard to leave Yippee. But, we'll come back some time, won't we, I mean, I won't have to leave Yippee forever, will I?"

"Not at all. Yippee and Lady Gervi are coming with us."

As if on cue, Lady Gervi came to the door. Looking in at the crowded room, she remained outside.

"Weeeeeeeee! Oh! Oh! Someone tell me, am I dreaming? Is it possible? Oh! Oh! Weeeeeeeee! Well, then, put me down, you big hulk. I must gather my things, and prepare myself. There's much to do, much to do …."

"Let's go," Heart said to the group. "I have all you need, right here, Violet. Enough histrionics."

"No!" Violet squealed, "I must …."

"HelperFriend, if you would kindly hush Violet so we can all *think!"*

HelperFriend put his hand over Violet's mouth, and she hushed. Her eyes rolled around expressively, but, thankfully, not a sound was heard.

Heart opened the door and HelperFriend, carrying Violet, stepped through the baffles, next Equuleus went out. Heart saw that the mechanical had lowered the hatch, and Equuleus went directly aboard.

Father Inventor got into his bell jar, while Key Man and Swen exited. Then she held the door while her father rolled outside.

The gaiety had come to a sudden halt as everyone formed a long line along the path of the *Heart!'s* soon departure.

Heart followed her varied and fascinating, group of passengers into the *Heart!*, assuring that Equuleus was comfortably situated, and his magnetics turned on. Then checking that Lady Gervi's safety harness was properly latched, that Yippee and the entirely overly excited Violet were in their little cubby holes, that Key Man was latched in, and Swen in his special place. After they were well and truly on their way, she would help Key Man and Swen out of their protective suits. No longer needed!

Then she stepped back out to wave to everyone and say a few final words. She waved, but no words came.

"I love you. I have nothing more to say than that I love you all!" She turned and went back into the *Heart!*

"Safety harness latched?" she asked HelperFriend.

"Safety harness latched," he affirmed.

She closed the hatch.

"Ready for take-off." She fired the engines, gave a sad wave and blew a kiss to her father, and without further ceremony, lifted off.

Chapter 28

With the exception of Violet's incessant babble, until even Yippee, it seemed, protested, and the nonstop cooing endearments between Key Man and Lady Gervi, and Violet's *additional* babble about, look how amazing that Key Man and Lady Gervi fell in love, and if they could do it, anyone could do it … with the exception of all of that, the journey was uneventful.

They landed at The Museum of Scientific Improbabilities and Unpredictable Oddities openly, no fear of detection by the Purists, with Martha and WonderMan One and WonderMan Two waiting for them at the back entrance, all three of them grinning, which was quite unusual for the WonderMen, Heart thought.

She turned off the restraining magnetics and opened the hatch. Heart unlatched her safety harness and helped Lady Gervi unlatch hers, Key Man was already out of his, and had let Swen out. HelperFriend let out Yippee and handed him to Lady Gervi, while Violet squealed and squawked to be let out.

Then, with all the pomp and ceremony he could produce, Key Man offered Lady Gervi his arm. She took it, and the two of them, attended by their dogs, stepped out of the *Heart!* followed by Equuleus, HelperFriend, and finally, Heart took Violet out of her cubby hole and exited, while watching Violet closely for any signs of reaction to the Earth environment.

Heart was sure she'd be all right in the real Earth environment but wanted to watch her closely, just the same, taking no chances. She'd told Key Man to watch Lady Gervi and Yippee for any signs of negative effects as well.

"*Ohhhh*," Lady Gervi said, a bit alarmed. "I feel very—heavy! Even Yippee feels heavy."

Yippee, apparently agreed, with a string of alarming sounding Yippee-ish.

"Me too, me too!" Violet ranted. "*Too heavy!*"

"You're all fine," Heart reassured. It's Earth's gravity. I told you about it. You're fine. You'll soon get used to it."

Martha had rushed up to them all smiles but stepped back at the sound of alarm and complaints. As soon as she heard what Heart said, she hurried up to them again. "Oh yes, Earth's gravity. Nothing to worry about. So glad to meet you, so glad to see you. Oh, Lady Gervi, I've heard lovely things about you! It's wonderful to have you here. And Yippee, what a darling!" Her irresistible smile of circles spread throughout the group.

"And *Violet!* Oh, my, Violet! It is such a delight to finally meet you!"

"You know about me? You know about me already?" Violet's ears twitched about to frame her face, engaging Martha with her wide, lavender eyes.

"Well, of course, dear! Your fame precedes you. *Of course!*" Martha smiled upon Violet with her own special smile.

Heart stood in awe of Martha's wisdom. *Ah! Violet would be her devoted champion forever!*

*   *

Ḣeart knew that Lady Gervi, Key Man, Swen and Yippee would take over her much-adored little room behind the sheltered wall of Key Man's workrooms as part of their living space, which she'd previously imagined would continue to be her own particular place, were she to stay on Earth an extended period of time.

Equuleus always had a place at The Museum of Scientific Improbabilities and Unpredictable Oddities. Even little Violet fit in everywhere— hanging out with Yippee, or as a most interesting and unusual hybrid mechanical and bio in the museum, appreciated by all those who loved Father Inventor's creations.

But where, Heart wondered, did *she* fit in?

The group had retired to the museum lunchroom to become acquainted, with Heart trailing after them. Martha immediately bonded with Lady Gervi, not only making her feel welcome but relating to her every bit as much as Key Man did.

However, as Heart's discomfort with her own sense of not fitting in grew, she noticed Martha watching her, and although she tried to nod and grin and appear to be engaged in all the conversation, she could not fake it.

"Carry on, dear friends," Martha suddenly said. "Key Man, I know you'll get everyone situated. I'm sure, Violet, you won't mind spending the night with Yippee and Swen. Heart and I must bid you good evening, as we have much to discuss and plan. We'll see you all on the morrow!"

Waving and grinning and hugging everyone as she went, she finally took Heart by the hand. They left the lunchroom and exited the museum by the back entrance, crossing the road to Martha's darling-gaudy little cottage.

"Whew! Exhausting, all that smiling stuff! I need to make a big pot of tea."

"I thought you loved it." Heart followed Martha into her kitchen. "I thought you loved all that smiling, and hugging and chatting and story-telling—stuff."

"I do. But, it *does* get exhausting. Then I escape here, to my safe-zone."

"Yes," Heart agreed, refusing to look at all the eyes in all the images in the front room that seemed to follow her right into the kitchen. "Definitely a safe-zone. So close, and yet so far, as long as everyone knows to leave you to your space."

"Oh, trust me, they do!" Martha giggled at her own, much more aggressive, side. She fussed about the kitchen doing one thing and then the next, but Heart didn't even pay attention, instead trying to picture an angry Martha.

Martha finally had a tray piled high. "Let's go back in the front room and settle on the comfy divan."

"All right," Heart said a bit reluctantly, not really inclined, at the moment, to be under all those two-dimensional and three-dimensional stares.

As they settled on the divan, Heart sat facing away from the wall, feeling strange and uncomfortable. She could sense Martha was about to spring something on her. She wanted to run away. She'd almost, she thought, rather be facing a multi-limbed bot—at least she knew what it was.

"It's so amazing, the Purists, undone, just like that!" Heart began, thrashing about for a subject. They'd all gone on and on about the Purists being undone in the lunchroom, and Heart didn't really want to talk about it—she wanted to go out and see it for herself. But she chatted on, as Martha went through her choreographed tea ritual. "All the Darling Undesirables, out of their prisons."

"Yes. Amazing things are happening," Martha agreed. "An amazing thing is happening right now, as we sit here, that has not hit the news yet. An amazing thing."

"What? What is it, Martha?"

"This very minute, as we speak, Jackson is turning off the dark energy in The Wall." Martha handed her a teacup, and Heart nearly dropped it.

"This. Very. Minute?"

"This. Very. Minute."

"How do you know?"

"Because he's talking to me, as we chat." Martha pushed a button on her vintage earring. Or, on what looked like a vintage earring.

"Here goes! Flipping a small switch for huge freedom," Jackson's voice entered the room.

Heart heard the echo of a switch being thrown. And she was certain she felt something release right into her bones. *"Martha!"* she whispered. "Did you feel that?"

"I did, my dear."

"Heart? *Heart?*" Jackson said.

"Here with me, dear boy," Martha answered, when Heart, too shocked at being addressed, said nothing.

"Back on Earth? Right." And he tuned out.

"The Wall—off? Off!" Heart exclaimed. "I can cross it? I can go under it? I can fly Equuleus over it? I don't have to be wrapped up in the paisley blanket?"

"That's right my dear. Not only over it and under it, but, all along The Wall, right now, people are making doorways and passageways. Which is why Jackson broke off so abruptly. He's directing a massive event, where The Wall, beautiful in its own right, is not going to be taken down altogether, but many charming walkways and roads are being built through it."

"Oh, Martha! *I can visit Eye!*"

"Yes whenever you please."

"Jackson is … he's …."

"I know, dear Heart. He certainly is. And you are too!" She couldn't resist crinkling her face up into all its happy "O's" and half-moons. "But! We have much to discuss, so … how's your tea?"

"My tea? … It's fine," Heart took her first sip to prove the point. "Fine. Discuss what? I want to contemplate Jackson turning off The Wall."

"I know you do, I know you do. I'm like that too! I like to contemplate things when they're new to me. But, I'm sorry Heart, you can't do that right now. Much needs to transpire. And for that all to happen, you must first learn much." She waved at the walls. "To begin, I must tell you that you are related to every single being on these walls."

"No," Heart protested.

"Yes. Every single one. The mechanicals and clockworks, you're not genetically related to, obviously, but every being in these images has contributed to some part of your present being.

"Of course, you are mostly bio, and it's your dark energy and dark matter components that make you impervious to environments that would destroy someone like me, who is entirely bio. Well, almost." She chuckled at her private secret. "If we had all the time in the world, which we don't, but some other day I'll go around the room and tell you how you're related to each individual in these images.

"But your bios are from your mother and your father, on the mantle there. The image that so fascinated you when you were last here.

"Now you need to brace yourself, my darling Heart. In that picture, with the light of love in their eyes, your parents are both *touching you*, as well. You may note, if you look close, that it appears your father is touching your mother, and she has her hand over his, and there's a glow in their touch. They are both touching you. She was four months pregnant with you at the time this image was shot." Martha stopped talking and watched Heart closely.

"What? No. That picture is—I don't know, really, as much as two hundred years old."

"More, actually. The sad part of the story is that your mother died of heart failure two months after this picture was taken. Your father, insane with grief, removed you from your Mother's womb and put you in stasis."

"Put … me … in … stasis?"

"Hid you away in his laboratory—where you have recently been, in fact."

Heart tried to picture what Martha was saying, and she could very well picture a fetus in the place where the top half of the clone was at the present moment. But again, it must be impossible. "Does this make any sense?"

"It makes perfect sense, dearest."

"But—*here I am!*"

"Yes. Thanks to your sister."

"My … my … *sister?!?*"

"Rose."

"Rose was my mother's name."

"Yes. And your sister's name. About twenty-five years ago, it looked for a while like the Purists' were getting tired of their nonsense. Raymond, your father, would come to Earth by way of the Mechanical Aurora Borealis, now and then. He felt the social environment had changed, and he thought he might be able to return to Earth. He also decided he wanted a child. But—not you. You were too delicate.

"Peter, who is his closest and oldest friend, told him that the illusion of the Purists being peaceful was not true. But Raymond had a longing, and he went forward with producing a test tube baby with his and Rose's genetics. He made sure that baby was petite like Rose and had her facial bone structure, but *his* heart, which is very strong.

"Of course, Peter was correct, and there was one right awful witch hunt for Raymond, as people were claiming to have seen Father Inventor. Which—they had."

"So he asked us, Peter, and Key Man, and me, *begged us!*, to raise the beautiful little Rose. Of course, we agreed. We adored her. The tiny room upstairs is her room."

"*Oh! Oh!* The tiny room for the tiny girl!" Heart cried, still trying to grasp the idea that she had a sister. "I accidentally eavesdropped on Key Man and Father, and they were saying, "she's so amazing. And, ego-centric that I am, I assumed they were talking about me, and then Key Man, said 'I remember when she was five,' and then I knew they *were not* talking about me. So … it was Rose."

Martha chuckled. "That must have been quite a shock to hear. But, you're right. That's who they were talking about."

"So, one day," Martha continued, "Peter took Rose to your father's laboratory. He regularly went there to cross over to visit The Mystic and occasionally to leave Rose there, when we felt things were not safe here.

"After a while, Rose would often request to stay at The Mystic's cottage. Well, I don't need to explain that! Stuck here, or be there in the beautiful forest, with her little friends, Zack and Amdrona, the two orphans The Mystic took in as her own."

"Zack and Amdrona … orphans," Heart repeated.

"Well … one day, when Rose was about twelve, Peter left her at the laboratory, because things were not good on both sides of The Wall. In fact, it was agreed that The Mystic, Zack, and Amdrona would hide away in the laboratory too if things didn't calm down.

"Anyway, being an exceptionally brilliant girl, definitely her father's daughter, she went exploring, getting into every nook and cranny she could get into. And she came upon you. There, in stasis for ever so long, with a label that read: 'Rose's baby.'"

"Oh, Rose became furious, enraged. She insisted that Raymond come to Earth and explain himself. She *demanded* he come to Earth. She was truly impossible. A beautiful sight to see!" Martha chuckled again at the memory.

"Well, he came. We hid away in the back of the museum for two days while she ranted at him for keeping this baby in stasis all that time. He tried to argue that she herself was not that much different, being a test tube baby from the bios of himself and his wife. But she said, no, it was *not* the same. You were a viable human, with half a year plus around two-hundred-and-thirty years of just—who knew what?—thinking? Feeling? She swore she would never talk to him again until he made you viable.

"And *she would not talk to him!* Raymond was grief-stricken that the little bit of interaction he'd previously had with her was gone, and, even worse, that she appeared to hate him. He didn't know what to do. The fact was, it was clear that you had your mother's heart. And—he couldn't bring himself to bring you out of stasis and let you develop.

"It was, candidly, hard on all of us. Very hard. Your father flew into a new frenzy of heart research. And he finally came to a stunning discovery. He figured out how to make a heart from components of the strongest hearts he knew, and he asked certain people if they'd be willing to donate a bit of their heart to the cause.

"Your heart, in Equuleus, is composed of genetic bits from your father, Peter, Key Man, me, and your sister, Rose."

Breathlessly, Heart whispered, "While I listened to my father and Key Man's conversation, Key Man said, 'all of our hearts are in her heart.' He meant it literally."

Martha nodded.

"But, wait, how does it happen that the strongest hearts are just—you all?"

"Well, of course, there are other strong hearts, but, yes, our hearts are unusually strong. As it happens, except for Peter, we are genetically linked."

"Genetically linked ... you're all related?"

"Yes."

"So ... you are related to me?" Heart asked, her confusion mounting.

"Yes."

"My, father's side of the family—You're my ... Aunt?"

"No."

"Then, what?"

Chapter 29

You, Heart, are *my* great, great, great, great, great aunt's niece."

"*I … oh … ah … oh … well … hmmmm ….*" And beyond that, Heart was not able to make a real word.

"I will let you contemplate that for a few moments. I have something to give you. I'll be right back. Don't go anywhere."

I couldn't stand up and go anywhere right now, Heart thought, *if the house were engulfed in flames.*

Martha soon returned and placed a package in Heart's lap. "For you, Heart. From *The Nieces.*"

Heart looked down at the package and began to unwrap it. The Nieces. *The Nieces. Ourbook* prophecy was being fulfilled, whether she liked it or not.

She slowly unwrapped the beautifully wrapped gift, and soon revealed a stunning plaid outfit, in royal purple and delicate lavender, in spiritual gold and sun-drenched yellow.

It was a plaid as she had never seen, and it pulsed, delighted, in her hands.

"Oh, excellent!" Martha said, observing the plaid's pulsing colors in response to Heart's touch. *"Excellent!"*

"The Nieces …."

"Yes, Heart. All through the years, down through the generations, 'The Nieces'—on both sides of the family, the delicate, beautiful, loving, artistic nieces of your mother, and the equally beautiful—except me, of course—robust, loving, scientific-minded nieces of your father …."

"Wait! You're *SOOOO* beautiful, Martha!" Heart almost shouted, coming out of her trance. "Sooo beautiful! You let me believe in myself that day in the museum when I was just about to give up. I mean, I was all but broken. I was going to give up. I only didn't because of Eye.

"But you treated me like a person. You and Peter winked at me. And that said, 'we love you,' like no one had ever. Not even Eye could show me that special secret love, only because he doesn't have eyes of course, but … Oh no, oh no, Martha, you will never, never, *never* get to say you are not beautiful.

"And if I'm your great, great, great, great, great cousin—*or whatever!*—then you'd better respect me, and *do as I say!!!"*

"Oh, Martha, among all the stunning plaids you've given me my whole life—and, when I was little, I didn't even know where they came from, you've now given me the most powerful, and precious plaid ever. You and the generations of *The Nieces*. My beautiful mother's nieces and father's nieces. This fabric, this map of life, all the plaids, alive, animate, protecting me, helping me forge my life, even when I've been alone. Or thought I was alone.

"You and *The Nieces*, down through the years, wove this mystical fabric, and you, Martha, my father's great, great, great, great, great, niece, you sewed it into my garments of protection and direction.

"So much makes sense now. Well, not everything. *But so much!!!*" Heart paused, exhausted. "Sorry. You were saying?"

They both burst out in uncontrollable gales of laughter.

"It makes sense," Heart finally whispered. "Where is my sister?"

"I'm coming to that." Martha reached around and picked up the picture frame that Heart thought she'd done something with the last time she was here, but saw nothing in the frame. Martha set the frame on the antique coffee table, beside the antique tea tray.

"Ready?"

"I have no idea!" Heart answered, still reeling from … *everything*.

"Let us visit the Gargantua."

"All right." Was her sister a Darling Undesirable? No. That wouldn't be right. She would have aged out years ago.

The interior of the Gargantua appeared in the picture frame. Hundreds of children were shown in rotating snippets, in classrooms, on a playground, in adorable beds shaped like hummingbirds and flowers.

"Oh, it's very sweet," Heart exclaimed happily. "Wonderful, Martha, but surely they cannot live forever on the Gargantua? Floating around in the sky. Or even on land. They need real outdoors, real sun, real flowers in real earth."

"Each step in turn, darling Heart. Each step in turn."

Suddenly, Peter's face appeared, more huge than life. "Hi, Martha. Well, well, and Heart! In Martha's cottage. Sooo good to see you! Have you been taking the tour?"

"We've just begun," Martha answered.

"Well, I see this means I probably have a few things to do. I'd better get at them."

"Yes, you'd better, my friend," Martha agreed.

"Bye now. See you soon!"

"Right-o!"

Peter's face clicked off and they were treated, once again, to a large group of Darling Undesirable children, their deformities of no importance to any of them, laughing and playing, a couple of keepers cuddling them, and playing with them. The shot was at a distance, and it was difficult to make out details. But one keeper turned, and Heart blanched.

"*There, there!*" she whispered, pointing. "There, Martha. *Keeper A.* The leader of the Purists. The most horrible human being."

"You mean, Rose?"

"*No! No! Keeper A. Keeper A!*" Heart was so agitated, she feared she would begin to shout, and Keeper A would know she'd been discovered. She'd try to escape and get the Purists agitated again.

Martha reached for the frame and shut the image off.

"Keeper A is Rose. Is your sister. Is, in fact, your baby sister. Technically."

"No! N*o-no-no-no-no-no!* She's … that's …." Oh, it all came crashing upon Heart. The shape of her mother's face in the pictures, the shape of Keeper A's face. The eternal image of her profile, meting out abuse, all her childhood. Yes. Beautiful. So Beautiful. Heart never denied that. But—a terrible, terrible beauty. A cruel beauty.

"No, Martha. If that is my sister, it's terrible! She's a terrible person. A mean person."

"Just exactly how so, Heart?"

"She put Eye in the deprivation chamber when I stayed at The Museum of Scientific Improbabilities and Unpredictable Oddities."

"Yes, Heart, that was bad. She regrets that, but I'll let her tell you herself."

"She was always punishing me. She was always singling me out."

"I completely understand, Heart. But let's look at it from her side. First, she demanded that her father 'give you life' as she put it. He finally did, at her insistence, but with the stipulation that she be responsible for you, as he could not.

"He said he would not put the three of us through more of his unnatural requests. Although we would have done it, and happily. But, anyway, Rose agreed. Then, your father hit upon the idea of putting your unnaturally strong heart, by dark energy means, in an unnaturally strong body."

"Equuleus."

"Yes. Equuleus. Well, then, you qualified as a Darling Undesirable. Legally an orphan, and, without a body part, most especially a heart, you were, by legal definition ..."

"A Darling Undesirable."

"Right again. So Rose agreed to do everything in her power to become Keeper A—no lesser station would suffice for any of us because we all understood the power plays of the most prestigious Darling Undesirable Facility ...."

"The Darling Undesirable Facility at Long Prairie."

"You are unraveling this mystery quiet excellently, my own Heart.

"Your father saw to it that Rose got hired on as an assistant to the previous Keeper A, who'd been saying she wanted to step down from the position. Your father has many, many strings he can pull. People have no idea that it is he who is behind the scenes.

"Anyway, Rose was a bit younger than you are now, only fifteen when she came into the assistant position. So, three years later, when the previous Keeper A retired, Rose stepped into the position. So very young for so much responsibility. *But so brilliant!*

"Because of the dedication she showed, your father then came to Earth in the Mechanical Aurora Borealis without telling her and set up a lab in the back of the clockworks wing in the museum. He started your heart, put it in Equuleus, took you out of stasis, and connected you to your heart by dark energy.

"*Pins and needles!* Peter, Key Man, your father, Equuleus, and I, were on pins and needles. What would happen?

"What happened is that you opened your beautiful eyes in that amniotic fluid and you smiled! Smiled at us, fully aware and present and just, brilliant and beautiful. Your heart, in Equuleus, beat strong and healthy, no doubt the strongest heart in the world.

"And so you were born. Oh, my, so sad and so amazing, your father sat and held you all night long, talking to you, loving you. You lay there, taking it all in, watching him, So, so alert, so beautiful!

"He had told Rose he was going to attempt to fulfill her demand, but … it was possible the worst might happen. So we hadn't told her about this incredible event. We didn't want her to see the worst if that's what happened. And I must say, my dear Heart, we really did anticipate the worst. Your father didn't but the rest of us did.

"For the next couple months he infused you with dark matter treatments, which treatments we'd all had and were familiar with. The two of you spent quite a lot of time in Rose's little room, where he sang to you and talked to you of your mother, and the stars, and Pink."

"That's why the room feels so familiar, that's why I love stars so much, that's why I always longed to go to Pink, Heart whispered. "And … and that's why I knew I had a mother, even if I was a Darling Undesirable!"

Martha nodded. "Yes, dearest of Hearts. But then your father told us he was going to give you dark energy treatments.

"The connection of your heart to you through Equuleus had been frightening enough and we protested vehemently, because, once again, we believed your little body would not tolerate this unknown. And we'd all fallen so much in love with you.

"But, he did it anyway. The results for him were *not* unknown. And the result sits before me, in all her shining glory, right now.

"Then, with Rose as Keeper A of The Darling Undesirables Facility at Long Prairie, you was 'discovered' on the doorstep, left there by your very own father.

"He arrived by way of the underground crystal matrix. Which, itself, is the result of another of his amazing inventions, a machine that digs through dirt like it's water, and turns all the rocks it encounters into a momentarily melted, hard as diamonds, completely enclosing surface, so that, even if the tunnel is quite close to the surface, it's extremely strong.

"In fact, your father was shocked by your cleverness when you figured a way to destroy a bit of the crystal matrix, in order to break out."

"Like father, like daughter," Heart murmured.

"Indeed. Entirely true. Anyway, Rose was soon dealing with many challenges. She's brilliant, but she was very young. We were far away. She knew she absolutely, under no circumstance, was to let anyone *EVER* come up with any sort of thought that either one of you were directly related to Father Inventor.

"So, first of all, she needed to assure that no one would ever think the two of you were related to each other. She worked hard not to show you any favoritism. Though she did plenty. I could list many instances that worried us, for one, the star dome. So what if Father Inventor gave the Darling Undesirables a bunch of money, we thought? It still drew attention to you.

"But—you so thrived under that dome. It not only saved your remarkable brilliance from turning to insanity under the endless restrictions of the Darling Undesirables law, but simply gave you an outlet for believing in yourself, and to learn more."

"Yes. It saved me. This is true."

"So. Anyway, Rose—Keeper A—was often horrible to you, in front of the other keepers. But she went to every single event you were in, again, against our advice. She hired Swen to also keep an eye on you. He soon refused payment, because he simply wanted to watch over you.

"She grew her rose garden in order to have access to the crystal matrix, to know what was going on at the other Darling Undesirables facilities, while keeping everyone else at a distance, insisting no one could go in her garden but herself and her trusted gardeners.

"Every gardener she hired was hypnotized to either not see the underground, or to think it was usual. She longed to have the garden a place where anyone could wander. But—it had a more important duty.

Heart nodded. "To keep in touch with what was happening at the other Darling Undesirables facilities."

"That's right."

"I guess," Heart continued, "I can understand all the, *ummm*, untruths you told me, like not knowing where the aurora came from and all that, to protect … well, everything. The museum and all the beings in it, including yourselves …."

"And *you*," Martha added.

"And me. Because we've never known when we were being listened in on."

"True, my dear."

"But I don't understand why, the day I first came here to the Museum of Scientific Improbabilities and Unpredictable Oddities, why that terrible fight between Keep … my sis … *Rose* … and Key Man?"

"An act, Heart, dearest, with everyone's apologies. A very big act, which, I must say, they pulled off excellently well. I was afraid it was a bit over the top. Or that one of them would start giggling. But, no.

"Well, Rose wasn't about to giggle because she was really, truly frightened about you. You were taking off and shapeshifting and doing things on your own, unpredictably.

"She was terrified you would escape, and she would never again see her sister—whom she loved more than life, and was willing to receive her hatred rather than risk the slightest chance of endangering her.

"We knew we must continue to have things appear to you to be as you believed—that Rose was sort of the 'bad guy' or you'd never trust us."

"True," Heart agreed. "Goodness, Key Man said some truly dreadful things about her. If this is all true, I don't even know how he could!"

"At Rose's insistence, Heart. It was hard on her, but she knew she needed you to fear her. You must not look like she favored you, no matter what."

"Which is why, when she talked to me, she almost always kept her profile to me—to not look me in the eye."

"Yes, Heart. Reprimanding you was *very* hard on her."

Heart fell into a stunned silence.

It was *All. Too. Much. To. Think. About.*

Finally, she said, "I'm rarely tired, Martha, but I feel incredibly overextended and exhausted. Would it be all right if I went upstairs and rested for a while?"

"Entirely, dear Heart. Sweetest of dreams."

Chapter 30

Heart went into the little fairy room with such a changed vision that she hardly felt like the same person. The little room didn't look the same, either. It still was tiny, and fairy-like.

But—everything in it … belonged to her sister. *Her. Sister.*

She had never, ever, once in her life imagined those words. She had imagined that maybe Eye was her brother. Had fantasized that one day, when she was grown, she'd do genetic testing and see that she and Eye were related.

But to even imagine that she and Martha were related—and in this extremely weird upside-down kind of relation? No, it had never—*could* never—cross her mind.

Everything in this room was her sister's. Or—Keeper A's. Depending on how she looked at it.

All these, gentle, beautiful, delicate things, the tiny, real, pastel books, this little cream-colored desk, this soft little round pale green rug that Swen had slept on, this pile of luxurious blankets and pillows—white and creme and pale green ….

Oh, wait, oh yes, there it was, *Keeper A's colors!* The off-white, the pale green, delicate fairy colors.

The last bit of convincing evidence. This. *EXACT* shade of pale, pale green. A nearly translucent seeming seafoam for little sylphs.

Heart lay down on the bed and turned to face the wall. To take in as little as possible. To try and think. Or not think. She put her hand under the giant pile of pillows, which she'd not done the other night and pulled out something …. A 3-D image. Of herself! As a small child.

When the light hit it, she heard her little girl self chirp, *"Stars! Stars! Stars!"*

*   *

When Heart awoke—and she had no idea at all how long she'd slept, but it was the deep, dark middle of the night—she heard voices downstairs. She moved about, there was something in her hand.

Oh! The picture of herself! Oh, my, what more could possibly happen? she thought as all the new information came crashing back into her consciousness.

"Come down here, Heart!" Jackson ordered from the bottom of two antique stairways.

Jackson!

I will when I'm good and ready, she replied in her mind. She quickly slipped into her new purple and golden plaid outfit and studied the effect in the mirror. Powerful and beautiful! All right, I'm ready.

But, she said nothing aloud. Instead, she crept down the stairs, thinking she might be happy to see Jackson, but instead, feeling quite nervous. There he stood, as she anticipated, by Martha. But also Key Man, Lady Gervi, Swen and Yippee were lined up, all clearly waiting for her.

"Hello? What's going on? Hello, Jackson, nice wake-up call. I say, what's going on? It's the middle of the night." She looked from one to the next. "Everyone's here but HelperFriend and Violet. Apparently, I've sprouted another head, or some such, during my brief sleep, the way you're all looking at me."

"The plaid," Martha whispered. "Astonishing!"

"I know, dear Martha. Thank you."

"Quite animated and astonishing," Lady Gervi agreed, with Yippee adding a counterpoint to her words, Swen nodding, Key Man grinning.

"Violet was acting out," Jackson more or less barked. "The clockworks man is keeping her subdued. Or at least restrained. They're on the *Heart!* Where you need to be, directly—along with this motley crew."

"*Hmmm* … number one, does Violet need restraining? She weighs two pounds. Number two, are we going somewhere? And number three, my friends are not a motley crew. My goodness, Jackson, I'm the one who just woke up, but it's as if *you* woke up with your nightclothes in a knot."

No one could resist a giggle.

"Right. Come along. It's almost 5:30—see the dawn? We need to be there by seven a.m."

"Where, where, *where?*"

"Didn't they tell you?"

"Well Jackson, I will say that I've been told more in the last couple days than I've ever been told my entire life. But about being somewhere by seven a.m. today, which must be a goodly distance, no. I've not been told."

"We're going to the UnderSea Cities. Let's get going, now."

"The UnderSea Cities! Oh my, that's big. That's amazing. I've never been there. Well, now, that is something I would like to do. I don't know why we're doing it, but let's go!"

Heart went out the front door, and everyone trailed behind, with Martha locking her door securely. "Sorry Martha, I didn't have time to make the bed."

"That's all right."

Heart was still so filled with all that Martha had told her about her life, that she completely forgot for the moment, Jackson's huge triumph. She stopped in her tracks, and turned, "Oh, Jackson, *The Wall!* You did it. You disabled The Wall! You're amazing!"

He actually smiled. Heart saw it, and no one could ever tell her otherwise. "I did do that, it's true."

Having crossed to the *Heart!* they all stopped and cheered. They'd cheered plenty yesterday, Heart was certain, when they first heard the news that all the people imprisoned in The Periphery on the other side of The Wall were free. But it was well worth another, early morning, cheer.

"Why are they cheering?" she heard Violet squeal. "Why?"

"I don't know," HelperFriend said in a weary voice. "Maybe because they're glad they're not with you!"

Everyone burst into laughter.

Heart poked her head around the open hatch. "Oh, HelperFriend, sarcasm!"

"Is that what it is? I thought it was frustration."

"Sarcasm and frustration go well together. All right, places everyone. Oh, oh, wait, where is Martha going to sit? And, where did she go? I thought she was going with us."

"She is," Key Man said. "She went to put a 'Closed for the Day' sign on the museum's front door."

"Excellent. But where is she going to ride?"

"Right over here," Mick said, coming around the *Heart!*

"Mick!" Heart couldn't resist giving him a big hug and turned to Jackson. "He's still your copilot!"

"Yes. He does the job."

"I'll say. He saved your life!"

"I don't know about that."

"You wouldn't be here if not for him."

"Well," Mick said, nodding and grinning, "there's that. By the way Heart, you look stunning! Your plaid is glowing."

"I know! It's brand new. It's a gift, like all my plaids, from Martha and *The Nieces.*" Heart grinned, looking from Mick to Jackson, while Martha came scurrying back out, checking to make sure the back entrance to the museum was also solidly locked.

"I guess the clockworks will have a party we'll have to clean up when we get back," she said, winded. "We've never all been gone at the same time."

"And we all know how much clockworks love to party!" Heart affirmed, smiling at Lady Gervi.

"Well, within limitations," Lady Gervi replied, quite ladylike.

"Let's go," Heart said moving to the hatch of the *Heart!* "Everyone knows their place. I'll follow you, Jackson."

"I'll project a map to you, Heart."

"Or HelperFriend and I will *follow a map*." Heart shook her head and rolled her eyes. "All aboard!"

Soon they were aloft and headed for the ocean. Before long, among much cheerful banter, the ocean loomed in the near distance.

"Ah, look at it!" Heart sighed. *"Just look!"*

"Well, that's rather alarming, is it not?" Lady Gervi said, clearly terrified. "It's bigger than all of Pink, and it moves!"

"Nothing to fear, my dear," Key Man said. "Nothing to fear. You've seen vids of the ocean."

"Oh, yes, that's right. I have. But, well, it's different when *it's real.*"

"One might say," HelperFriend said quietly.

Heart looked over at him and was surprised to discover that if he had blood running in his veins, his knuckles would be white, as his gear-spinning hands gripped onto the edge of the instrument panel.

"Course correction," she heard Jackson bark over the communication system. She looked at the map. She'd drifted off-course with the sighting of the ocean.

"Correcting," she replied. "We have to stay attentive, HelperFriend."

"Sorry, Heart, sorry. Oh now, what is that?"

Heart looked back out to see the Gargantua at some distance, hovering above the ground.

"That's the Gargantua."

"Well, it's just, 'things too big to be believed day,'" HelperFriend said.

"Or 'HelperFriend practicing sarcasm day,'" Heart replied.

"I rather much wish I'd stayed at the museum," Lady Gervi murmured.

Yippee started making some disturbing sounds, and Violet, who had thankfully seemed to fall asleep, woke and began adding chatter to the general hubbub.

"All right everyone," Heart said, "This is your captain speaking. Calm down. Be quiet. I need to hear orders. There isn't anything frightening here. And trust me, I know. I've seen frightening." She connected with Jackson. "Not sure where I'm putting down, Jackson."

"Oh for … do you have me in sight?"

"No. Wait, yes."

"Then follow me."

"Right." She followed Jackson's craft, and just as the *Heart!* touched down a short walking distance from the Gargantua, the Mechanical Aurora Borealis opened up the skies and came down upon the Gargantua.

A great flurry ensued inside the aurora, and Heart then knew why her father had not been particularly upset by her departure yesterday. He would see her today.

*   *

Heart flipped on communication again. "The aurora borealis, Jackson! My father is here!"

"Of course."

"What 'of course?'"

"Don't you know anything? Don't you know why we're here?"

"To look at the ocean? To visit the Gargantua? Maybe to visit the UnderSea Cities, although I believe most of my passengers will not be doing that."

"Right. You've not been told anything. Well, I won't spoil the surprise."

Peter's voice cut into their communication. "Please prepare to board the Gargantua."

"Let's go!" Heart released her safety harness, released everyone's magnetics, and opened the hatch. Equuleus stood and was first to exit. Key Man released his safety harness and opened Swen's cubby hole, who leapt out with doggie enthusiasm.

"I've seen the ocean," Swen said. "I've even been to the UnderSea Cities for a story once, when I was a young pup, long ago. But I can't wait to see this Gargantua, which can't be seen from my safety niche." He went bounding out then back in. "*WHOA!* "That's bigger than big!" and bounded back outside again.

Key Man offered Lady Gervi his hand. "I believe Yippee and I will stay here for the time being," she said demurely.

"I will not let anything harm you in any way, my lady. In addition, you wanted to come to Earth to learn new things. I will grant you that this has come suddenly, but it is a great opportunity. Further, I believe you may be a bit more disconcerted staying out here alone with your little Yippee."

His infallible logic prevailed. Without further discussion, she tucked Yippee under one arm and offered Key Man her other, and cautiously exited.

Violet continued to mutter under her breath. Heart could only assume that had to do with a real, true fear. She opened Violet's little safe place, and holding her in one hand, she turned to Helper-Friend. "And you, my friend."

"Cannot I not stay here?"

"You heard Key Man. More fearsome here alone, than being with us."

"What's keeping you?" Jackson growled. "Peter is waiting."

"Just a bit of fear and trepidation from the new folks. Lots of very big things, never before seen."

"Whatever. Let's get a move on."

HelperFriend released his harness and stood. "You really want me to do this?"

"I do."

He stood and took her hand. They joined the others waiting for her to lead them. All except Equuleus, who had gone on ahead.

Down from the Gargantua came a ramp like none other. Wide, long, beautifully lit, with carved wooden railings and art objects all along the gradual incline.

Heart smiled as Lady Gervi actually moved ahead of Key Man, her long, svelte gear legs taking her to the ramp in several easy strides. She stopped at every art object and had a brief chat with Yippee about each. And good thing, too, Heart thought, or Key Man would never have caught up with her.

Swen loped back and forth between Lady Gervi and Key Man, delighted with his new family, on an amazing outing.

"Well, I don't know what all the fuss is about. Just don't know. Some big long ramp, what's so scary about that?" Violet said.

"You didn't see …" HelperFriend started, but Heart shook her head.

"Didn't see what?"

"The best part yet," Heart said.

Heart looked over her shoulder and saw Martha and Jackson and Mick bringing up the rear. When they were all finally gathered in a little anteroom-like space, which was quite cozy for them, a door closed and they were whisked up several flights in an elevator transport.

"*Whoooooooaaaaaaa!* HelperFriend, Lady Gervi and Violet all cried, each in their own register. Which made Heart, Key Man, Martha, Mick, and Swen laugh aloud.

Jackson, hands behind his back, made no sound.

"Will someone please poke him and see if he's alive?" Heart begged.

"Not if you gave me the world," Mick answered.

The door whooshed open, and there stood Peter, grinning, with open arms, "Heart, Key Man, Martha and … everybody! Welcome to the Gargantua!"

Heart gave him a big hug, and whispered, "Thank you for saving the Darlings, my dear doorman!"

He returned the hug. "It's only just begun! Prepare to be amazed!" He winked and gestured for everyone to follow him. "Come along, you don't want to miss it, you don't want to miss it!"

Heart fell back to walk with Jackson, "don't want to miss what?"

"You'll soon see."

She moved over to Martha, "Don't want to miss what?"

"You'll see, but we have a bit of a walk if I'm not wrong. We must be at the front of the Gargantua." Martha's short legs pedaled like they were on rollers, and Heart decided there was no point in trying to get anything out of anybody who knew anything.

They finally came to a place where they could see the ocean, where Peter stopped for a moment. "From here, in the night, the UnderSea Cities give an amazing light show. You won't believe the beauty until you see it!"

"*Ahh!*" Lady Gervi said, fully converted to all things gigantic on Earth. She looked down at Key Man in sheer adoration.

Smiling, Heart looked out toward the ocean, imagining what it might be like in the evening when night fell, when she saw something she could never, never be prepared for. Twenty feet in front of her a door slid open, another transport, Heart surmised. Out stepped her father! He'd come down from the aurora.

She made a move to go to him when from another hall, around the corner, came running a petite, svelte beautiful young woman, long, dark hair flowing about her shoulders, huge smile radiating on her stunning features.

"Daddy!" she cried, throwing herself into the open arms of Father Inventor.

Heart thought she would melt right through the floor. She just—*stared.*

Equuleus came to stand by her, as everyone moved to let him through. And Jackson, on her other side, put his arm around her shoulders.

She looked at him, shock still written on her face. "How long have you known? Have you always known?"

"No, Heart, no. Just recently. The Mystic told me a couple days ago."

"Oh. Martha told me last night. That's why I was so deep asleep. Trying to … to …."

Heart's father and her … *sister!* turned to look at her, and, together they hurried up to her. Everyone, even Equuleus, stepped away.

"Finally!" Keeper A … Rose … *her sister* … sighed, enfolding Heart to her in a life's worth of withheld love.

Heart looked to her father, who stood there, face beaming with joy.

All around her, Heart heard sniffles and soft whispers. Many around her knew her story much better than she did. A most peculiar sensation.

"All right," Rose said, "we have so *much* to talk about, but right now, we must not miss the big event."

Heart stepped back from everyone. She couldn't process this fast. Too much to think, to remember. To forget. She just couldn't process this fast.

Rose was still smiling at her, gesturing for her to come, when the transport whooshed open again, and out stepped The Mystic, Zack, and Amdrona.

"Oh! Rose," Amdrona cried.

Rose turned, but it was Zack who flew up to her and swept her off her feet hugging her close to him. "*Ahh!*" he sighed, as she buried her face into his shoulder, hugging him for all she was worth. "Now, my Love?"

"Yes, now," she murmured.

He kissed her a kiss that had waited since childhood, and, though long, was sweet and childlike.

"*Ohhhh!*" Key Man and Lady Gervi and Yippee and Swen and Violet cried.

"*Bee-aaa-uuu-tiii-fullll,*" Violet squealed.

But, wait! Heart thought. *WAIT!* There was someone else who came off the transport, blocked by all the people gathered, quietly standing by.

Heart pushed through the crowd and threw her arms around Eye. "You're here! You're here!"

"Of course," he laughed. "Wouldn't miss this event for anything, even if I can't see it."

Heart turned, looking for Butterfly, almost completely overshadowed by all the activity. "But here are your eyes," she said, enfolding Butterfly in her embrace. "Oh, I don't care why we're here, as long as you're here!"

"Is it possible you don't know yet why we're here?" Eye asked, incredulous.

"Everyone keeps asking me that!"

"Well, then, it'll be a lovely surprise," Butterfly said.

"I've had plenty surprises to last a good, long, while."

"This one ..." Eye said, then raised his voice as dozens and dozens of Darlings came off transports and up ramps, "is really going to be in the running as the winner."

Peter managed to come into the middle of their group. "All right now, everyone, let's get settled. I've tried to keep a bunch of seats together, but if you don't get in them, it's not my fault."

"Come along, Mother," he said to The Mystic.

Heart's eyebrows raised up almost to her hairline. *MOTHER!?!*

Heart moved along with everyone and found herself sitting between Jackson and Eye, with Butterfly on Eye's other side, and Zack on the other side of Jackson.

She leaned across Jackson and said to Zack. "Peter called The Mystic 'mother.'"

"Yes, dear Heart."

"The Mystic is Peter's mother?"

"That's right."

"Well, you can't know who's related to whom around here." She turned to Jackson. "Are you related to me?"

"No, Heart, I'm not."

Right at that moment, her father began speaking. "Welcome everyone, I'm so, so, so deeply happy that this day has arrived, and that each and every one of you is here. I've dreamed of this day, though I dared not imagine it as anything other than a dream, for many years."

Heart leaned back to try to surreptitiously take in the delicately beautiful woman she'd spent her lifetime trying to avoid. How different she looked now! Her long, dark, gorgeous hair tumbling about her shoulders, when Heart had only ever seen it severely pulled back. And that smile! Heart had never seen "Keeper A" smile.

But now as Rose glanced up at Zack, her face radiating with a love-filled smile *Ah! There!* Heart saw her mother's face. So disguised by not only her darker coloring but even more by the oppression of keeping her sister safe, her emotions tied down.

"I can *see* her beauty, Heart," Eye whispered in her ear with prescient insight. "And, just so you know, I forgave her everything. *Everything!* in the moment The Mystic told me the same things Martha was telling you, as Jackson turned off the power to The Wall. The moment we were all freed."

As her father continued to speak, Heart took Eye's hand and wrote upon it her gratitude and love for him, in their innocent childhood language.

"But today," her father continued, "*has* arrived, and the moment has arrived. For years I've been working with the UnderSea Cities, who have been imagining with me a home for all, *all* the Darlings and their keepers. A home like no other, centered on love and care. And so, without further hesitation, I present to you the *Home of the Darling Desirables!*"

He stepped aside, and, as everyone watched in stunned awe—even those who had been told what to expect, there was no way to be prepared for the ripples far out to sea, and then, slowly, slowly, a vast island rose from the ocean depths.

Father Inventor continued, "I've worked on Pink for years with the scientists of the UnderSea Cities, while they and many residents of the cities, seeded the ocean carefully bringing this solid, verdant, island into being as a home for all the darling children, and their children's children, for any and all clockwork or mechanical or hybrid or bio beings to live in harmony and safety, whatever their special needs, and whatever their particular talents."

The island continued to rise from the sea, sparkling in the sunlight, verdant with beautiful plant life, and, even more surprising, what looked like little houses.

"All the plants you see have been developed to thrive and grow either submerged in water or out of water. Yes," Heart's father said as if answering her unspoken question, "Those are little houses, all constructed underwater by our wonderful friends, the inhabitants of the UnderSea Cities. They are watching this event now too, so let them know your appreciation."

He didn't have to say it twice as the whole of Gargantua broke out in cheerful pandemonium. Peter came up to her father and gave him a big hug. "Well done, well done, my friend," he said.

Then Peter turned to everyone, "My friends, welcome to the *Home of The Darling Desirables*.

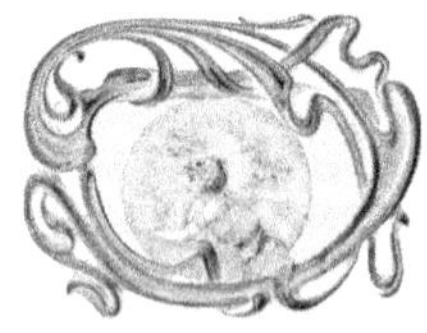

Chapter 31

When that island came out of the sea, when that sign appeared above it in beautiful stunning lights, *"Home of The Darling Desirables,"* when everyone around Heart cheered and cried, and danced, when she saw those little charming houses, the very ones she'd seen in her dreams her whole childhood, the ones she told Eye about so many times in their nightly chats, the little houses that Eye "saw" better than anyone, and had carefully explained to Peter, so that they were perfect replicas of Heart's dream, when she heard all the Darlings around her, laughing and jumping up and down, whether they understood what was going on or not, but were simply contagiously happy—when all of that happened, Heart never, ever, wanted to leave that precious, beautiful island her father had quietly been bringing into being all these years.

Maybe one day, but not now. Of course, Swen and Key Man and Lady Gervi and Yippee needed to go back to The Museum of Scientific Improbabilities and Unpredictable Oddities with Martha. Heart talked Jackson into taking the H*eart!* back with those passengers a few days later, when the celebration began, *somewhat!* to subside.

While everyone was preparing to take airboats to the Darling Desirables Island, their new home, Heart slipped into the Gargantua and up to the top to watch through the massive windows Jackson take off in the *Heart!* and head east with her precious friends.

"Shall we have a little talk?" Peter asked, quietly joining her.

Heart turned from the window as the last speck of the *Heart!* disappeared beyond the horizon. "I'd love that, Peter."

They sat facing on the two luxurious divans, and Heart realized she suddenly felt shy.

"Ask me anything," he encouraged.

"Where to begin?" Heart wondered aloud. "All right, so, first of all, The Mystic is your mother."

Peter nodded. "That's right."

"And you seem very close with my father. So—how long have you been friends?"

"We've been friends since childhood, that's true, Heart. I haven't thought about it in terms of years, but give or take a few years, it'd be about two-hundred-and-forty-years."

"So—The Mystic is even older."

"Sure. Mother would be, let's see, around two-hundred-and-seventy-five. My, my, she's getting up there!" Peter chuckled.

Heart was flooded with questions and insights. "So, in the *Battle at the Darling Undesirables Facility at Mountain's Edge*, when the computer simulation said it could not compute a simulation with Father Inventor's 1-1-2080, it was referring to me. That's when my father removed me from my mother's womb and placed me in stasis."

"Oh! That information was not to be revealed, but I guess the AI was under undue pressure. Yes, that would be right, Heart."

"All right, then. What I really, really want to know is, can you tell me anything about my mother?"

"I can, Heart. I can tell you many things about your mother."

Heart heaved a huge sigh. "I … I can't talk to Father about her. It's too painful for him."

"I understand, Heart. But you can ask me anything about her. Well, just let me talk about her for a while. Picture the most beautiful girl on the planet. Something about her … well, it's in both of her beautiful and brilliant daughters, which I am so blessed to have in my life. She moved in light.

"There was something translucent about her. Light shone from her and through her. Pale, delicate beauty. Anyone could have known she would not stay on Earth too long, I've often thought.

"She had a laugh like stars giggling. She'd look at you, and … and you were never the same. Her loving look just … changed something in you, shifted something inside.

"She came into our lives, mother's and mine, when she was looking for an herbalist to mentor her. Well, Mother is and was the best herbalist on Earth. But Rose, your mother, had a touch with flowers. Uncanny. Mother used to say that Rose could make flowers grow on a stone, and I believe it was true."

"It sounds, Peter, as though you fell in love with her," Heart observed simply.

"I did, Heart. I am not shy to admit I fell hopelessly in love with her and dared to dream she might fall in love with me. Mother saw my hopeless condition and told me it was not to be.

"I remember it was one of the very few times I have ever been angry with her. How dare she say that? But, of course, she knew what she saw in the future. And, as it transpired, the minute I introduced her to my best friend, who had been away for the summer studying, at the ripe old age of seventeen, longevity at the Longevity University on a summer scholarship, they fell in love. And … it was more than that. They—recognized each other. I was there, I saw it.

"Well, young, and callow, and jealous, I hated myself for introducing them, but, of course, one cannot stay the hand of fate.

"Though Rose was only fifteen, the two of them bonded and, whether I liked it or not, they fell in love.

"The rest, as they say, was history."

Heart reached out and patted his hand. "But you had the blessing of her in your life. Which is more than I've had."

"So true, dear Heart. So true. And I have the blessing of you and your sister, who, except for her dark coloring, has your mother's very features."

"That's true. I *did* finally see it, blocked as I'd been by my fear of … 'Keeper A' and only having ever seen that picture on my father's library mantle on Pink of my mother. But I've really been haunted trying to figure out who I'd met who had her features."

They shared a quiet moment, contemplating the beautiful Roses. Then Peter asked softly, "I feel you have some other burning question."

"I do, Peter. I … I'm wondering about Jackson. He lived in The Periphery his whole childhood. Who were his parents?"

"The great question we've all asked, Heart. My mother came upon two little babes in the woods one day while truffle hunting—Zack and Amdrona. Every year Mother would take them to that spot on that day to commemorate their arrival. They called it their birthday. And on that day, eight years later, they came upon the baby Jackson, looking so like Zack, it's always been assumed that they're related. But for all her psychic powers, Mother could never get a clear picture of where they came from.

"Jackson was always so independent. Always wandering off. As soon as he could, he took to living in the forest, coming around to check on Zack and Amdrona. He'd bring buckets of rare mushrooms and other forest edibles. He's always been a mystery. Well, they're all a mystery. Then, about five years later, Xavier turned up in the midst of Mother's herb garden on that same day—their 'birthday,' darling little freckle-faced child."

"Oh!" Heart gasped. "Xavier, too. Strange and mysterious."

"Indeed," Peter agreed.

They paused, each with their own loving, sad, reflections on Xavier.

Heart finally broke the reverie. "I've been putting other things together, too. For instance, I realized Rose—*my sister*—must have been the informant, the mysterious person who always knew things. Who knew, for example, there were one-thousand clones."

"Yes, that's right, Heart."

"So she acted like she was in with Loruza, but she wasn't."

"Well, she never really behaved as though she was sharing any energy with Loruza. That poor young woman is truly not sane, though she can do a fabulous imitation of sanity."

"Yes, she can."

"She always hated Rose, but she had to tolerate her because the Clone thought so much of her."

"But … Loruza is still out there," Heart said. "And probably still has some of her minions, some bots, maybe a few clones. Maybe even a few Purists."

"True, Heart. But I wouldn't bother putting energy into those thoughts."

"I'm just making an observation. Recalling her ability to be so sweet and attentive to me and to Eye …."

At that moment, Rose stepped off the transport, taking in the two of them together.

"May I join you?"

"Please do," Peter said, patting the seat beside him.

Rose sat by him, and Peter affectionately put his arm around her.

They were so comfortable together! Heart took in the energy between them, considering Rose's childhood, when Peter was, essentially, her surrogate father, with Father far away, exiled on Pink.

Rose reached across and took both of Heart's hands in her own. "I love you *so much*, my little Heart. And I pray you will forgive me the ungraceful hardships I visited upon you. Will you?"

Heart looked into the amazing eyes that had been shielded from her during her entire childhood. "I will. I … I mean," Heart stuttered, shy, confused, "I do. I do more than forgive you. I thank you. Well, that's inadequate. But I'm in awe of your strength. How you could have done what you did—all those years of my childhood. Protecting me. How could I be so blind? So self-involved?"

"No, no, dearest. You were a *child*, in a very weird world. A child filled with guileless love. I used to watch the surveillance vids of you giving the saddest, most broken darlings love. Those with short lives, who would never leave their little beds. You spent hours hugging them and singing to them.

"Ah! In my very private room, I'd sit and cry, so moved by you. You've always been, simply, about love." Rose moved to sit by her and put her arm around her. "All I ever longed for was the day when you might say you loved me, too."

Heart felt tears–her rare, rare tears–welling up and spilling out. "Oh, I do, my darling sister. I *do love you!*" She hugged her close.

"*Now where are you?*" Violet's voice shrieked over the intercom.

Heart and Rose burst into giggles.

"Goodness, how did she do that?" Peter turned on visual. "We're right here, Little Miss Lavender."

Violet poked her ears at the vid screen. "Well, get down here and party—*I mean it now!*"

"We'd better do as she says," Heart said, standing. "We'll have no peace otherwise." She looked at Peter gratefully. "Thank you, Peter. Thank you for sharing your wisdom, and your love. You've been the doorman to much more than The Museum of Scientific Improbabilities and Unpredictable Oddities in my life."

Chapter 32

Four Months Later

Though Heart did not care for ostentation, her father insisted on having built for her a small rather castle-like structure, citing her household as a practical need for a variety of rooms—Equuleus had to be able to move about freely, HelperFriend was not small and must have a suite of rooms of his own. She'd finally convinced Violet to be happy with a little, rabbit-sized room of her own—*whew!*—easier said than done.

And then there was the Clone!

Her father and Key Man reassembled him after Heart agreed to have him as a member of her household, on his sworn promise to behave himself, and—

he must no longer look nor sound like her father. He attempted to protest, but, upon the threat of being homeless, he agreed to cosmetic alteration.

Heart let him choose his face and voice, both of which were a bit over the top in her estimation, but, in the end, not only was he elated with his new self, his character changed dramatically for the better, as well. Pleasant and self-assured, the Clone named himself "Martin" for no known reason. He became helpful around the house, and *surprise!* was especially good with the older Darlings, going for long walks with them around the island, and proving to be an excellent instructor.

He had his own room next to HelperFriend's suite, and they became inseparable pals. Heart's home and life wese full to overflowing. And, although her childhood picture had been of her living in the same little home as Eye, to have him nearby, living with Butterfly was nearly as good.

In the four months since *The Darling Desirables* island rose from the sea, Heart had done so much, she could hardly track it.

She'd planted thousands and thousands of flowers in the loamy, wildly fertile soil. She planted a few trees. She started three levels of schools. She organized and hired dozens of people to care for the Darlings, who were no longer called "keepers." They were christened "Darling"—"Darling Teacher," "Darling Cook," "Darling Gardner," "Darling Doctor," so on and so forth.

Then she started in earnest recruiting "Darling Surgeons," and "Darling Genetic Fabricators."

Rose lived nearby with her life-long love, Zack, in one of the charming pastel houses with big windows all around and thousands of roses in their yard.

Heart and Rose brain-stormed for hours, imagining ways to make the lives of the *Darling Desirables* better and ever better. And when she was not doing that, Rose could be found out along the shore, tending to her roses encircling the entire island, with each and every Darling finally *inside* her glorious garden.

Heart and the people of the UnderSea Cities built a beautiful building in the open space behind the pastel homes. The sign over the wide entranceway read: *Heart of Health & Wholeness.*

And then Heart recruited like mad. Her father told her she could spend any amount of money to retain the best doctors, the best surgeons, the best healers, money meant nothing to him. He'd simply sell another patent or invention.

She made offers no surgeon or doctor or healer or mystic, or miracle worker could refuse. They came from everywhere, vying for the opportunity. They offered to come for free, just to be there with the cutting edge medical, surgical, and genetic science.

She established an amazing brain trust, where the world's genetic research was housed. And then, not entirely unlike what she'd done for the residents of Pink, she began having the Darlings made whole.

Each *Darling Desirable* resident was given detailed information of their bio-genetics if they wanted it. They were counseled regarding the various procedures that would make them whole—if they wanted it. It was a matter of each Darling's personal choice.

*   *

Ḣeart handed Butterfly a large, sealed envelope. She knew what it contained and was anxious to see Butterfly's reaction.

Knowing this was the report on her genetic makeup, Butterfly tore at the seal and rapidly read through the medical jargon.

"Ah! Here! Here it is, Eye, it says; 'anomalous genetic material … not human but humanoid … If this genetic information were pure, (which in this individual, it is not), the individual would be quite small in stature, likely not more than one to two feet tall, and there's every indication it would possess wings or wing-like structures.'"

"*Sheesh!*" Butterfly said, "would it kill them to write: 'This being is fay'?"

"Oh, Butterfly," Eye exclaimed, "you were right!"

"Of course I was right. Did you doubt me, Eye?"

"No, never, my dear. But now it's proven."

"Indeed!" Butterfly turned to Heart. "I want my wings, Heart."

"I knew that's what you'd say! I want you to have your wings too. I'll discuss this with my team and see who best to work with you. As we don't have any other Darling with the potential of growing wings, we have to have the very best doctors."

"I want my wings right away, Heart."

"Patience, dear Butterfly. Patience."

After Heart interviewed a variety of genetic research scientists, and hand-picked those few who were willing to believe in other humanoid species—and, why doubt it, with the genetic information right before them?—she made the first appointment to move forward with Butterfly's request to be made whole.

The genetic research scientists took bits of Butterfly's peculiar shoulder nubbins and hemmed and hawed over their findings until they agreed they *might* be able to grow wings for Butterfly, because it certainly did appear as though that's what would happen if the genetic information was properly turned on.

However, they were cautious to do a wing-seed technique on Butterfly's body. It was not understood like arm-seeding, or leg-seeding, or spine-seeding, or organ seeding, or teeth-seeding. Or even brain seeding, all of which they had done many times.

They told Butterfly that they would try to grow the wings first in the lab, before committing her to major surgery. And, as she had insisted would happen, beautiful gossamer wings began to grow in the lab. They were small, but they were viable, and it appeared they would grow large and beautiful, once properly implanted.

Heart was studying the beautiful wings in their enclosed lab environment, filled with wonder at their beauty, when Eye came up to her.

"Are they truly amazing?" Eye asked.

Heart looked around, for Butterfly, but soon realized that Eye was alone.

"They are indeed amazing, Eye. In every way. Miraculous."

"Yes. Well …."

Heart turned to Eye. "What's wrong?"

"Nothing, Heart. Butterfly will finally have her wings. It's … it's …."

Heart led him outside and they walked along the little flower-strewn path outside the laboratory. "Tell me," she urged.

Eye sighed deeply. "As you know, I've insisted I don't want eyes."

"I do know that, yes." Heart had had to content herself with her number one goal not being fulfilled, that Eye would have eyes. But her father reminded her that she *had* accomplished her goal, which was not to *make* Eye have eyes but to bring about the possibility that Eye *could* have eyes.

"It seems Butterfly has gotten it into her mind that she wants me to have eyes … to see her wings. You know, Heart, I'll do anything for her. But you also know how I feel about attempting to get eyes. As long as I don't *know* that I cannot have eyes, I can tell myself it's possible. But if I'm told there will never be a chance to have eyes, then, well, that'll be hard. Anyway, my world is beautiful with the sights I create in my imagination.

"But if Butterfly has wings, she'll be whole in her mind. And in my mind too, for that matter. We'll be—we'll no longer be the same. She'll be whole and I won't be.

"I'll feel inferior. She may not even like me anymore. So—I guess I must learn if I can have eyes. But

I … I don't really want to know the details like I hear you spell it out to others. No, I'd rather not hear all those details.

"Hearing is my sight. What I hear is extremely graphic. It's not like I can look in another direction and see something that makes the bad picture go away. Images stick in my mind for a long time.

"I know this is asking a lot, Heart, but, dear Heart, will you stand in for me when it comes to the doctors' verbal report? If it's not good, just tell me something like, right now's not the best time, or, they're working on this science."

"Of course, Eye, I'll do that for you." Heart couldn't argue with his negative expectation—she'd never known of another Darling who didn't have any eyes at all. She would do as he requested.

She made the appointment with the doctors, and then she sat with Eye while he had all the testing and imaging that needed to be done, without Butterfly knowing about it. After all the tests and diagnostics, Eye left, with a promise from Heart that she would be very circumspect when the results came in.

But much to Heart's amazement, the doctors called for Eye to return to their offices at once.

She entered.

"Where is Eye?" the lead surgeon asked.

"He feared the worst, and asked me to stand in for him, to receive his report."

"That's too bad," he replied. "I think he'd really like to hear this from us. It's hard to believe he's never been told before, but that young man is, in common terms, completely wired for eyes! All he needs are eyeballs, basically. This is rather simplistic, but the point is, we'd love to give him eyes. Ask him what color he'd like."

"Oh! Oh, thank you, you wonderful, beautiful doctors. I'll tell him immediately!" Heart rushed out to find Eye, and found him before long, dawdling along the fenced walk.

"Sit by me," she said, unable to keep the excitement from her voice.

"Oh, no, already! That didn't take long."

She led him to a rustic little bench and they sat.

"No, it didn't." She grabbed Eye's hand, "Brace yourself, Eye. I'll quote the doctors word for word: 'that young man is wired for eyes, all he needs are eyeballs. We'd love to give him eyes. Ask him what color he'd like.'"

Eye gasped. "No, Heart, no, it can't be true!"

"It's completely true, my dearest friend. Utterly, completely true."

"Blue," Eye said. "I'd like blue eyes."

Chapter 33

Both Butterfly's and Eye's surgeries went well, for which Heart was profoundly grateful, but now the moment had arrived for the unveiling. They opted to do both at the same time, which was what Butterfly wanted, although Heart would have preferred Eye not to have to share his moment of sight.

And, just in case anything didn't go well, Butterfly and Eye opted to have only Heart, aside from the surgeon, present for their unveiling.

First Butterfly's healing wraps were removed. Her little wings, though perfect, were very small. "Oh my," Butterfly cried, "they hurt very badly. Why is that?"

"It *is* major surgery," the surgeon said. "Although they should not be unduly painful."

Heart looked over Butterfly's head with a worried expression. The surgeon shrugged and slightly shook his head. "They really ought not hurt too badly for long."

Butterfly was looking over her shoulder at the wings in the large mirror on the wall. "They're … too small!" she said, her voice filled with disappointment.

"You saw them in the lab," Heart said.

"They looked so wonderful, I didn't even think how literally small they are."

"They will grow, dear."

"You must be very careful with them," the surgeon said. "They are quite fragile. We hope they'll get stronger as they get bigger. But it's been rather a surprise how delicate they are."

Heart could read Butterfly's disappointment in her face and in her words. And, worse, she knew Eye worried about her disappointment, while he sat there, waiting his turn.

"I'm sure they're beautiful, dearest," he said, tension and sadness in his voice.

"Shall we see how things went with these beautiful eye implants?" The surgeon began to remove the healing wraps without waiting for an answer. "Now keep in mind we had to do rather extensive cosmetic surgery with eyelids and so …."

"Thank you, doctor," Heart spoke up. "Let's not make any mind pictures with these details." She had already told him not to do what he was about to do. At least he understood enough to keep the rest to himself. "Are you ready, Eye?" Heart patted his hand. "We don't have to do this right now."

"Let's get it done. If Butterfly is disappointed, and I'm disappointed, I'd prefer to have it all at the same time, rather than drawing it out. No more not knowing. I just … want to know!"

"All right. Continue, doctor."

Butterfly was not in the moment with Eye, Heart observed sadly. But, whatever—good or bad, I'm here for him.

It seemed to take forever to remove the healing wraps, but finally, Heart saw—*closed eyes!* Just that was so shocking. Her little Eye, with eyelids. Quite beautiful, too. The doctors had said they would implant eyelashes eventually, but they wanted the eyes to completely heal. Even without eyelashes, his eyelids were amazing!

"You can open your eyes now," the doctor said.

"I … I don't know how!" Eye whispered.

"Ah, yes, true. You have to learn how to open your eyes—you'll train those little muscles. Not to worry, you'll learn. I will manually open them, gently. Don't jump. Eyes are very sensitive to touch." The surgeon, standing in front of Eye, opened his eyes, then stepped aside.

Heart, sitting right in front of him, gasped. She could see her dear, sweet, Eye *see her!* With the most beautiful blue eyes, ever. *"Butterfly!"* he exclaimed.

"No, no, Eye, I'm not Butterfly!"

"That's Heart, Eye, *I'm* Butterfly."

Heart was dismayed by how hurt Butterfly sounded.

Eye laughed. *"I know! I know!* I was teasing. *Teasing*, you silly girls. I know exactly where each of you is sitting, and I know what you look like, whether I have physical eyes or not. You both ought to know me better. Now I'm the only one laughing at my joke, which, *I see*, is not very funny."

"Oh, Eye," Heart sighed. "You … have eyes."

"Are they pretty?"

"They're beautiful! And … *You can see me!"*

Eye took her hands, and, for the first time ever, looked deep into her eyes. "Yes, my dearest Heart, I can see you. And—it *is* miraculous! But, I've always seen you. You look almost exactly as you do in my mind's eye. Although, curiously, perhaps slightly less dimensional. Well, that's hard to explain!

"But, Heart, what's important about this moment is that you see me seeing you. You can see my deep, abiding, brotherly love for you in my eyes. *That's* what's important!"

Heart, shocked by Eye's truth, nodded. "You're right. Strangely selfish of me."

"No Heart, not selfish. It's what I've wanted, too. I could never explain, because I never, ever, believed it was possible that I could have physical eyes. *No!* Never, until this very minute when, I really can see you, physically, did I for one fleeting second believe I would ever have physical sight. Not selfish, Heart, but loving. Because when a person loves themselves, they cannot help but love others."

"Thank you," Heart said simply, becoming aware of Butterfly's slight perturbation. She signed their secret language, "I love you," in Eye's palm, and before he could even respond, she stood and left the room.

"*Me too you!*" he called after her.

She heard him say to Butterfly as she walked down the hall, "*Now!* Let me see those gorgeous, delicate wings, sweet Butterfly."

She paused, listening.

"They're too small," Butterfly said in soft disappointment.

"They'll grow, my darling. Turn around. Oh, Butterfly, they are *exquisite*. Perfect shape, delicately pearlescent. Just beautiful. Imagine them the size you want them, and soon, that is how they will be."

Heart slipped away as the two bonded in their new state of being.

She took a long walk home, feeling deeply, quietly, happy and fulfilled. Happy, and yet sad. Lonely-sad. Key Man and Lady Gervi, Rose and Zack, Eye and Butterfly—all around her, there was love.

Yes, love! She so believed in love, the unconditional, love-for-everyone kind of love. But what about romantic love? The kind of love for one particular person, with whom you shared all your secrets, your joys, your fears? The one special person who championed you, who had your back. Who told you your very small and delicate wings were perfect and beautiful?!

There had been Xavier, who loved her in that complete and precious way. Maybe that was her life's quota. His love for her was so, *so* special. Much more, she was certain, than many people ever had in their whole, entire lifetime.

But then … her mind *would* go to that moment, in the crystal matrix, when they rescued the Darlings, that moment when Jackson fell to his knees and embraced the terrified, deformed, sad darling children, and unabashedly cried tears. That moment when she *finally!* fell utterly into the depths of unrecoverable love. With Jackson.

If she were to be truthful with herself, was it not Jackson, all along? From the moment when she was facing death on Equuleus, about to fly into the aurora, with the Purists' bomb close at hand—that moment when Jackson reached up to kiss her cheek, and she turned and kissed him right on his lovely, stern mouth, very much surprising them both.

Curiously, at this moment, she discovered herself passing Jackson's modest little cottage. Pale blue, quiet, with a few gentle lights coming on in the gathering night. She could see the forms of the two clones moving about inside, a second-generation clone, and the third generation clone he had cut in half when he rescued Heart and the two children in the crystal matrix. Jackson had reclaimed them, and given them a home in his modest home, after turning off The Wall.

After that, after he was no longer an active soldier, Jackson had become a stalwart defender of the Darlings, traveling the world. He was rarely here in his little home, but out in the world, searching for homeless unloved children one minute, and banging on doors to recruit the most elite and skilled surgeons, the most brilliant research scientists, the most knowing healers, the next minute.

He was unabashed. He didn't care about manners. He only cared about the children.

Heart chuckled with affection, at how his one-man crusade touched the world. Everywhere, all around the world, could be seen gigantic 3-D vid-posters with the word *"RIGHT!"* above a very … Heart had to admit … *verrrrrry* attractive image of Jackson, looking, *as only he could!* tough and gentle, with a caption underneath: "Give the Children Life & Love—It's just … *RIGHT!*"

Jackson hated the posters, but no one knew who produced them. They were offered free from an anonymous source to anyone who put them up. Many of the posters were motion-sensitive, sounding out Jackson's *"Right!"* whenever anyone walked by.

At least he was in her life, even if not *"in her life."*

She came to her own home and walked past the *Heart!*, sitting quietly and neglected in its parking stall. She'd been so busy, she'd not even started up its engines in a couple of months.

She returned to it and climbed into the pilot's seat, recalling how important it had been at one point in her life to be allowed to pilot alone. And now—the thought hadn't even crossed her mind in months! She looked down and saw the little box Xavier had left there so long ago.

She picked up the box and wandered into the quiet house. Violet was off visiting Yippee for a few days—that was another relationship that might end up in complete togetherness. When Violet wasn't visiting Yippee, most of the time, Yippee was here.

Equuleus had taken up the habit of midnight flights as everything was so gloriously breath-taking all around them in the night.

She passed by the kitchen where Helper-Friend and, she had to remind herself, "Martin," were making up recipes, their new favorite pas-time.

"*Hey!*" She said softly as she passed.

"Come try this amazing dessert we've invented, Heart," Martin begged.

"Kinda tired, my friend. I'm going to go up and relax a bit. I might be down later."

She exchanged a look with HelperFriend, who, as always, read her transparently.

He stepped out into the hall and put his hand on her shoulder. "Eye?"

She smiled. "Amazing, HelperFriend. Perfect. Beautiful blue eyes, *eyes that saw me*. Very, very ...."

"Special," he said.

"Yes. Special."

"But ... you're sad ...." HelperFriend observed.

"Happy-sad, dear friend."

"Oh. Lonely-happy-sad," HelperFriend said, with telepathic empathy.

"A little, yes."

Wordlessly, he hugged her.

"Thank you, dear. I'll be fine, you know."

"Of course, Heart. You will be very happy, soon."

Heart wended her way up the little winding stairway and stepped out on the balcony that overlooked the UnderSea Cities—*exquisite!* Their night lights sparkled, danced, and shined up through the water into the night sky.

She looked up, as she did every, single, night, to send love to Pink. *Love to Pink and your sweet moon! Love to Father and to all The Folks,* she prayed her nightly prayer.

Then she recalled the little box in her hands. She opened it and out sprang a whole bevy of stars. There was the 3-D of her nine-year-old self, chirping again and again, *"Stars! Stars! Stars! Stars!"*

But—where had all these twinkling stars come from? And then she remembered the hands full of HelperFriend's tears that had been poured into the box. They had transmuted into—*STARS!*

But, wait! They were not random, they were in a constellation. It was … *it was Leo!* Oh, how could she have almost forgotten her beloved Leo?

She closed the box and looked up to the sky, looked right in the heart of Leo, and, as she did, its heart came out of the constellation and shot toward her. At least, that's how it looked.

Had she had an experience like this before? It seemed, *it seemed* she had some memory—or maybe just a dream, but it was so much like this … if she could only recall ….

The shooting star became ever brighter, came ever closer. It was not an illusion. It was real! It jetted across eons and lightyears and distances greater than imagination.

It came right toward her, Heart, on this tiny, little planet, flung off to the edge of a remote corner of the universe, but somehow, the star knew her, it came to her and then, *Ping!* a light appeared before her—so very familiar. And yet, completely unfamiliar.

The Light Being began to speak with a voice of many delicate chimes. "Ah, Little Star, how proud I am of you! You've planted a myriad seeds of love on this little planet, and they've taken root! They've grown into Love. You have done exceedingly well."

"I … I only do what I know. It's not … not … do I know you? Somehow this feels familiar. But, of course, it can't be real. I'm sleeping, I've fallen asleep and I'm having a very real dream."

"No, Little Star. All the rest is a powerful dream that you're creating. An excellent dream, made of love. *This moment is what is real.*"

"But have we—encountered before? Have we met before? You feel …"

"We have met before, and before, and before, and we will meet again, and again, and again …."

The being began to fade, to become smaller, to recede.

"Wait!" Heart cried. "Wait! I remember you! I remember you! I promised I would never forget you, and I haven't! I remember now. Don't leave, I have so many questions!"

The many chimes, ever fainter, jingled as if chuckling. *"You … will … forget … me … again … and … you … will … never … forget … me."*

The star flew back to the heart of Leo, Heart watched it every bit of the way, and *she knew what she saw.*

"Where are you, Heart?" Jackson's voice called from the bottom of the little winding stairs. "Why don't you answer?" He came up the stairs, muttering under his breath because the stairs were narrow for his broad shoulders. He stepped out on the balcony.

"Why didn't you answer me?"

Heart shrugged, still in the "real" place with the heart of Leo, feeling odd and tingly, as if covered in stardust. Which she was.

"You're sort of … *glowing*." Jackson looked at her, hard. *"Glowing."*

"I thought you were on the other side of the world," she said.

"I was."

"What brought you here?"

"Eye's eyes. His eyes were revealed today, yes?"

"Yes."

"Well, I wanted to … to be here for you, if … *hmmm*, not sure why now."

"You wanted to be here with me because you knew Eye's eyes were my most important goal. If it went badly, you wanted to be here for me, and if it went well, you wanted to be here for me. Because he'd be with Butterfly. And I'd be alone."

"My, I've said it quite succinctly," Jackson observed. "Yes, that's me talking. Yes."

"It's the latter." Heart turned from the constellation Leo to face Jackson. "It went so, so, *so* perfectly—everything I ever dreamed, and more. And yes, I walked home sad, because he and Butterfly are together. I'm very, totally happy that they're together. But—I walked home alone."

"I ... know," Jackson said.

Heart sighed, looking out at the UnderSea Cities. She felt Jackson leaning toward her as if magnetically drawn. She felt him daring to console her, maybe even kiss her cheek.

And as he did so, she turned and kissed him on his lovely, stern—*oh! Not so stern!*—mouth. She let the little box softly slip to the floor as she wrapped her arms around the man she had always adored. The box fell open and her own childish voice called out, "*Stars! Stars! Stars! Stars!*"

"*Oh my stars*," Heart eventually whispered, "why do I always have to be the one to make the move?"

"Because I'm an idiot," Jackson replied, folding his arms ever more closely around her. "But, Heart, why didn't you answer me? I was at the bottom of the stairs, calling you and calling you."

"I ... I was talking to my Star Man," Heart said, the memory already fading.

Right at that moment, Equuleus flew around them, whinnying. "*FINALLY! Finally, you discover each other! Worlds have been waiting for this moment!*" With a great burst of wings, he performed a series of pirouettes in the dreamy, mystical lights that shot up into the night sky from the UnderSea Cities.

Heart and Jackson watched Equuleus's performance, mesmerized. Then Jackson turned to Heart and said, *"I'm your Star Man!"*

And he … *winked.*

About the Author

I live in a forest in the Pacific Northwest with a few domestic and numerous wild creatures, where I create an ever-growing inventory of books and stories.

When you support my work you help support ten acres of natural forest, and all its resident fauna. *All the creatures and I thank you!*

If you would like to receive my newsletter, **Home of the Heart**, send a note to: Blythe@BlytheAyne. com. You'll receive occaional news of new releases, giveaways, and other goodies.

Or, if you have questions, comments, or observations, I'd love to hear from you!

Blythe@BlytheAyne.com

www.BlytheAyne.com

9 781947 151208